ISBN: 978-1-923184-00-8 (ebook)

ISBN: 978-1-923184-01-5 (Paperback)

Cover: Yummy Book Covers

Map: Holly Dunn Designs

Interior formatting: K. Elle Morrison

She's a Keeper

Ali K. Mulford

For my Kiwi, thank you for falling in love with me even with monkey poo in my hair

And for my two little wildlings who I first dreamed up under an avocado tree in the middle of the jungle

Content Warnings

Note for readers:
This book contains brief themes of parent loss, mention of cheating (not between main characters), injury, menstruation, and spiders, as well as (not so brief) sexually explicit scenes

PRICKLE ISLAND
ZOO
KEY
TOILETS
FOOD
SHOPPING
FREE WIFI
GIFT SHOP + ENTRY
ENTRY
CAFÉ
VET HOSPITAL
PLAYGROUND
REPTILE HOUSE
THE PECKISH PEACOCK
SAVANNAH
AVIARY
BABOONS

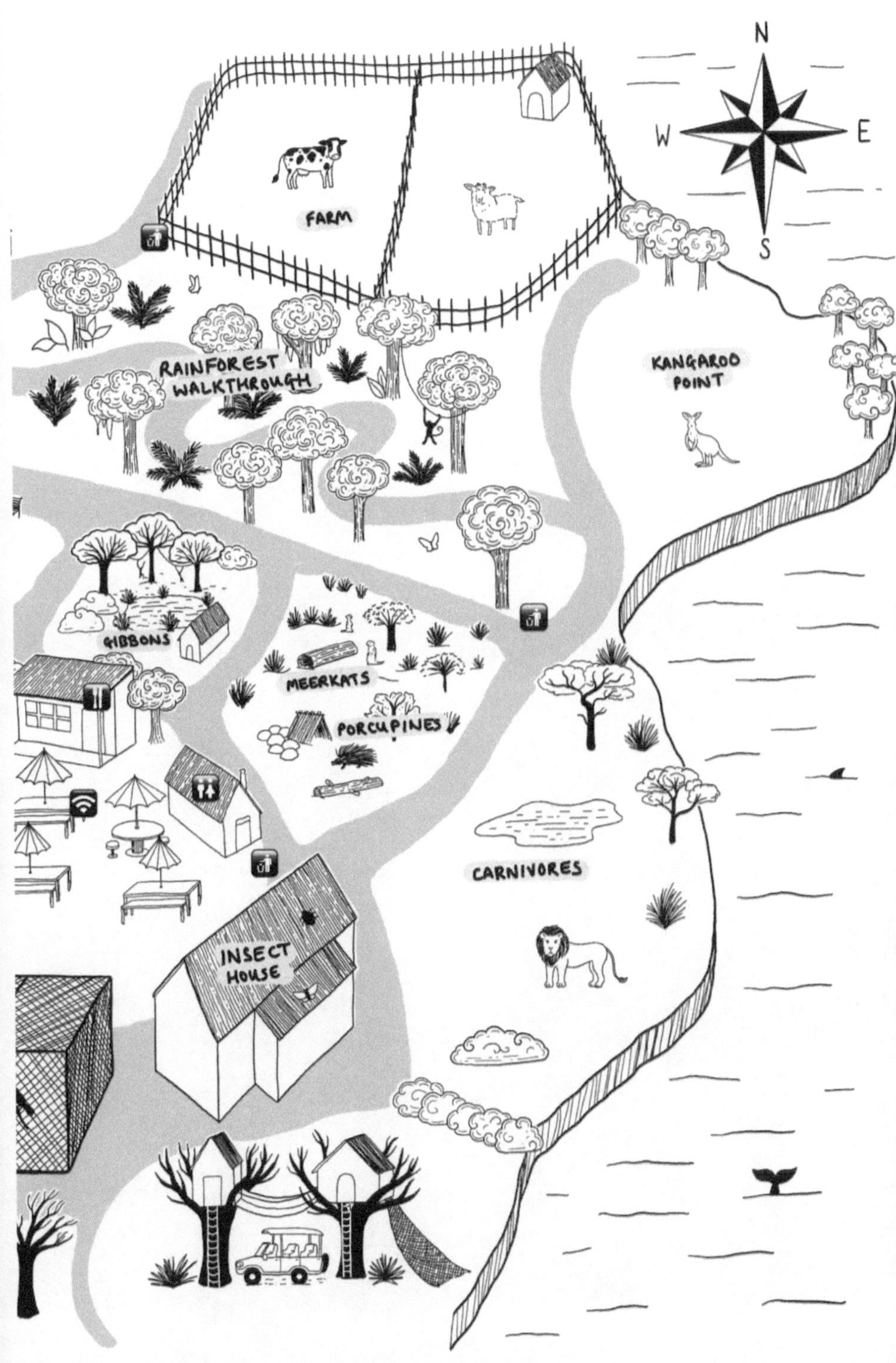

N
W
E
S
FARM
RAINFOREST WALKTHROUGH
KANGAROO POINT
GIBBONS
MEERKATS
PORCUPINES
CARNIVORES
INSECT HOUSE

MEET THE ZOO TEAM

Evelyn Lachlan (she/her) CEO of Prickle Island Zoo

Hawk Lachlan (he/him) Carnivore Keeper

Lark Lachlan (she/her) Primate Keeper

Finch Lachlan (she/her) Head Veterinarian

Dove Lachlan (she/her) Birds Keeper

Heron Lachlan (they/he) Hoofstock Keeper

Crane Lachlan (he/him) Reptiles and Inverts

Wren Lachlan (she/her) Farm Animals

Aya (she/her) Food Prep Manager

Kiwi Slang Guide

As defined for me by my Kiwi partner. If you don't like the definitions, then you can get stuffed ;)

- Cracker of a day - great day/ beautiful weather
- Tramping pack - hiking backpack
- Sweet as - no problem / all good / you're welcome / thank you
- Kumara - sweet potato
- Pub - bar / establishment serving alcoholic beverages
- Rugby pitch - playing field for rugby
- Gumboots - rain boots / rubber boots/ Wellington boots
- Uni - university
- Pack of stubbies - pack of (usually 6) short-neck beer bottles
- Cuppa - cup of a hot drink, often tea or coffee
- Packing a sad - sulking (person) / break down (equipment)
- Have a yarn - have an informal chat
- Buggy - stroller
- Puffed - out of breath due to physical exertion
- Dairy - corner store / convenience store
- Mates - friends
- Bloke - man / fellow / chap
- Boozehag - person who drinks to excess, often used in jest
- Bloody - expletive used for emphasis
- Plaster - Band-Aid
- Egg - silly person
- Chocka - crowded / full
- Pash - kiss passionately (pash rash = red marks around the lips from excessive kissing)
- Scody - nasty / rank / gross
- Wanker - unpleasant person / arrogant person / person who masturbates

- Knickers - panties / women's underpants
- Wop wops - a place that is far from anything
- Limpet - clingy/clinger
- Crook - sick / ill
- Torch - flashlight
- Having a lark - playing a prank / engaging in good-natured mischief
- All Blacks - New Zealand men's Rugby team
- vivid - permanent marker
- OE - Overseas Experience, an extended journey overseas for work or holiday
- Mean fry up - awesome meal consisting of fried foods such as sausages, eggs, and bacon
- Necking - to drink alcohol quickly / kissing and caressing
- Getting on my tits - annoying me / getting on my nerves
- Pōhutukawa - native New Zealand tree with bright red flowers, known as the New Zealand Christmas tree as it often flowers around Christmas

STAFF
PRICKLE
ISLAND
ZOO
ZOO

Lark

I woke up with a scaly noose around my neck . . . Well, the baby boa's tail didn't quite make it all the way around.

"Nice try, Matilda," I said, unwrapping the snake from my throat and giving her a kiss on the top of her scaly head. I knew she didn't mean it. "You get any bigger and I might have to let you go out on display." I glanced over at the miniature terrarium in the corner of my sloping room. Sure enough, one clamp was dislodged and the screen lid had shifted just enough for Matilda to squeak through.

Technically, she was my little brother Crane's snake since he was the reptile and invertebrates keeper, but I had an empty terrarium just sitting in the corner of my room, so

Matilda became my involuntary roommate until Crane finished building her on-display enclosure to my exacting standards.

I rolled out of bed, careful not to hit my head on the sloping concrete wall of my makeshift room. Hopping into a clean pair of khaki shorts, I let out a snarling yawn and yanked on my button-down emblazoned with "Prickle Island Zoo" in orange embroidery. My bedroom door was actually just a chain-link fence that I'd covered with canvas and polka-dot curtains for some added privacy. Sliding it open, I trudged down the iron grate steps, following the coffee scent wafting up from the kitchen below.

"Do you think hot French girl will be back this summer?" Finch asked as I stumbled into the kitchen.

"Kitchen" was a generous word for the space. It was really a metal tabletop and sink that had once been used to prep monkey food. A microwave, hot plate, mini fridge, and toaster had been added, along with my favorite appliance of all time: a coffee maker.

I grabbed a triangle of peanut butter toast off my older sister's plate as I walked by. "Hey!"

"I only want a little piece," I mumbled as I dusted crumbs off my shirt.

"Then go make yourself your own *little piece*," Finch said, pulling her plate closer and wrapping her tattooed arms around it, her many rings clinking against the porcelain.

"Do I even want to know who 'French girl' is?" Hawk asked from his spot beside the coffee maker, where he worshipped at the altar of caffeine.

"You remember that bartender at the Salty Dog?" Finch asked, waving a circle around her short hair like a halo. "The one with the blonde shaggy bob?"

Hawk shrugged, his eyes still half-closed with sleep. "The

island gets overrun in the summer. They've got to come back at least three years in a row before I bother learning their names."

Finch laughed. "True."

With tattoos from her jaw down to her knuckles, dyed black hair, and multiple facial piercings, Finch was the rebel of the family. Her name was actually *Goldfinch*, but no one called her that. She was also the smartest of all us Lachlan siblings. She started taking university classes at the age of thirteen and was the youngest person ever in the state of Connecticut to get her veterinary degree. Now, at twenty-eight, she was the head veterinarian for the Prickle Island Zoo.

"Remember your promise," I mumbled as I munched on Finch's stolen toast, wishing my sister had picked crunchy peanut butter instead of smooth.

Finch threw her hands up in the air. "I promise I won't sleep with Sparkles, okay?"

"Sparkles?" Hawk asked.

"The hot French girl," Finch said, as if it were obvious. "The unicorn of last summer."

"Damn, could she wear a neckerchief!" I crooned, holding a dramatic hand to my chest and fluttering my lashes.

"Serious insta-love for Lars," Finch taunted.

Only Finch could call me Lars and get away with it. Everyone else called me by my birth name: Lark. *Yeah, my mom and dad had a thing for bird names . . .*

I shot Finch a pleading look.

"But if she returns this year," Finch amended, holding her hands up, "I promise I won't sleep with her."

"Thank you, oh magnanimous lesbian," I said with a bow, tipping my imaginary cap to her.

Nine months out of the year, the island population was so small, I could count everyone on two hands. But in the summer, when all the rich families moved onto the island, shop owners, workers, and niche staff for the wealthy came as well. Crowded ferries full of tourists poured in every day too . . . and that was when Finch's fun began.

"I'll have plenty of chauffeurs and nannies and sailing instructors to pick from anyway," Finch said with a wave of her hand. "I don't need to go after Sparkles. I'll be playing my own game."

"So long as that game does not involve zoo volunteers," Hawk reminded Finch as he refilled his mug.

He gave Finch the "no sleeping with zoo volunteers" speech at the start of every summer . . . and every summer she had an excuse for why she broke that rule. I had no such problem. Most of the volunteers were college students seeking extra credit who were more focused on taking Instagram pics of the enclosures than actually helping clean them.

"Speaking of," I hedged as Hawk rolled his eyes, "can you *please* give me a volunteer who can lift a bale of hay this year? Or at least one who isn't afraid of wielding a broom without breaking a nail?"

Hawk always assigned me the glam girls who constantly asked for a baby monkey to raise, as if I would just snatch one from its mother to give to them.

"The volunteers are randomly assigned as always," Hawk said in his exhausted monotone, rubbing the heel of his palm into his eye. He'd taken on a lot of the behind-the-scenes stuff since our father passed away ten years ago, and the extra responsibilities on top of being the carnivore keeper had worn away all of his once-friendly personality into something more befitting one of those grumpy, old Muppets. "You'll get who you get and you won't throw a fit."

Finch rolled her eyes. "Thank you, Scout Leader Hawk."

Sunshine peeked above the windowsill as the gibbons whooped in the distant trees. I smiled at the early beams of sunlight. I loved this time of year, when I rose with the sun instead of before it . . . Monkeys didn't follow daylight savings and all the animals needed to be out into their daytime enclosures and fed before the nine a.m. opening time, no matter how much we all begged our mother—and zoo matriarch—to push the opening to ten.

"If I don't scare any volunteers away this year, can we at least talk about my Guatemala trip?" I pleaded. I'd been desperate to go for the last three years since Mariana, a Guatemalan wildlife biologist, had come to do a placement at the zoo. She was an absolute goddess of a human being and was probably the only person on earth who was more obsessed with primate fun facts than I was. She'd invited me to go on her annual howler monkey research trip for the last three years . . . and for the last three years, our funding had been rejected by the Westworth family.

The Westworths were one of the richest families in New England, and they owned the entire island, including the zoo. So, despite the fact that it was my great-great-grandfather who first moved out to the island, our home, our zoo, and our livelihoods depended on the Westworths' goodwill.

"If we get the funding *and* if Aya gets back from vacation before then," Hawk said.

"So that is a tentative yes?" I asked hopefully, but Hawk just shook his head. "Dove got to go to Indonesia last summer, but you keep rejecting my trip. It's not fair!" The fact my little sister got to go on a conservation trip before me was still a massive point of contention between us.

"It cost less and her animals are easier to cover than yours," Hawk reminded. "If you are willing to let Dove take over some of the primates—"

"Not going to happen."

Hawk shrugged. "Then neither is Guatemala."

I wanted to shout at my older brother some more when the radio on the kitchen island crackled to life. "Hawk, the boat's early," our mother's voice rang out. "Can you get the truck and go grab the new volunteers?"

Hawk cursed and chugged his coffee before grabbing the radio out of the line of docks that ran along the windowsill. "Copy. I'm on my way now." He hastily rubbed his cowlick, trying to flatten his bedhead.

Mom's voice came through the radio again. "Lark, are you going to deal with Loki before he wakes up the whole island?"

"You can barely hear him over the howlers," I grumbled as I snapped at my brother and he threw me my radio. "I'm on my way, Mom."

The radio barely had time to scratch before Mom said, "No, you aren't."

I frowned and walked to the kitchen window, lifting up on my tiptoes and staring uphill toward the house at the top of the zoo. Mom stood in the window, lifting her mug of tea at me in greeting. "Hi," she said through the radio. "Loki. Now."

"Fine." I mimed an overly exaggerated thumbs-up out the window and turned to my snickering siblings. Doing Loki's enclosure first would mess up my well-orchestrated morning routine. My whole fine-tuned schedule would be thrown out of whack by Loki's wahooing. "One of you needs to plant a tree outside this window," I muttered. "What's the point of moving out of your family's home if your mom can still spy on you?"

There was a time when all nine of us had lived in that three-bedroom house up the hill. But when we built the new rainforest exhibit and moved the nearly century-old capuchin house behind a bamboo hedge, Hawk had immediately set about turning it into a second dwelling for us. Now, Hawk, Finch, and I all had our own bedrooms and the house was mostly conventional . . . apart from the drains in all the floors and a few random chain-link walls.

A loud hooting call rang out across the zoo and I skidded across the kitchen in my woolen socks to where my shoes sat in a lineup of muddy work boots. "Frickin' Loki," I muttered.

Finch shrugged. "He's a teenager. He'll grow out of it."

"Why couldn't he have grown out of it *before* the start of summer?" I yanked on my boots and quickly tied my laces. "He had to pick the only time when the island is full of grumpy rich people who don't want their tennis matches interrupted by a hormonal baboon!"

Hawk followed me out the door, snatching the keys to his flatbed truck off the magnetic hooks on the wall.

He called over his shoulder, "Don't forget I need you to check out that ulcer on Ace's side today."

"And I need more of Jackie's ointment!" I called.

Finch nodded with a yawn and meandered through the door, not bothering to lock it behind us. For nine months out of the year, the only people in the zoo were my family members and our animal diets manager, Aya. Anyone who wanted to steal my stuff would have to scale one electric fence and three barbed-wire fences to get in. The only thieves I actually might have to worry about were the furry and feathered kind.

I took off at a clip uphill toward the baboon exhibit, the whole zoo coming to life with excitement at seeing the first khaki shirt of the morning. Squawks and hoots and growls sounded all around me as I headed downhill to the loudest morning alarm in the world.

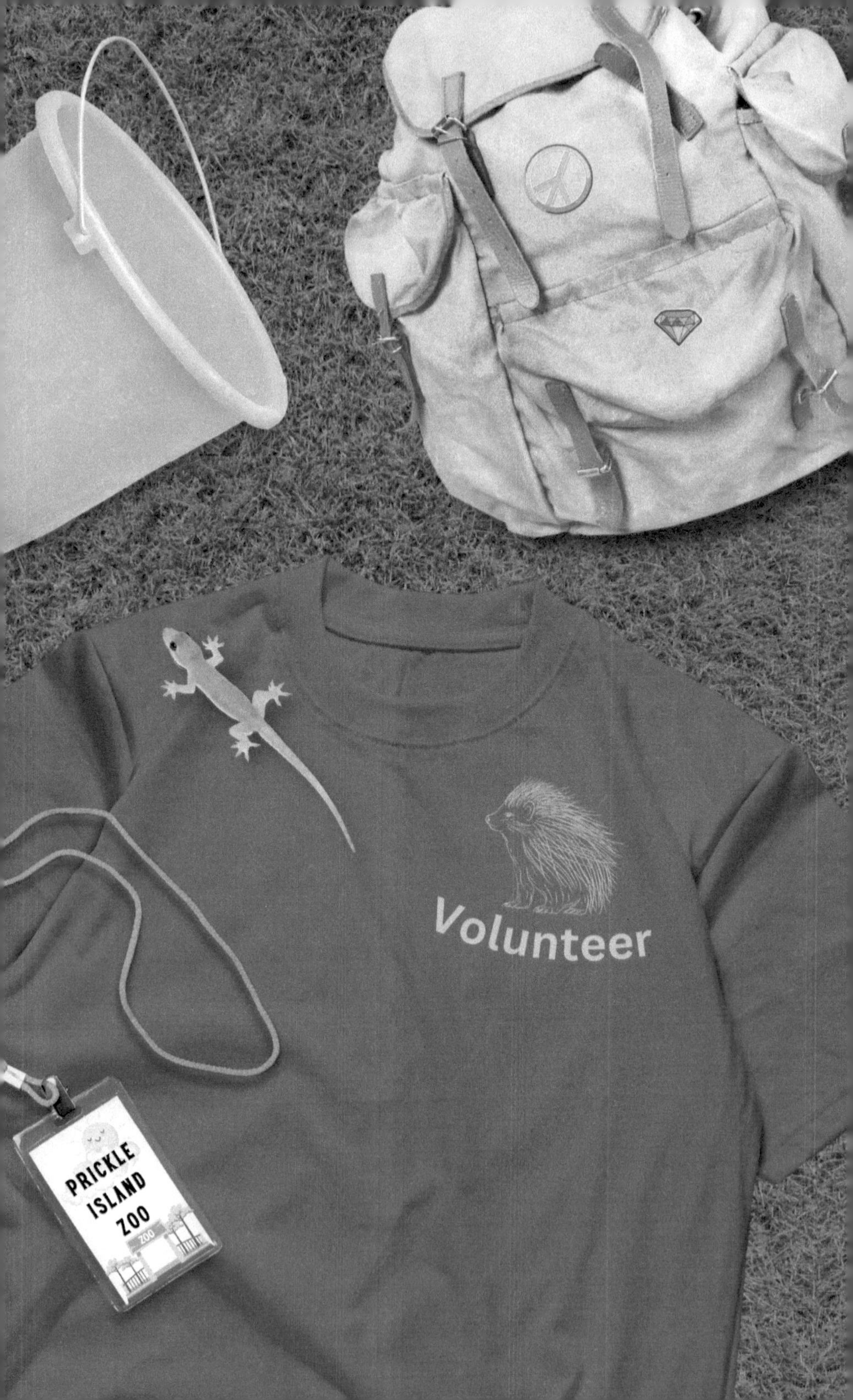

Volunteer
PRICKLE
ISLAND
ZOO
ZOO

Chapter Two

Logan

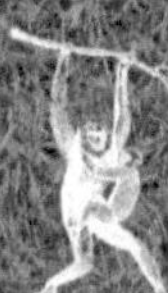

It was a cracker of a day. The sun was glinting off the ocean waves as I rode the ferry through the harbor and out toward Prickle Island. I took a photo of the plaque at the front of the ferry that told the story of a man named James Lachlan, who'd introduced a family of porcupines to the island in the mid-1800s, which was how the island was named. In a bubble at the bottom of the plaque in neon yellow were the words: *Fun Fact! A group of porcupines is called a prickle!* The word prickle was designed all spiky to emphasize the zaniness of the word.

I locked my phone again and the picture of *her* came up. Every time I saw Kelly's smiling face, I reminded myself I needed to change that photo . . . . but then my phone would go into my pocket and I'd forget until the next time I pulled it out and I cringed all over again. I wondered what she was doing—

Nope. No. She had cheated on me—*several times*—and it was over. I wasn't going to be that guy moping over a fucking photo. She wasn't worth it.

By the end, we barely had a shell of a relationship. The life we had together was just an unsuccessful performance of what two people of a certain age did when they paired off. I knew I'd move back home and take over our rural family business one day. Kelly knew she'd never leave the city. It was always doomed to fail. But every time I saw her photo, I was reminded that youthful chapter was over and the next was about to begin and this summer was all that was left of the in-between: one last adventure before it was time to move home and face my responsibilities.

As I leaned my elbows on the railing of the ferry, the wind whipped my shirt back, ballooning it out like a sail. A middle-aged man wandered over and leaned on the railing beside me. He wore a polo shirt and navy trousers with embroidered pink seahorses, looking like he'd stepped out of the pages of a preppy yacht club magazine.

"Let me guess," he said, arching his brow. "You're some sort of watersports instructor?"

"What?"

"Why you're coming to the island," he said, nodding down to my tramping pack that was leaning against my leg. "Water-skiing or sailing?"

"Neither."

"Tennis coach?" He eyed me up and down. "Come on. It's got to be something athletic." He stuck out his hand. "I'm Jimmy. I'm one of the golf instructors on the Westworths' northern links."

I didn't know half of the words in that sentence, but I stuck out my hand and said, "Logan. I'm here to volunteer at the zoo for the summer."

"The zoo?" Jimmy looked at me like I'd just told a really bad joke. "Isn't that for college kids?"

I tried not to grimace. I'd gathered as much as I waited in the ferry terminal with all the others who clearly looked a decade younger than me.

I shrugged. "It didn't say there was an age limit."

"Hey, it's okay," Jimmy said, clapping me on the shoulder like we were old friends. What was it with Americans and physical affection? "Who wouldn't want to spend a summer petting lions and shit?"

The appeal of the zoo had been less about proximity to lions and more about being far, far away from home. I'd quit my job to move back home and figured while I was between jobs and sans girlfriend, it was the perfect time for one last trip before I had to face the music of what a mess my family was becoming. I saw an online advertisement about the zoo when I was drunk at three a.m., which drunk me decided was fate and I applied. Honestly, I didn't really think it through. I saw the advert and said fuck it, one more cool thing before boring small-town life forever.

Of course, I didn't say any of this to Jimmy and instead asked, "So you move to the island for the summer each year?"

He nodded. "I'm an employee of the Westworth family. They fly me out for the summer in case they or their guests want lessons. Some of the other island residents are permitted by the Westworths to use the course too."

"How gracious of them."

Despite being from halfway around the world, even I had heard of the Westworth family. They were one step below Rockefellers and Vanderbilts. They owned the whole island, including the zoo, and rented part of their land out to visitors and other rich families in the summertime. Still, bringing a golf instructor with you on your summer holiday seemed completely mad.

"Where are you from, Logan?"

"Aotearoa, New Zealand," I said, and his eyes lit up like I'd just told him I was the King of fucking England.

"A Kiwi!" He leaned in, suddenly far more interested in me than he was two seconds ago. "Like *Lord of the Rings* and kangaroos?"

I sighed, not wanting to explain that kangaroos were from Australia and not New Zealand and that we weren't at all alike and it was actually annoying to clump us all together, but being a Kiwi—and someone who didn't do confrontation—I just nodded and said, "Yes."

"*Yis*," he said, mimicking my accent. "I love how you say *yis*." I grimaced, but Jimmy carried on, pointing out to the blip of an island that was slowly pulling into view. "Let me give you some tips on the good parts of the island for people like us to visit and the ones you want to stay away from if you aren't wearing designer loafers and a sweater around your neck."

"Sweet as."

"Sweet as what?" Jimmy asked.

I shook my head. "It just means cool." Technically, the saying was "sweet as a kumara," but then I'd have to explain what a kumara was and I really didn't want to go down the whole token Kiwi rabbit hole that I'd had to do on the flight from LAX to JFK . . . and on the train . . . and in the taxi.

As we drew closer to the island, Jimmy carried on ranting about the dos and don'ts of Prickle Island and I began to wonder, what was I doing here? Of all the wild things people did to get over a breakup, I thought I'd win for traveling to a zoo on an island off the coast of another country. At least it would all make a good story at the local pub one day.

But that little gnawing voice kept popping up in the back of my mind: maybe this was all a big mistake.

STAFF
PRICKLE
ISLAND
ZOO
ZOO

Chapter Three

Lark

"Great," I muttered as I stared at the drain overflowing with monkey excrement. "Just great."

"I-I don't know what happened," the perky volunteer I was assigned, Madison, said. She wrinkled her button nose at the brown liquid as it spilled onto the path and trailed in rivulets into the bushes. "I tried to fish everything out with the scooper, but it's not draining."

Madison was the sort of volunteer that I dreaded being put on my roster. She was eighteen and wore enough makeup to be walking a red carpet, her hair always perfectly slicked back in a high ponytail, and her nails . . . Just like when I decided which girls I should crush on, you could always tell with the nails.

Madison's perfect ombre manicure was never going anywhere near a pile of monkey poo, which meant I would be doing all of my normal work *and* looking out for this walking incident report.

No shame to the ones who could do the glam *and* the work, but volunteers like Madison effectively doubled my workload, and I was about to break out into hives at being so behind my schedule.

I hated summers.

"Three months. It's only three months," I muttered under my breath. Soon, the crisp fall air would be rolling off the ocean and the island would go quiet again. Then it would just be my family and Aya running the zoo.

"Huh?" Madison asked.

"Nothing," I replied, wiping my forearm across my sweaty brow and putting my other hand on my hip as I frowned down at the blockage. "Why don't you go take a break, Maddie? I've got this covered."

I waved out my sweaty shirt. It was still early morning and already the humidity was killing me. The temperature would make me even slower. If I was lucky, I'd finish my shift two hours late at this rate.

"Oh, whew," Madison said, as if she'd been working for five hours and not thirty minutes. She bounced off to the nearest patch of shade, leaving behind a whiff of floral perfume that I could smell even over the stench of the over-flowing drain.

Why couldn't I have a volunteer who, just once, knew how to use a pressure washer? Madison had whined the whole way up the hill that her arms were going to fall off and she was carrying two *empty* buckets. Just my luck. At least Madison seemed oblivious to my grumpiness, so I wouldn't be called into a meeting with Hawk this summer about making a volunteer cry . . . again.

I frowned back at the drain, grabbing the scooper and fishing around the murky brown water.

Nothing.

Whatever was clogging the drain was high up in the pipe. I glanced up to the capuchins happily munching their leaves in their day enclosure, none the wiser that their bowel movements the night before were ruining my day. I needed to get this over with quickly before the spider monkeys started to riot from waiting for their breakfast, and I couldn't just leave a drain spewing poo all the way through the zoo on the first day of summer. My sweet, sweet summer schedule I'd so perfectly planned down to the minute was already falling apart on day one.

"Screw it," I said, frowning at the brown water and rolling up my sleeve to the shoulder. I crouched down and stuck my hand into the opaque water, feeling for the drain hole. Brown liquid was all the way up to my shoulder before I felt the blockage. "Aha!" I said victoriously, yanking the wad of hay, leaves, and feces out of the drainpipe, relief washing through me as the water finally drained away.

Someone cleared their throat from above me, and I looked up through the fence to see Hawk standing next to the most handsome man I'd ever seen in my entire life. He had black hair, dark eyes, sun-kissed olive skin . . . and a horrified expression on his face.

I blanched, dropping the poo wad back into the drain with a loud *plop!* and grimacing as I held my gross, wet arm midair away from my body.

"Uh, Lark," Hawk said, gesturing to the man next to him. "This is Logan Anderson. You've got an extra volunteer this summer."

My mouth dropped open as I scanned from Logan's hiking boots to his blue jeans to his fitted charcoal V-neck that hugged his broad, muscled chest. "*He's* my volunteer? How old is he?"

"Ouch," Logan said with a smirk that made butterflies dance low in my belly, which was very odd considering I usually wasn't attracted to men. Did wanting to lick those gorgeous dimples mean I was attracted to him? No, this guy was like Hollywood leading man-level attractive. People of all sexualities probably would've had butterflies if he smiled at them. *Don't overthink it, Lark.*

I realized Logan was still staring at me as I ogled him.

"Oh, I-I didn't mean you're old. You're *older*, I mean," I scrambled, trying and failing to put a sentence together as I appreciated—okay, fine—*gawked* at him. I couldn't quite place him. He looked like he could just as easily be about to enter a work meeting or pull out an axe and start chopping wood. "I just mean most of the volunteers are late teens and you look older and . . ." I twisted my torso to the side, as if that would hide my poo-stained arm from him.

What the hell was I doing? Was I seriously trying to look *cute* while covered shoulder-deep in monkey poop?

"I'm thirty-one," Logan said.

"Thitty?" I asked, quirking my brow at his unusual accent.

"He's from New Zealand," Hawk said, hooking his thumb at Logan with a smile. Ugh, Hawk seemed to like him. That was definitely taking hotness points away from the man.

"Sorry, thirrrrty-one," Logan said like a pirate, and I frowned. "I'm taking the winter off—well, your summer—to travel around and I've always wanted to visit this area, so what better way than as a volunteer?"

"You wanted to visit Connecticut?" I asked incredulously. I mean, the state was fine, but I thought international travelers would want to visit New York or Boston, not a random Hamptons-wannabe island off the shoreline. Something about that answer had my spidey-senses tingling. Logan was clearly hiding something. People who looked as gorgeous as he did didn't just fly to Prickle Island Zoo to sweep enclosures for the summer.

Hawk's hand landed on Logan's muscled shoulder. "I thought I'd get you someone who could actually lift a bale of hay this year. That's what you wanted, right?"

"Right," I said, sizing up Wolverine's body double. "Good. Awesome. That's . . . good." I looked all around me, trying to find an excuse to escape the situation. "Well, you go get your volunteer T-shirt and get settled in, and I'll, uh, see you on shift tomorrow, Logan. I'm . . . I'm going to go wash my hands now."

"Good idea," Hawk said, and I darted him a glare that told him he'd be hearing about this impromptu visit later. If he didn't watch himself, I was siccing Matilda on him.

I trudged past Madison, who looked up from her phone just long enough to add, "Check out the hottie in gray." Before I could answer, she scrunched her nose, catching a whiff of me. "OMG, you smell like death."

"It's a zoo, Maddie!" I threw my hands in the air and rushed toward my house hidden behind a hedgerow of bamboo. "Smelling awful is part of the job! I should've been an herbivore keeper," I muttered, thinking of my younger siblings who only ever smelled like straw and horse manure. But knowing my luck, I would've still made an ass of myself in front of sexy Kiwi lumberjack.

Madison trailed behind me. "So, who is the guy?"

"A problem," I muttered. "That's what he is."

STAFF
PRICKLE
ISLAND
ZOO
ZOO

Lark

"How are the vet volunteers?" Mom asked as she passed the salad bowl.

It was Sunday, or as Mom called it: Sunday Funday Fondue Day. A bright orange ceramic pot of cheese fondue sat in the center of our long dining room table, a present from my grandparents for my parents' wedding in the eighties—a time when fondue sets had already long gone out of style. But that was my parents: quirky, fun-loving, and knew exactly what they wanted out of life even if it wasn't trendy.

For a family that all lived and worked in the same location, we actually didn't organically spend much time together because we were all so busy. Having our Sunday Funday

Fondue Day family dinners was mandated by Mom so that we could all actually catch up outside of zoo hours. Granted, most of the conversation was still about animals anyway.

Our whole family was neurodivergent in one form or another—and thank God too because I couldn't imagine a neurotypical person growing up in this household. Crane and Heron had already entered into a rousing game of "It's feces but what species?" in which Heron would try to identify the creature who stained Crane's khakis. My money was on an iguana.

"The new volunteers are good," Finch said through a mouthful of fondue-covered bread. "Eager as ever, but one is surprisingly knowledgeable—real horse people energy. I'm already planning her letter of rec in my head."

"Ah, the coveted letter of recommendation," I teased.

"You got a hot guy for once," Finch said, giving me a nudge with her elbow.

"Shut it," I gritted out.

"Why are you so flustered?"

"I am completely un-flustered."

"I'm just appreciating—"

"Jeez," Hawk said, scrubbing a hand down his face. "Should I have put him with the twins instead?"

Heron looked up from where they were feeding their blue-tongued skink, Guava, under the table. "The Australian?"

"He's from New Zealand," I said at the same time as Hawk. I glared at my brother as he smirked back at me knowingly.

"Same thing," Crane said.

"It's not the same thing," I snapped, hating how easily my younger siblings got under my skin. Why was I even defending this random, ridiculously attractive stranger?

"Besides, we don't hate all Australians," Mom interjected,

as if there were a microphone in front of her face and she was being forced to make a comment on the record. She nudged Crane to pass the bowl of Caesar salad before adding, "We only hate one Australian family."

"Fucking Madigans," Heron said, and Mom smacked them with a dishcloth. "Who names a kid Newt anyway?"

Gaz Madigan was an Australian zoologist who was once best friends with our dad back in the day. That was before Gaz moved back to Australia and opened the Madigan Mountain Wildlife Park. He took all of our dad's ideas down to naming all of his kids after animals. I still thought they had eight children—one more than our own family—just to spite Dad.

When the Madigans started their reality show, it was intended to be a conservation show like *Crocodile Hunter*—which was honestly blasphemous considering the Irwins were conservation royalty and no one would ever hold a candle to them. But of course, when the Madigans couldn't hack it, they turned the show, *Madigan Mountain,* into a melodrama-filled, reality-TV-like, low-budget, wannabe Kardashians. After that, Gaz started distancing himself from our dad, pretending like he didn't even know him. We never really knew what went down between them, only that one day, Dad started hating Gaz, and Mom never explained why.

"Didn't you always want to go to New Zealand, Lars?" Finch asked, and I knew she was trying to goad me as she swirled her spaghetti around her fork. "Maybe if you stop acting like Mrs. Trunchbull to your volunteers and you're actually nice to the hot Kiwi, he'd offer to show you around one day."

"I wanted to go to New Zealand to meet Cate Blanchett in a flowing dress with elf ears on," I corrected. "Not some well-dressed lumberjack dude."

"Yeah, but, I mean, you like dudes too," Finch taunted with

a wink. "Hence the comment about your volunteer being a hottie . . . and actually age-appropriate for you. Win-win."

I turned to Crane, desperately trying to change the subject. "How's Matilda's enclosure coming along?"

"I think it's almost ready."

I arched a brow at him. "Really?" In order for Matilda to go on display, the enclosure would need to meet my exacting standards, and thus far, I'd found a reason to shoot down the request every time Crane said the enclosure was ready. Especially considering it was accessed through the pygmy marmoset exhibit, and if all the doors and latches between the marmosets and the terrarium weren't snake-proof, Matilda would be like a kid in a candy store.

"She's going to be five feet long before you ever think it's good enough." Crane groaned. "I'm still working on getting the plants right. There's not a lot of time at the end of the day to be building new enclosures." He glanced at Mom. "When is Aya back?"

"She's in Japan until July," Mom said.

Crane shook his head. "I still can't believe you let her go."

"Her sister was getting married!" Mom set her cutlery down and gave Crane that mama bear look she did so well. "Of course I let her go."

Aya was the only full-time employee besides my family. She basically *was* family. She and her wife, Kirby, were twenty percent of the zoo's wintertime population.

Finch leaned into me. "Don't think I didn't notice that little deflection," she whispered. "I think the hot volunteer has got your panties in a twist."

"Who did you get paired with?" I asked, ignoring Finch and kicking Dove under the table.

Dove peeked up from her phone for all of two seconds and said, "Huh?" while her thumbs kept typing.

"Never mind," I muttered, looking at Finch. Even though there were only two years that separated me and my sisters, Finch and I had always been close and Dove and I had always hated each other. I mean, we loved each other, but she was also my mortal enemy so . . ."Why do I even bother?"

"I'm talking with my friends, Finch, jeez."

Finch shrugged and chucked a piece of bread at Dove. The twenty-four-year-old didn't even lift her head as she swept crumbs out of her lavender-streaked hair.

"Goldfinch Lachlan!" Mom scolded. "Seriously? You're nearly thirty and you're still throwing food around the table like a toddler."

"It got her attention," Finch said with a grin, the piercings in her lip glinting in the light.

"She seriously has a phone problem," I added.

Dove stopped typing and slammed her phone on the table. "I do *not* have a phone problem," she hissed. "I've been cleaning out bird cages all day and I just want to talk to my friends, which I can't do in person because we live on a fucking island!"

"That's right," I growled at her. "You hate being here *so* much. Always thinking about yourself over our family like a selfish princess."

Dove's mouth fell open and I swore, she looked like steam might start curling out of her ears. "Oh, here we go about duty to the family again!" Dove screamed. "You sound like you're in the fucking mafia. Not all of us get off on checklists and keeping on schedules and being fucking boring like you, Lark." She grabbed her phone off the table and stormed upstairs.

"Hormones," Crane said, and Finch and I simultaneously kicked him under the table while Hawk threw another piece of bread at him.

Mom dropped her head into her hands and rubbed her

temples. "I'd say I live with a bunch of wild animals, but we all know they're less trouble than you all."

She bent over to grab the piece of bread that fell on the floor, but her rescue dog—some strange mix of collie and pitbull named Phoebe—had already wolfed it down.

"And this is why we don't have a reality show like the Madigans," Finch said with a laugh, and the whole table groaned.

Volunteer
PRICKLE
ISLAND
ZOO
ZOO

Chapter Five

Logan

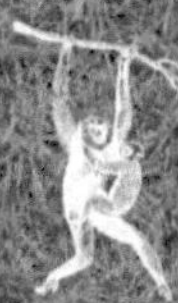

I'd expected a lot of things when I booked a ticket halfway around the world to an island off the coast of Connecticut . . . but an adorably surly zookeeper wasn't one of them. Lark was gorgeous—from her freckly sun-tanned skin to the no-nonsense way she pursed her full lips to her strong, stocky figure that looked like she knew her way around a rugby pitch. While Kelly had been an artsy fashionista who never wanted to leave the city, Lark looked like the kind of woman you'd meet solo-tramping in the forest: vibrant, determined, and too focused on the path ahead to give anyone else the time of day.

I raced after Lark, intent on not looking useless in front of her. Hawk had said she always got stuck with people who couldn't pull their own weight, and I had accepted that as a strange sort of challenge.

I had no idea why, but I needed to be good at this.

After everything I left broken back home, I needed to feel like I was doing something right, even if it was just hefting two buckets in each hand. Two were filled with chopped fruits, another pellets, another filled nearly to the brim with dried corn, and I had to be careful not to swing my arms or it would spill everywhere.

"Don't spill those," Lark said, as if reading my mind. Despite her words being sharp, they were undercut by a honeyed timbre that made me want to be bossed around all day long just to hear it. Her sandy-brown ponytail whipped around as she nodded at the buckets. "They're specifically weighed, and I don't want to have to go back to the kitchens to start all over again."

"Aye, aye, captain," I quipped, which seemed to incense her even further and made my smile widen. I continued to entertain myself, poking the bear by giving her a wink.

Lark let out an indignant huff, turned back around, and kept hurtling uphill at breakneck speed. I raced after her, knowing the fact I easily kept up bothered her too. I rolled my shoulders back and switched my grip on the buckets, careful not to trip in the too-big gumboots I'd been given.

It reminded me of mornings spent feeding farm animals before my shifts at my parents' café. Well, technically, it was a café, art gallery, craft store, and community hub, as many small-town New Zealand stores had a tendency to be. Sometimes, we sold the neighbor's knit beanies and homemade soaps, sometimes we hosted the local teens' new band, and sometimes we displayed the watercolor art of a newly retired man whose wife had forced him to find a hobby and stop bothering her. I wondered what they were selling now. I'd moved to

Auckland for uni, met Kelly, and never really came back except for Christmases, but when I did visit, I was immediately passed a bucket or an apron and I'd get stuck feeding the chickens and making flat whites in the café.

I thought Lark expected me to be irritated by her putting me to work, but to me, it just felt like home.

"Careful, these steps are uneven," Lark said to the ether, but I assumed it was directed at me, even though she stared straight ahead.

"Got it." I shook my head. I couldn't believe I flew halfway around the world just to carry more buckets. Remind me never to make life decisions at three a.m.

The other volunteer, Madison, trailed behind, swinging her empty bucket with one hand while she typed on her phone with the other. Madison dawdled, clearly unbothered with keeping pace, which I was grateful for. The second she saw me, she'd started flirting with me, finding excuses to touch my arms and playfully lean into my shoulder. I didn't come all this way just to rebound with the first pretty girl who was young enough that it was entering Leonardo DiCaprio-level creepy . . . I glanced at Lark. I didn't come here for anyone for that matter.

That wasn't the point of this trip.

But the mostly female volunteers at the volunteer house clearly hadn't gotten the message that I wasn't interested, and I stayed holed up in my bunk bed for most of the night while the rest of them went out drinking with the tatted-up veterinarian. I couldn't believe the vet and the uptight keeper racing ahead of me were actually related.

As we rushed up the hillside, the morning sun still low in the sky, I asked myself for the millionth time: What the fuck am I doing here? I should be back home, helping in the café, doing renovations and winter projects in the slow season, not playing zookeeper with a bunch of Americans. I rolled my shoulders and kept walking, chasing Lark's perfectly round ass up the hill.

Shit, I really shouldn't be thinking about her ass . . . or how perfectly round it was . . . or how I heard a little buh-dum, buh-dum of bongos in my head as her cheeks went up and down.

Shit. Shit. Shit.

A single tattoo peeked above the back of Lark's shirt: two monkeys, their tails rising from the collar. Something about this buttoned-up woman having a tattoo sent a flare of excitement through me. How many other tattoos did she have? And where? I kept my eyes fixed on her neck tattoo. At least it kept me from staring at her ass like I was a teenager.

I came here to have a break from dating, to think about my life, to have one last adventure before needing to stick closer to home . . . not to pack a semi for the first woman over twenty that I saw.

"How old are you?" I blurted out as I caught up to Lark at the slippery, algae-covered steps cutting between two old concrete buildings.

Very smooth, Logan. Very smooth.

"What?" she asked, her breathing a little ragged as she took the steps two at a time. The breathy way she spoke did not help calm my cock down.

"I told you yesterday that I'm thirty-one," I said, putting a little extra emphasis on the "R" so she'd understand me. I watched her shoulders bunch at the way I said it, and I'd bet a pack of stubbies that she was scowling right now. "How old are you?"

"Twenty-six," she said. "Twenty-seven in August."

Good, I thought. *Good? GOOD?* I silently yelled at myself.

Her age shouldn't matter at all because I wasn't in the market for a rebound chick and this particular woman seemed like she absolutely loathed me. I was definitely not being promoted to Don Juan status anytime soon—nor did I want to be! Dammit, Logan.

"Have you lived here your whole life?" I asked, desperately trying to change the subject.

Lark took a moment to reply, reaching a strip of dirt that cut through the grass and walking at twice the speed, as if she were trying to outrun me and my weird questions. "If you want to know about my family's history, you can read the plaque at the visitor kiosk by the porcupine playground," she said.

"Can you slow down there, tails?" I finally said, huffing and puffing as she reached another flight of stairs. "Are we trying to run away from something? There's no lion on the loose I should know about, is there?"

Lark turned so fast, her ponytail smacked into her eyes. "I'm walking a normal pace," she gritted out.

"Are you normally this jolly in the mornings? I can grab you a cuppa—"

"It's been a busy morning," she said tightly. "With several unnecessary disruptions."

"Look, tails, I know you're packing a sad because I got paired with you and for some reason, you really don't like me, but we can still have a yarn every now and again."

She stared at me for several seconds, folding her arms. "We're definitely not speaking the same language." She looked me up and down, her eyes snagging on my arms before drifting back to my face. I knew she tried to do it faster than I could spot it, but I noticed, and it did nothing but stroke my ego. A once-over by someone as attractive as Lark Lachlan felt like a victory worth celebrating. I pressed my lips together to keep from smiling, wondering if maybe she made me carry these heavy buckets just to appreciate my arms.

"What in the hell does having a yawn mean? Tired?"

"Yarn."

"Yawn," she repeated back.

"Yarrrrn," I said, knowing she was about to make another pirate comment. "It means to have a chat."

"Aye, aye, captain," she said, echoing my earlier retort and saluting me as she turned around.

Her radio fizzled from her belt, and her hand instinctively reached for the volume dial and turned it up.

A young male voice called through the radio, "Crane to Heron."

She turned the dial down and rolled her eyes. It was one of her teenage twin siblings. I'd spotted their golf buggy barreling up the hill earlier this morning.

"Do you all have bird code names?" I asked as I followed her up the stairs and reached a blissfully flat stretch of path. I would never need to work out my calves again. Lark's were like perfect little bricks sticking out of her shapely legs. If I wasn't a leg man before, I guessed I was now.

"They're not code names," she said. "My birth name is Lark."

"What's it like having the name Lark?"

"What's it like having the name Logan?" she snapped in the adorable, grumpy way that made her ponytail swish emphatically with each word. "I'm pronouncing that right? Low-gon?"

"Fair point," I said with a chuckle. "What are all your siblings' names?"

"Hawk, Finch, Dove, Heron, Crane, and Wren." She rattled them off like she had done it a million times before. Big families were already intriguing, then adding the names and living at the zoo on top was sure to be a spectacle.

"You know," I said, "you remind me of the Madigans."

Apparently, that was the wrong fucking thing to say

because she let out a little growl and balled her hands into fists at her sides. We went down and uphill five more times before I began to wonder if she was purposefully making me walk in circles as punishment.

"Are we lost, tails?"

We climbed up the last flight of concrete steps and ducked behind a cluster of tall grasses until we reached a heavy iron door seemingly built into the hillside.

Lark nodded to the buckets in my hands and then to the door. "You can put those down now." She was puffed in a way that clearly denoted she'd been hustling up the hill just to annoy me. "Why do you keep calling me tails? Is that like a *Sonic the Hedgehog* reference because I'm walking fast?"

Well, I couldn't admit it was a Sonic reference now. I took a step forward without thinking and brushed the hair that had escaped her ponytail aside and trailed my pointer finger down the tattoo of the two monkeys on her neck. Her skin pebbled beneath my touch, and I grinned.

"When you're walking, only the tails peek up above your collar," I said.

She stepped out of my touch and rubbed her hand over the back of her neck. "Oh."

"Do you have any other tattoos?" I asked and then realized that was probably a personal question and I should just shut up and get to work digging a giant hole to jump into. I came here to have an experience, one last travel memory, not to flirt with a hot zookeeper who was clearly uninterested in me . . . except for when I casually touched her.

"No other tattoos," she said. I was about to turn toward the door when she added, "I used to have my nose pierced though."

"Why'd you get rid of it?"

"Monkeys kept picking it out," she said.

I chuckled and she just stared at me. "Oh, you're serious?"

"Some of the monkeys are aggressive groomers," she added, as if that were a perfectly reasonable explanation.

"Speaking of, aren't the lemurs waiting?" I asked, nodding to the door.

She reached for the handle and paused, as if debating saying something. "Lemurs aren't monkeys." She gave me a warning look. "Neither are the gibbons. If visitors call them monkeys, you can politely correct them, but if you call them monkeys behind the scenes—"

"You'll throw me to the lions?" I joked. She narrowed her eyes at me. "You'll give me more of the silent treatment? Is this because I saw that little *plumbing* incident yesterday?"

"I'm not giving you the silent treatment!" she said, exasperated. "And no, I don't normally stick my arms up sewage drains, but I had a bunch of shit—no pun intended—to get done and it needed to happen, and if you think I'm embarrassed, I'm not."

I loved that she swore almost as much as me—it seemed to be a keeper thing. She was tough as nails and it was starting to make a lot of sense why they hired other people to do the customer service side of things over the summer.

"Welcome to zoo life," Lark said. "And I'm not ignoring you. I'm just focused on work and you're . . . distracting."

"That's one word for it," Madison said with a smile as she finally caught up to us. She held her phone up to her face and checked her makeup in the camera. She placed her hand on my sweaty bicep and said, "The lemurs are so soft, you're literally going to die."

"And that's . . . a good thing?" I asked, eyeing Madison like she had two heads.

Madison launched into an anecdote about lemurs, but my eyes stayed glued to Lark. She pulled a key from her giant carabiner and unlocked the iron door, yanking open the rusty lock with practiced ease. She leaned her shoulder into the door as she undid the bolt and then threw her whole weight back to yank it free and . . . Damn, none of that should be sexy, but it absolutely was.

I didn't think khakis and boots would do it for me either, but here I was, lusting after a woman who'd had her arm up a shit pipe the day before. What the fuck was wrong with me?

STAFF
PRICKLE ISLAND ZOO
ZOO

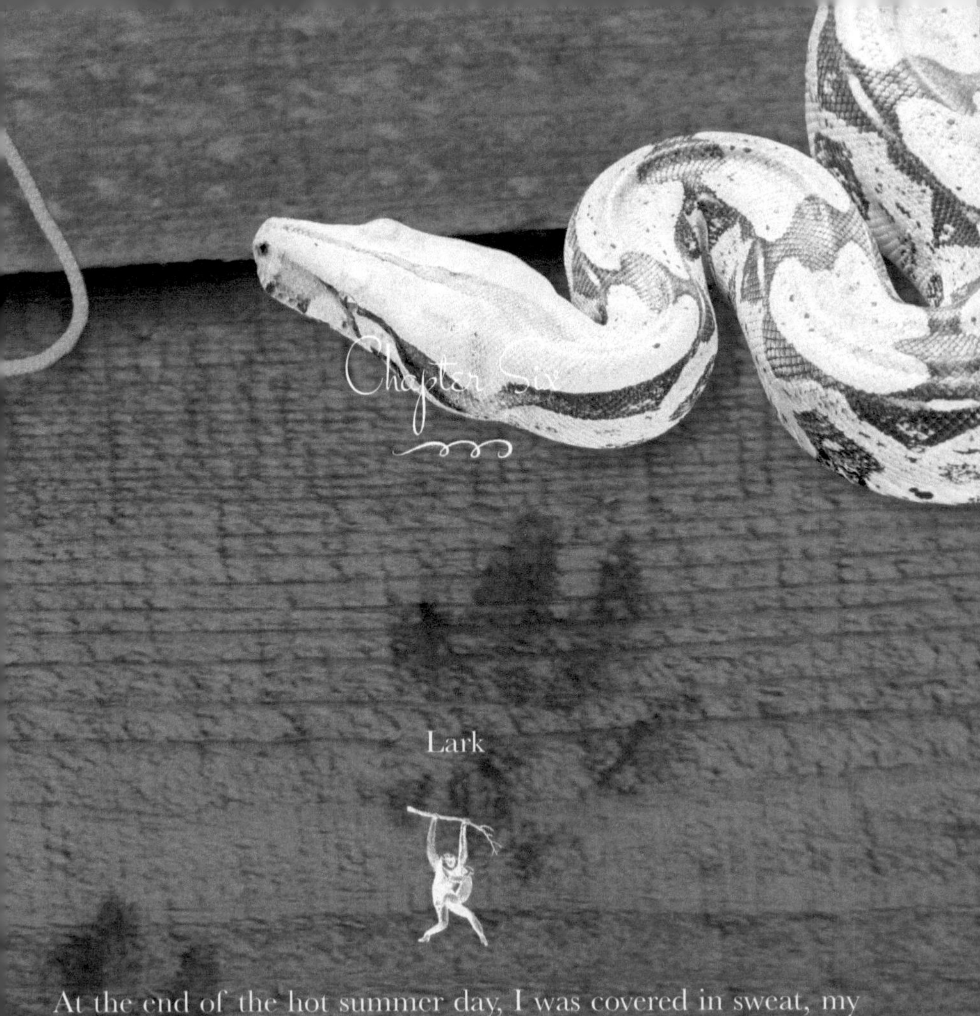

Chapter Six

Lark

At the end of the hot summer day, I was covered in sweat, my boots caked in mud, and my clothes speckled with the splash-back of hosing down enclosures. I was so ready to peel off my thick socks, have a shower, and curl up on the couch with a hard apple cider and a baby boa constrictor.

"You can head back to the volunteer house now," I said, not making eye contact with my Kiwi shadow. I could tell by the angle of the sun that we were at least two hours over the end of our shift—just as I had guessed. Madison had left long ago, but Logan seemed determined to finish out the day with me. "If you don't head down now, you'll only have burnt bread rolls left for dinner."

I saw his broad shoulders rise and fall from my periphery. "I can go grab something at the dairy instead," he said.

"Dairy?"

"That store down the road that sells the ice creams and stuff?"

"Oh, the general store," I said, wondering why he called it a dairy but also wanting to just get this day over with. I'd learned too many new Kiwi slang words already today and I was exhausted. I knew any questions would only prolong the time between now and me taking my boots and bra off.

Logan lingered behind me, and I glanced at him with an arched brow, wondering why he hadn't headed off yet.

"I was going to ask," Logan hedged. "I noticed in the staff directory Heron's pronouns are they/he—"

"Don't make me go off," I said, whirling as my shoulders bunched to my ears. Here it was. I knew there was something about this guy that would put me off. "Every single species we work with has examples of reversed and fluid gender roles as well as intersex individuals. All of these perceived notions of gender are a giant spectrum that humans have tried to shove into two ridiculous boxes based on ever-changing cultural norms . . ."

Logan's eyebrows practically hit his hairline as he said, "Sorry, just to be clear, this *isn't* you going off?"

"I'm not going to let any bigot mess with my family." My hands balled into fists at my sides, my mind preparing to launch into a whole bunch of statistics and biological facts that would eviscerate him.

"What I was going to ask," Logan continued slowly, like a frightened gazelle. "Do they prefer for 'they' and 'he' to be used interchangeably, or do they prefer we use 'they' but are okay with 'he' as well?"

I blinked at him. Goddammit. That was actually a really thoughtful question.

"I'd say they prefer 'they' ninety percent of the time, with a sprinkling of 'he' for fun every now and again."

"Sweet as," he said, rubbing the back of his neck. "Anything else you need a hand with?"

"No."

"Any other gender and sexuality statistics you want to throw my way?"

I narrowed my eyes at him. Yes. I had several, but I hated that he knew that. I also noted by the questions he was asking that he was trying to stall me. Why, I had no idea.

We kept walking, Logan trailing me like he had since dawn. He'd kept up during the whole shift and was actually useful, even though it was his first day. He didn't ask too many questions, but when he did, he asked the right ones, which made me both begrudgingly respect him and hate him even more. Why did he have to be good-looking *and* competent?

This whole day was breaking my brain. I didn't like guys. They made sense from a distance, like an impressionist painting. I could appreciate their attractiveness, even had a few fantasies about fictional men every now and then, but I didn't want to hook up with a real-life one!

And yet, everything Logan did today was kind of turning me on, and it enraged me. I was worse than a tiger in heat and was starting to think I should ask Finch to run bloodwork on me to make sure I didn't have a sudden hormonal imbalance.

"I just have the buckets left to do and then I'm done," I said tightly as we neared the prep kitchens and the giant industrial sinks we used to scrub down our buckets. "You can go."

"Let me wash them," Logan offered, taking the handle from the stack of empty buckets. I was too tired to clench my hand around them before he snagged them from my grip.

"It's my job," I said, reaching for the buckets, but he just held them higher out of my grasp like a kid playing keep-away. "You'll do it wrong."

"Is there a specific bucket-washing protocol I don't know about?"

"I have a system," I muttered, and he only grinned.

"Of course you do." He cleared his throat, trying to suppress a laugh. "Are you always pricklier than a porcupine, or is it just around me?"

"Excuse me?" My shoulders bunched around my ears again. "I am. Not. Prickly!"

Okay, maybe shouting it at him wasn't really helping my case. Still, I was about two seconds from shoving a porcupine quill up his ass. Let's see how prickly he thought I was then!

Logan lifted the hem of his shirt to wipe across his sweaty brow, revealing a peek of his muscled torso. Sweet baby Chris Hemsworth. He was more ripped than a pair of holey jeans.

The Greek god didn't seem to notice me gaping at him. By the time he lowered his shirt, I had sent a message to my face to stop drooling like a panting dingo.

"Look, tails," Logan said, his crinkling eyes finding mine as I desperately tried to shove the image of his body out of my mind. "The volunteer house is not exactly the place I want to go to relax at the end of the day."

I let out a rough laugh. Now *that* I understood. The place was party central. I felt like I needed a tetanus shot just walking into the volunteer house. I'd rather wash buckets than go down there too.

"Why don't you just go for a walk or something?" I countered. "Go down to the *dairy*."

"I think I've had enough recreational walking for the day."

I shifted my weight from foot to foot, my legs exceedingly tired as I said, "Touché." His eyebrows pinched together in a fake puppy dog face that was actually really sweet and completely unfair because he knew I was a zookeeper and had a thing for making sad animals happy. "Okay, fine," I said, dropping my hands from where they were still reaching out. "But I'm showing you my system first."

His smile was enough to make my legs a little shaky as he said, "Can't wait."

Okay, I definitely needed some iron supplements or an exorcism or something because the way those dark eyes were watching me made my stomach do little somersaults.

STAFF
PRICKLE ISLAND ZOO
ZOO

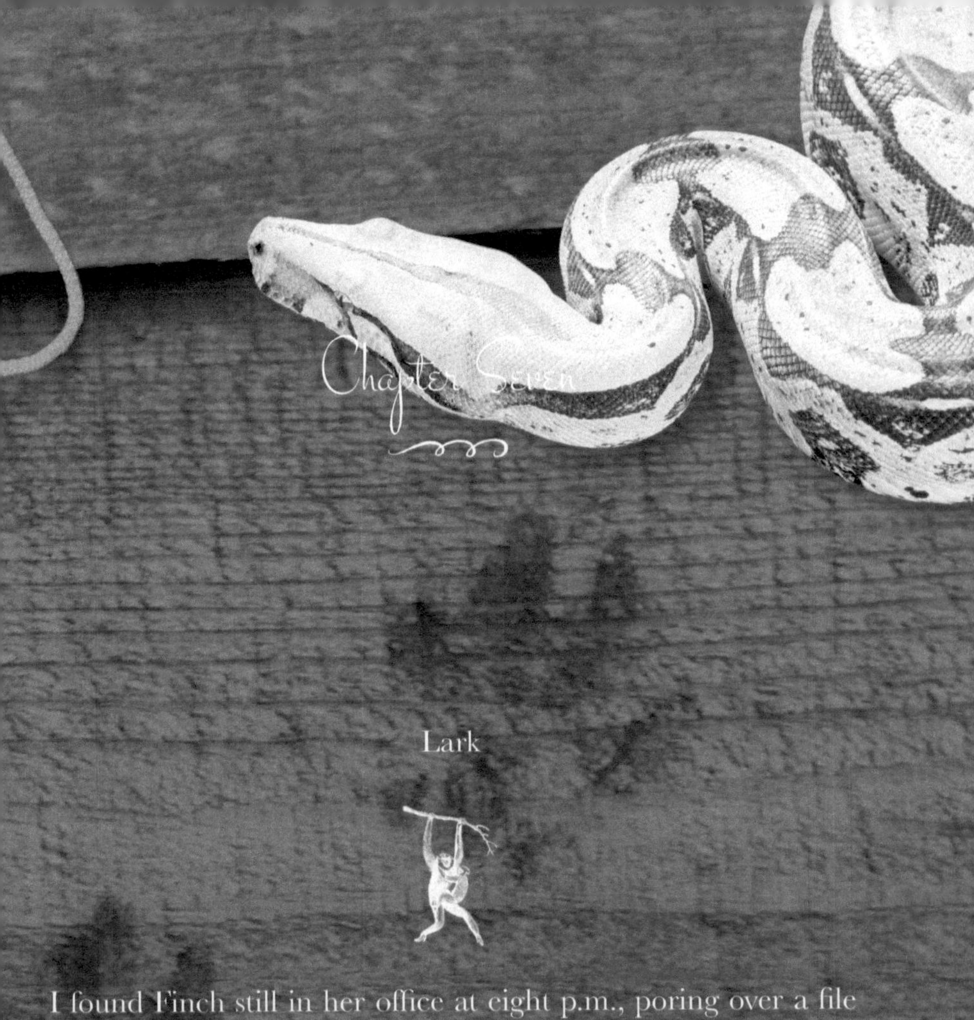

I found Finch still in her office at eight p.m., poring over a file on her desk. I wandered in and dropped into the empty desk chair across the room crowded with crates, boxes, and stacks of paper.

"You want me to heat up some ramen?" I offered as she looked up from her papers with bloodshot, unfocused eyes.

We kept a stash of emergency food in the vet hospital kitchens. The kitchens were mostly used for heating up animal formula and prepping food for the patients, but we had a few random jars of peanut butter and a bunch of instant noodles there for the inevitable late nights. Sometimes, we'd end up sleeping on the floor in here if an animal was particularly sick and the idea of going even the five-minute walk away was too far. It was also easier during baby bird season when the entire shoreline brought their rescued water birds to the vet hospital and we needed to crop feed them every two hours through the night. I crossed all my fingers and toes that there'd be no tropical storms during this year's season.

Eventually, Finch was planning on turning the attic into her own apartment. Hawk was helping her, but who knew how long it would actually take with our crazy schedules.

"I'm good," Finch said as I swirled my legs around the desk chair. "I just got sidetracked reading up on this study about . . . never mind." She looked at my face and I tried to perk up a bit. "I want to hear how your day was. You look like you got bitch-slapped by a baboon today."

"Not today," I muttered, though it had happened to me three times before. Freaking Loki.

"How was having Logan on the primate run?" she asked with a too-pleased-with-herself smirk. "Have you lifted your tail and let him sniff you yet?"

I folded my arms and leaned back in the chair. "I hate him."

"You mean you hate how much you *like* him," Finch corrected. "Flustered hottie syndrome. I should write a case study. Animals aren't the only ones who get all loopy for a potential mate."

"Don't say mate," I shot back. "And I don't like him."

"But you think he's hot," she said matter-of-factly. We exchanged glances, her eyebrows raising more and more with each passing second until I finally relented.

"Really hot." I groaned, pulling my hoodie strings tighter until I could barely peek out of the face hole. "Which I find infuriating because I don't hook up with guys, and even if I did, I don't hook up with volunteers."

"Uh-huh," Finch said, chewing on the end of her pen cap. "Did he keep up with your routine?"

"Yes." I dropped my face into my hands. "He even offered to wash my buckets."

"Well, I'll be damned," Finch said, slapping her knee. "That's practically going steady in zoo land."

"No, we're not *going steady*," I grumbled. "It's just the hottie goggles. He'll do something annoying and dickish soon enough and then I'll get my wits about me again."

"Or . . . he keeps being really nice to you even though you're being really mean to him—"

"I am no—"

"That wasn't a question," Finch said, doing her best Miranda Priestly as she pointed her chewed pen at me. "So you're going to do the Lark thing where you're mean to him until he's mean back and then you can justify that he's an asshole and stop liking him?"

"I hate you."

"No, you don't." Finch flashed her Cheshire cat grin, the piercings in her cheeks accenting her smile.

"I'm going to bed," I muttered, rising from my chair. "It's late."

Yes, eight p.m. was late when you woke up at four-thirty a.m.

"Have sweet dreams about you-know-who," Finch taunted, waggling her fingers at me.

I flipped her the bird as I walked out.

As I wandered down the path to the old monkey enclosure, I saw the volunteer house at the bottom of the hill lit up with party lights strobing out the windows. I had half a mind to stomp down there and bust them for underage drinking, or at least remind them that they would be waking up at dawn miserably hungover or not. I'd tell them they'd have no one to blame but themselves like the absolute buzzkill I knew I was.

Or maybe I should just go pointedly leave a giant box of condoms on the doorstep . . . We did nickname the place the Bunny House for a reason. The libidos in there were the worst of any primates in the entire zoo.

But then I thought Logan might be there and I really didn't want to see him with his tongue down a college girl's throat. The thought made me queasy. Although . . . the sight of him kissing someone else would at least let me get the sight of his ab muscles out of my mind. If he lifted his shirt to wipe his brow one more time, I was going to need a fire extinguisher for my lady bits.

I put off the Bunny House scolding for another day. I was only a handful of years older than a lot of them and still, I got more comments of "you remind me of my mom" or "you are just like my teacher" than any of my other siblings. If Logan saw me there now, he'd probably call me more than just *prickly*.

I passed the meerkat exhibit, all of them curled in a ball behind the glass window in their den. The porcupines were out wandering the exhibit while the meerkats slept, enjoying their evening apple slices. Porcupines were just like spiky puppies, and the way Logan had said it made it sound like he found my prickliness just as adorable.

I spotted Hawk's pickup truck pulling into the front of the zoo, probably having just finished his Monday night perimeter check. I had a sneaking suspicion my brother was going to stop in the kitchens to do some food prep before turning in for the night. But I was starting to sense a pattern with his little weekly act of altruism and so I decided to intervene. Little did Hawk know, I'd already finished the primate run's food prep just so my brother didn't spend all night weighing out monkey food for me.

I wandered over to our house, smug knowing I'd beaten my brother at his sneaky game. I speed-walked the rest of the way, looking forward to decompressing from the day curled up on the couch with a bowl of popcorn and Matilda snuggling on my lap . . . Yes, snakes can snuggle.

PRICKLE
ISLAND ZOO
ZOO
Volunteer

Chapter Eight

Logan

Last night's sleep on the rickety bunk bed had been made even worse by the fact that a bunch of drunk uni students were trying—and failing in spectacular fashion—to discreetly hook up in the bunk room. Volunteers weren't allowed to roam the zoo at night, so we had to stay in the house until morning, but we were allowed to use the back patio. I didn't smoke, but I'd found myself outside, leaning against the building and staring up at the strange constellations in the night sky. So different from the Southern Cross I was used to.

There were a lot of dumb things that my mates and I had done after a breakup, but this blew all the others away. I searched for that feeling of sadness, of heartbreak, but it didn't come. And a little voice spoke into my mind: *You have to really love someone to have your heart broken by them.*

Kiwis had a penchant for adventure—it was why you found one of us in every tramping hut and hostel all over the world. But coming to this zoo was beginning to feel like a quarter-life crisis. Was this my Ferrari and hair plugs moment?

The bass of the music thumped so loudly that the wall vibrated against my back. Cackles of drunken laughter echoed off the metal ceiling. I thought for the hundredth time in the last twenty-four hours that maybe I should just leave.

This whole thing was a massive mistake.

I should go home and face the music—no more adventures or running off. It was time to be the responsible one and step up, not leaving my little brother struggling to keep up the family business. And my dad? Who knew if his health was as bad as I feared. No one in my family would talk about it. I only had a terrible gut instinct that he wasn't well and I'd be needed at home soon . . . and that had freaked me out enough to wind up here of all places.

When Hawk passed the volunteer house, I practically leapt off the wall.

"Hey!" I called a little too loudly, jogging after him. "Do you need some help?"

Please say yes. Please say yes. If I had to stay in the volunteer house for one more second, I might completely lose my mind.

I took one of the milk crates out of his arms. They were empty but still, I didn't want him to say no, so I was trying to be useful.

He chuckled. "Not having fun with the volunteers?"

He and I were roughly the same age, and he seemed to understand the exact predicament I was in. Hawk was a handsome-looking bloke, and I bet he had a bunch of volunteers throwing themselves at him every summer. He seemed equally disinterested in them too.

"Not really my thing," I said, swinging the empty crate in my hand.

"It dies down after the first week or so, once they realize that they can stay up until two a.m. all they like, but the howlers, lions, parrots, and gibbons will be waking them up at four a.m. regardless. Until then, we've got some earplugs in the med kit. I recommend you use them." He gave me a sideways glance. "You look like you're in need of rescuing tonight."

"Please say you really need help with something?" I asked, eagerly bouncing on the balls of my feet. "I'd be eternally grateful."

"I do actually," he said with a nod, and my shoulders sagged in relief. "You can help me do some diet prep."

"Okay," I hedged, not knowing exactly what that entailed, but if it wasn't Jell-O shots and having drunk people make me repeat the word "deck" all night, then I was in.

We walked up the hill and into the prep kitchens. If an airport hangar and an old barn had a baby, that was what this place was. It had giant walk-in chill rooms and freezers and a whole wall that looked like a shrine to white buckets. A long metal workbench sat in the middle of the room along with an assortment of digital scales, knives, and giant chopping boards. There was a table with grow lights and rows of seedlings that made me wonder if they kept a garden somewhere and another table stacked high with containers of something that was *moving* . . . I cringed as I realized they were mealworms. Gross. A giant plastic tub of water sat in one corner, holding huge branches of leafy trees, and I identified the leaves as the same we gave to the howlers each morning.

"Wow. This place is like an entire botanic garden."

"We try to grow as much as we can here to cut down on

costs," Hawk said. "Having to ferry it over from the mainland only adds to the price. Food is definitely our biggest expense."

"I can only imagine," I said, gawking at the massive space. Around the corner, stacks and stacks of pellet bags sat on the upper platforms along with a forklift.

"We'll start with the bir—" Hawk opened the rolling fridge door. "Of course," he said as he frowned at a stack of labeled buckets in the corner.

"What?" I poked my head into the room, appreciating the chill on the balmy summer night.

"Lark already prepped the primate diets," he said.

"And that's a bad thing?" I asked, scanning the shelves that were overflowing with crates of fruits and vegetables.

"She can't just let me do a nice thing for her one night a week," he muttered.

"That sounds like her," I said with a nod and then realized maybe that was overstepping some sort of sibling line where Hawk was allowed to say those things, but I, a stranger, was not. "Sorry—"

"No, no, it's true," he said with a chuckle. He pulled a plastic tray of apples back to reveal a case of beer. "Drink?"

"Sweet as, cheers," I said, excited to have something better than a warm bag of wine to drink.

Hawk grabbed two bottles and slid the apples back.

"We keep them hidden for when we're doing tours," he explained. "I can't imagine the Westworths' private guests would like seeing cases of beer in here." He shrugged, opening his bottle and dropping the cap onto the metal table with a clink. "But I'm technically off the clock. I think we can handle chopping a few apples."

We lifted our bottles to each other, and then I took a long sip. "I think of any job, you all have earned a drink after a long day."

"I think my sister, Finch, embodies the 'work hard, play hard' philosophy more than the rest of us." He laughed as he sipped his drink. His sister did seem like a bit of a booze hag, but I wasn't about to say as much. "Here." He took another sip and then set his drink on one of the lower shelves. "We'll be pulling all the blue crates first."

I took one last swig of my beer and then helped him haul all of the fruit out onto the table. He turned on a touch screen above the metal table and showed me how to read the different diet sheets, what size to cut things, and where to put the different pieces of fruit. We set about chopping, taking sips of beer in between pieces of fruit.

"How's the primate run?" he asked knowingly.

"It's good," I hedged, and he laughed.

"Lark hasn't made you cry yet, so that's good."

"She makes people cry?" I asked incredulously.

"Sometimes." He shook his head, probably remembering some particular instance. "Though she doesn't mean it. Not really."

"I don't find her that intense," I said with a shrug. "She's just focused."

"I'm sure it would piss her off to know you're not scared of her," Hawk added. "She's a real hardass, but she cares more than any of us too."

"I know," I said, more to myself.

"You know?" Hawk arched his brow, and I suddenly felt like I'd stepped out of line again. I really shouldn't be talking to this guy about his sister. Hawk seemed like the only person around here who I could actually hold a conversation with, and I didn't want to ruin it by being a creep. "I just mean, when you see her with her animals, you can tell she cares."

Hawk hummed in agreement. "I think she thinks that if everything is perfect, it will get easier."

"What?"

"Life." He gestured with his knife to the surrounding room. "Someday, she'll realize that no matter how perfect her routines, no matter how well she takes care of us, there won't be a level of perfectionism where she wins a trophy and then finally gets to be happy. Sorry," Hawk added quickly. "That's too deep for food-prep conversation."

I chuckled. It seemed like the Lachlan siblings all had psychology degrees from the way they talked. Maybe that was the same thing that endeared them to working with animals.

"I . . . I don't know if I'm going to stay for the summer," I said tentatively. "I didn't realize this was mostly a university program, and I don't really think I fit in here, and—"

My phone buzzed, a message from my mom who was just waking up in New Zealand. Hawk glanced over to my phone, which I'd placed on the bench beside my beer bottle.

"Is she the reason you want to go?" He smirked and nodded to the lock screen. "I don't blame you."

"Nah." I grimaced at the smiling picture of Kelly, mid-jump at the beach because she thought it would be "quirky." She made me take at least a hundred of them to get the perfect "candid" shot, and she put her favorite of that hundred as the lock screen of my phone, replacing the generic Southern Alps photo that had been there before. I once again made a mental note to change it as I turned my phone over. "She's the reason I came here in the first place. Well, one of the reasons."

"Ah," Hawk said, clinking his beer bottle against mine again. "Now *that* I understand too."

"I can't imagine there's a lot of options for you on an island," I said. "No Tinder for Prickle Island?"

"Not unless you have a thing for octogenarian duchesses." He shook his head as he put a lid on one of the buckets and slid it across the bench to make room for another. "It's fine," he said. "I'm not looking for anything serious. This life really isn't for everyone, and I doubt I'm going to stumble across a woman who wants to live in a zoo for the rest of her life."

"I know how you feel," I said, and he shot me a look. "Okay, well, not exactly, but Kelly and I broke up because I needed to move back to my hometown and she wanted to stay in the city. There are not a lot of potential girlfriends who want to live in the middle of nowhere." Hawk nodded in agreement as he finished the last of his drink and set the empty bottle down. "Do you think you want another beer?"

"I don't think we could handle more than three with the space we have," he replied.

"You've already had two?"

He looked at me like I was speaking German. "What?"

"You've already had two beers?"

"We have three bears," he said.

"Oh, *beers*," I said, over-emphasizing the word. "Not bears."

"Ohhhh." His shoulders shook with laughter. "Say bear beer."

"Bear beer."

"They sound exactly the same," he said.

"No, they don't," I replied. "Besides, only one ever makes sense in context."

"Unless you're having drinks at a zoo," he replied, belly laughing harder.

This was a different side to the gruff man I normally saw stomping around the zoo, stone-faced like his sister, and it was kind of nice to actually have someone to talk to.

Hawk's face sobered slightly as he smiled at me. "I think you should give it another week before you call it quits," he said. "It's nice having another guy around here for once. And yes," he added, nodding to the fridge. "I'd like another bear."

PRICKLE
ISLAND
ZOO
ZOO
Volunteer

Chapter Nine

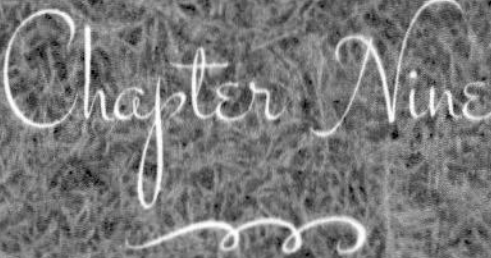

Logan

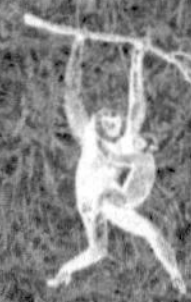

The roar of the howler monkeys in the morning was so loud, I couldn't even hear the scrape of Lark's shovel dragging across the concrete of the enclosure. "Do you ever get used to it?" My voice was hoarse from having to shout to be heard.

"Used to what?" she shouted back.

Well, that answered my question.

The monkeys paused, making my ears ring, and I said, "How can such a little monkey make such a loud sound? I feel like a giant monster is about to burst through the trees."

A spark ignited in Lark's eyes as she turned toward me. "They actually used howler monkey sounds for the dinosaurs in Jurassic Park," she said with glee before remembering that—for some reason—she didn't like me and plastered back on her signature frown.

I loved that she couldn't control her need to share that fun fact with me though. She turned all bright and shiny when she was talking about animals, as if her inner child came bounding out before she could tamp it down. It seemed like the truest version of herself.

Note to self: ask Lark for more animal fun facts.

One monkey dive-bombed me from the top of the enclosure, a fluffy black cannonball that smacked the air out of my chest. I tried to keep hosing down the mixture of food scraps and poo toward the drain, but I found myself continually flinching, as if bracing for the impact of another monkey falling from the sky. Pretty sure my orange volunteer T-shirt had muddy footprints all up the back and shoulders now. I looked like I got run over by a mob of howler monkeys, but it was just the same one again and again and again.

"He always does that," Lark said, pointing to the howler who was making a game of climbing to the top of their enclosure and jumping down on me.

"Who is that?"

"Not Stephen."

"What's his name?"

"That's his name." She gestured to the whiteboard through the chain-link and sure enough, three names down was "Not Stephen."

"You named a monkey 'Not Stephen?'"

She shrugged. "He was born a few months after another monkey we named Stephen and they looked so much alike, we couldn't tell them apart." She gestured to another monkey hanging from his tail at the top of the enclosure, munching on a bundle of fresh leaves. "Probably because Stu is the father of both of them. You can see the resemblance, right?"

I blinked at her. Yeah, I could see the resemblance. They were all bloody howler monkeys. That was the resemblance. But I asked instead, "You can tell the rest of them apart?"

She looked at me like I was speaking in Klingon. "Can you tell Madison and I apart?" she asked with an arched brow. "All of their faces are different. After a few months, Stephen and Not Stephen started looking less alike, but the name stuck. I kept thinking we'd rename him, but we never did."

"I only know that the baby's name is Emma." I nodded to the black little fluff ball that clung to its mum's back.

Lark smiled up at her. "Emma is our first baby howler in years, and she's my favorite new addition to the zoo . . . well, her and Matilda."

"Who's Matilda?"

She ignored me and kept shoveling. I could see her schooling herself, as if she were having a little pep talk in her brain that she wasn't meant to be sharing this stuff with me.

Still, I saw how she peeked up at the mother monkey, Darcy, beaming like a proud mum as Emma ventured off her mother's back and started to explore little by little. Darcy seemed to keep Emma within tail-grabbing range and whenever the baby walked too far, she'd grab her by the tail and yank her back again with the same exasperated expression as a human mother just trying to finish a meal without her toddler running off.

Darcy wandered down the tree branch and onto the feeding platform where Madison was meant to be putting out the fresh fruit. All the while, Emma clung to her mum like an immovable backpack.

Madison handed out pieces of fruit one at a time to the

troop, holding her phone in the other, clearly trying to get a good shot.

"Maddie," Lark warned as Madison held a piece of papaya back from the biggest monkey to get a longer shot.

Lark's mouth opened to say more, but before she could get it out, the monkey launched forward, yanking Madison by the hair and snatching the piece of fruit.

Madison screamed, tripping backward over her bucket. Lark and I launched forward at the same time. Lark shoved Maddie back up to her feet, and Maddie smacked against the chain-link fence hard but managed to cling on and keep herself upright. Lark's gumboots skidded across the slippery, wet concrete and her arms started windmilling.

As Lark tipped over, I dropped to my knees, catching her upper body like a rugby ball. The slimy concrete, however, was even less forgiving than a rugby pitch, and I knew when I looked down at my knees, they'd be covered in scratches and bruises. Lark's head slammed back against my forearm with the momentum of her fall, and I was certain I'd just saved her from smashing her skull against the concrete.

Lark stared breathlessly up at me, and the way she looked at me made my whole body buzz like a plucked guitar string. My eyes instinctively fell to her full, parted lips as she caught her breath. My fingertips pressed tighter into the soft skin of her side, where they had slipped under the hem of her shirt. For a second, I half-considered just leaning down and kissing that breathless mouth, suddenly so keen to have my lips on hers—

"Oh. My. God." Madison's sharp voice cut the spell and I watched as that buzzing moment between us disappeared from Lark's eyes like a hypnotist snapping their fingers.

What was I doing? What was I *thinking*? I quickly pulled my head back as Lark bolted up out of my grasp.

"Please don't sue. Please don't sue," Lark muttered under her breath as she raced over to Madison's side. "Are you hurt? Are you okay?"

Madison held up her phone, a video of the attack playing on a loop on her screen. "This is seriously hilarious," she said, suddenly all better. I gaped at her as she patted Lark's arm and looked at me. "Wow. That was some Marvel-level heroics, Logan."

"I could've handled it," Lark said, pinching the bridge of her nose.

"You're welcome?" I replied, rising back to my feet and cringing as I saw my bloodied knees.

"Maddie, it's almost time for our lunch break." *It wasn't anywhere near our time for a lunch break.* "Why don't you head off a little early and take a long lunch?" Lark asked, moving to the heavy iron door and unbolting it for the volunteer.

Madison was glued to her phone again and only gave a perfunctory, "Uh-huh." Clearly, she was unaware she almost smashed her head open on the concrete and nearly caused Lark to do the same.

Madison wandered off, sloshing in her gumboots through the disinfectant solution without looking up. I thought she might bite it again on the wet concrete between enclosures, but she managed to stay upright.

"That kid is a liability," I said.

Lark waved a hand down at my bloody shins. "She's not the only one."

"Are you *mad* that I saved you from cracking your skull open?"

Lark folded her arms across her chest, and I was determined to not look down at the swell of her breasts that peeked from the V of her shirt, which had accidentally popped open during her fall. "I could've grabbed her without falling if you hadn't gotten in the way and without getting my knees all bloody."

"Oh, really?"

"Really," she bit out. "I've been navigating this place my entire life. This isn't my first rodeo with an overly confident volunteer." Her fingers stretched and clenched at her side again, as if she were trying to keep herself from scolding me. I was impressed by her level of self-control when I was trying my best to goad her into a playful spat. I loved when she got fiery, but she clearly didn't want to play as she said, "Come on. Before you bleed all over my clean floors."

"You're mad at me for bleeding now too?"

She put her hand on my back and gave me a nudge toward the door. The light shove didn't move me an inch, and she looked to where her hand had been on my bright orange T-shirt.

"Are you made of freaking marble?" She stared at my bicep like she had X-ray vision. "I'm making you carry the buckets the rest of the summer," she added. "Can't have you losing those guns."

A smile twisted my lips. I'd had women compliment my body before, but never one who was excited—not to have my big arms around her, or lift her, *or pin her down,* but to have them carrying heavy buckets up and down hills all day long. And for some weird reason, I liked that. A lot.

"There's a med kit in the hall," she said.

"I can do it if you want to finish up in here," I offered. I knew she'd be grumpy all day if she fell behind her self-imposed schedule. She seemed to be the only keeper at the zoo who had a laminated and color-coded one hanging in every enclosure.

"Just let me." She blew the stray strands of sandy-brown

hair off her face. "I have a way I like the Band-Aids to be orga- nized and I don't want you messing it up."

Of course she had a plaster system. That surprised me none. Like all things Lark Lachlan, she was purposeful and methodical down to her medical kit organization.

I followed her to the little food prep table built into the long hallway. She seemed to notice the top buttons of her shirt undone as I trailed behind her and hastily re-buttoned them. When we reached the table, she opened the creaking metal cabinets and fished out a clear plastic container that looked more like a giant toolbox than a medical kit . . . I supposed keepers sustained all sorts of random injuries on the job.

"Sit," she instructed, looking at the plastic chair. She set the kit on the bench and washed her hands vigorously with the industrial-grade cleaner. "If Hawk or Mom finds out about this . . ."

"I won't tell them," I promised.

"I'm sure Maddie is already sharing that video with the entire internet." She groaned. "This is a disaster. I knew she wasn't ready to go into an enclosure. She doesn't have any chill."

I nodded. You couldn't be loud or jumpy around animals, even farm animals. There was a certain kind of masseuse-level calm that people who worked with animals were able to harness. Madison had none of that.

"Hawk keeps nagging me about letting volunteers be more hands-on and giving them more experiences so they promote the program. It's important to our funding. Ugh. And the howlers are the easiest troop too. The spider monkeys are too grabby. Too many limbs. The squirrel monkeys are bitey and smell like urine. The marmosets are fine but are flighty and hard to get a photo with. This whole thing is ridiculous," Lark groused to herself, opening the med kit. "I figured the howlers would be our safest option for her since she was so desperate to 'have a monkey selfie.'" She put on a high, whiny voice that made me chuckle. "I should've known better."

"It seemed like a fine call to me."

"That's because you've got chill animal vibes," she said. "Like, you've got baboon-level chill."

I didn't know what that meant, but I felt like I'd passed some sort of test. I hummed and gave a nod. "I grew up on a farm."

"Aha!" She pointed her finger toward the ceiling and then toward me. "That explains a lot."

"Well, technically, it was a farm slash café slash community hub for the little town I lived in. My family does a little bit of a lot of things."

Nodding, she said, "That I get too. Zoologists, business owners, customer service reps, conservationists, tour guides, café owners, construction workers, gardeners, chefs . . . we do it all around here too."

She rifled through the collection of Band-Aids and selected two large oval ones. I hoped that this conversation might unlock another level of tolerance between us, if not friendliness even. Maybe I was just overthinking things, but it seemed like she'd been more cold with me than the other volunteers and certainly more than the other staff and locals who frequented the zoo. Lark would outright *smile* at crowds of zoo visitors and then scowl at me in the next breath.

"Take your boots off," she instructed, and I did as she asked, shucking my boots and then rolling off my wooly socks. It was still early and I hoped they didn't have too much of the sweaty foot smell yet. I mean, Lark was literally one-arm swimming in a feces pond the other day, so she probably wouldn't care, but for some reason, I didn't want to have stinky feet around her. Droplets of blood had already stained my socks, and I grabbed a paper towel from the dispenser and wiped up my legs.

"Here," she said, taking out a little spray bottle. "This stings a little, but you don't want to get an infection as that floor is normally covered in monkey poo, so . . ."

"Yeah, I get it," I said as she crouched and sprayed the disinfectant onto my cut knees. She looked up at me from between my spread legs and my mind short-circuited. "You okay?"

"Perfect," I gritted out, knowing she was asking about the stinging but wishing she were about to reach for my belt buckle. Those full lips, the way she balanced one hand on my thigh . . .

Focus on the stinging or the monkey poo or the frozen fucking tundra, anything other than the hot woman crouched between your legs, you stupid bloody egg. I couldn't be getting accidentally hard in front of her, especially when her face was this close to my crotch. And definitely not after she was finally talking to me in more than monosyllabic sentences.

Lark cleaned up the rest of my knees with an antiseptic wipe and covered them with the oval plasters, then she rose and made quick work of cleaning up the bench area.

"Well, Maddie is officially on fruit-chopping duties for the rest of the summer," she said, reaching up and straightening her ponytail in a way that shouldn't be sexy but absolutely fucking was. Everything she did was sexy. She couldn't help it.

"Are you sure you can trust her with a knife?" I asked.

"I'll make her wear the knife safety gloves," she said with a laugh. She nibbled the inside of her lip and glanced down the hallway. "You want to meet the spider monkeys?"

I don't know why, but the way she asked me felt like a big deal. Maybe this was her way of thanking me for shredding up my shins to save her? Maybe she just wanted to spend her lunch break with me? Maybe I was overthinking this and she did this with all the chill vibes volunteers . . .

Still, my responding smile and nod made her light up even more. "I would love to."

This was something special, and for some reason, she was sharing it with me.

STAFF
PRICKLE
ISLAND
ZOO
ZOO

"That was fun," Logan said, swinging his arms back and forth like he didn't know what to do with them. I needed to give him more buckets to carry.

I double-checked the padlock, yanking on the thick metal to make sure it didn't open. "You're a natural," I said with a shrug. "I think you and Jacob are besties now."

Logan chuckled. Jacob, the four-year-old spider monkey, had climbed all over Logan like he was a jungle gym. I had to pull out a foraging box treat for Jacob just to get him off so we could get out of the enclosure. Logan had handled the invasion of his personal space like a champ. Most people would've been provoked by it, would've tried to shift away or move them off and started a dangerous chain reaction. But Logan moved around the enclosure with surprising ease. And okay, fine, maybe I was testing him to see how he could handle it a little bit.

The radio on my hip scratched and I heard the tail end of my name as I twisted the volume up. Unclipping the radio from my belt with a click, I held it to my mouth and waited for the beep. "Go ahead."

"Uhhh . . ." Crane's breath crackled over the radio. I hated when he started his radio calls with a long breath. I wheeled my hand around in silent command to speed it up. "We've got a Code Aardvark at The Peckish Peacock."

"On my way," I said, tugging on the lock instinctively one last time before taking off at a jog toward the lunch pavilion.

"I didn't know you had aardvarks at the zoo," Logan said, easily keeping up with me without even having to jog.

"We don't," I replied. "That's why we use it as a code word. It means there's a minor issue with a visitor at the café." I picked up my radio and asked, "Can you describe the nature of the problem?"

"A kid's got his knee stuck in the porcupine and I need an extra pair of hands."

"What?" I shouted into the radio, suddenly picking up into a run. "Shouldn't that be a Code Blue? Do I need to get a med kit?"

How the fuck did a kid get into the porcupine exhibit, and what did it mean to have his knee *stuck*? I had a bunch of awful images of impaled porcupine quills. Had some parent dangled their kid over to get a better look? This was why we couldn't have nice things!

I burst through the side path and jumped over the knee-high fence to the back of the café. I bolted around the corner, relief flooding through me as Crane's voice came back through the radio, confirming the sight in front of me.

"The playground that's *shaped* like a porcupine," he said, bored. "Not an actual porcupine."

My shoulders drooped as I spotted Crane across the pavilion, standing next to two worried parents looking up at a small child who'd somehow managed to scale the giant fake quills and end up on top of the playground. "You could've freaking started with that," I grumbled but didn't say it over the radio.

There were too many visitors around, and the last thing I needed was to be told off by Hawk or my mom for complaining over the radio during operating hours. Why couldn't the kid have gotten stuck on the elephant-shaped slide? We didn't have any actual elephants in the zoo, so at least then I would've known what Crane meant.

I raced over to the child, who looked about four with a mop of blond hair and a concerned expression, though he wasn't crying at least. I was about to start climbing the fake quills, wondering how on earth I was going to get up there, when Logan bounded forward and hauled himself up on top of the playground with his beefy biceps. He hooked one leg over the top of the quill, balancing himself as he bent forward to the worried kid.

"Wow, you climbed so high," he said in an impressed voice. "Are you a superhero?" The little boy shook his head, his concern easing a little. "Are you sure you're not Spider-Man?" Logan goaded, and the boy's face broke out into a smile.

"No," the boy said with a giggle.

"Okay, Spider-Man," Logan said, making the boy laugh more. "I'm going to help you get down, alright?"

The boy nodded as Logan maneuvered the boy's knee backward and out of the tight space where the two quills met. The mother standing beside Crane let out a sigh of relief that made her whole body drop forward. Once the boy's leg was free, Logan pulled him up over the edge and lowered the boy down by his armpits to his dad's outstretched hands. Rescue successfully completed, Logan jumped from the porcupine structure, where the boy's mom hugged him and profusely thanked him.

Okay, she really didn't need to be groping him like that . . .

Logan gave her a nod, stepping out of her touch, and gave the boy a high five in the most adorable way that made my stupid ovaries do a little dance. Of course he had to be good with monkeys *and* children. Of freaking course. He also spared me from making an ass of myself in front of a crowd of people as I attempted to pole dance my way up a massive porcupine structure.

My little brother gave me a salute, and I nodded back. Emergency avoided. I picked up my radio and stalked back behind the café, leaving Logan to be showered with his well-earned praise. "You found him," I said to my brother over the radio. "You're the one filling out the incident report."

"Oh, come on." Crane moaned. "You're better at it than I am."

Hawk's voice sounded over the radio. "Looking forward to reading that report tonight, Crane."

I was about to head over toward the rainforest walkthrough when Logan reappeared by my side.

"Thought you could lose me, tails?" he asked with a wink.

"The marmosets get lunch at twelve o'clock," I said, as if that were answer enough. "I didn't want to fall behind schedule." Logan let out a little harrumph but kept following me. "That was impressive, by the way," I added sheepishly. "You should consider a career in firefighting." I tried—and failed—not to think of him posing for one of those calendars . . .

"You would've handled it without me," he said with a

shrug. "But seeing as I'm taller, I figured I would make it up there first."

"I probably would've made an ass of myself," I said. "Thank you for sparing me the embarrassment."

"When Crane said a kid with his knee stuck in a porcupine, did you think—"

"Yep." I let out a loud laugh, shaking my head at the ridiculousness. "Never thought I'd hear that radio call, but you've got to be prepared for anything around here, I guess."

The back of Logan's hand bumped against mine as we walked over toward the rainforest walkthrough. It was only an accidental touch, but it made the back of my hand tingle. I had the strange, sudden urge to reach out and hold his hand— which would look totally unhinged and be completely inappropriate. I stuffed my hands in my pockets instead. He needed to stop being so cute with monkeys and children. It was really confusing my libido. I walked faster, trying to think about my sore feet and not about the attractive distraction beside me.

STAFF
PRICKLE ISLAND ZOO
ZOO

Chapter Eleven

Lark

Two weeks later and Logan was still hanging around me like a golden retriever shadow. He'd started prepping all the diets in the evenings to escape the volunteer house, even beating me out to the prep work a few times. We'd entered into an unspoken battle to see who would get to them first. Most of the time, I let him win because I wouldn't want to spend my evenings in the volunteer house either.

I was still mad at him for being distractingly good-looking, and even when shark week came and went, my hormones still all had little Logan-shaped glasses on. But I was done falling for people just to have them leave at the end of summer, so I put a leash on my stupid hormones . . . which was really hard when Logan kept wiping his sweaty brow with the hem of his T-shirt in an act that I swore made "Pony" by Ginuwine play every time he did it.

"How are there no visitors here today?" Logan asked. He snipped leaves into a basket beside me, none the wiser that I was busy thinking about what he'd look like shirtless.

"It rained this morning," I said with a shrug.

"But it's beautiful out now."

"The weather an hour before opening is always a predictor of numbers, even if it changes in the afternoon," I said, wanting to launch into the statistical analysis I had conducted two years ago on visitor behaviors and patterns, but I refrained. "I guess they think they need the whole day to visit and don't want to waste their money, but I like these days because it means less time spent telling people off for trying to poke their fingers into enclosures and more time making enrichment. They're going to love their veggie popsicles."

Logan snorted. "You're an animal extrovert and a human introvert."

I glanced at him and our gazes snagged. He had gorgeous brown eyes that turned almost a honeyed amber like a squirrel monkey's in the right light. Most people would probably be offended by being compared to a squirrel monkey, but for some reason, I knew that Logan would take it as the compliment it was.

Oh god, I was still staring into his eyes, thinking about squirrel monkeys.

I tore my gaze away and began hacking into the kale in front of me with my scissors.

He cleared his throat. "Does most of the produce in the kitchens come from here?"

"No. We still have to supplement from a mainland supplier,

but Mom wants us to one day be able to grow a good bulk of our fruit and veg at least."

The greenhouse was baking even with all the windows and doors open, and the leaves were all beginning to look sad and wilty. The rest of the five greenhouses were filled with everything from tomatoes to bell peppers to exotic tropical fruits that didn't mind the heat one bit, but this greenhouse had some accidental kale regrow from the winter, so we were quickly making use of it.

"Your mum has quite the green thumb," Logan said. "I bet my mum would love some tips."

"Is she a gardener too?"

I'd given up trying not to talk to Logan. He made conversation too damn easy, and every time we were together, I forgot more and more to treat him like I did the other volunteers. He was always around even when he didn't need to be and actually half-decent company, especially compared to Madison, who was currently standing outside the greenhouse, so focused on filming an AMA that she almost walked straight into an electric fence.

"Yeah, Mum grows a bunch of the food for the family and the café," Logan said, filling up his bucket with produce. "But it's nothing compared to this place."

"This is what semi-retirement looks like for an ex-keeper." I chuckled as I waved my scissors around. "Mom was meant to step back and do more of the big picture stuff—proposals for the Westworths, liaising with other zoos, event planning—but Evie Lachlan is *not* a desk job person. I think this whole place was a manifestation of her anxiety from sitting too long."

"A pretty productive retirement crisis," Logan added. "Why can I imagine you doing exactly the same?"

I gave a huff of mock offense even though that is *exactly*

what I would do. I didn't know how to sit still. I couldn't ever imagine having a desk job, let alone an idle retirement.

A chorus of high-pitched screeching cut through the air and the sound flooded my whole body with ice. I dropped my bucket and ran on instinct. Something was going on with the howlers. That wasn't a normal sound.

"Are we following you or . . . ?" Madison called from far behind me as I bolted, but I ignored her, too focused on running as fast as I could.

Logan, to his credit, didn't say a word, chasing after me as I pounded the concrete with my heavy boots. The sounds grew louder and more frantic, and I wondered if a brawl had broken out or if a visitor had jumped the fence and was harassing them . . . A million worst-case scenarios flashed through my head.

My lungs burned and legs ached as I ran. I spent most of my day speed-walking, so sprinting really shouldn't have been so hard, but have you ever sprinted up a steep hill before? Brutal.

But the panicked noises kept me going, even as I was determined to add a new cardio routine into my schedule, as if I had any more time in the day. Terror gripped me tighter as the sounds continued. This wasn't a passing fight. Whatever was happening was still ongoing.

When I turned the corner, all other thoughts tumbled out of my head at what I saw. It took me a second to make sense of it with all the commotion within the enclosure, but then I saw it: there, resting on the top of the enclosure, was a wayward balloon probably from some rich person's garden party. The string had dropped through the chain-link roof and a little black fluff ball was tangled up in it.

"Emma!" I screamed and ran faster.

Volunteer
PRICKLE
ISLAND
ZOO
ZOO

Chapter Twelve

Logan

Her scream was like a knife to the chest. Lark permitted herself that one split second of horror before launching into action. There were certain types of people who knew how to react in an emergency: firefighters, nurses, and I was now adding keepers to that list. She radioed her siblings to come help her even as she unlocked the door one-handed and bolted into the anteroom. I followed after her silently, knowing she was in her element and to wait until she had directions for me. She moved with military precision, running through the gauntlet of anteroom doors like a ninja warrior. I was getting pulled trying to keep up.

When she opened the howler door, I could see that Emma

was still moving, still wriggling and screeching for her mum. Darcy was in a panic, yanking Emma over and over to try and dislodge her from her trap, but that was only creating a tourniquet around her waist and neck.

Lark pulled out her Leatherman and flicked open the blade. She tried to climb up the chain-link one-handed, but her boot slipped.

"Here," I said, squatting down and grabbing her around the thighs. I hoisted her up so that she was sitting on my shoulder, my arms banding around her shorts to hold her steady.

She didn't make a single sound of protest, only a nod of confirmation that yes, this was a better plan. Her gaze remained locked on Emma above her.

"Get ready for it," she said.

"What?" But even as I asked, the troop all descended on us, biting and yanking at our clothes. "Motherfucker," I growled, trying to shake one off my leg. Fuck, they were strong. One of them was going to take a chunk out of me.

"It's okay, it's okay," Lark said in a sweet, hushed tone even as she was being ambushed by an angry monkey mob.

When she cut Emma free, she fell limply into Lark's arms. No more fluffy backpack. Fear curled in my gut that maybe she'd broken an arm or even paralyzed herself from where the string cut into her neck.

"Hey, hey, hey!" Hawk shouted, bursting into the enclosure and yanking a monkey off of my side.

Adrenaline poured through me, my heart thundering in my ears.

"We've got to take her to the hospital!" Finch's voice sounded behind us.

Lark tucked Emma into her shirt, and I carefully lowered her down. Even in my panic, I noticed the way her ass slid down my chest and hip, and I was definitely going to hell for that.

Hawk was recalling the troop into their nighttime enclosure with the lure of early dinner and those fruit ice blocks we'd made for them earlier. Darcy, of course, wasn't interested. Hawk had to get in between us and Darcy so that we could get out the door without the mother monkey following us.

"We're bringing her back, Mama, don't worry," Lark reassured her. "She's coming back."

We exited the enclosure, leaving Hawk behind to deal with the rest of the troop as we raced Emma through the zoo to the vet hospital. Lark and Finch rushed into the exam room, and I hung against the wall, feeling completely useless.

"Logan." Lark barked out my name without looking up. "Can you go finish making the enrichment and throw the scavenger balls over for the baboons? And go find Maddie and give her something to do? And tell one of the tour guides I won't be there for the rainforest tour and that you'll assist them?"

I stared at her in shock for a second. She was asking me to take over part of her shift? I mean, granted, it wasn't any actual direct contact parts. Still, for Lark, of all people, to trust me with it was a really big deal.

"I'm on it," I said and left without another word.

The adrenaline easily carried me through the next few hours like no time had passed. I did everything on Lark's shift that didn't involve a key: washed buckets, prepped food, raked leaves, made enrichment, filled in paperwork, and even gave a few impromptu tours to people who did end up coming to the zoo even though it was raining in the morning.

The whole rest of the shift was a blur. The sound of Lark screaming Emma's name haunted me. I anxiously scrubbed the buckets until my fingers were raw. That was the only way I knew how to help and so I was doing it as best as I could.

When I'd exhausted all of my helpful ideas, I made my way back down to the vet hospital. I found Lark in one of the smaller treatment rooms. Emma appeared to be either asleep or sedated, wrapped up around a hot water bottle and a bunch of fleecy blankets in a giant carrier on the table.

"Is she going to be okay?" I asked, and when Lark looked up at me, I could see the exhaustion on her face. She was clearly in the throes of an adrenaline crash. She looked like she'd had ten cups of coffee and hadn't slept in a week. Her eyes were bloodshot and rimmed with red. The thought of her crying made my soul crack.

"Nothing's broken," she said, bouncing her leg up and down. "But Finch says she needs to stay down here until she gets full mobility in her arms again. She thinks Emma sprained something and wants to put her left arm in a cast for a week. If she can't hold on to her mom, she could fall and injure herself even worse." She kept shifting, kept moving as if she were about to combust. "I'm going to fucking kill the owner of that balloon." She took a shuddering breath and all the pent-up energy in me snapped.

I shut the door, reaching her in two strides, and pulled her into a tight hug. Her whole body trembled against mine, her arms limp by her sides for a second before she lifted her hands and wrapped them around me.

"Today was really scary," I murmured into her hair, the surprising smell of lavender wafting from it, along with a healthy dose of hay and monkey poo. "Are you okay?"

"Not really." Her words were muffled into the fabric of my shirt, and I felt breath by breath as her whole body eased in my hold, the tension finally ebbing as she melted into me.

My hand swept soothing circles down her back, and every-thing about that moment—her warmth, her smell, the buzz that filled my veins with having her pressed up against me—felt so incredibly right. I burrowed into my deepest sense of calm, as if I could pull the anxiety from her body with this hug alone. I could've stood there forever, breathing her in, feeling her chest rise and fall against my own.

"Lars?" Finch called right before she opened the door.

Lark ripped herself from my grip to lean back against the wall. "Yeah?" she asked right before her sister opened the door.

Finch glanced back and forth between us with suspicion. "I wanted to show you the lab results, but if you're busy . . ."

"No," Lark said, practically fleeing from the room before hastily tossing over her shoulder, "Thanks for covering for me today, Logan."

The door shut behind her, and I was left standing there with goosebumps still rippling down my arms, my whole body vibrating in the wake of her touch.

STAFF
PRICKLE
ISLAND
ZOO
ZOO

Lark

Three months out of the year, the normally bare parking lot of the Salty Dog was overrun with cars, golf carts, and e-scooters. I'd walked the twenty minutes over from the zoo with Finch and Dove—the conversation dominated by the mating rituals of bowerbirds—you know, normal sibling conversation. We waited on the seawall for Hawk to arrive from the ferry terminal, where he had to go pick up some bulk orders of toilet paper. I swore each visitor used an entire roll.

A week had passed since Emma's accident, and I'd spent every waking minute not on my shift being with her. It took Finch threatening me with a blow dart to get me to leave the hospital for team drinks. I really hoped Emma's arm was back to its normal backpack self tomorrow morning. We took her cast off before we left for the night, letting her get used to it being off while she slept, and we'd assess her again in the morning.

She'd taken to living on my shoulder, smushed up against my face whenever she was off her hot water bottle in her little sleep carrier. I knew she missed her mom and I couldn't wait to get her back with Darcy, but we'd have to do the reintroductions to the troop slowly. We couldn't just chuck her in there and hope they'd all accept her again.

The whole thing left a permanent knot in my stomach. It had also been a very good distraction from that hug with Logan. That hug, *the* hug, the one I reenacted when I fell asleep spooning my pillow . . . yeah, I was too focused on Emma to think about that at all.

Hawk's rusty red pickup pulled into the parking lot and up onto the grass right beside the Salty Dog to claim what we liked to call a "locals-only parking spot." But when I spotted who sat in the front seat, my mouth fell open.

When my eyes landed on the short, dark hair and that dimpled grin, I froze.

"Hey!" Hawk called, leaning out the door. "I brought Logan along."

"Oh really, Captain Obvious," Finch said, her sarcastic expression morphing as she shot a glance my way. "You look like you're about to go full baboon on someone."

"I might," I gritted out.

Logan's freshly washed hair was slicked back off his face, a lone wet strand falling across his forehead. He wore a navy-blue button-down with the sleeves bunched up, dark jeans, and work boots—and fuck if he didn't look like some outdoorsy photoshoot from *Men's Health* magazine.

"What do they put in the water in New Zealand?" Dove

asked, leaning past Finch to get a better look at the gorgeous man striding over to us. "I love being the only straight sister."

"Lark is bi," Finch reminded as she hooked a finger into Dove's belt loop and yanked her back. "Down girl. I should've brought my tranq gun."

Logan's eyes landed on me, and I was suddenly keenly aware that I still had baby howler monkey shit in my hair. I had to do a final check on Emma after my shift and didn't want to waste time showering before team drinks. Besides, none of my siblings would've noticed or cared—Dove's clothes were covered in mud splatters from pressure-washing the bird baths today and Finch's scrubs stunk of piss from one of the dingoes waking up from anesthesia. But Logan . . . Logan looked like he'd showered, which in keeper terms was like him showing up in a tux. I bet he smelled like soap and clean linen and just a little bit of sweat from the hot summer's night and . . . curse my traitorous hormones. I hated my brother for bringing him.

"Hey," Logan called to us, his eyes still stuck on me.

"Hey!" I called back a little too loud, my voice an octave higher than normal.

When Hawk got close enough, I grabbed my brother by the elbow and yanked him to the side.

"Just need to chat about some zoo stuff. We'll meet you in there," I called to Finch with a wave, and she led Dove and Logan into the Salty Dog.

"Zoo *stuff*?" Hawk echoed.

I waited until the others pushed through the creaking wooden door and the bell above jangled before turning on Hawk with a furious gaze. His smile fell and his face turned into that wary, guarded one where he knew he fucked up but wasn't sure how yet.

"What are you doing inviting a volunteer to our staff

drinks?" I seethed. "Aren't you the one with the whole 'no volunteers' speech every summer?"

"It's just Logan. He's older than the other volunteers," Hawk said. "I felt bad leaving him with a bunch of freshmen doing shots of Goldschläger and vodka with Capri-Sun chasers." I screwed up my face and thanked all the party gods I never had the traditional college experience. "Plus, he's a nice guy and I like him."

"Then take him on a date on your own time," I snapped. "But this is *team* drinks."

"It's family drinks," Hawk countered.

"And he's not family."

"And you and Finch bring summer friends along all the time."

I couldn't argue with that.

We called them "summer friends" because that was the only time we had them. For the rest of the year, our siblings were our only friends on the island. We'd occasionally take the boat into town and hang out with some of the locals on the shoreline, but they were more acquaintances than actual friends.

Something about summers on Prickle Island was magical. It was like adult summer camp. People grew really close to each other really quickly, and then summer would be over and the spell would break and we'd promise to keep in touch but never did. But I got used to those summer friends and always looked forward to the new ones.

Summer hookups, on the other hand, were Finch's forte, and she'd made an art form of sleeping with every eligible queer woman on the island by the end of each summer. Most of my ill-fated relationships involved falling madly in love with the wrong girls, imagining they'd stay after the summer was over, and then having my heart stomped all over when they inevitably left. Luckily, I'd grown out of that a few years ago and had resigned myself to the fact that my longest-lasting relationship would be with my vibrator.

"What's so wrong with Logan anyway? He's really nice," Hawk said, pulling me out of my rabbit hole of thoughts. "Or is it just because you're attracted to him?"

"I am *not*!" I held my hand to my chest in dramatic offense. "I mean, I have eyes. He is the Hollywood kind of handsome. It's just . . ."

"Just?"

"I don't know. He irritates me."

"Because you like him," Hawk taunted.

"I don't *like* him," I gritted out. "I don't like guys."

"Honestly, Lars, maybe you should—"

"Just get drunk and kiss him and then I can move on," I said with a nod. "Yeah, maybe."

"I was going to say just be his friend," Hawk said with a frown. "But whatever you want to do, just don't tell me about it."

"Oh, come on! You're supposed to talk me out of this!" I shouted, and a few of the bar patrons walking through the parking lot looked over at us. My cheeks flamed as I lowered my voice. "What about the 'no sleeping with volunteers' rule?"

"That's a Finch rule."

"What?" I barked. "When? Why?"

"Because I know you're not going to make your way through the entire Bunny House," he said with that infuriating smile that made me want to punch him right in the mouth. Stupid older brother. "You can have your one freebie of the season."

"Can you just place him with someone else? Heron or Crane or D—not Dove," I corrected, remembering the way she stared at him like he was a corner piece from the brownie pan.

Something in me had snapped. I was sick of thinking about Logan, sick of fantasizing about him holding me in his arms, his hands on my body . . . It was enough to make me want to pull my own hair out. Something had to be done. I couldn't keep going on feeling like this.

"You really want me to move him with someone else?" Hawk asked. "You know he'll know it was you who asked for it, right?"

"Ugh, no." I rubbed my forehead. "Okay, back to plan A—get drunk and kiss him."

"There's the Lachlan spirit," Hawk said, patting me on the back.

I rolled my eyes. "We're a weird family."

"You're just now realizing that?"

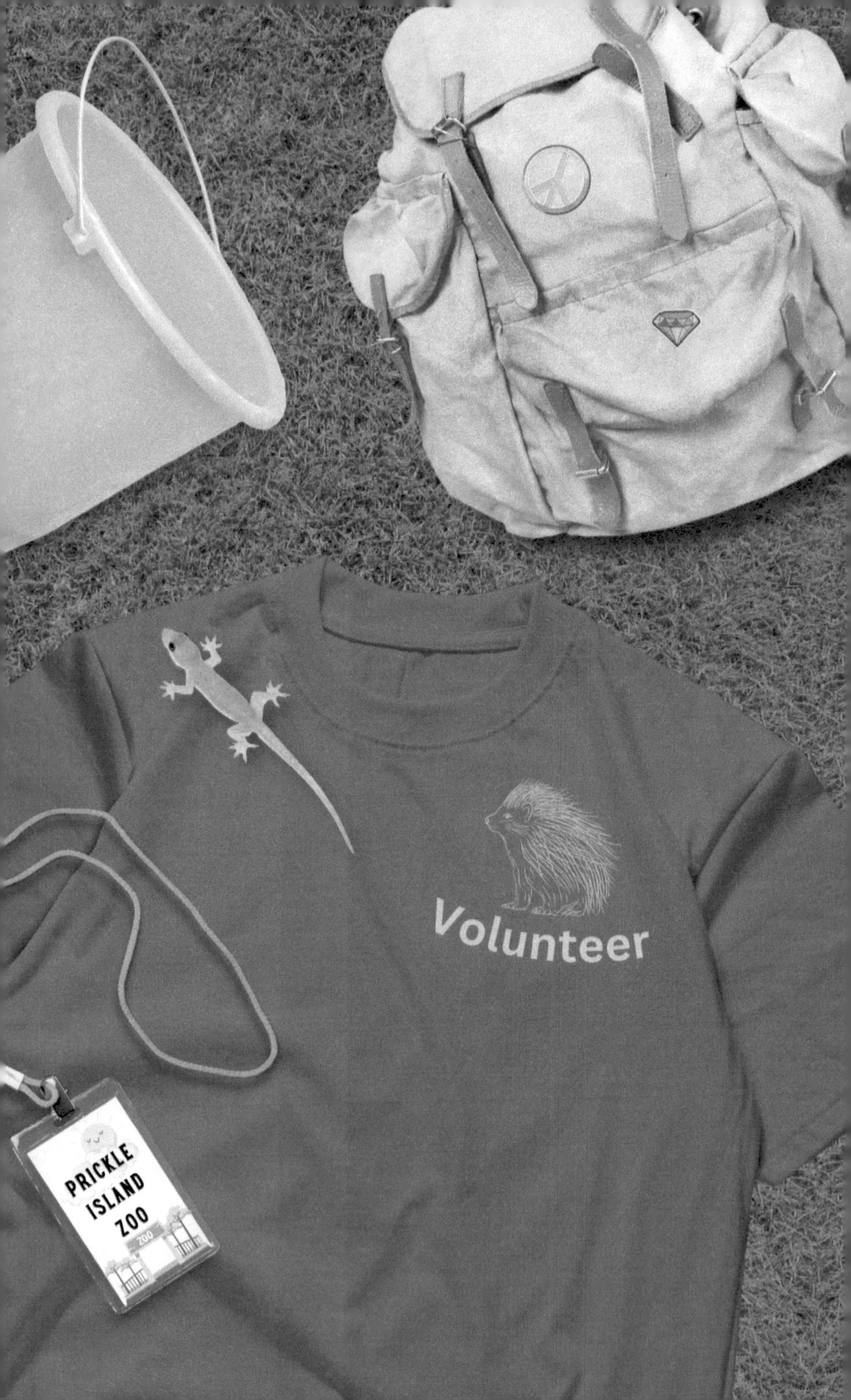

Volunteer
PRICKLE
ISLAND
ZOO
ZOO

Chapter Fourteen

Logan

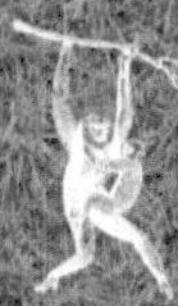

The Salty Dog seemed like it had once been a nautical-themed pub that had given up on the decor about two decades ago. A few fishing nets and buoys still clung to the corners, but otherwise it looked like a contemporary pub with a mishmash of furnishings: velvet couches, ornate coffee tables, and ten different kinds of barstools lining the bar.

"These are the rejects from the fancy houses up on the point," Dove said, sweeping a lock of her purple hair behind her ear and smiling up at me. "Whenever one of the rich, old ladies decides to redo her living room, we get to pick through it before the junk gets sent to the mainland."

"That explains the candelabra," I said, tipping my head to

what looked to be an up-cycled mahogany wardrobe now stuffed with an assortment of glassware. Vases and sculptures dotted the top of the wardrobe—a strange opulence contrasting with the sticky concrete floors and chipping black paint on the walls.

"Kirby!" Finch called to the bartender, an older Black woman with short white-blonde hair and bright fuchsia lipstick.

"Lachlans!" Kirby called, waving her bar rag at us. "I'll be right over."

I followed Finch and Dove through the horde congregated around the door. The place was chocka, filled to the brim with the oddest assortment of patrons. "Who are all these people?" I asked.

"Summer staff," Dove and Finch said at once.

"Nannies, gardeners, masseuses, yoga instructors," Dove said. She pointed at three women wedged into a two-seater couch, frantically typing on their phones. "Social media managers."

"People bring social media managers on their summer holidays?"

"Clearly, you've never watched *Real Housewives*," Dove replied. She continued pointing around the room. "Personal trainers, stylists, housekeepers, chefs . . . Some of them work for the island estates, others come and open their restaurants and art studios along the main road just for the ferry tourists."

We wove through the crowd to a back staircase that was roped off with a sign that said "Reserved." Finch climbed over the rope, then Dove. I followed them up the steep steps to a mezzanine that looked down over the pub. There was a large seating area of leather couches, upholstered ottomans, and wingback chairs, plus a giant TV mounted to one wall.

"They use this place for private parties," Dove said. "But on Wednesdays, it's ours."

I blinked, remembering it was Wednesday. I'd lost track of the days since flying over. Every day since I'd arrived had been a blur. It was nice being so exhausted at the end of the day that I could sleep through the thumping music and not-so-subtle hookups. But Hawk had been right too. The volunteer house had calmed down a lot since the first week, and most of the time, everyone was asleep before 10 p.m.

I dropped into one of the leather chairs and smoothed my hand down the arm, wondering how expensive it must be. I felt like I should be wearing a smoking jacket with a Cuban cigar held between my teeth.

Kirby walked up the steps holding six longneck beers, four clasped in her fingers and two held to her body with her elbows. She set them down, passing me one and perching on the arm of my chair.

"And who is this?" she asked to Dove in a thick British accent.

"Logan's one of our volunteers," Dove said.

"You brought a vollie to drinks with you?" Kirby's eyebrows lifted into her hairline and she glanced from the sisters to me. "I mean, look at him, I don't blame you . . ."

"He's on Lark's team this summer," Dove added, and Kirby threw her head back and cackled with laughter.

"Poor sod."

"She's not that bad," I protested, feeling strangely defensive of her.

Yes, she had a system for everything and held herself to a ridiculous standard and her work ethic was enough to break anyone who wasn't bitten by a radioactive spider, but that just made her even more incredible.

Finch spit her beer back into her bottle. "*Not that bad?* That might be the nicest compliment one of Lark's volunteers has ever given her."

I glanced between the three of them. Were we talking about the same Lark? She was certainly a bit cold to me at the beginning and understandably frustrated with Madison, but she seemed like the most caring person I'd ever met. The way she treated her job, the way she held Emma, the worry in her eyes when one of her animals was sick . . . . Underneath that grumpy exterior, I knew there was a mushy khaki-colored heart.

People didn't wake up to clean animal poo at five a.m. if they didn't care. There were a lot of easier jobs that paid a lot more. It was what my dad had always told me about our family business: there was a million jobs that would be less work; if you didn't love this job deep down in your bones, it was time to go do something else. So I left and did something else. But now, after years away, I was starting to miss that life. It still was there deep down in my bones just like my dad had said. I bet Lark would like my dad—

Dammit, why was I thinking about Lark meeting my parents?

I caught myself and tried to focus back on the conversation between the sisters and Kirby about the latest island gossip. It seemed like a conversation I shouldn't be privy to. Hawk had invited me and I hadn't really thought twice about it, eager as always to get out of the volunteer house, but judging by Lark's reaction, this wasn't a normal thing . . . and the way Kirby reacted to having me there made me think maybe I should make a quick exit and go.

But then Lark came stomping up the stairs, her frown morphing into a strange look of determination when her eyes landed on me. She still wore her work cargo shorts but had changed into a baggy Gorillaz T-shirt and Birkenstocks. I arched my brow as she marched straight over, snagging a beer off the table and dropping into the chair beside me. She leaned forward, perching her elbows on her knees, her leg pressing against mine in a way that sent fire through my entire body.

She pinned me with a look, her hazel eyes hard as she said, "Hi."

"Hi," I replied, trying not to sound flustered as I took a sip from my drink.

Hawk whispered something to Finch and looked in our direction as Finch rolled her eyes. A Lachlan sibling game of telephone was happening on the couch across from us.

Kirby patted me one last time on my shoulder and gave Lark a wink. "I shouldn't be leaving the punters to themselves," she said.

Lark waved at her. "Keep the drinks coming, Kirby."

Kirby did a double-take at Lark. "I'm sorry. Who are you and what have you done with Lark Lachlan?" she asked. "Is this *Freaky Friday*? Have you swapped bodies with your sister?"

"Whatever you've got," Lark said, ignoring Kirby's snarky comment. "Who's up for shots?"

Kirby looked to Hawk for confirmation, and he just shrugged. "Whatever you've got."

"That baroness just had a boozy garden party and has graciously donated the leftovers," she said, winking at Lark. "I'll bring up some tequila." She shook her head in disbelief. "I've got to tell Aya about this."

Aya was the zoo's wildlife nutritionist and Kirby's wife who, according to Lark, was away for part of the summer in Japan. I was secretly grateful to Aya. Her being gone meant I could do the diet prep in the evenings and save myself from the volunteer house.

The rest of the Lachlan siblings went back to talking about their animals and the things they needed to do tomorrow and the observations they had planned for their one-eyed bear, but

Lark . . . Lark kept staring at me like I was a riddle she was going to solve.

"Cheers," she said, clinking her beer bottle with mine a little too aggressively. She didn't wait for me to reply. She threw her head back and chugged her entire beer.

I shook my head, bemused. Work hard, play hard, I guessed.

PRICKLE
ISLAND
ZOO
ZOO
Volunteer

Chapter Fifteen

Logan

This was a bad idea. This was a really awesome, really bad idea, I thought for the millionth time as I walked side by side with Lark. Every few paces, my hand shot out and kept her from weaving off the boardwalk and into the midnight water below.

The woman seemed determined for some reason to single-handedly drink the Salty Dog dry. I wondered what had happened today to make her flip this switch? Had something happened with Emma I didn't know about? Lark had been more distant and distracted with taking care of Emma in the vet hospital, but I hadn't heard any news and none of her siblings seemed different. If it were an animal thing, all the

Lachlans would be in bad spirits. So maybe she just needed to unwind?

These keepers partied hard enough that I might need to make them all honorary Kiwis. It was two a.m. before Kirby cut us off and kicked us out the door, and when we'd walked out . . . Lark hooked her arm through my own and slurred, "I'm going for a walk, wanna come?"

I'd told her I thought she should get to bed, considering she needed to be awake—and sober—in three hours, but she just ignored me and wandered off on her own. I'd looked back at her siblings, who just shrugged at me.

"Have fun, you two," Finch had called, giving me the distinct impression that they all wanted me to go with their sister—which was probably a huge mistake—but I wasn't about to let her wander off into the ocean on accident, so off I went, chasing after a drunk zookeeper.

"Easy," I said again, steering Lark back closer to me. "Shouldn't you be getting back to your place now?"

"The ocean breeze helps sober me up," she said, stumbling toward the seawall that looked like it had been battered by a fair few storms in the last century. She leaned against the wall and sighed, staring out over the moonlit ocean. "Isn't it beautiful, or whatever people are supposed to say . . ."

"Or whatever?" My lips twisted. "Lark, what's going on? Why are we here?"

"Look, let's just kiss and get this over with."

My mouth fell open as I stared at her. "What?"

Her hooded eyes finally shifted to me. "Let's just kiss, and then we can move on," she said.

"Move on from what?"

"We'll kiss and then we'll be like: oh, that wasn't as amazing as I thought it would be." Her head bobbled as she spoke. "And then we can stop thinking about kissing each other all the damn time."

"Why do you think I'm thinking about kissing you all the damn time?" I asked even though my eyes were now stuck on her perfectly plump lips.

"You're not?" She sounded relieved. "Oh, thank God."

"I didn't say that." My shoulders shook with amusement. "But I also don't really understand this plan of yours."

"I don't really understand it either." She groaned, tugging at the hem of her baggy T-shirt. "Okay, let's just pretend this didn't happen. I redact that. Strike it from the record." She swirled a finger in the air as she straightened, her shoulders rising and falling in resolution, and it was so goddamned adorable. "I like women," she said matter-of-factly before hastily adding, "and hypothetically men too. Sometimes. It's complicated. It doesn't really matter. The point is . . ."

She wobbled and my hands went out, hovering in midair, readying to catch her. "What is the point?"

"This isn't funny." My smile seemed to infuriate her further. She marched the last few steps up to me and pointed her finger in my chest, filled with drunken bravado. "Keepers don't sleep with volunteers," she said, backing me up into the wall. "I don't care that I randomly keep thinking about you grabbing me and kissing me. It's a rule."

My smile widened as I stared down at her, and I wanted to grab her and kiss her so badly right then, giving her what she wanted, but instead, I just said, "Okay."

"Okay," she said, her gaze falling from my eyes to my lips. "Okay," she repeated. "That's that." Then, she grabbed me by the collar of my shirt and pulled my face down to hers.

Our mouths collided in a sloppy kiss, and my hands instinctively shot out to either side of her waist, spinning her and leaning her against the rock wall. My lips moved over hers, slow and burning, not letting her move them faster. I was determined to savor her as she let out a little breath that made my whole body loosen and tense all at once. My tongue dipped into her mouth, the taste of tequila and lime on her tongue. Her hands clenched tighter in my shirt, and I suddenly realized what the fuck I was doing and took a giant step back.

"Shit, I'm sorry. I . . ." What was I supposed to say? I wanted to kiss her. I wanted to find a bed bigger than the one in my tiny bunk room and make her moan those little breathy sounds over and over again.

But we were both drunk and tired and probably doing something that we'd regret in the morning. I hovered my hands in midair, unsure if I should reach for her again or offer to walk her home.

Lark brushed her messy hair off her face. "Good, that's over with now," she said, sounding less victorious and more deflated. "You should go back to the Bunny House. I'll see you in the morning."

I took a step toward her. "Let me walk you home," I said. "It's a long way back around the boardwalk."

She kept walking in the opposite direction instead, and I followed her with my hands out like I was trying to herd a toddler. As we turned the corner, a set of stairs cut up through the stone wall leading to a chain-link fence topped in barbed wire. She held up the keycard clipped onto her cargo shorts pocket.

"I'm already home," she said. "Come on, you can cut through the penguins on your way back to the volunteer house."

"I never thought I'd hear that sentence." I shook my head and smiled, hating that my eyes were lingering on her ass as she climbed the steps up to the zoo gate. I was going to need to take a *long* cold shower before I went to bed tonight.

STAFF
PRICKLE
ISLAND
ZOO
ZOO

Chapter Sixteen

Lark

I was never drinking again. When my slithering escapee alarm, Matilda, snaked around my arm and squeezed, I finally relented. Man, she was getting big. I wasn't ready for her to be getting so big. The thought momentarily sidetracked me from the pounding in my head. The reek of booze seeped from my pores and acid burned up my throat. Someone dropped a metal water bottle against the concrete downstairs and the vice around my head tightened even more.

If it were any other day and any other job, I'd have called in sick, but I knew that wouldn't work for two reasons: first, all of my siblings knew I was severely hungover from being a stubborn asshole and I, therefore, would get none of their pity.

Second, today we'd see how Emma was doing with the cast off her arm and if she was ready to be reintroduced to Darcy and then the rest of her troop. This was a big day for the two of them, dammit. I had to get up.

There weren't a lot of things that could make someone get out of bed when the entire room was spinning, but knowing that a cute little black puffball was waiting for me was one of them. Damn her adorableness. The thought of the look on her little face searching for me to bring breakfast out the carrier window was just too much.

"Curse you, cute monkeys," I grumbled, rolling to put my feet on the floor and immediately stopping to hold my head in my hands. This was a million times worse than that time we took the ferry in the storm and I had to sit below deck with no windows and puked my guts up the whole ride . . . Better plan: don't think about puke right now, not when someone just poured lighter fluid into my guts.

I grabbed my khakis, belt, and wool socks from the cupboard, needing to take a long breath between each leg of my cargo shorts and holding on to my dresser for dear life. Seriously, was the whole house shaking? By the time I padded down to the kitchen, holding the walls for stability, Finch and Hawk were gone. A piece of peanut butter toast, a bottle of Gatorade, and two Tylenol sat on the bench, a sticky note above it in Finch's handwriting saying: "Drink this, dumbass."

Great. The biggest party animal on all of Prickle Island was calling *me* a dumbass. That had to be bad.

I took the Tylenol, chasing it down with the red Gatorade that I then cradled like a toddler with a juice box. The smallest nibble of peanut butter toast was too much. My stomach muscles clenched. "Ugh. No. Stop it," I commanded my stomach, yanking open the kitchen window and hanging my head out. The cool, misty morning air revived me a little, the strong scent of salt water hanging in the breeze.

And then I remembered—the docks, the seawall, and Logan's perfect kisses.

"Oh no," I groaned, leaning my forehead against the cool glass pane.

I was going to have to see him today, and it was going to be super freaking awkward. Why did I think kissing would help me get over him? Now, all I wanted to do was get under him! Shit.

The gibbons whooped their morning song through the zoo, and I remembered again: Emma.

I stumbled to the door, yanked on my boots, and headed off to the veterinary hospital two buildings up.

I opened the door to the loudest, most piercing sounds imaginable. Whoever thought rock concerts were loud had clearly never heard fifteen Amazon parrots in a tiled hospital room. I shut the door and took another breath before diving into the wall of shrieking sounds. Five a.m. was too early for the fifteen-piece feathered bagpipe orchestra that was going on in the vet hospital.

This was just plain mean. If I ever became a supervillain, this would be my form of torture: forcing my hungover victims to clean cages of screeching parrots. The devil's got nothing on me. My life is downright sadistic.

I cringed as I walked through the wall of echoing sound, my brain feeling like it was being stabbed over and over again with each screech. The chemical smell coming from the surgical rooms made my stomach twist into hot knots. It smelled way too much like the shots I was doing last night. The scent filled my nose and mouth, and I had to swallow the bile rising up my throat as I finally made it to the carrier that had become Emma's makeshift hospital room.

I lifted the towel and opened the latch without looking, "Good morn—"

Before I realized what was happening, Emma darted to my shoulder and clung onto my cheek in her normal position . . . only this time she landed with a wet *shlunk*. The stench was overwhelming as I stared into her carrier.

She'd had explosive diarrhea everywhere.

Clearly, those painkillers had messed up her bowel movements. And now I had a shit-covered monkey clinging to my motherfucking face, her wet tail wrapped all the way around my neck to hold on, and the smell so much sharper and more acidic than even her normal monkey poo. Oh, how I wished for normal-smelling monkey poo right now.

My stomach clenched and I gagged. I needed a toilet. Now.

I tried to move Emma, but her little claws dug into my nose and hair. This was where she sat for breakfast and she was *not* going to be moved. I threw open the door and ran into the too-bright hallway that seriously made me wonder if I was being abducted by aliens and pounded on the locked bathroom door.

Finch was wearing sunglasses as she sauntered out of her office but otherwise seemed normal as she leaned against the doorframe. "Morning, sunshine."

"Open. This. Door. Now," I panted between every word.

"That bathroom is for vet staff only."

"I swear to God, Finch, if you don't open this fucking door," I growled, my stomach bubbling like a freaking fish tank.

"Okay, okay," she said, pulling the clump of keys from her pocket and walking ever so slowly over to the door. I knew she was trying to torture me for last night—and it was working.

"Come on, come on," I whined.

"What's a matter, Lars?" Finch asked as she opened the

door and I stumbled into the darkness and dropped straight to the bowl. "Was it the . . . tequila?"

At the word tequila, I spewed my guts up into the toilet, projectile vomiting like something straight out of *The Exorcist*. Alcohol burned up my throat and nose as my shit-covered baby monkey clung to my hair.

"I'm sorry, Emma," I cried through bouts of nausea, feeling like the worst fucking surrogate monkey mom ever. "I'm sorry," I said, rubbing a hand down her wet, stinky back. "I promise I'll never do this to you again."

"Don't do this to yourself again either," Finch chided. "Expensive tequila tastes just as bad as the crappy stuff when it's coming back up, huh?"

My stomach lurched again. "Stop saying tequila." I moaned, the porcelain feeling cool against my cheek. I didn't care that a bunch of asses had probably touched it. I was already covered in monkey shit.

"Do you want me to get you an IV drip going?" Finch taunted, but I ignored her. "Cuz I'm allowed to treat all kinds of wild animals and you're certainly acting like one today."

"Thanks for taking an eon to open the toilet, Finch," I said. "You're so cruel."

"Nah," she said with a click of her tongue. "If I was truly cruel, I'd have called Logan to come up and meet you here covered in monkey shit and vomit, gorgeous."

"Please tell me you didn't," I said, spitting into the toilet one last time before leaning back against the cool white tiles.

"Don't worry," Finch said. "Hawk has commandeered him for the morning. Told him he needed some help with the outer fencing. Big bro bought you some peace."

I looked up at the ceiling and whispered, "Thank you, Hawk!"

Finch kept staring at me, a quizzical look on her face. "This Kiwi guy's really got you all messed up, hasn't he?"

"No," I said, but as my stomach roiled and my head spun, I decided there was no point in lying. "Maybe."

"Was he a good kisser?"

"Yes," I moaned. "Like fireworks kind of good."

"Well, you're screwed, then," Finch said. "Maybe you should just throw in the towel and date him."

"We don't date volunteers."

"We'd make an exception for you."

"Why are you always making exceptions for me?"

"Because you haven't had any fun in years, Lars, and it shows," Finch said. "You're so uptight and responsible and grumpy, and maybe you need to get all 'happy butterflies and rainbows and freaking fireworks' over someone."

"And when he leaves at the end of the summer and my heart breaks into a thousand tiny pieces?" I asked. "How sunshine and rainbows do you think I'll be then? Besides, he is *so* not the type I get crushes on. He's not even the right gender!"

"Oh, come on, Lars." Finch pulled her sunglasses down to glare at me over the rim. "You've liked multiple genders since you were a kid! You had a Team Jess poster on your wall, for crying out loud."

"Everyone was a little straight for Milo Ventimiglia back then," I muttered. "You remember that Fergie video?"

"What are we, eleven? Uh . . ." Finch searched the ceiling as if there'd be an answer there.

"The one with her in the frilly underwear?"

"Oh yeah!" Finch snapped her fingers. "God, I love women."

"Well, I thought I always fell into the 'attracted to men in theory, but only want to date women' camp," I said, rubbing my throbbing temples. "And Logan is messing up everything I thought I knew about myself."

"Nobody's taking your rainbow card, Lars. Queerness isn't a one-size-fits-all thing," Finch said in that sing-song older sister way she always did when she was telling me off. "Bisexuality doesn't have to be a fifty-fifty split."

"It's not fifty-fifty at all! I'm ninety-five percent attracted to women, five percent to Lee Pace, Emma D'arcy, and Vico Ortiz, which leaves exactly zero percent for Logan Anderson, and yet there he was all hot and sweet and muscly, and I'm *not* handling it well."

Finch waved her hand up and down at me. "Clearly."

"I feel like I'm thirteen!" I shouted and then lowered my voice as the sound pinged around the echoey space. "This is all new and weird and I don't like it!"

"Maybe new and weird will be good for you too." Finch shrugged, and I gave her the finger. "Who knows? Maybe you need to stop labeling it, Lars. He's here, he's hot, and he clearly likes you if he was willing to kiss you after watching you stick your arm up a shit pipe—"

"Hawk told you about that?" I groaned, but Finch ignored me and carried on.

"*And* you said he's a good kisser." She counted her points on one hand, looking around the room as if she could tally up the value of the man. "I mean, the answer is staring you straight in the face, Lars."

"The answer is staring me straight in the face, Finch," I echoed. "No sleeping with volunteers and no getting my heart broken by summer friends. I'm not doing it."

"Fine."

"Fine."

"Enjoy your tequila voms solo, then," she said, turning and stalking back to her office.

My stomach surged and I scrambled back to the toilet. "Stop saying tequila!"

STAFF
PRICKLE
ISLAND
ZOO
ZOO

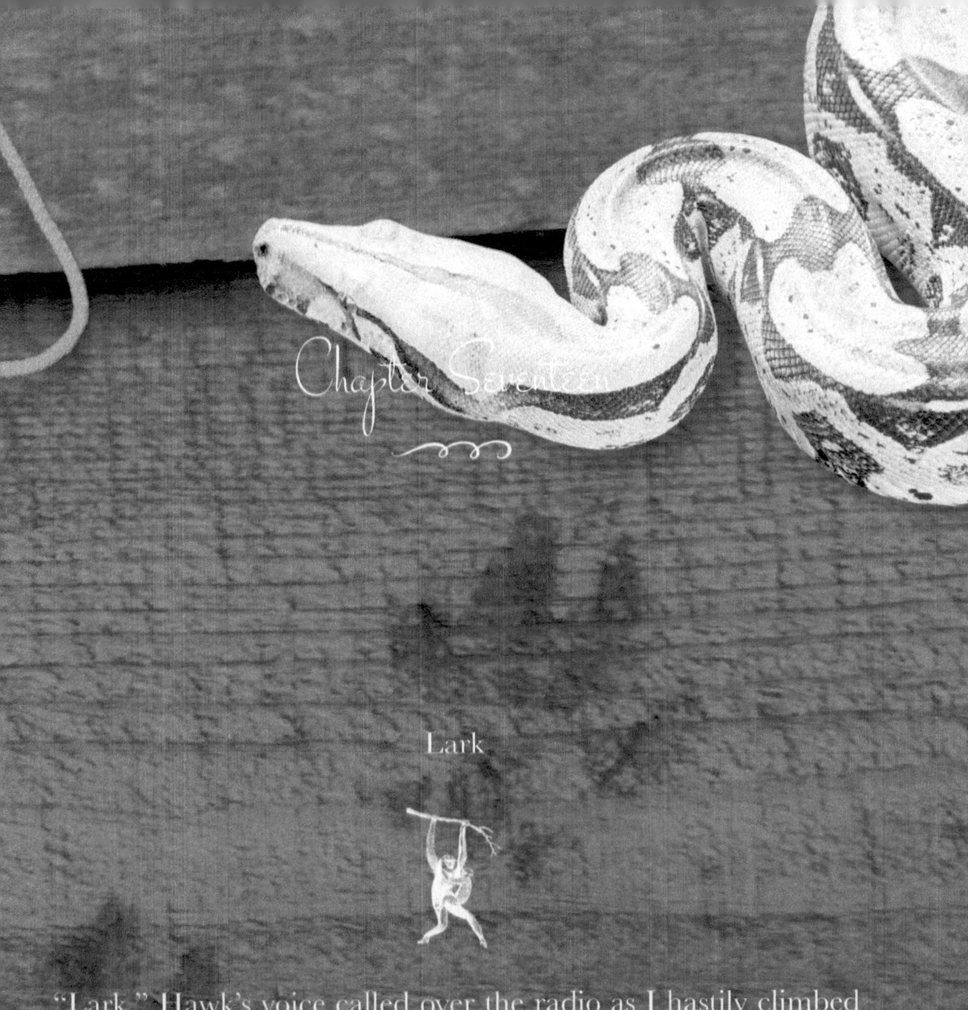

Chapter Seventeen

Lark

"Lark," Hawk's voice called over the radio as I hastily climbed out of the shower and almost slipped, bare-assed, onto the floor of the vet hospital bathroom. Normally, I'd just roll with the monkey poo, but being covered in my own vomit *and* explosive monkey diarrhea was one step too far.

Since Finch had unlocked the bathroom for me, I was taking full advantage. Plus, Emma needed a wash too, so I'd let her cling to my cheek as I soaped her up, peeling one limb at a time off me to wash. She held on like a champ, and I was starting to feel good about her prospects of being reunited with her mom today.

Of course, right as I thought that, Emma leapt onto the

towel rail as I skidded across the floor to my radio lying on top of my shorts. "Oh, *now* you're an independent little monkey?" I grumbled at her. I swore, if she knew what sticking your tongue out meant, she would've done it.

I grabbed my radio and said, "Go ahead," hating the way I knew my voice would echo. They probably thought I was pooping . . . I mean, they wouldn't have been that far off, but . . .

"Can you come to the mid-camp office?" Hawk asked.

Oh god. He was calling me to his office? That couldn't be good. Was he still with Logan? Did he and Logan talk? Did Logan tell him about what happened between us last night?

Oh, sweet baby flamingoes, *last night*. The memory flooded back into me again. I practically demanded that we kiss. Then I told him I couldn't sleep with him. Then I shoved him against a wall and kissed him anyway. Then he spun *me* into the wall and kissed me and holy guacamole, it was so deliciously good. Even drunk and barely able to keep upright, I remembered how hot that kiss was.

If Logan was in that office, I would die. I started rapidly brainstorming ways to fake my own death and escape on the ferry and start a B&B in Vermont under a punny pseudonym when Hawk's voice crackled over the radio again. "It's about Guatemala."

My whole body sagged in relief, and then I realized I was still standing naked in the middle of the room with a baby howler monkey waiting for her breakfast. "Give me five minutes, I'm just feeding Emma," I said, which was technically about to not be a lie.

I jumped back into my clothes, feeling a lot lighter after the shower. My shirt was relatively unscathed and my spirits were buoyed by Hawk's radio call.

Guatemala! I was saved.

Was Aya back from her vacation? Was Hawk finally letting me go on one of Mariana's research trips? Mariana spearheaded one of the biggest conservation groups in the country and did a bunch of work on howler monkey research. I practically danced out the door, hoping my constant pestering to go on this trip had finally paid off. I grabbed Emma and went to get her bucket of food that I'd left in the hallway in my haste to use the toilet.

"You seem more chipper," Finch said, taking a bite of an apple.

"Hey," I said, pointing at the gala apple I'd helped offload from the truck the day before. "That's for the capuchins."

Finch took another bite. "It's better than the red delicious ones in the Peacock," she said with a shrug. "Besides, I thought we talked about putting the troop on a different diet?"

"I would fight with you more," I said with a smile. "But I'm going to Guatemala and I never have to look Logan in the face ever again and you can't get under my skin right now."

"Ooooh." She snickered, wiping her mouth with the back of her hand. "I bet I can when you find out the details of your trip, Larsy."

My face fell. I was hoping I'd waltz into Hawk's office and he'd hand me a plane ticket and I might be able to pack and leave without seeing Logan at all. Whatever Finch knew was souring my stomach all over again.

"Go," she said, walking over, taking Emma from my shoulder, and placing the little puffball on her own. "I'll feed the little excrement tornado."

I rolled my eyes. "She likes the porridge room temperature, not warm."

Finch pointed her finger to her several veterinary degrees prominently displayed in her open office doorway. "I think we'll survive," she said.

I gave one last look between Emma and Finch and bounded out the front door, cutting through the blissfully empty pathways waiting to be crammed with roaming hordes of visitors after nine a.m. I hustled up to the mid-camp office, which was behind the invertebrate house.

I didn't look at the spiders and tarantulas as I went. Fuck spiders. I knew I should love all creatures being a keeper and all, but seriously, fuck spiders. I didn't know how Crane dealt with them, let alone *loved* them. I wanted to like them . . . Logically, they were cool. They played an important role in insect control and had fascinating adaptations, *but* creepy, crawly, hairy things were gross AF and you could never change my mind.

When I walked into Hawk's office, I found him sitting at a desk that looked like it hadn't changed since the 1980s. We probably owned the oldest desktop computer on the Eastern Seaboard. Everything was dusty and decorated in clashing beiges and tans. It had been our dad's office, and when Hawk took over, he hadn't changed a thing. The place was a weird sort of grimy shrine to Dad now.

Hawk pushed off the desk in his rolling chair and leaned back with a smile. "It's happening," he said. "I just talked with Mari and got approval from the board and you're going. You fly out on Monday for two weeks. The Westworth research grant will be funding your trip and making a sizable donation to the howler monkey conservation fund."

"Yes!" I leapt up and down, clapping my hands with glee like a little kid. I didn't care enough to act cool in front of my big brother. He knew how badly I wanted this. Hawk, Finch, and Dove had all been on research trips via the Westworth grant fund, and I was so ready to add my name to the family conservation legacy. Plus, I'd been dying to travel forever and to see the absolutely gorgeous Mari again, and *this*, this was my chance.

"I would remind you that you'll be going as an ambassador of the zoo and by extension, the Westworth name and to behave as such," Hawk said, pulling out a manila folder with a giant stack of forms to be filled in. "But you're not Finch, so you don't need that speech. Mom's got her travel kit for you," he added. "And I'll get her to grab you both clean uniforms too."

I paused from the solo dance party I was conducting around the room. "Both?"

Hawk grimaced as he pulled out a second manila folder. "The grant had spots for two people," he said. "Mari confirmed that two people would be more help and it means more money for their fund, but . . . she wanted me to preferably pick someone who also speaks a little Spanish."

I folded my arms across my chest. "I'm the only one of us who speaks any Spanish."

"Actually . . ." He drew the word out like he was desperate not to say what followed. "There *is* one suitable volunteer who happens to know some as well."

"No," I said. "No. No. No. No. No." The words flew out of me like a staccato curse and I shook my head vigorously. "Please, for the love of God, Hawk. Tell me that Logan Anderson does *not* speak Spanish." He frowned at the floor and then displayed what in primate terms we would call a "fear grimace." "No!" I would sell little bottles of maple syrup at my Vermont B&B. I'd call it The Cozy Moose Lodge and serve moose-shaped pancakes for breakfast. I blinked and came back to reality. "You can't be serious?"

"Mari said she has ambitious plans for the scope of this trip and needs an extra pair of hands to make it work," Hawk said.

"Then I'll just do two people's worth of work," I barked. "I'm used to it."

"And I would feel safer knowing my little sister wasn't traveling internationally for the first time on her own."

"I am *perfectly* capable of taking care of myself."

"You got pantsed by a spider monkey last month."

"Spider monkeys are incredibly strong!" I snapped.

"*And* going by yourself means less money for your favorite conservation project."

My lip curled. He had me there. "I'm not opposed to traveling with someone, just pick another person! I can translate for the both of us. What about Heron?"

"We need them here," Hawk said, placing his elbows on the desk and steepling his fingers in the posture of a boss about to fire someone. "We're all going to have to take on some of your run while you're away."

Guilt gnawed at me. I felt like a shitty sister and teammate leaving them so I could go gallivanting off in the jungles of Guatemala, whether it was family tradition or not. Plus, the Westworths' annual zoo gala was coming up and I usually played a big part in planning that event too. Maybe I shouldn't go. Maybe I was being selfish. Could my family even handle two weeks without me?

Back when Mom and Dad were young, the zoo had enough money to hire a whole team of help, and they would go off on all of these ambassador adventures all over the world, raising money for local wildlife and bringing vet supplies. But since Dad died, the zoo's owners, the illustrious Westworth family, had started giving us less and less in funding for full-time staff, let alone these trips. It was a miracle this trip had been agreed upon at all.

My brain raced through options. "I can find a summer staff member from one of the estates to come with me."

"And leave their well-paid job to go trekking through the jungle with you?" Hawk chuckled. "That's a tall order."

"Then a different volunteer."

"You want Madison as your travel companion?" he asked, arching his brow.

"No," I muttered. "Ugh, come on, Hawk! I've been waiting for this trip for three years."

I did want to travel to Guatemala, yes. But I also had it in my head that maybe Mari and I might end up having a two-week-long love affair when I went over too. We did share one drunken kiss three years ago, and I'd still kind of held on to the idea that maybe she'd be into it . . . That felt really pathetic now that I was thinking of it again. But whenever we messaged, she never mentioned she was seeing anyone and . . . I hated how much I sounded like Finch when I thought about it.

My sister was the one who would travel to a different country for a hookup, not me. But the idea of Mariana had lived in my head for a long time. I couldn't bring along a distractingly hot Kiwi guy when I was trying to woo an equally hot wildlife biologist. This was like the setup to a bad porno.

"I thought you liked Logan," Hawk said. "At the Salty Dog, you seemed pretty into the idea of spending more time with him. I thought you'd be happy."

"It's . . . really, really complicated," I muttered, rocking back and forth onto my heels. "Last night, we—"

"Whoop!" Hawk plugged his ears and started loudly singing. "I don't want to know what my little sister got up to last night thaaaaaaaaaanks."

I rolled my eyes and yanked one of his hands from his ear. "Hawk. Seriously?"

"Okay," he said, grabbing the two manila folders and dropping them back into the squeaky, ancient filing drawer. "Look,

I can cancel the tickets. We can try again another year when we have more staff." He reached for the curling knot of beige phone cord, ready to call this whole trip off.

"No." My hands shot out, and I cringed. "No, don't. I'll go. I'll bring Logan."

A little voice in my head was screaming at me: *What in the fluffy moose pancakes are you doing? Have you completely lost your mind?*

But this was my dream. I wanted to go to another country and work with animals like my parents had, and I probably wouldn't have another chance for a very long time, maybe never. My hangover seemed to come back twofold, my stomach turning to acid, and I grabbed my head. I was about to spend two weeks in the jungle with the most infuriatingly hot man I'd ever met. And now I knew he was a good kisser too.

STAFF
PRICKLE
ISLAND
ZOO
ZOO

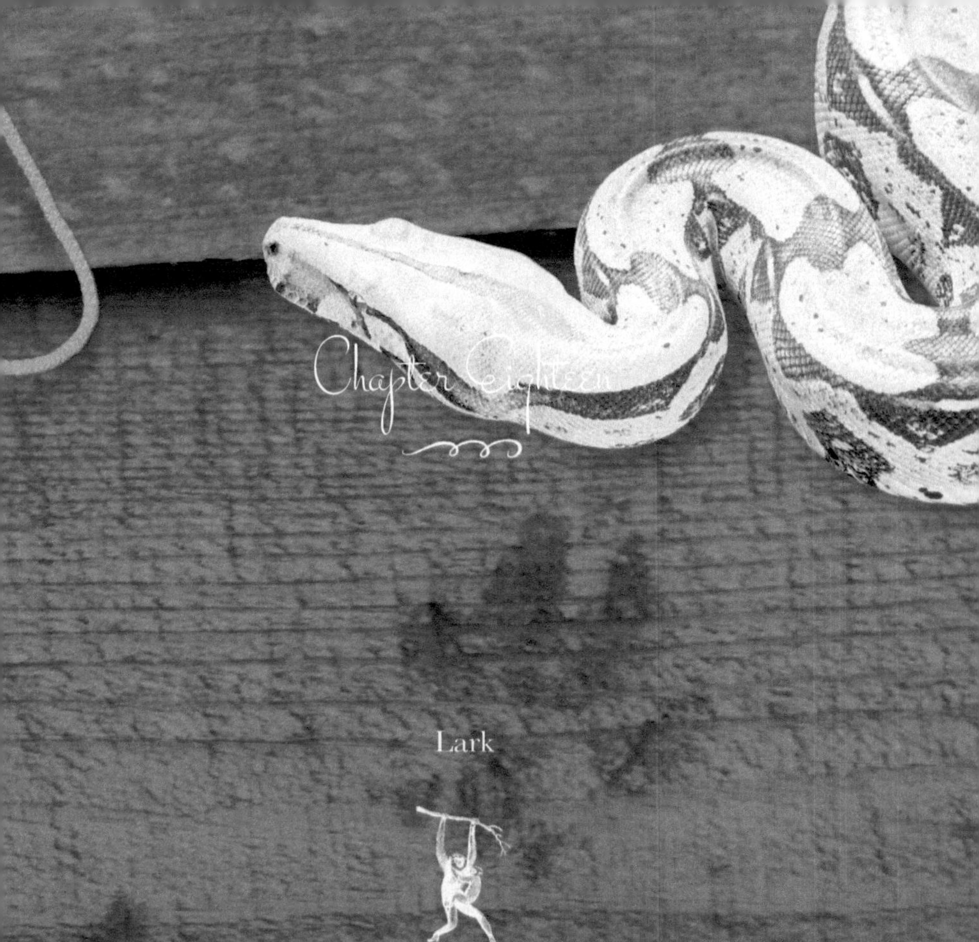

I licked the salty French fry grease from my fingertips, my stomach finally feeling a little more settled. Nothing like the burnt fries and leftover fountain soda from the zoo's café to fix a hangover. I sat on Mom's countertop like I used to when I was a little girl and she needed to put a Band-Aid on my knee. Phoebe sat on the floor below me, her tail thumping hard on the tiles as she looked up at me with those big puppy dog eyes, hoping I'd drop some food.

"The greasier the better," Mom said, waggling her finger. She grabbed my empty paper bag of grease and soda cup and dropped them in the trash. When she returned, she passed me a cup of coffee. "Here."

"Thanks, Mom." I sipped the heavily sweetened coffee and the pounding in my head lightened a little more. At twenty-six, I should've still had a lot of partying left in me, but I swore this hangover would last all week. Finch's and my tolerances for alcohol couldn't be more different. I never understood how someone could drink all night long and then act semi-normal in the morning. The drinking genes must've skipped over me.

"It's nice to know you're human," Mom said with a laugh. "All the others do stupid things that stress me out all the time, especially Finch and Crane," she muttered, more to herself. Ah, yes, the two problem children of our already wild bunch. "I never worried about you . . . and so that was starting to stress me out."

"Well, being in a different country for two weeks will add some stress, I'm sure," I said, pursing my lips and blowing on the coffee as I cradled the warm mug. "Although, now I'm thinking maybe I shouldn't go."

"Oh, you're going," Mom said, shaking her finger at me. "Even if I have to tattoo a FedEx label on your forehead, you're going." I snorted and took another long sip of coffee. "You've been talking about traveling to a different country *forever*."

"But it's so close to the gala—"

"I've been organizing that gala for over thirty years."

"But there's the catering and the waitstaff will need safety training and we need to plan which animals to bring out for the guests and—"

Mom held up her hand. "*Thirty years*, Lark Lachlan."

Mom dug through her medicine cabinet, bags of dog treats and pill bottles of Phoebe's medicine tumbling out. I really needed to reorganize Mom's cupboards again. Ever since I moved down to the old monkey house, she'd let this place go feral.

"Here it is," Mom said, brandishing a small canvas bag. "I think these are still good from Dove's trip to Indonesia." She pulled out the packets and read the expiration dates. "Yep. Okay. We've got your standard painkillers, antiseptic, motion sickness tablets . . ." She held up a packet of white pills. "These are to make things go when you're stopped up. And these"— she held up a packet of blue pills— "are to make things *stop* going."

"Great," I muttered, praying I didn't have to repeat the white pill/ blue pill conversation with Logan. As the staff member, I was going to be in charge of his safety as well. I was pretty used to having conversations about poo . . . like pretty much every day of my life. I may be the all-time heavyweight champion of "It's feces but what species?" . . . but Logan didn't need to see that side of me any more than he already had.

"Bug spray." Mom pulled out a bottle and showed it to me. "Strong enough to burn your first layer of skin off. Bite relief. Aloe. Antihistamines just in case you're allergic to something random." She looked up from the bag and sighed, a warm smile on her face. "I'm glad you're taking up the family tradition and going off to have an adventure."

"You know you could come with me?" I offered, hoping she had one more wildlife biology trip in her. "You know some Spanish."

"I've had my fair share of adventures," she said, glancing off to a photo of her feeding a baby rhino in Namibia. "Too many, some might say. I don't think my knees would be very happy being squeezed into a sardine box for eighteen hours anymore."

"It's not that far to Guatemala."

She swept a lock of my hair behind my ear, ignoring me. "Now I want my kids to have their own stories to tell and to carry on their father's legacy."

There it was—that tinge of sadness in her warmth that never really went away. I'd lived most of my life steered in the direction of my family's legacy even before my dad died. His death only made my true north even stronger. Most of the choices I made each day were to take care of my mom and my siblings and to be the kind of Lachlan that would make my dad proud.

This trip would definitely make him proud . . . if only it were just me going.

"I really wish Logan wasn't coming." I groaned, remembering again.

"Because you have a crush on him?" Mom asked with that knowing look.

"Maybe," I muttered. There was no point in lying to Mom. She could always see right through the bullshit, even with the best liars among us, and I certainly wasn't one of them. It's what made her a good keeper and an even better parent: she pushed when we needed pushing, she supported when we needed supporting, and she rescued when we needed rescuing. I was determined to never need her rescuing.

Sighing, I set my coffee aside. I pulled my hair back up in a ponytail as I said, "I wasn't supposed to have a crush on someone like him. He's messing up all of my hypothetical future plans."

Mom playfully smacked me with the travel med bag. "Only *you* would be mad at someone for making you like them," she said. "It's okay to like someone you didn't expect," she added. "Your great-great-grandmother thought she'd marry a gentleman. Instead, she met a man setting porcupines loose on a private island off the coast." She chuckled and shook her head. "Falling for the right kind of wrong person is in your blood, honey."

"You're talking like I'm going to marry this guy." I picked

up my coffee again and took another careful sip. "If I pursue him, it'll be just a casual hookup." This felt like a weirdly honest conversation to be having with my mom, but considering she literally used to write papers on animal promiscuity in mating bond behaviors, I knew she'd understand with a biologist's detachment. "He's going back to New Zealand at the end of the summer."

"Lark," Mom said in that "get ready for me to drop some wisdom because it's coming whether you like it or not" kind of way. "You, as always, are a million steps ahead of yourself right now. Give yourself some time with him. Get to know the guy. Maybe he's nice. Maybe he snores like a bulldog and has a weird way of brushing his teeth and has really strong opinions on the correct way to pronounce GIF and you'll be over this crush by the time you get back from your trip." Mom zipped the med bag back up, smiling at my laughter. "Believe me, there's nothing like two weeks with no internet and no showers to truly know if you really like someone or not."

My stomach dropped. I probably would see him brushing his teeth and share a room with him and get pushed a million ways closer to him. Travel brought out the real side of people —the "I'm too tired to keep pretending" kind of real side. Surely, there'd be something there that would turn me off. Then I could go back to fantasizing about the hot French girl at the bar and stop daydreaming about Logan wrapping his arms around me and murmuring words into my hair.

"And you'll make sure Crane doesn't move Matilda?" I added, giving her the "I'm watching you" eyes.

"I think her enclosure—"

"It's not ready yet."

"At some point," Mom said, placing a hand on my forearm. "You're going to have to trust Crane with her, honey. He's a good keeper. It's time to let her go."

"Not yet."

"Lar—"

"If you want me to go off and have adventures, then Matilda stays in her terrarium in my room until I say so, deal?"

"You're a good keeper, but you would've made an even better hostage negotiator," Mom said. I kept my gaze hooked on hers, waiting for verbal confirmation. She threw her hands up in the air. "Fine."

"Fine." I gave a definitive nod. "Then I will go to Guatemala."

Mom cupped my cheek and kissed the crown of my head. "I love you, you responsible weirdo," she said. "Now go have an adventure worthy of the Lachlan name."

Volunteer
PRICKLE
ISLAND
ZOO
ZOO

Chapter Nineteen

Logan

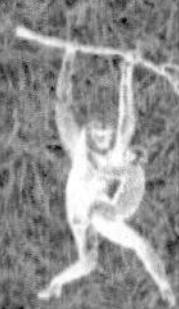

We stood in uncomfortable silence as Hawk's truck pulled around the corner and drove off back toward the zoo. Rain pelted down in sudden bursts, and the ocean was frothing and choppy. No one else seemed to be waiting for the ferry, which made the situation even more awkward because I was huddled next to Lark under the tiny awning, waiting for it to roll in.

My tramping pack rested against my leg, and my arms made a swishing noise against my rain jacket every time I moved them . . . which was a lot because I was jittery as fuck standing next to Lark. We hadn't talked about the trip. I'd noticed she'd already been slightly more aloof with me since Emma's injury, but I just figured it was because she had a lot on her mind. But since Hawk asked me if I wanted to go to Guatemala—*and since we kissed*—she'd started acting like I didn't even exist anymore.

I didn't know how much of it was that she didn't want me coming with her and how much of it was guilt or embarrassment over our drunken pash. She'd told me on the wharf that night that she thought about me grabbing her and kissing her.

It had consumed my thoughts ever since.

I'd considered doing it every day, but, reading the room, Lark seemed colder to me again and I didn't think it would be welcome. But just because she didn't want me, didn't mean this whole trip had to be awful. I'd asked the universe for one more adventure before I had to move home, and now I was getting two for the price of one.

Lark stared straight ahead at the horizon, her eyes tracking the bobbing boats in the distance.

"Are we just going to not talk to each other for the next two weeks?" I asked, folding my arms across my chest, and then shoving my hands into my pockets, and then running a hand through my hair. I needed to stop fucking moving.

"We can talk," she said, doing a similar arm gymnastics routine. She let out a long sigh through her nose and finally looked up at me. Her hazel eyes peeked under the hood of her rain jacket, her button nose barely visible above the zipper. "I'm sorry I kissed you and then hugged you after Emma—"

"Technically, I initiated that hug."

A thrill of excitement shot up my spine, knowing that hug had been more than just a casual, friendly hug to her too. How could it have been? The way she perfectly molded into my arms? My skin tingled as if it could remember how good it felt to have her pressed against me. Had I misread her cold shoulder toward me lately? Maybe it didn't mean she was disinterested at all. Maybe it meant she really wanted me . . . Maybe that was *a lot* to read into a hug.

"Still . . ." She chewed on her lip in a way that made me desperate to reach out and pull it free. "It was unprofessional," she continued. "If I led you on, I'm sorry. I shouldn't have done it. It won't happen again." She punctuated each sentence with an adorable nod before turning back to the ocean.

"I'm not sorry," I said, my fingers buzzing with the need to touch her again. "For any of it." Silence stretched on between us. So long I was beginning to wonder if she'd even heard me over the roar of waves and pounding of rain. I bounced on my toes as I said, "Well, this trip isn't going to be awkward at all."

"You're the one who wanted to talk." Lark watched as the ferry twisted sideways and began closing the distance to the dock. I was not looking forward to getting on that thing in this weather. "Why don't you tell me why you're here?"

"I'm waiting for a ferry."

"No, why did you come to Prickle Island?"

"Oh." I sighed. "I . . ." I debated telling her some sort of whimsical story but decided it was better to just tell her the truth. Pulling out my phone, I showed her the lock screen of Kelly mid-jump, smiling. The one I *still* hadn't changed. Lark narrowed her eyes at the photo like she was staring at a *Magic Eye* picture, trying to make sense of it. "We broke up recently," I admitted. "And I decided I needed to go on a trip to clear my head before I moved back to my hometown."

My words lingered for a beat before Lark replied, "Shit. Sorry." She swung back and forth onto the heels of her boots, both of us moving like we were an old couple sitting in rocking chairs. "So you're moving back in with your parents?"

"Technically, I'm moving in with my brother as it's his property now," I said. "But my parents are still there too. I'm moving into the old farmhouse on the corner of their property . . . It's less pathetic than it sounds."

Lark gave me a look. "I literally live in an old monkey enclosure," she said. "Your life doesn't sound pathetic to me."

"Yeah, but monkeys are cooler than cows and sheep," I added and felt like I'd just won a gold medal when she smiled at me. "Everyone knows that."

"It's true," she said. "But at least you get your own house. I've still got to live with my siblings. What I would give to have my own place." The rain fell faster, bucketing down against the shelter, and I noticed the way Lark shuffled a little closer to me until her sleeve brushed against mine. "Hawk's building a new house for himself at the top of the zoo," she said. "I think he kind of hopes we'll all have our own houses and families there one day. Easier to convince us to stay when we can all have our own places, I guess."

"And do you want to stay?" I asked.

She looked at me sideways and then back out to sea. Little droplets of water clung to the hair escaping out of her hood. "Nobody's ever asked me that," she said. "I don't know. Hawk will definitely stay. Finch probably will . . . Dove will be out of there in the next few years, I bet. The twins . . ." She snorted. "Who knows? And Wren will definitely stay too."

"You answered every one of them but you," I gently reminded.

"Yeah," she said. "I know."

I wanted to push her further on it but knew by her mono-syllabic responses that she was over the conversation, so I tried to steer it somewhere else. "Which of the primates at the zoo is your favorite to work with?"

She turned her whole body to face me at that. Her eyebrows shot up and her cheeks dimpled in a way that made me shove my hands back in my pockets just so I didn't grab her face and kiss her.

"You want me to pick *just one*?" She huffed. "That's so unfair. Can we at least break them down into new-world and old-world monkeys . . . and apes . . . and marmosets?" she added.

"I'll allow it." I let out a deep laugh. "Only for you." A clanging bell tolled in the distance and the ferry pitched to and fro as it drew closer through the mist, slowing as it expertly pulled up to the dock.

"Okay, well, I'd say baboons have got to be my favorite old-world monkey. They're absolute cretins sometimes, but they're also so intelligent and ours have a fascinating troop structure. I was thinking I should write a paper on the unique dominance hierarchies . . ."

She kept going, and I just stared at her in wide-eyed bemusement, trying to keep up with her excited tangents. A second ago, I couldn't get a full sentence out of her. Now, she was talking too fast to comprehend. What did "tumescence" and "cryptic oestrus" fucking mean? It didn't matter. At least she was talking to me and not acting like she wanted to bite my head off anymore. I couldn't help but smile at the way she lit up like a bloody firework, the passion pouring out in her every word.

This might be my favorite Lark Lachlan hack: ask her about primates.

The ferry bell rang again, and a man dressed head to toe in yellow rain gear clambered down. Lark finally took a breath from her excited ramblings long enough to look at him.

"Oh, we should go," she said, grabbing her heavy backpack and swinging it onto her shoulder with ease. Damn, she was strong. I stared at her perfectly muscled calves as she hiked down the steps and out onto the wobbling dock. Did I have a thing for calves now? No, I just had a thing for *Lark's* calves . . . and her eyes, and her hair, and her adorable, stubborn scowl.

Oh boy, I was about to fly to a different country with the most attractive woman I'd ever met—who may or may not actually be into me even though she clearly doesn't want to be—and just the thought made me equally hard and terrified. Lark carried on debating the pros and cons of picking howler monkeys as her favorite new-world primate, and my mind started daydreaming ways I could get her to talk like that to me for the rest of the trip. As I stepped onto the slippery, rocking docks, more focused on Lark's calves than keeping my footing, I knew for certain that I was in such deep shit, it wasn't even funny.

PRICKLE
ISLAND
ZOO
ZOO
Volunteer

Chapter Twenty

Logan

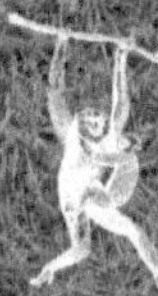

The second leg of our trip from Florida to Guatemala City wasn't particularly long—well, all flights are short compared to getting anywhere from New Zealand—but Lark started fading midway through her Lonely Planet book of common Guatemalan phrases.

Her head dipped forward and then up again, over and over, until it looked like she was going to a rock concert in slow motion. Finally, I gently reached over and tipped her head into my shoulder, and she let out the cutest hum before she started to do these little sleepy snortles as she settled her head into me. The scent of her lavender shampoo wafted from her hair, and I breathed her in deeply . . . three times before I realized I was huffing her hair and stopped. I pulled out my phone from my shorts pocket, careful not to jiggle my shoulder and wake her.

I took a couple of selfies, making goofy faces that I was going to show her when she woke up. I tilted the camera a little more in her direction each time. She let out a little hum again, and I glanced at her sideways right as the camera took another photo.

When I saw the image of myself looking at her . . . it was something I wasn't expecting. There was a calm in my face, a steady sort of happiness that surprised me. I looked at her like she did it all the time and like I loved when she did it too . . . There was something special about this stolen moment, something that made me warm and nervous all at once. I tucked the phone away, worried one of the flight attendants would walk by and judge me.

Was this cute or kind of serial killer-y? The fact I wasn't sure was a problem.

Maybe I should delete it, I thought as I pulled out my phone again.

Kelly's face popped up as the lock screen lit up, and something about it turned my stomach. She couldn't be there anymore, her smile mocking me, our relationship feeling so fake and so far away now with Lark's head on my shoulder.

I opened my phone up again and immediately changed the lock screen image to the last one I took: the one of me glancing at Lark as she slept.

A flight attendant walked down the aisle with the drinks trolley. Each row, she'd pause, look at the person, and decide whether to ask for their drink order in English or Spanish. When she got to ours, I could see the wheels turning for a second with my dark eyes and hair, my tan skin, before she asked for my order in Spanish.

My response was only, "Coke, por favor," but it was enough to make her reply in English, "With ice?"

Dammit. I felt like I had failed a test. It probably didn't help that I spoke Spanish with a New Zealand accent. Lark's accent was similarly laced through her Spanish, especially in the way she said her "R"s. Neither of us were good enough to pass as fluent in the language, though Lark seemed to understand everything people said, whereas I only caught most of the words in each sentence, which was enough to get around but not enough to carry on a full conversation.

The flight attendant passed me my Coke and asked if Lark wanted anything, and I realized I had no idea. But, I also didn't want to ruin this moment by waking her, so I just shook my head. The flight attendant carried on, and I settled back into my chair, trying not to breathe too deeply or make Lark's head rise and fall too much.

Something about this moment seemed to press itself into my memory even as it was happening. The smell of her shampoo, the warmth of her cheek, the little soft breaths and hums she made as she slept . . . my mind was savoring them, tucking them away like treasures I would take out and look at later. And I knew then, that despite my intentions for this trip to rediscover myself as a single person again, it was already too late. I was falling for Lark Lachlan.

I read on my phone for a few minutes before a rough patch of turbulence made Lark's head roll off my shoulder and she bounced up straight. She rubbed her eyes and blinked down at the guidebook in her hand with a yawn. Slowly, she seemed to shift from her sleepy self to her shoulders tensing and going into full planner mode again.

"Did I miss the drinks?" she asked, eyeing the Coke I still hadn't touched because I didn't want to jostle her sleeping head.

"I got you a Coke," I said, passing her the little plastic cup.

"Oh," she said, looking between me and the drink in surprise. "Thanks."

I shrugged. "No worries." And I went back to reading on my phone as if the last ten minutes hadn't changed everything inside of me.

PRICKLE
ISLAND
ZOO
ZOO
Volunteer

Chapter Twenty-One

Logan

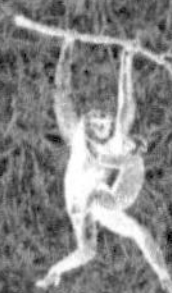

Was it possible to get seasick from too much travel? We took the ferry to the mainland, got a taxi to the airport, took a big plane to Florida and a medium plane to Guatemala City and a tiny plane to Flores, then got on a jam-packed bus out toward Yaxha National Park, then onto an even smaller and more tightly packed shuttle out to a giant house in the middle of the jungle called Finca de los Monos Saraguatos that had a howler monkey painted on its side . . . Well, at least we knew we were in the right spot.

The place looked to be an eco-hotel with little paths fanning out to villas around the property. The giant house in the center of the villas served as restaurant, rec center, and hostel for backpackers. Beside the main building was a large, crystal-clear pool ringed by hammocks that looked so deliciously refreshing, I was desperate to jump into it.

By the time we climbed the ten minutes up the winding forest path to our villa, I'd not only forgotten every word of Spanish I'd ever learned, I'd forgotten English too. There was a lot of hand gesturing and patient smiles with the receptionist as she passed us our room key. I knew she spoke intentionally very slowly, and I was embarrassed I was still missing every third word, but luckily, Lark seemed to understand her just fine and she was kind with my clumsy pronunciations, which I was grateful for.

When the receptionist told us that Mari would meet us tomorrow morning for the longer part of our journey, I winced at the word "longer." The last twenty-four hours weren't the long part?

The entire world spun from a whole day's worth of travel and no sleep. I had the distinct impression I smelled like plane disinfectant and feet. Prickle Island was hot, but here, with the humidity, it was sweltering and my entire body was sticky and scody as.

Great, I'd finally gotten on speaking terms with Lark— thanks to many primate questions—and now I smelled like old corn chips and BO.

Lark seemed equally exhausted when we spotted the two twin beds in the airy room. She pulled back the mosquito netting, flicked on the squeaky fan, and collapsed onto the nearest bed. The rounded walls of the room were covered in speckled clay, painted in a warm coral color that stretched up to the thatched roof. A hammock hung out on the deck, looking out to the teeming, beautiful jungle beyond.

Everything felt so surreal . . . except for the heat—*that* felt incredibly real.

I dropped my pack on the tiled floor next to Lark's, who was already drooling on her pillow, her boots hanging over the edge of her bed. I was desperate to join her in the land of the sleeping, but first I was even more desperate to shower before I stunk up the whole room. I turned around the space, searching for the shower, which was . . . out on the back balcony.

The outdoor toilet was separated from the outdoor shower and sink by a privacy screen, but otherwise was open to the elements. The only thing staring at me would be a humming-bird or coatimundi though. A pump of body wash, shampoo, and conditioner was mounted to the wall, and fluffy white towels were placed on the wire shelf above, along with a sign warning guests to shake out the towels before using them.

Right. I hoped they meant some sort of innocent beetle and not a venomous snake or scorpion. I might have freaked myself out Googling every possible creature that could kill me in this jungle, and by tomorrow evening, I would be about twelve hours too far from any hospital if one of the wankers decided to bite me.

I hastily stripped off my clothes and hung them on the balcony to air out the funk. The water that came out was pleas-antly cool when I turned the tap on. I doubted anyone was craving hot water around here anyway. The shower revived me enough to actually appreciate the lush greenery and the song of birds flitting through the trees. The jungle was otherworldly and breathtaking, like I'd been dropped into the middle of a movie. I couldn't believe I was here.

I'd signed up for a summer at a zoo in Connecticut, not trekking through the Central American bush. Why had I so quickly abandoned my zoo plans to come here? I probably could've convinced myself it was the loud volunteer house or the long work hours or eating the same burger from the Peckish Peacock for lunch every day, but, as I washed the shampoo out of my hair, I already knew the answer was drooling on a pillow in the room behind me. Hawk had said Lark was going and since I knew a bit of Spanish, maybe I'd like to go with her . . . I hadn't even waited for him to finish his sentence before I said yes. When he'd given me a knowing smile, I'd just said I'd always wanted to travel to Guatemala, citing this old New Zealand soap opera quote, but I knew he saw straight through me.

Lark was coming, and whatever hypnotic spell she had over me, I knew I wanted to be wherever she was.

I was about to turn the shower off when I heard a squeak from across the balcony. A parrot or a monkey maybe? I turned to shoo away whatever animal had gotten a little too curious of this outdoor shower arrangement when I came face-to-face with a suddenly very awake Lark.

STAFF
PRICKLE
ISLAND
ZOO
ZOO

Chapter Twenty-Two

Lark

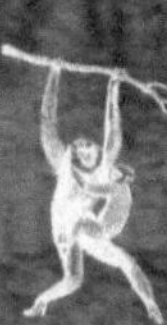

Sweet Hootie and the Blowfish.

Logan was standing in front of me butt-ass naked. *I* saw Logan Anderson naked. All of him. I saw IT—his little Logan, though there was nothing little about it.

My toothbrush fell out of my mouth and clattered to the slat boards below my feet.

"Oh my god," I said, covering my eyes and turning to the door. "I-I'm sorry!" I scrambled for the handle. "I thought you'd gone out for a walk—"

"You didn't hear the shower?" he asked, amusement in his voice. I knew if I peeked through my fingers, he'd be smiling at me. He took a second to just stand there, the cocky bastard, free-balling it while I frantically studied the hinges on the door.

I knew two things about Logan I hadn't known a second before: one—judging by his tan lines, he wore boxer briefs, and two—holy abs, Batman, he was ridiculously cut. That peek I got when he wiped his sweaty brow did *not* do him justice. Okay, fine, and three—he was very generously well-endowed which, considering I'd only ever slept with women whose cocks were quite often purple or vibrating, reconfirmed that maybe I didn't have a thing for all men, but I *definitely* had a thing for Logan.

"Lark," he added in a voice I swore was sexier and deeper than it had been a second before. I was having so many inappropriate thoughts right now.

Why did my name sound so good coming out of his mouth suddenly? He didn't say the "R," and it sounded soft and beautiful, more like "Lock," which I thought was way cooler. Most of the larks at the zoo were complete assholes anyway. Although, that would make my name sound like Lock Locklan, and I was sure there was a knock-knock joke in there somewhere—

Logan cleared his throat and snapped me from my anxiety spiral.

"I'm covered now," he said.

I peeked through my fingers to double-check before turning to face him. He had a fluffy white towel slung low over his hips, and that V of muscles set every single one of my nerve endings on fire. My eyes were still Gorilla-glued onto his happy trail when he cleared his throat again, and I wanted to leap off of the balcony and flee into the Guatemalan hills.

"Sorry. Sorry," I said like the scatterbrained disaster that I was.

Why did he have to look like that? I held Logan's dark gaze a little too intently, shouting at my peripheral vision to stop checking out the rest of his glorious man chest. I was too focused on not checking him out—anymore—because Logan said a whole sentence to me and I had no clue what it was.

"What?" I grimaced. "Sorry. Jet lag."

His smirk told me he *knew* it wasn't jet lag, especially considering we were still in the same freaking time zone. "I said I'm going down to the restaurant to grab a coffee. Do you want one?"

"Coffee. Right. Ooh, yes. Caffeine." I moaned. "Please."

"Sweet as," he replied, and I had to remind myself it was a Kiwi saying and he wasn't complimenting my ass before I accidentally muttered, "Likewise."

He took a step toward me, and then another. He smelled of vanilla shampoo and soap, and I wanted to wipe away the droplets of water from his chest with my tongue. The lack of sleep really made my mind into a slut . . . Yep, that was the only reason.

When Logan walked so close to me that his towel brushed my knees, I sucked in a breath and started to instinctively lean in.

"Can I . . . ?"

I wanted to reply with, "Yes, you absolutely fucking can," but then he gestured to the door behind me that I was blocking with my horny, ogling body.

"Oh. OH," I exclaimed, darting to the side and setting some distance between us. "Sorry. I'm in your way."

I nearly toppled over the sink jumping away from him, and his hand shot out and grabbed my elbow to keep me upright. He really shouldn't touch me while he was mostly naked because it was making my knees all wobbly.

"Whoa," he said.

His warm hand on my forearm made my whole body

pebble with goosebumps. I really couldn't have him touching me right now unless that hand planned to travel southward to my lady parts that were more soaked than Logan's chiseled body. His palm was rough and calloused as it slid up my bicep, leaving a trail of tingles in its wake before he released me and put his hand on the doorknob.

"Aha," he said, tipping his head to a metal hook hanging from the back of the door. "I'll make sure to lock it next time, sorry."

"Sorry," I echoed through gritted teeth, pretty sure my cheeks were now redder than a mandrill's ass.

When Logan left, I picked up my toothbrush from the balcony floor and washed it off in the sink. I took a long time brushing my teeth, afraid I'd accidentally walk in on Logan changing and see him in all his naked glory a second time. Then I would have no choice but to throw myself at him like a horny bonobo. It wasn't until I heard the metal of the screen door shut that I finally stopped brushing. My dentist would be so proud.

With Logan gone, I decided that I should probably take a shower too since I smelled foul—and that meant something coming from a zookeeper. I reached up and switched the hook into the metal loop, locking the door. The accidental peep show was going to be one-sided.

Logan hadn't returned when I got out of the shower. I pulled on a light sundress and cotton underwear. The room swayed under my feet and exhaustion crept in again. I was sleepy and grumpy—and now more than a little horny—and that bed looked super soft and inviting.

I got in, lying belly down, my wet hair still wrapped in my towel, the smooth sheets rubbing against my bare, freshly shaved legs. I should've probably gotten my phone out and called Mom to let everyone know I was alright. Or texted Mari and told her I couldn't wait to see her tomorrow. But instead, I closed my eyes and all I saw was Logan's tanned skin, muscled chest, and dimpled smile that made my whole body tingle and ache.

I lifted my head off the pillow and glanced around. No one was there and the main house was a decent walk away . . . Besides, I could be quick. I dipped my hand under the waistband of my underwear. I was already so ridiculously turned on it would only take a minute . . . and then maybe I could finally focus on something besides that happy trail below Logan's towel.

·I parted my flesh with two fingers and circled my pulsing clit, imagining Logan's naked body and how badly I wanted it pressed against mine. I imagined his fingers were my fingers, his mouth licking its way down my body and sucking on my hard nipples. I turned my face into the pillow, letting out a little panting breath. My pussy muscles fluttered, pushing me closer, and I wished it were Logan's cock they were clamping around. I was moving my hand faster when the screen door screeched open and I instantly went limp, pretending to be asleep.

"Lark?" Logan called, stepping into the room. I didn't move. "Coffee?"

I pretended to yawn and stretch, blinking open my eyes in a *hopefully* convincing act, but when I rolled over and looked at Logan, I swore there was a mixture of surprise and lust in his eyes. Did he know? How could he? Probably because I was acting so freaking weird. *Stop acting so weird!*

"Thanks," I said, reaching for the mug of hot coffee with my non-masturbating hand, as if the hand alone would incriminate me.

"I'm . . . ," Logan said, looking everywhere around the room but at me. "I'm going to go for a walk to check out the grounds. Apparently, there's a waterfall." He spoke twice as fast as normal, the words vomiting out of him as he lifted a visitor map and frantically shook it as if in evidence. "I'll let you get back to, uh, napping."

Oh. My. God. He knew.

"I think I'll head down and get some lunch in an hour," he continued, not looking in my direction. "Want to join me?"

"Okay," I squeaked in a way too high voice.

"Okay," he said. "See ya." He practically bolted toward the door.

Just when I thought seeing Logan's not-so-little Logan was embarrassing, he'd somehow caught me rubbing one out like a horny teenager. I slapped my hand to my forehead and, as I did, looked down to see my nipples poking out from the fabric of my dress so hard, they could cut glass and my sundress tucked into my wet flamingo-print underwear.

My stomach dropped and I thought I might throw up. I'd just been sitting spread-eagle in my soaked underwear in front of the man I just saw naked. I briefly thought about maybe pushing him off one of the mountains we were climbing tomorrow just so I never had to make eye contact with him again. That B&B in Vermont was sounding very tempting. I rolled over and buried my face in my pillow. How the fuck was I going to make it through this trip?

Volunteer
PRICKLE
ISLAND
ZOO
ZOO

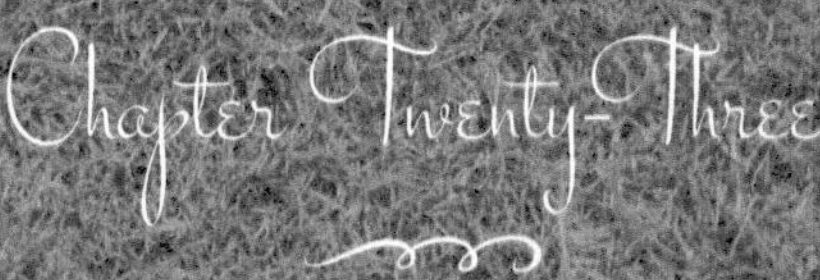

Chapter Twenty-Three

Logan

She was definitely touching herself. Fuck me. There was no doubt in my mind that was what she was doing.

At first, I thought maybe she'd just gotten dressed too quickly and tucked her dress into her knickers, but her bright red blush and rock-hard nipples and super-fake wake-up yawn told me everything else I needed to know. She was wanking off right after she saw me naked in the shower—just the thought made me want to turn around and help her finish the job.

I needed to touch her, to taste her, to be inside that sweet, wet pussy. God, it made me feral thinking of her, and I was one hundred percent not that kind of guy. I was the friendly, sometimes awkward, make you a cup of tea kind of guy, not the storm into the villa, pin her down, and eat her out kind of guy. But fuck, maybe Lark Lachlan would make me reconsider.

I stopped midway down the path and turned to pretend I was fascinated with the foliage as a couple walked past me. I was so hard, like about to come in my pants kind of hard. She wanted me. Lark wanted me. *Me,* of all people. I knew it now for certain, even if she kept saying it was inappropriate and against the rules and whatever else. I saw the way she looked at my cock, like she couldn't wait for—

"Beautiful day," the guy said in a British accent as he passed me.

"Gorgeous," I gritted out with a curt nod.

I didn't look back at them, hoping he didn't want to strike up a friendly conversation. Normally, when I traveled, I'd make friends with just about everyone. I swore you could stumble across fellow Kiwis in just about every travel destination on earth. But right now, I needed to get a handle on the situation that was tenting my shorts.

Lark wanted me. I tried to rationalize it away, coming up with a million different other explanations, but I knew that was what was happening.

However much Lark tried to convince herself—and me— she wasn't into the idea of the two of us . . . the last hour confirmed otherwise.

Those pink flamingo undies. Of course, she had animal-print underwear. All I could think about was those bare thighs clamped together and how much I wished they were clamped around my hips instead. How was I supposed to sleep in the same room as her? I thought I had my desire for her under at least a little bit of control, but *now* . . .

I walked faster, turning away from the forest trail that the map showed looped around the hills and promised a waterfall with a lookout at the top, and instead turned left to the main house, where I was going to find the nearest bathroom stall and wank like a fucking animal while thinking of Lark doing the same.

We ate dinner out on the patio, a giant fan blowing away the mosquitos and calming my still-roaring sex drive. The citronella torches that were lit all around us shooed away the rest of the biters. I also wore a ridiculous amount of insect repellent, which didn't seem to deter the yellow fly that bit me at lunch. Now I had a lump the size of an orange coming out of my forearm. What was it with the bugs here? They were playing on a whole other level.

Lark sipped on her mojito as I nursed my second Cuba libre, which was loosening my tongue and making me use more and more Kiwi slang words that made Lark laugh. I'd never really been a rum drinker, but I thought I would become one if all the drinks tasted this good.

I leaned back in my chair. My belt was tight after eating the best fucking tacos of my entire life. Those masa tortillas were next-level delicious. Even after our plates were taken away, though, Lark and I stayed, watching the bats swooping down over the pool and listening to the frogs croaking through the forest. We'd ordered another round of drinks, and I was glad that the night wasn't over yet. I just wanted her to be near me, to steal a little more time when she was open and happy and talkative.

Our conversation had started off a little stilted after our earlier run-in, but we managed to power through, neither of us admitting anything to the other. At least my bathroom wank had dulled the lust that kept me teetering on a knife's edge around her.

Lark dropped her chin into her hand and watched me as I finished explaining to her what "Couldn't plan a piss-up in a brewery" meant. At some point, she'd stopped laughing and was just staring at me.

"What?" I asked.

Her shoulders dramatically rose and fell, and I could tell she was getting a little tipsy. "Nothing."

"No, go on," I goaded. "What were you thinking about? Are you worried about Emma?"

She shook her head. "I know Finch will take good care of her. Dove will too," she added, as if giving her little sister even a modicum of a compliment was painful.

"So what are you thinking about?"

"You and me."

I nearly spat my drink back out. *Way to play it cool, Logan.* This could be it. Maybe we could finally see if all of this static between us would actually turn into a spark. "What are you thinking about you and me?"

She frowned around the rim of her glass as she took another sip. "Nothing I should be."

"Now see *that*"—I pointed at her—"I disagree with. I think you're thinking exactly what you should be."

Her lips quirked into a begrudging smile. "There are rules."

"Zoo rules," I added. "And right now, we're not at the zoo and I am not your volunteer."

"We're still here on *behalf* of the zoo."

"And I am here as your travel companion and field research assistant." My smile widened. "Are there any rules about either of them?"

"No." She leaned her elbows on the table and searched my

face with her signature grumpiness that made me want to just grab her and kiss her so badly, it hurt.

Who were we kidding? She liked me. I liked her. All the rules and reasons that I shouldn't kiss her right then and there were starting to fade further and further into the distance.

"Maybe in Guatemala, the rules are different." I nudged her just a little more.

"Only in Guatemala," she said pointedly, "they might be."

"Might be?"

"I'm thinking about it," she hedged, swirling the straw through the ice of her drink. "I haven't decided yet."

I knew I had two choices right then: be the guy who pushed her into something because I was so desperate to have her or be the guy who gave her some space to decide exactly what she wanted. And as much as I wanted her right then more than I wanted to breathe, I knew I was going to be the latter, dammit.

I downed the rest of my drink and feigned a yawn. "It has been a *long* day," I said, stretching my arms over my head. "Multiple days, really. I think I'm going to go peruse the 'take a book, leave a book' shelf and hit the hay."

"Okay," she said, sucking the remnants of her mojito noisily through her straw. "I'll see you up there."

It took all of my strength to stand and walk away from her then. The ball needed to be in her court. She needed to think about this. And yes, I had visions of her getting naked and slipping into my bed that night, but she was already a long way from the zoo Lark who hated even looking at me right now, and I didn't want to ruin it. Maybe Guatemala would work its magic on her. Maybe, even if only for two weeks, she'd want to be mine.

STAFF
PRICKLE
ISLAND
ZOO
ZOO

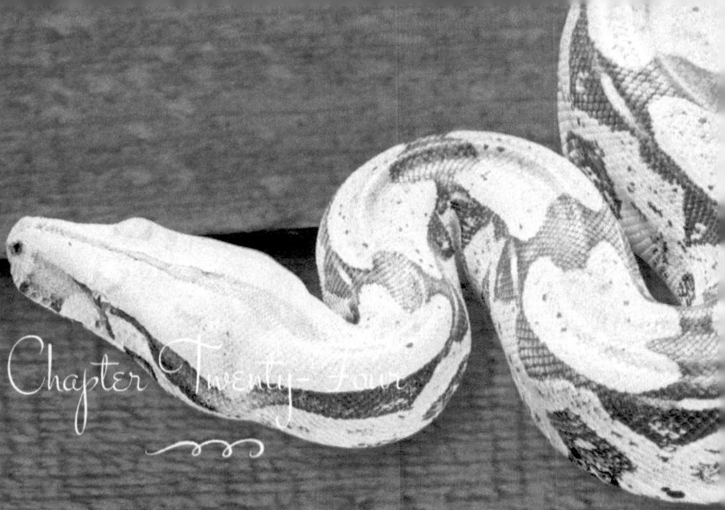

Chapter Twenty-Four

Lark

I woke up before dawn, needing to pee after too many mojitos. Clumsily rolling out of bed, I tried to feel my way blindly to the outdoor toilet and bumped into the wall three times before I found the door. I really didn't want to turn the light on and wake Logan and have him listen to me peeing . . . like he hadn't seen me in much grosser situations than that.

The moonlight combined with the floodlights from the big house were enough for me to make out the basic shapes of everything. I tiptoed over to the toilet, the sounds of insects and croaking frogs infinitely louder than inside. I imagined this was probably weird for most people, but most people didn't grow up in a zoo. Being around a bunch of wild animals while I used the toilet was pretty par for the course in my life.

I flushed and went to wash my hands, feeling for the pump soap in the darkness. While I washed, my legs suddenly started to itch, and then burn, and then sting with crazy pain. I reached for the light switch, blinking back against the bright white outdoor light. I stared down at my legs to see a swarm of black ants covering my feet and crawling up into my pajama pants.

I screeched, jumping out of the river of ants and into the doorway, yanking down my pjs and sweeping my hands frantically down my legs. I kicked my pants out the open door, jumping up and down on the balls of my feet as I flicked the ants off my legs in the darkness of the hall when . . . the light turned on.

"What the—"

I froze in the most ridiculous position, like I was a freaking circus mime. I was standing in my zebra-stripe underwear, my braless tank top rising above my belly button from the literal "ants in my pants" dance I was just doing. I crossed my hands over my crotch like that would hide anything and sheepishly said, "Ants."

Logan's brows pinched together and he stared down at the floor. "Oh." He rushed forward, pushing past me and punting my pj pants the rest of the way outside. He kicked the last few ants out with his bare feet and shut the door. "I do *not* want those bloody things getting inside." He turned and looked me over as my face tingled in embarrassment. "Are you hurt?"

"A few bites," I said, awkwardly tugging down the hem of my tank top.

Logan crouched and swept a hand down my bare calf, and I was keenly aware of how close his head was to my nether region. "I don't see any bumps," he said before rising again.

It was only then that I realized he was shirtless and standing so close that the bow of his pajama pants was brushing my lower belly. "D-didn't you have a shirt on before?"

"I got hot," he said with a shrug.

Yeah, you did, I wanted to reply but held it in. I couldn't be hitting on a man in my zebra-print underwear. I had the sudden urge to word-vomit to him that a group of zebras was called a dazzle, but that would only draw more attention to my ridiculously non-sexy panties.

"Well, now we know," I said, stumbling to steer the conversation. "Always turn the light on when you go outside at night here."

"Noted," he said with a sleepy chuckle that I wanted to hear over and over again. Was there any way to ask him to put his lips to my ear and make that sound again without it being considered hitting on him? "What time is it?"

"Five a.m.," I said. Despite being in a different country, we were still in the same time zone as Connecticut, and it was still my normal wake-up time.

"You can take the zookeeper out of the zoo, eh?" He smiled and shook his head. "Do you even know how to sleep in?"

"Not really," I said. "I mean, we do get days off and sick leave and stuff. We just cover each other's shifts but that means more work for the others, so I usually just work every day."

His eyebrows lifted. "You work every day?"

"Didn't you grow up on a farm?" I asked, feeling suddenly defensive, and he held his hands up.

"No, no, I get it," he said. "I'm just impressed. You care a lot about your family and your job."

I folded my arms over my chest, not wanting him to get an eyeful of my peaked nipples under my tank top. It was underwear or nipples. I couldn't cover both. He'd just said something really nice to me and I didn't need my two witch hats getting in the way of an actual compliment.

"I don't know about that," I hedged.

"I do," he replied. "I see you with them. I know you've got a soft, squishy side that you try to hide from people, especially volunteers."

I rolled my eyes. "I should really go put some clothes on," I said.

"Mm-hmm," he replied but didn't move an inch, his eyes filling with heat as they held mine.

My cheeks burned and I broke our gaze, turning back toward my bed.

Logan's hand shot out and grabbed me by the crook of my arm. He spun me so fast I barely had time to register it before his hand was at the back of my neck and his lips were on mine. He gave me one slow, soft, lingering kiss that made my stomach flip, and then he let me go.

His eyes darkened as he said, "Want to go watch the sunrise from the lookout?"

My mouth bobbed open and I struggled to choke out the word, "Okay."

"Okay," he said with a nod. "I'll go put some clothes on too."

I stared at him as he walked off like he hadn't just kissed me, like it was just a normal thing he did all the time. Was ant venom hallucinogenic in Guatemala? Was I still asleep? Butterflies danced low in my belly as I tried to walk like a normal, respectable person and not a giddy cartoon character over to my pack and fish out my shorts and sports bra and T-shirt.

Logan yanked on a shirt next to me then turned his back. He dropped his pants, revealing the fitted boxer briefs I suspected he wore, muscled thighs, and a toned ass. I turned back to the hook where my pack hung and tried not to think about his perfectly sculpted behind as I dressed. Maybe what he said last night was true. Maybe the rules *could* be a little different in Guatemala. Maybe I wanted to find a way to bend them just a little bit more . . .

He'd just kissed me and all I could think about was how I could get him to do it again . . . without being attacked by a swarm of ants.

STAFF
PRICKLE
ISLAND
ZOO
ZOO

Chapter Twenty-Five

Lark

The shadowed predawn jungle was beautiful and filled to the brim with wildlife. Butterflies and hummingbirds flitted through the trees, a troop of spider monkeys moved across the canopy, and in the distance, the howlers sang their haunting morning chorus. It smelled of morning dew, rich soil, and mulching leaf litter.

The whole forest was so beautifully surreal. Shadows lifted from the trees, and the temperature and humidity slowly started to rise, making me shed the long-sleeve shirt I wore over my tank top and tie it around my waist. I noticed Logan's eyes tracking the movement but couldn't bring myself to look at him.

He'd just kissed me, and it had been soft and slow and yet so freaking hot, and now we were walking through the jungle to watch the sunrise together like something out of a fairy tale.

Four giant wooden beams and rusty metal steps appeared through the forest—the lookout. We climbed up the steps in silence. The dawn seemed too perfect to interrupt with conversation. The view opened up, looking out over the mountains to a waterfall far in the distance. I sucked in a breath at the sight. Parrots flew through the trees as the pink morning sun lifted above the horizon, and my eyes welled. I never thought I'd see this. Any of this.

We stared out at the forest in silence, watching as more wildlife erupted from the canopy. The sun rose until it was beaming in our faces, basking us in its golden glow. The sight filled me with awe—the kind that I knew would stay with me my whole life. This moment would forever be imprinted into my brain and had officially secured itself a spot in the highlight reel of lifetime experiences. It was bittersweet too, something about it tinged with the thought of going back to my life at the zoo. I didn't want this to be the only time I ever had this feeling. I wanted to stare out at sunrises in other places from other corners of the world. I wanted to be filled with this quiet, life-changing wonder again.

Logan reached over and grabbed my hand, threading his fingers through mine.

"What are you doing?"

"Holding your hand."

"Why are you holding my hand?"

He shrugged, offering me a soft smile. "Because I want to." He leaned his shoulder into mine and stared down at our clasped hands. "There are a lot of things I've been wanting to do."

I hummed, my throat suddenly going dry. The kiss we just shared flashed to the front of my mind again. "Like?"

He pulled our joined hands off the railing, making me turn toward him. His face was lit in sharp shadows from the early morning sun. His smooth skin was golden, more perfectly lit than any camera filter. His full lips were curved, his dark brown eyes roving my face. When he leaned down, I instinctively lifted onto my tiptoes and brushed my lips against his.

He let out a satisfied breath and murmured my name in a way that made my whole body tingle. Releasing my hand, he reached for me, one hand bracketing my jaw, the other sweeping around my back to pull me into his hard chest. My knees turned to jelly as his lips landed on mine. This kiss wasn't soft and slow like before. This one was hard and frenzied. He licked his tongue into my mouth with a groan, seemingly desperate to taste me.

My eager hands tugged on the hem of his T-shirt as he kissed me more feverishly. We were doing this. We were really doing this. This felt weird and amazing and so, so right. Maybe it was the magic of sunrise . . . Maybe it was the magic of Logan and me together—this strange little spark that had always been there and was now growing into a roaring inferno between us.

Logan must've sensed my wayward thoughts because he paused and pulled away. "Where did you go just now?" he asked, a smirk forming on his swollen lips.

I let out a surprised giggle and shook my head. "Nowhere."

"Liar." He rested his forehead against my own. His hands covered mine and held them against his chest to stop their frantic roving. "Lark?"

"Yeah?" I panted, my chest rising and falling so fast, my whole body feeling like I might combust if he didn't put his lips on mine again.

"Is this what you want?" he asked carefully. "Because half of the time, it seems like yes, and half the time, it seems like no, and I'm going to need a one hundred percent yes, you're into this before I keep randomly grabbing you and kissing you like a bloody fool."

I swallowed. Here it was. Plain and simple. I couldn't blame tequila or fire ants or jet lag this time. I couldn't lie to myself or to him anymore. However ridiculously I danced around it up until this moment, he'd laid it all bare with that one statement.

"Yes," I said, holding up a resolute finger to make my point. "Only in Guatemala, but yes, I one hundred percent want you to keep grabbing me and kissing me . . . and other things."

His smile widened for a split second before his hands were back on me, one snaking into my hair, the other raking down my back to cup my ass as his lips worked over mine. I moaned into his mouth and his hand dropped lower, hooking under my thigh and lifting me up. I koala-ed around him, holding on with an embarrassing squeak, and he smiled against my lips as he backed me up onto the lookout ledge, pinning me against one of the posts that held up the awning.

"You are so fucking adorable," he said against my mouth.

"And sexy," I added pointedly. "Like vixen goddess sexy, right?"

He chuckled as his fingers pressed tighter into my ass. "You are the sexiest woman I've ever met and you don't even know the half of it." He rocked his erection against the seam of my jean shorts, and my eyelids hooded with desire. "I've wanted you since the moment I saw you roughhouse that door to the monkey enclosure."

I shook my head and laughed. "That is a very random time to pick."

"Not from the angle I was standing at," he said, his teeth grazing my bottom lip.

I rocked my hips against him, the friction from the seam of my shorts already giving my pussy its own little heartbeat. Logan's lips skimmed up my jaw to the shell of my ear as he moved my ass up and down along him.

"Were you thinking of me?" he murmured, his hot breath in my ear making my nipples even harder as they rubbed against his chest. "Yesterday, when I brought you coffee, were you thinking of me?"

The embarrassment I thought would rise in me again was nowhere to be found, not when he asked it like it turned him the fuck on.

"Yes," I said as he nipped at my neck. "I was thinking about you."

"Did you come?"

My core turned to molten heat at the question. "No, I was rudely interrupted by the object of my fantasies."

His hand snaked under my tank top and found my peaked nipple. I arched into his touch and moaned so loudly, I thought I scared away a few parrots. Logan groaned at the noise and rocked into me harder.

"Would you like me to remedy that situation?" he asked before his lips returned to mine.

"Ye—"

"Lark!" a feminine voice shouted through the jungle. "You up there?" she called out in Spanish.

"Shit, Mari," I said, shoving Logan back like we were two teenagers about to be caught by our parents. I stared at Logan, his hair mussed, his lips swollen, his chest heaving . . . and his very evident erection straining against his shorts. "Make that go away," I hissed.

"I was trying to," he grumbled, turning around and flicking his hard-on up into the waistband of his shorts.

"Lark!" Mari called again.

"Mari!" I called back, sweeping my hair off my face and leaping back onto the lookout platform from the railing. I straightened my clothes, yanking my long-sleeve shirt back on to hopefully hide my Everest nipples.

I didn't look at Logan as I turned to the steps and ran toward Mari.

I was pretty sure I was two kisses away from being fucked in the middle of the jungle, and I thanked the bad-timing gods that Mari hadn't tried to sneak up on us as a surprise. My inner muscles clenched. I'd have to apologize to my pussy later. I owed her two promised orgasms . . . Well, technically, Logan owed her, and I was definitely going to make him fulfill those promises.

Volunteer
PRICKLE ISLAND ZOO
ZOO

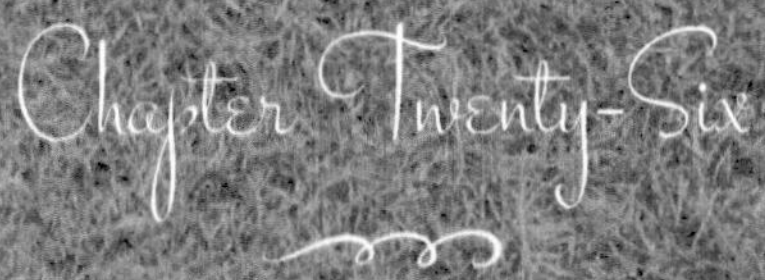

Chapter Twenty-Six

Logan

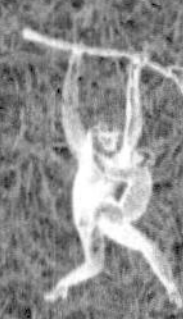

Well, there was no competing with her. Mariana—Mari—looked like a Victoria's Secret model dressed as a safari guide, and I swore Lark's pupils turned into little love hearts when she saw her. Mari wore a gray, collared polo shirt, a baseball cap with a howler monkey embroidered on the front of it, thick khaki trousers with a million pockets, and leather tramping boots. She looked cool and smart and obviously unbeatable when it came to Lark's affections.

I hadn't ever competed with a woman for someone before . . . that I knew of, at least. With a guy, I'd just have gone full night club bouncer on him and puffed out my chest and flexed my muscles, which now I was thinking about it, was very much like the baboons at the zoo. None of that alpha-male bullshit would work against someone like Mari. In fact, it would probably make Lark tilt onto Team Mari even more.

All of my explicitly detailed fantasies about fucking Lark in every corner of our villa now vanished with the way she bounded over to Mari and threw her arms around her. Lark buried her head in Mari's shoulder, and they rocked from side to side together, talking over each other about how Lark was finally here and it was all really happening. They spoke in such rapid Spanish, I could barely catch every few words.

Great, I was going to spend the next two weeks watching Lark fall in love with biology Barbie.

Mari finally released Lark from their bear hug and turned her eyes on me.

"Hi," she said with a broad smile as she shook my hand.

"Mari, this is Logan. He's one of the zoo volunteers. He's from New Zealand," Lark added, as if that were the synopsis of who I was as a person: Logan. Volunteer. New Zealand. That was what I'd been reduced to now. "Logan, this is Mari, director of the Guatemalan Wildlife Conservation Network and team leader for the black howler monkey research project."

"And your host for the next two weeks," Mari added with a wink. *How* was anyone that good at winking? Lark tucked a loose strand of hair behind her ear, and I would've stomped into a line of swarming ants to get her to do that when I looked at her again.

Mari gave me a friendly smile. "You ready for tomorrow?" she asked, sizing me up. "You look fit enough. Have you ever slept in a hammock before?"

I clenched my jaw so hard, I thought I might crack a tooth. "I'm sure I can manage," I gritted out, already planning how I could run up the mountain tomorrow or offer to carry all the bags or some other act of strength to prove I wasn't completely useless.

"I've got the supplies in my truck." She hooked her thumb to the forest trail behind her. "If you don't have space in your packs, you can leave some of your things in the lockers here. You've got a night here on the way back too."

"I thought we were leaving today?"

She snorted. "No, we've got to be way out of here by this time of morning," she said, like my question was ridiculous . . . Well, maybe she didn't and it just sounded that way because the woman I wanted to be with was staring at her like she was a supermodel. "We've got to leave here at midnight tonight to make it to the camp before sundown tomorrow." She glanced at Lark, flashing her beautiful white teeth. "Trust me, we don't want to still be hiking when the sun goes down in the middle of the jungle."

"Aren't we in the middle of the jungle here?" I asked, and both Lark and Mari erupted into laughter, which made me clench my jaw even tighter, and I started planning my explanation to a jaw physio . . . if there was such a thing.

"You'll see what I mean tomorrow," Mari said, linking her arm through Lark's. "Come on, let's go have breakfast. Let Jorge sleep."

"Jorge?" Lark and I asked at the same time as we turned to see a man leaning against one of the lookout posts with his arms folded.

A little house sat right beside the lookout that I'd somehow missed in the early morning shadows. All the blood drained from my face as Jorge lifted his chin to me with a half-smile that told me everything I needed to know: he'd heard Lark and me on the lookout before.

"Oh my god," Lark muttered, turning in a circle like she didn't know which way to run.

"Great," I snarled, giving a sheepish, apologetic wave to Jorge before walking toward Mari.

Lark plastered on a fake grin and gave Mari a squeeze, saying, "We'll meet you down there. I need to grab my sunhat from the villa. Grab us one of the tables by the pool."

Mari threw her arms around Lark again and pulled her into a quick, tight hug. "Okay, I'll go get the coffees."

"You're a saint," Lark said as Mari jogged off back down the trail, moving over roots and under vines with the practiced ease of a field biologist. When Lark turned from Mari's direction, her warm smile disappeared and her expression turned pure ice queen. She glanced at Jorge and then at me before tilting her head, beckoning me to follow.

We walked far enough that we were out of his earshot before she whirled on me and said, "Why are you being such a dick to Mari?"

"You mean your girlfriend?"

Lark's mouth fell open. "She is *not* my girlfriend."

"But you wish she were," I countered. "I don't blame you. She looks like she moonlights as a high fashion model."

Lark guffawed. "Are you seriously jealous right now?"

"Shouldn't I be?"

"No!" she spat back. "We were just—"

"We were two seconds from fucking when she arrived."

"And?"

"And," I growled. "That means something. Or at least I thought it should."

"First of all," she said, and I knew I'd just dug my own grave. No good conversation starts with "first of all." Lark squared me with a look. "It doesn't mean anything, Logan." She threw her hands up in the air. "Second of all, I'm not going to deny it anymore. Yes, you're hot and I want to fuck you." My dick went hard again as the words tumbled out of her mouth. "Well, a little less since you were an asshole to my friend." That doused ice on my newfound arousal. "And yes, I wanted to be with her in the past because she's fucking gorgeous and smart and *nice*," she said pointedly. "But right now, the horny spotlight in my brain is pointed directly at you, even if I hate it."

I pressed my lips together, trying to hide a smug, satisfied smile.

But Lark wasn't done. "But it doesn't matter who I want to sleep with!" She groaned, clearly exasperated. "I don't want to feel anything for either of you!"

I narrowed my eyes at her. "Why not?"

"Because I need to go home to a job and a family that needs me and neither of you will be in that future, so let's just have our Guatemala-only hookup and then move the fuck on!" Her cheeks had flushed beet red, and I hated how hot she was when she was righteously furious. But it was true. I was heading back home at the end of the summer to my own family drama. It was a poorly kept family secret that Dad's health wasn't doing great and that my brother needed more help running all the many family businesses. Even if I wanted to drop everything and be with my hot zookeeper, I couldn't. And she loved her job and her life at the zoo. I wasn't going to mess that up for her either.

I rubbed the back of my neck. "You're right."

"Wow." Her eyes widened. "I didn't think I'd ever hear you say that."

"Shoot your shot with Mari if you want," I said, even though my insides were turning green with possessive asshole jealousy. "But I'm not going to stop randomly grabbing you and kissing you until you tell me otherwise."

"I'm not shooting my shot with Mari!" she shouted, and

Jorge whistled from uphill. Lark stormed another few steps down the path.

"Sorry, Jorge," I called with a wave. I wondered how often he got woken up like this. I grabbed Lark, spinning her into me and planting a kiss on her that promised more. Her ice melted just a little as I worked my mouth over her lips. "I'm sorry. I just—"

"Let's just have a fun trip," Lark said with a nod. "No strings. No jealousy. No feelings." She counted her demands on her fingers. "And only in Guatemala," she warned. "When we get back to the zoo, *this*"—she waved her hand between us—"never happened."

I nodded and followed her gorgeous ass down the trail, dangerous hope reigniting in me. "Only in Guatemala."

STAFF
PRICKLE
ISLAND
ZOO
ZOO

I couldn't believe I was giving up on my pursuit of Mari for anyone, let alone a man. When did the world tip upside down? But my heart was the captain of the cheer team right now, and the way Logan had kissed me had her full attention. I'd been honest when I told him that he was the only one I was thinking about right now.

God help me.

"Mmm," Mari hummed, digging into her eggs. "I love the breakfasts here."

I piled a serving of refried beans into a tortilla and added my eggs on top in a makeshift breakfast burrito that tasted like heaven. The caramelized plantains were to die for; the coffee was ridiculously strong, and it only cost a handful of quetzals. This place was heaven.

Mari dumped three spoonfuls of sugar in her coffee before stirring it and taking a sip. "So, you've got two more months before you fly home, Kiwi?" Mari asked Logan.

He nodded and quickly swallowed his mouthful of food. "Yep."

That seemed to be all he wanted to contribute to the conversation. Despite my confession that he was all I was thinking about, he still seemed pretty standoffish around Mari.

"Do you know kiwi birds actually do have wings?" I interrupted the awkward silence. I put two fingers on my shoulder and flicked them up and down. "They're just really tiny, flappy vestigial things that don't really do anything—"

"Does she do this with you too?" Logan asked.

"Hey," I grumbled, swatting him with my napkin. "You know animal fun facts are my love language."

"As they are mine," Mari said, giving me a wink that made Logan scowl and go back to his food.

I leaned over and murmured in English, "Now who's being the prickly one?"

That got him to at least stop moping.

Mari and I continued to dominate the conversation, catching up and talking about what we'd been doing over the last three years. Logan mostly focused on his plate, but his knee kept pressing into mine under the table.

"Oh," Mari said. "I forgot to tell you about Miguel!"

She took out her phone and showed me a photo of her with a guy standing in front of an old church in Antigua.

"Ooh," I said, admiring the photo.

"We've been dating for three months, so it's still pretty new," she said. "He works at the university with me. He's in the chemistry department." She put her hand on her chest and made a swoony face as if being a scientist was equivalent to being a billionaire model.

My smile widened. "He sounds amazing."

Suddenly, Logan's surly mood evaporated into thin air. He leaned in and looked at the photo and flashed a genuine smile. I had to fight the overwhelming urge to roll my eyes. Men.

"How did you two meet?" he asked with actual warmth.

I gave him a pointed look. *Oh, I see, you and Mari are besties now that you know she has a guy and isn't going to be flirting with me.* I nudged him with my knee and he nudged me back. I went to nudge him again as Mari told us about their meeting during Semana Santa, but Logan's hand landed on my knee, sliding up my thigh and halting all of my protests.

My throat bobbed, and I grabbed the slick glass of ice water beading with condensation. His fingers squeezed and then rose a little higher. His pinky finger brushed the seam of my jeans, and I practically choked on my sip of water.

We'd laid it all out there: I wanted him, he wanted me; I didn't want Mari, and Mari didn't want me. Logan and I would have a quick, messy vacation relationship and then we'd go back to reality. That was all it would be. Then I could move on with my life and forget about him.

Of course, we'd finally confessed how badly we wanted to sleep together right before we'd have an ever-present third wheel for the next two weeks. Terrible timing. I wasn't exactly sure how many secret hookup spots there were in the middle of the jungle. We'd probably stumble into a bunch of thorns or get attacked by a giant snake if we ventured off from the farm we were going to.

Logan's hand shifted, cupping me through my jeans, pressing his middle finger in, and I practically dropped my glass onto the table.

"I need to go to the toilet," I said, rising too quickly from the table and jostling it. "Sorry," I added.

"Should we go for a swim after breakfast?" Mari asked, nodding to the pool. "You can go change into your swimsuit."

"Sounds great," I said through a faux smile. The last thing I needed to see was Logan shirtless and wet again. The next two weeks were going to be lady blue balls times a million.

"You want to go sit by the pool?" Mari asked Logan as she stood up.

"I think I'm . . . going to just sit here a little longer. Still working on this coffee," he replied, staring straight down into his empty coffee cup.

My lips curved into a mischievous grin. At least I wouldn't be blue balls-ing it alone. If I was going to suffer, so should he. I hustled off to the toilet, praying that on this research trip, Mari would need to be up at the lookout *alone* for several hours at a time, or was a really heavy sleeper, or something because I'd finally admitted to Logan how badly I wanted him and it was going to kill me to waste our whole "only in Guatemala" time together.

STAFF
PRICKLE
ISLAND
ZOO
ZOO

Lark

We left at midnight in Mari's truck and drove down a bumping road to an even bumpier road until the path was too narrow for a car anymore. She pulled off-road to where a little farmhouse sat amongst the jungle, a handful of other cars parked next to the tall grasses amongst the field.

Pulling out her research permit, she whistled and was greeted by a chorus of barking as five dogs ran off the porch in our direction. A face appeared in the window and they waved, whistling and calling the dogs back.

"Wait here," Mari said, running off to the house with all of her documentation.

Logan and I stood there in sleepy silence, shuffling from

foot to foot as the stars winked out above us and the sky turned from pitch black to deep blue. He reached over and took my hand, threading his fingers through my own. I squeezed his hand in response, letting him know I was thinking the same things. This was an incredible, once-in-a-lifetime experience and I was getting to share it with him.

Mari emerged a couple minutes later with two men walking their motorbikes toward us. "Lark, we're riding with Diego," she said, nodding to the man closest to her. "Logan, you'll ride with Carlos."

"Two of us are riding on the back of that?" I asked, staring at the motorbike that looked like it had seen better days. I'd noticed as we moved out of the bigger towns, there were fewer and fewer cars and more and more motorbikes.

"You'll go in the middle," Mari said.

I found her accent easy to understand, but Diego's and Carlos's were nearly impossible for me to decipher. I thought I'd be doing better with my Spanish, but obviously everyone around me had been using their white-lady Spanish on me.

Mari warned me to be careful of the muffler as I got on the motorbike. I wasn't sure what I was meant to do with my hands. Was I supposed to hug Diego? My thighs were sandwiched around my pack, which sat between me and him, and Mari was around me with her pack on her back. Was this even safe? Probably not. I had just settled on a polite hip hold when the motorbike lurched to life and we took off down the narrow trail through the jungle.

Logan looked equally terrified as he held on to the bar jutting out of the seat behind him. His pack rocked and bounced as we rode over gnarled tree roots and weaved around large rocks. My chin knocked into my pack three times before I found a position where I wouldn't be so easily jostled. Mari was saying something to me about tree species, but I couldn't hear over the roar of the engines. We drove over a dried riverbed, bumping and jockeying over the stones. My stomach twisted into a knot with all the bouncing, along with a healthy dose of fear. My thighs were killing me from holding on to my pack so tightly.

We rode like that for hours, deeper and deeper into the jungle, until my legs were so numb and cramped that I could barely feel them. We hit a huge bump that made Mari claw into me. My right leg dropped from the footrest and banged into the muffler. I thought maybe I'd gotten away with it. I lifted my leg, trying to act like nothing had happened, when a hot, searing pain flashed through my inner calf.

If it had been an inch higher, I would've been protected by the thick fabric of my shorts; a few inches lower, and my boot would've protected my foot. But instead, it felt like I had a burn hole the size of a cantaloupe on my leg. I didn't look down, too embarrassed to say anything. What was there to do anyway? I'd get my travel med kit out when we got to the hiking part of our trek. Maybe I could change into my pants without anyone even noticing.

I gritted my teeth through the pain as we kept flying through the now midmorning jungle. Droplets of weeping fluid from my burn wound trickled down into my sock. That couldn't be a good sign.

When we finally reached the base of the mountain, I wanted to drop to my knees and kiss the ground, but instead, I wobbled over to the nearest tree on drunken legs and propped my pack against my shins to cover the burn.

Logan looked like he'd gone pale, seasick from the bumpy ride. He immediately started stretching his arms and dropped into a crouch.

"You did well," Mari said as she waved farewell to the drivers. I couldn't believe they were about to turn around and make the whole trip back like it was nothing. "Did you see the ruins?"

"Huh?"

"The ones I was telling you about?"

"Oh." I realized that was what she was pointing at in the darkness. "Yes. Beautiful," I lied. I'd thought it had just been a hill and I couldn't hear her. I made a mental note to pay more attention on the ride back. The ride out had just been about hanging on for dear life.

"Let's break for some lunch," she said, perching on one of the larger stones on the dry riverbed. "Then we start hiking."

I craned my neck up to the mountain above us and swallowed. "Great," I said, feeling less confident with every breath. The burning pain in my leg was insane, and I was afraid to look down. "You two rest. I'm just going to pee." I hooked my thumb toward the forest behind me.

"Follow the riverbed," Mari said, pointing. "It curves around the corner. Make sure to really stomp your feet as you walk."

"Awesome," I said, turning and trudging over the unsteady rocks. Logan's eyes narrowed at me curiously.

"Why don't you leave your pack?" Mari called.

"I, um . . . wanted to get changed into my pants for the hike."

"Good idea." Mari nodded. "Lots of thorns and black poisonwood along the trail."

I gave her a thumbs-up, ignoring Logan's eyes on me and following the riverbed down and around the corner. Once I was out of sight and out of earshot of Mari's continual stream of fun facts that rivaled my own, I unclipped my pack, flipped the top open, and began searching for my med kit.

My fingers closed around the canvas bag Mom gave me

and I'd just pulled it out when a voice behind me said, "Let's see it."

I whirled to spy Logan, arms crossed and frowning at me. "See what?"

"I saw your leg slam into the muffler an hour back, tails," he said.

I twisted sideways, hiding my injury from him. "I don't know what you're talking about."

"Lark Stubbornness-Personified Lachlan."

"That is an even stranger middle name than my actual one," I said, trying to move the conversation somewhere other than my careless injury.

Logan took the bait. "What's your middle name?"

"Irwin."

His eyebrows shot up. "What? Why?"

I shrugged. "Because crocodile hunter was taken."

I could see the wheels in Logan's mind turning, trying to decide if I was telling the truth. But when I shifted my weight and winced, his eyes dropped back to my leg. "You're trying to distract me."

My lips curved into a frown as I muttered, "It was worth a shot."

"How bad is it?"

I groaned and rolled my eyes, turning my ankle out to get a good view of the injury.

"Shit," Logan muttered.

The skin had gone bone-white, a blackened layer curling around it in a disgusting halo. Clear liquid beaded all along the softball-sized circle on my leg.

"Shit," I echoed, moving more frantically through the med kit. "This is just perfect. My first day of the research trip and I have a giant fucking burn hole in my leg and—"

Logan's hands came over mine, stalling them. "It's going to be okay."

"I know it's going to be okay," I snapped, rifling through the supplies. "I can handle a minor injury. With minor painkillers and limited bandaging," I added with a groan. "I don't want them looking at me like I'm the pathetic American who can't even ride a motorbike. I'm supposed to be the ambassador for the zoo. I'm supposed to know what I'm doing, and this—"

Logan closed the distance between us and silenced me with a kiss. Damn him, it was a very effective way of shutting me up. His lips hovered over mine for a second longer before he said, "Let me help you." He took the case from my hands. "Sit down."

I sat and let him swab my leg with iodine and bandage it. It still hurt like a motherfucker, but at least I didn't have to look at it anymore. When he was done, he kissed the inside of my knee in a way that made me forget all about my injury and wish he were trailing his lips higher. Thank you, evolution, for making my sexy-time hormones override my pain receptors right now. Biological imperative cocktail at its finest. Just the look in his eyes when he glanced my way was enough to make me forget everything else except how he promised that he wouldn't stop grabbing me and kissing me.

"No one's been eaten by anything, have they?" Mari shouted from up the riverbed.

Logan hung his head. Clearly, his thoughts were following the same train as mine. "These next two weeks are going to be torture, aren't they?"

"Uh-huh," I said roughly. "Are you already thinking of ways we can sneak off?"

"Yep," he said.

"Any good ideas?"

"Nope." My shoulders drooped, and he added, "But I do know we have one sweet night alone at the eco-hotel before we leave." His voice dropped an octave as he pinned me with a look. "And I'm going to fuck you against every surface in that place."

I clamped my knees together and bit my lip.

Mari called out again, and I was about to claw the rest of my skin off in sexual frustration.

"Time to hike a mountain with a burn hole in my leg," I muttered.

"I don't know why, but even that is turning me on right now."

"You better walk in front of me so you're not staring at my ass the whole way, then."

"Your ass is the only thing getting me up that mountain," Logan countered with a grin. "Let's go, tails."

Volunteer
PRICKLE
ISLAND
ZOO
ZOO

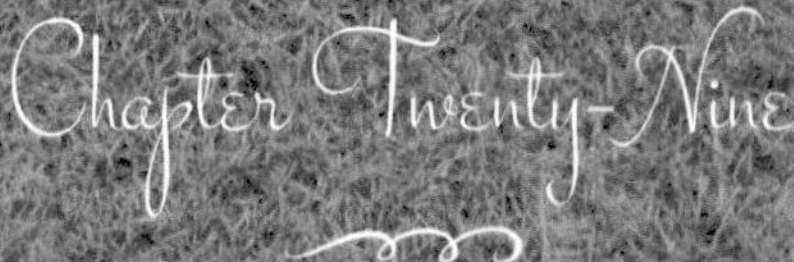

Chapter Twenty-Nine

Logan

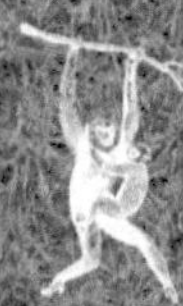

By the time we'd hiked the three hours up the mountain to our next water break, I knew that Lark was hurting. By the time we finished the last two hours, she was leaning far to the side with each step, and it took all of my strength not to run up and sling her arm over my shoulder . . . but I knew she'd hate that. She was far too proud to receive that kind of assistance. I knew she wanted to stride into the campsite with the pride of a fifth-generation member of the Prickle Island Zoo.

The sun was starting to set by the time we arrived at the campsite. The research site was four wooden posts covered by a roof thatched in palm leaves. A pond sat downhill from the hut, and the fields around had been cleared of trees. Two white-and-gray horses grazed in one paddock, and a braying donkey wandered beside it. Their paddocks were made up of two lines of barbed wire twisted around stakes in the ground. One narrow section was empty, the barbed wire surrounding only a large, gnarled tree, the only one still standing in the field.

Lark practically ran the last stretch to the fire pit before collapsing onto the nearest log. She dropped her hands onto her knees and panted a few breaths before she unclipped her chest strap and waist belt and let her pack schlump to the side.

I was desperate to get my feet out of their sweaty leather prisons. I sat on the log beside Lark, shucked off my boots, and peeled my wet socks off my feet. My skin was marked with little indentations, and my feet were so swollen that my toes were little stubs. I was pretty sure I was going to lose my big toenail. The top was an angry red, and the base was beginning to purple. My blisters had blisters even though I'd tried to wear in my tramping boots before my trip. I should've just brought my old ones. Yeah, they had a hole in the toe, but they'd survived three of New Zealand's Great Walks with no blisters. Now my feet looked like two spoiled hams.

Mari dropped her pack against a pole under the hut and walked casually to perch on a log across the fire pit from Lark. This was when her expertise in the field was clear. The first hour, we'd all managed about the same, but Mari had pulled way ahead by lunchtime and had to take the rear afterward so she didn't lose us. Lark and I were both physically fit people, but Mari was an absolute fucking machine, and it was brilliant seeing her so at home that even despite her being my rival for all of two seconds, I was heartily impressed.

"The river looks crystal clear, but if you see me drinking out of it, don't do what I do," she warned. "That's locals' water only unless you want to be crapping everywhere."

"Noted," I said with a huff.

She pointed to a giant steel pot and metal cooler on a long stone workbench that was positioned under a little thatched awning. "Boiled water," she said. "Only boiled water."

"Boiled water only. Got it," Lark said dutifully, as if she were taking mental notes. My cheeks dimpled as I shook my head at her, and she mouthed, "What?" at me.

"We'll hang the hammocks up over there." Mari hooked her thumb toward the hut behind her. "I suggest you sleep with long sleeves if you don't want to be covered in bites when you wake up. You brought bug spray?"

Lark fished through her pack like the Girl Scout she was and produced three different bottles. "Yep."

Mari rolled her shoulders a few times and stretched her neck. "Poop tree," she said, pointing at the lone tree beside the horses and donkey. The hill undulated down so we couldn't see the base of the tree from where we sat.

"Poop tree?" I repeated, making sure I hadn't just completely forgotten what words meant.

"Yeah," she said. "That's the toilet. There should be some toilet paper hanging off one of the branches. I brought more in my bag too."

"And where do we, um, put said toilet paper?" Lark asked, peeling her socks off with a moan that made me have to clear my throat. That sound alone was giving me a semi, and I dropped my face into my hands, trying to think of really unsexy things, like the poop tree, and not the sound she just made. There were no bathroom stalls around here that I could sneak off to deal with a hard-on right now.

"Just leave the toilet paper there," Mari said. "It's biodegradable. The ants will take it."

"The fucking ants," I muttered, thinking of the way they tried to carry Lark away like she was a giant bloody leaf the other night.

Mari quirked her brow at me. "You'll be grateful for them when you wake up in the morning and all the shit is gone."

I blinked at her. They were efficient little bastards, I'd give them that. Who needed a toilet when you could have an army of ants carry your excrement off?

Mari stretched her arms over her head and leaned side to side as if she'd just gone for a quick jog. Then, she stood and said, "I'm going to get the hammocks set up. Then dinner and sleep. We'll meet the farmers tomorrow."

On the trek up the mountain, Mari had explained her relationship to the farmers in the region: the area abutted a national park but was technically private land that had been divided up between seven farms, each having plots along the trail here. The farmers lived up in the mountains during the week and down with their families in town on the weekends; some shared farms with brothers and cousins and took turns with who tended the land. Sometimes, there were twenty men living up here, sometimes two. Judging by the two horses and donkey in the paddock, I'd wager at least three were here currently. How come we didn't get to ride horses?

I eyed Mari from across the open space, and then my eyes landed on Lark. "How's the leg?" I asked softly enough that Mari couldn't hear.

"It hurts," Lark said, letting out a slow, wincing breath. "But I'm fine."

"If it's any consolation, I think you're incredibly impressive, tails," I said. "If it were me, I'd be bitching and whining the whole way up this mountain." I shifted off my log and moved to sit next to her. We stared out at the setting sun as the jungle came to life with evening birdsong. "Why do you always feel like you have to be the strongest person in every room?"

I didn't know why I asked it. It just kind of tumbled out of my mouth.

"We're not in a room," she countered in that cheeky, defiant way of hers.

"You know what I mean."

She sighed, reaching for a stick and mindlessly trailing it through the dirt. "I don't know," she hedged. "I've always been that kid—the responsible one. It got me a lot of brownie points for being sensible amongst my chaotic siblings. Of course, that probably made me swing even more into the organizer role. So much so, my mother worries about me now," she added with a smile.

My shoulders rose and fell with a half-laugh. "I can imagine she's more comfortable with the chaotic ones than she is with a . . ."

"Buttoned-up know-it-all?" she offered. I laughed as I studied her face. "That's what my siblings think of me."

"That's not how I think of you."

She pursed her lips, her brow furrowing, and I leaned over and smoothed the crease between her eyes with my pointer finger.

"How do you think of me?" she asked carefully, pausing between each word as if she were debating taking it back.

"I think you're smart, caring, hardworking, tough, gorgeous," I said, leaning my shoulder into her. "I think you'll sacrifice your own desires for your family, and I think you're working yourself raw trying to make someone proud and that someone isn't you."

She winced as my words landed home, and my gut clenched. That was too harsh. I wanted to apologize as soon as I said it, but she beat me to it.

"My dad," she said, the words coming out hoarse, and I had to ball my hands into fists to not pull her into my chest. "It's for him and for all of my family after he died."

"How did he die?" I asked softly, pressing my knee into

hers a little more, as if to anchor her there in that moment. She stared off in silence, watching Mari tie up her hammock. "We can talk about something else."

"No," she said, clearing her throat. "No. It's fine."

There she was, being the tough one again.

She took a deep breath and said, "He died of a heart attack. Ten years ago." She tossed the stick and dropped her elbows to her knees. "Hawk was the one who found him."

"Shit," I said, knowing that wasn't a particularly helpful or comforting thing to say.

I felt the overwhelming urge to give Hawk a bear hug the next time I saw him. It made a lot of sense. He was a lot like Lark: tough, hardworking, sometimes cold even, but when you got to know him, he was kind and deeply caring. Must be a Lachlan family trait. It was a lot like my family too. We stuffed it all down, kept plowing forward even when things were breaking us. We didn't complain, didn't talk, just worked harder.

"I think Hawk took it the hardest," Lark continued. "We all grieved him in our own ways. Hawk took over his office, put all of his energy into continuing Dad's legacy. Finch got lost in her studies . . . and hooking up with every eligible girl on the island. Dove leans on social media and being online and everywhere but in her actual body. Wren got really into her art and crafting. The twins probably had the healthiest response of just lighting a bunch of shit on fire and beating each other up."

I snorted. "That sounds very healthy."

"Light pyromania really helps heal the trauma when you're nine."

"And you? How did you cope?"

Lark shrugged. "I worked," she said. "I focused on my job and made sure everything was running smoothly and had the optimized schedules and the very best routines. The things I wanted kind of disappeared." She didn't sound sad about it, only resigned. "I decided I was going to help Hawk build the future my dad saw for us."

"And what was that?"

"All of us living at the zoo," she said. "All of the siblings having their own houses on the property, running the place together, building it back to its former glory. He wanted to buy the zoo from the Westworths, own it outright without their patronage . . . It seemed possible back then when thousands of visitors flooded the zoo every summer. Now, we constantly live in fear that the Westworths will sell it to make way for another golf course."

"But didn't your great-however-many-grandfather found the island?"

"He did," she hedged. "Sort of. Technically, it was already land owned by the Westworths, though none of them had ever been out to the island at that time. He became the caretaker and started the zoo as a private collection on their behalf. My dad always wanted to make it truly ours."

I watched the sun dip below the tree line. The parrots that had flown from tree to tree were now replaced by bats zipping around, lit up by Mari's torchlight.

We sat there in silence for a long stretch before I finally asked, "What were all the things you wanted before they disappeared?"

Her eyes welled with tears, and I hated that I'd struck that nerve. I didn't want to be the one who made her cry, but it also seemed like this conversation was long overdue, one she desperately needed, and one her siblings might not be fully equipped to have with her.

"I wanted to move somewhere new," she said, her voice wobbling. "I wanted to meet new people. Experience new cultures. Pick the place in the world I wanted to call home instead of the one predestined for me." She took a shuddering breath. "But now . . . I'm careful. Hardworking. Putting the family and our name above my own selfish needs. I'm being the person I should be."

"Maybe the person you think you should be is killing the person you need to be," I said. "Maybe sometimes, you need to put *your* happiness ahead of everyone else's."

Her bottom lip trembled, and she nibbled at it. I clenched my hands into fists to not pull it free.

"You sound like Dove. Maybe that's why I'm so hard on her," she said with a sniff. "She knows how to do that, and I don't. Even after Dad died, she still feels like she can leave, and I just . . . can't. I can't do that to Dad."

Her voice cracked, and my soul cracked with it. When a tear slid down her cheek, I reached out on instinct and wiped it away with my thumb. The gentle gesture just made more tears spill down her cheeks, and I grabbed her and pulled her into my chest, letting her tears stain my sweaty shirt.

"I'm sorry I smell so gross," I whispered into her hair.

"I'm used to gross smells." She sobbed into my T-shirt. Her arms wrapped around me, and I buried my lips in her hair that still smelled like the vanilla shampoo from the hotel. I swept a hand in soothing circles down her back, wishing I could somehow pull the pain out of her from the strength of my hold alone.

I knew on any other day, at any other time, she never would've been so vulnerable with me. But after days of traveling and no sleep, she was tired enough that I was able to crack through her defenses. The Lark that was underneath was so beautiful and real and raw that I knew whether we called this a two-week fling or not, the feeling of this moment, with my arms around her, would stay with me for the rest of my life.

We held each other like that for a long time as the sky darkened before Mari's shouted swears pulled our focus.

I hated the feeling of emptiness I had as Lark pulled out of our hug and called, "What's wrong?"

"One of the hammocks is broken," Mari called back with another curse that I didn't quite understand. Something about grandmothers? "They're all doubles," she added. "Think you two can share for a night until we can fix this one?"

Lark's mouth fell open beside me, and she called, "No," right as I shouted, "Yes!"

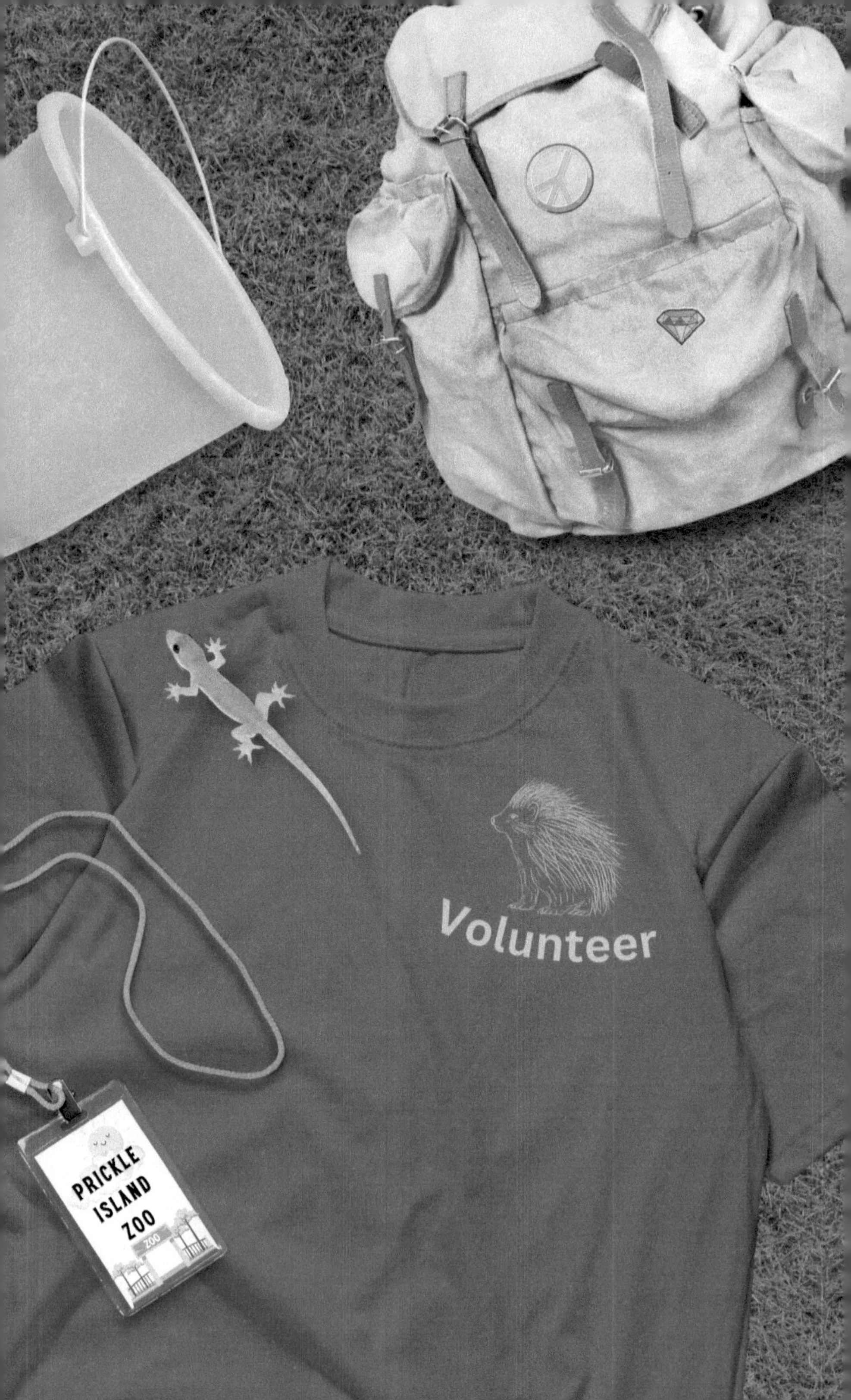

Volunteer
PRICKLE
ISLAND
ZOO
ZOO

Chapter Thirty

Logan

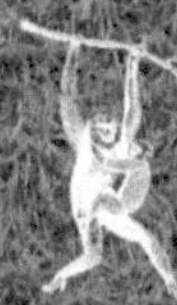

Two people were *not* meant to sleep in one hammock . . . even
if it was a double, whatever that meant. There was no way to
be a gentleman and put a pillow between us. We didn't even
have pillows. And after Lark had poured her heart out to me
about her dad and her squashed dreams, I just wanted to keep
holding her all night long anyway.

We ate our lean dinner quickly: tinned chicken and trail
mix . . . delicious. I was too tired to care. Behind the rainwater
tank, I changed into my fresh pair of quick-dry pants and long-
sleeve merino shirt. There was a bucket and soap for a rudi-
mentary PSC wash—pits, sack, and crack—but after a whole
day of tramping, it didn't really do the job. Mari promised us

we could bathe in the pond in the morning, and I looked forward to not smelling like I'd just been rolling in a pigsty. No amount of deodorant I swiped under my arms would make me smell like *deep river* or *steel bonfire* or whatever the fuck name they gave to men's deodorant that smelled nothing like that. Why couldn't they make a deodorant that just smelled clean without trying to make it gunmetal blue like men were all magpies? Probably because we were. I'd grabbed this one off the shelf with one look and didn't even read the label.

Okay, my brain was officially delirious.

With my head torch on, I scanned the dusty red ground around me as I headed toward the "poop tree." A bunch of little reflective eyes looked back at me, and I decided it would be sadistic to look any closer at them. I didn't want to know.

I was just tall enough to be able to climb over the barbed-wire fence if I stood on a rock beside one of the stakes. Still, I cupped my junk as I swung a leg over. The last thing I needed was to be dangling by my nuts off a barbed-wire fence . . . I hoped Lark wasn't watching my less-than-elegant dismount over the other side.

The pieces of the Lark puzzle were finally starting to fit together. It made a lot of sense now why she cared so much about schedules and routines and duty to her family. I understood that feeling more than she knew. It was why I went on this trip, why Kelly and I broke up. My dad wouldn't say it out loud, but I knew he wasn't doing too good, and I knew there'd be a time when I was needed closer to home. Kelly didn't want to move out to the wop-wops. Hell, she didn't even want *me* moving back to the middle of nowhere. It only took that one more crack in our relationship before it finally imploded.

Lark and I were cut from the same cloth in that way—both of us feeling responsible for our families. I'd told her it was okay to put her happiness first, but really, I was telling myself, even if I knew I wouldn't take my own advice and she wouldn't either.

The poop tree was surrounded by lines of ants, and I had to jump over the rows of them like a really unfun game of "floor is lava" to get to it. The tree had a line of toilet paper rolls hanging from it, waving in the wind like flags. It was the most healthy, robust tree I'd ever seen, and I wondered if it was because of all the "fertilizer" it got fed every day.

The jungle rustled with some strange noises and the horses and donkey, lit up by my torchlight, twisted their ears to the sound. Suddenly, I didn't want to be pissing in the middle of the jungle at nighttime and quickly finished and did my ant-hopscotch back to the hut.

Mari was clearly fast asleep already, judging by the loud snoring coming from her hammock along the far post of the hut. Lark was already in our hammock, and I wondered if she was also asleep. There was no delicate way to tiptoe into a shared hammock though. When I pulled down the side to climb in, she cheeped and clung onto the opposite edge.

"Sorry." I grimaced, trying—and failing—to drop gracefully onto the other side. When I sat down, the whole thing swung wildly back and forth. I turned off my head torch and hung it on a nail on the post above us.

"Just get in," she whispered, still trying to cling to her side as I lifted my legs and leaned back. I pulled the other edge up. We were all elbows and shoulders, jostling in weird ways, trying to figure out how to both sleep without touching each other. She got me in the ribs, and I hip-checked her, the whole hammock rocking like a kid on a swing set.

"Lark?"

"Yeah?"

"You can't cling onto the side like a fucking limpet all night," I said.

"I don't know what that means, but sure I can," she countered.

"They don't have limpets where you're from?" I shook my head. Now wasn't the time. We were both exhausted and just needed to sleep. "Doesn't matter." I slid one arm under her shoulders. "Let go."

"No."

"Aren't you exhausted?"

"Yes." Still, she didn't let go.

"Then why don't you just resign yourself to the fact that we're both going to end up squashed together in the middle of this hammock?"

"Because I'm stubborn," she said, and I was sure if I still had my head torch on, I'd see her bottom lip stuck out.

"Yes," I said. "Yes, you most certainly are." My hand curled around her side, and I gave a little tug of encouragement. "Come on, tails."

Finally, she released the far edge of the hammock and I bicep-curled her into me. Her cheek rested on my chest, her arm slinging over my side, her leg covering mine.

She hummed as she melted more into me, and my cock twitched. Even at the point of exhaustion, he still was ready to climb a few more mountains. But the feeling quickly ebbed to the quiet warmth of her pressed against me.

"Isn't this better?" I murmured into her hair.

"Mm-hmm," she hummed, sleep already making her voice distant. Her limbs were slack against mine.

"Little koala bear."

She yawned. "Koalas aren't bears; they're marsupials."

"Shh," I said with a chuckle. Even half asleep, she couldn't help herself.

If I hadn't been trekking uphill all day, I might've found it hard to sleep, but with Lark's soft body pressed against mine, the steady rise and fall of her chest, and my aching muscles demanding rest, sleep found me quickly. My arms tightened around Lark one last time, and when I was sure she was asleep, I kissed the top of her head and then drifted off to join her in the land of the blissfully unconscious.

STAFF
PRICKLE ISLAND ZOO
ZOO

I woke up in the predawn light to the roar of howler monkeys in the distance. Their loud calls accompanying the squawk of birds and buzz of morning insects sounded just like home. One thing that was nothing like home, however, was the hot, unconscious man curled around me. Logan and I had become intertwined like we were playing a game of Twister in our sleep. My thigh had slipped between his legs and was pressing against his morning erection. I closed my unfocused eyes and leaned into him again. Waking up in this strange, new place was disorienting. My body was so tired, my brain discombobulated.

Logan's forearm had found its way against my pussy and just the pressure of it made me instantly throb in a way that made me wonder if I was awake or if this was all a sexy dream. I had half a mind to just rub myself against his forearm until I came and satisfy my early morning horniness. But despite being intertwined, I wasn't a hammock creep, so I tried to roll over and separate the two of us.

Instead, I rolled right out of the hammock and toppled to the ground, collapsing on the dusty earth with a grunt.

"Shit!" Logan whispered, peeking over the edge of the hammock. "Are you okay?"

The sun hadn't risen yet, but the sky was bright enough to see the outline of his face against the lightening sky. Of course he had to wake up to witness my clumsiness. Why couldn't I fall into a heap silently?

"I'm fine," I said, rising and dusting myself off as embarrassment burned through me.

"It's too early for whatever you're doing," Logan grumbled. "Come back to bed."

"It's a hammock."

"'Come back to hammock' doesn't have the same ring."

"I . . ." I twisted around, searching for a good excuse to not climb back into that hammock and torture myself with his closeness. But then again . . . he was awake now and Mari wasn't, so . . .

I sidled over to the hammock and tried to climb in slowly but ended up just collapsing in with all of the grace of a newborn giraffe. The hammock rocked wildly, and Logan's arms instinctively wrapped around me as we tried not to laugh. We froze as Mari's snoring paused and snickered when it picked back up again. I felt like a teenager sneaking around as I stifled my laugh in Logan's shoulder.

He swept a lock of hair behind my ear, his fingers lingering in my hair, and I wondered if he was having the same thoughts as I was. The hardness pressed against my hip certainly seemed to indicate so. Soon, Mari would wake to the sound of the howlers and the brightness of the rising sun, and I decided I didn't want to waste this moment.

I reached a hand to Logan's jaw and he instantly closed the distance, his mind clearly going to the same place. His lips met mine in a soft kiss, his tongue tracing over my bottom lip before dipping into my mouth. A moan caught in my throat and I reminded myself I needed to be quiet . . . or at least wait until the next roar of howler monkeys.

My hand trailed down Logan's side and I cupped him through his sweatpants, letting him know exactly where I wanted this to go. His breath hitched as he rocked into my palm, his hand sliding down my side in mirror action and dipping into the waistband of my pants. My whole body trembled as his fingers parted my flesh.

"You're so wet," he whispered as his fingers trailed lower, swirling in my heat and spreading it back up to my aching clit. He circled his fingers over that throbbing button, making my hips tilt into his hand.

I slid my hand into his pants and grabbed him, pumping once tentatively as he thrust into my fist. It was only then I realized I'd never done this before. I'd had sex, but never with someone with a working cock. I mean, I'd seen it done on the internet, though I knew that was probably not the best representation of what sex with a man was actually like . . . and I was starting to wonder if there was a method to this whole thing that I didn't know about. How complicated could this be? I watched monkeys do it every day——

"Where have you drifted off to?" Logan murmured against my lips, his tongue coaxing me back to the present.

He rocked into my grip again, and I slid my hand up and down his shaft in matching rhythm.

"Is this good?" I asked.

He hummed against my mouth, a deep throaty sound that made my hips press my pussy harder into his fingers. The hammock swayed as I kept up the movement. Logan's fingers circled me one more time before dipping to my slick entrance and pushing inside me. My breath caught and he consumed my moan with his mouth, his fingers slowly massaging me. He dropped the heel of his palm to my clit and kept circling me while his fingers pumped in and out. Fuck, he knew what he was doing. I'd heard a lot of men were useless at finding the clit, let alone paying any attention to it, but not Logan Anderson. He played me like a freaking violin.

"Faster." His whisper was tinged with pleading as I started pumping his cock in quicker strokes. "Yes." The word was more of a guttural noise than a word, and I moved faster as his fingers worked over me.

His mouth trailed from my own as he lowered his head to my nipple, which beaded beneath my braless shirt. Closing his lips over me, he sucked me through the fabric, and my head fell back against the hammock so hard that it made the whole thing bounce. His teeth tested my sensitive flesh as his fingers fucked me in a frantic rhythm. I bit the inside of my lip, trying not to cry out as I edged higher and higher toward release.

"I'm so close," I mewled, riding his fingers as I chased my climax. "I—oh god, I'm going to come."

With one final pull on my nipple, I shattered, my pussy clamping around his fingers, my teeth digging so hard into my lip that I tasted blood as wave after wave of pleasure coursed through me. With his fingers still inside me, Logan thrust frantically into my grip one more time, choking out a groan as he buried his head into my shoulder. I felt him spill over my fingers, a sticky heat coating the inside of his underwear as his own fingers pulled out of me.

My whole body trembled with the echoes of that orgasm,

our chests rising and falling in rapid unison as we came down from that high. This moment was different from all the others before it for so many reasons, not the least of which because that was an impeccable morning orgasm. Logan's and my hands lingered inside the waistbands of each other's clothes. We'd need to get up and get changed before Mari woke up and saw the evidence of what we'd done. I'd find an excuse to wash the clothes in the pond . . . but I took one more moment to just enjoy the sweet afterglow of rocking there against Logan. He lifted his head and his lips found mine again, kissing me in that sloppy, sated way.

I smiled against his mouth, already wishing we had the rest of the day to see what other naked acro-yoga we could do in this hammock together. I wanted to say a million things to him too, tell him all of the disparate emotions bubbling up inside me, that this thing between us shifted the moment he made me come . . . but instead, I just kissed him, hoping my mouth could tell him all the things too delicate to speak aloud.

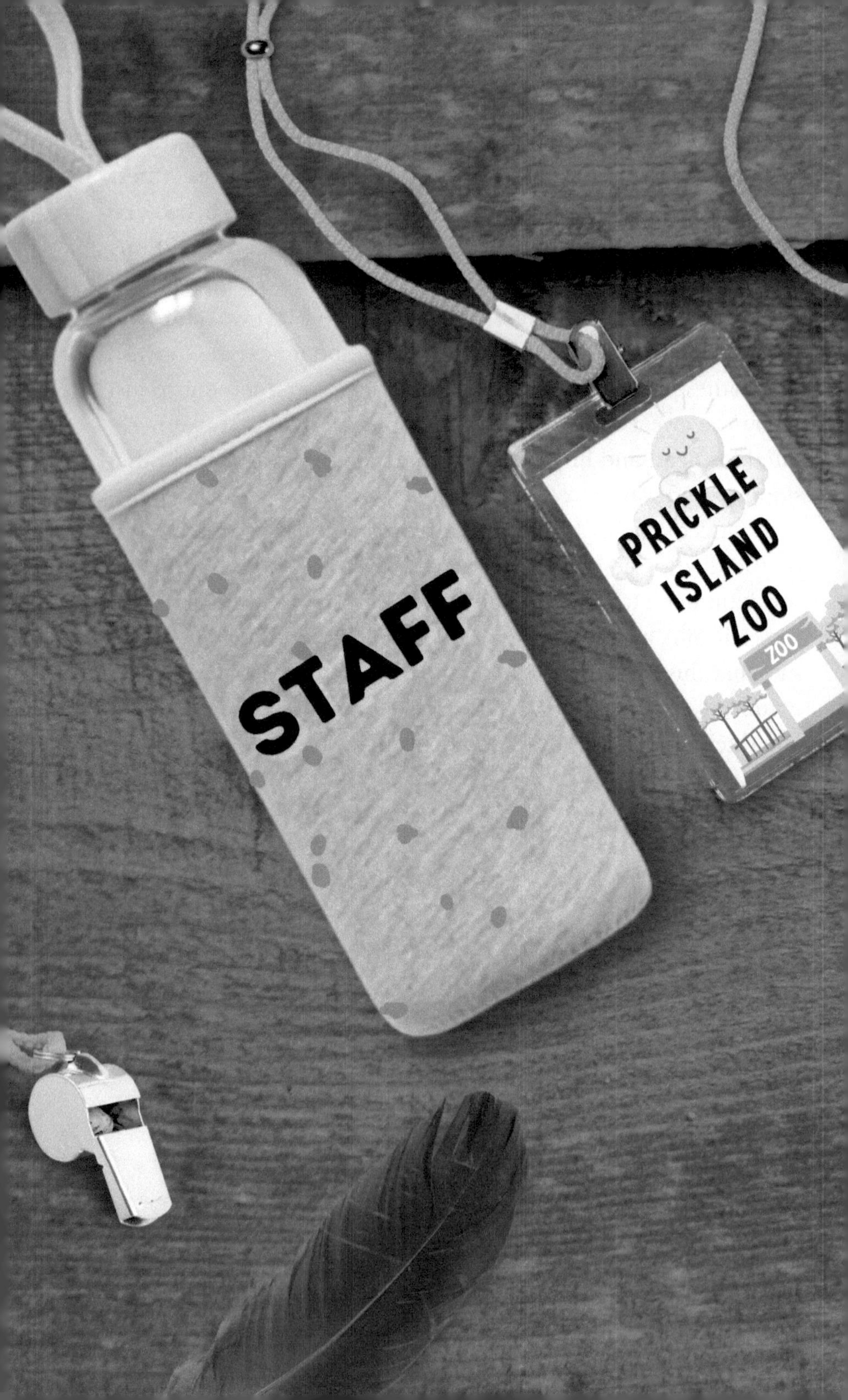
STAFF
PRICKLE
ISLAND
ZOO
ZOO

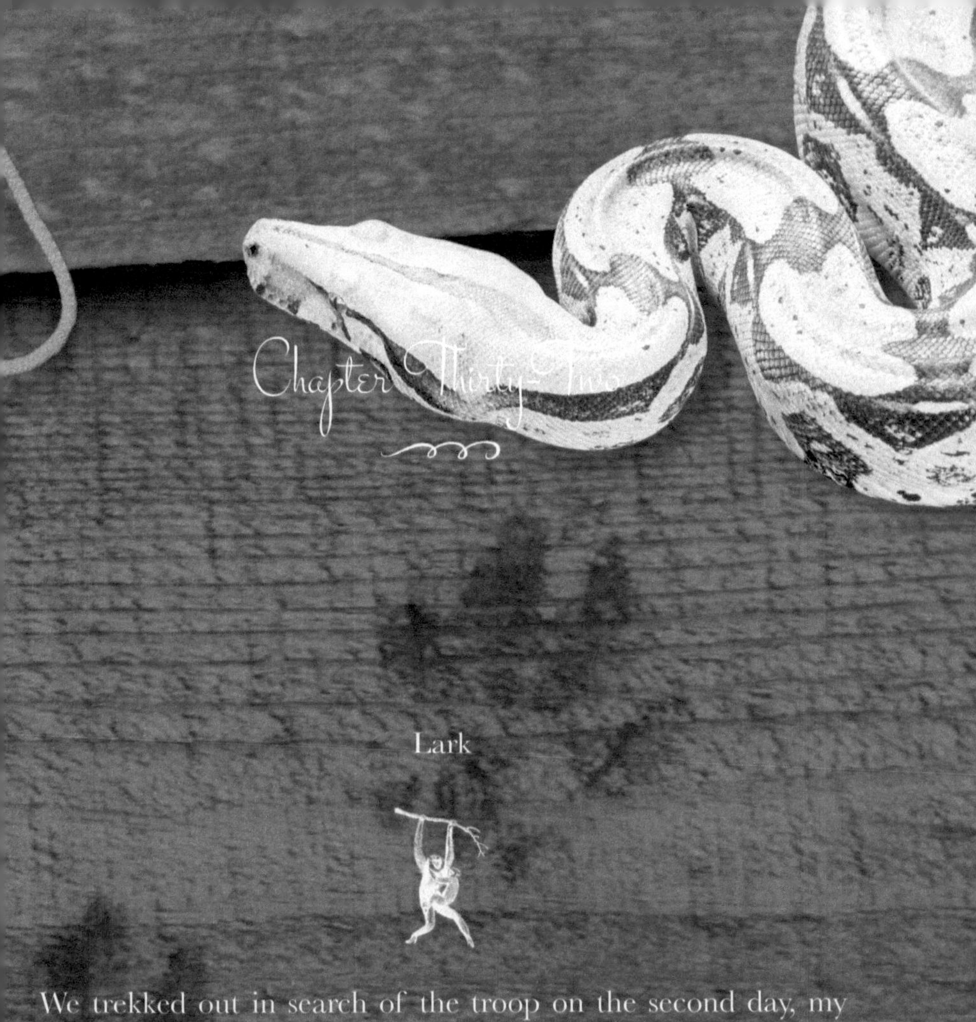

We trekked out in search of the troop on the second day, my feet still sore from the massive hike the day before. The burn on my calf was still weeping and gross, and now flies were swarming the leg of my pants. Awesome. I cleaned it with iodine again in the morning and tried to air it out, but it was determined to stay wet and nasty. The fact Logan still looked at me with those bedroom eyes made me wonder if he was severely dehydrated. I couldn't believe we managed to hook up in a hammock in the middle of the freaking jungle. This would give me the upper hand in every future game of Never Have I Ever.

When we got to the ridge, we followed the spine of the

mountain down and up to another hill across the valley. Mari made a point to tell us to shuffle through the deep leaf litter, and I started thinking about what would happen if I got bit by a venomous snake this far from a hospital.

Nope. Better to not think about it. *My burn would be the only injury,* I told myself, as if I could command it to be true from sheer stubbornness alone.

At least the vagina gods were smiling upon me. I was pretty sure getting fingered in the jungle was at the top of the itchy lady parts no-no list. I definitely made sure to go pee afterward, but still . . . I thanked all of the goddesses that the only thing my pussy was, was happy.

When we got up to the top of the hill, we were greeted by two men. They had their T-shirts flipped up like they were trying to get cool, and honestly, it made me really want to do the same. They wore thick jeans and baseball hats with roosters embroidered on them. One held two shot glasses of coffee and offered them to Mari and me.

Ooooh, coffee. I was profusely thankful, which made them laugh. Too bad there wasn't one for Logan, but I wasn't about to share. The coffee was so strong, it made the hair on my arms stand on end. It woke me up better than a slap in the face, and I wasn't nearly as tired as I had been two sips before.

They said something to Mari that I couldn't quite understand and gestured for us to take a seat under the shade of one of their avocado trees. The trees weren't planted in rows like in the orchards I was used to. They grew all around and through the forest. Mari worked tirelessly to help them maintain these ecological corridors for the native wildlife to pass through.

I sat next to Mari, expecting Logan to do the same, but the men gestured to him and he followed them off uphill. I sat there, enjoying the cool shade and mopping the sweat from my brow for a second before turning to Mari.

"Why are we here?" I asked. "Why did they leave with Logan?"

"They want us to sit on their land and bless it with our fertility." She said it so matter-of-factly, I thought for a second, she was kidding.

I tried—and failed—to hide my shock, gaping at her like she just told me I was a secret princess.

She chuckled and shrugged. "Women are powerful."

Well, at least we could agree on that.

"You don't have any rituals of luck or superstitions?" she continued, laughing at my stupefied expression.

I thought of the first few that came to my mind: spilled salt, broken mirrors, sidewalk cracks, dandelions, shooting stars, find a penny . . . Yeah, I grew up with a fair few superstitions and things I did for good luck too.

"Look!" Mari pointed across the valley, practically bouncing up with excitement as two scarlet macaws flew across the canopy.

I sucked in a breath. The sight filled me with complete awe. They were gorgeous flying against the green of the trees. We sat there watching them for a long time while I wondered how one actually went about blessing land. It would be just my luck for lightning to strike this tree tomorrow or for it to become riddled with pests after we left. I had this weird sense that I wanted to be good at bringing the tree luck. This was my literal *Fern Gully* moment, for crying out loud.

I decided to instead just sit and stew in contemplation. If Logan were here, I knew he'd laugh at me for trying to get "being good luck" right, as if there were a manual for being lucky.

Mari seemed content to watch the trees, writing something in her little pocket notebook about the flora and fauna. She was a lot more comfortable with silence than I was, but the heat was helping me get there. I loved how everyone here gathered around in the shade during the hottest parts of the day and just hung out. Napped in hammocks, played music, worked on art projects and embroidery. I didn't know how to do it—take a break. Everything felt jittery and wrong just sitting around and talking about nothing in particular for a few hours each day. It felt almost wasteful. But here, you were weird if you didn't do it. And the heat pretty much demanded it anyway, so I just stared out at the trees with her and thought.

Fertility. Luck. Who knew if I had either of those? I hadn't really ever thought about the words before that moment.

Staring out over the jungle, the midmorning heat making sweat bead on my forehead, the roots of the avocado tree undulating under my legs, I started thinking about it. I'd floated the idea of kids around before, even thought maybe past girlfriends might be the ones to start a family with, but the relationships always ended before we ever even discussed it.

I liked the idea of being pregnant and had watched enough animals giving birth over the years that I knew it wasn't nearly as screamy or dramatic or devoid of poo as the movies made it out to be. Birth was gooey and bloody and shitty and still kind of magical in its own amazing way, and watching all the animal moms around me and the ferocity of their love for their babies made me want that for myself one day too.

As I sat watching the scarlet macaws and Amazon parrots fly against the blue sky, I started imagining what it would be like to have kids. It couldn't be all that different than raising baby monkeys, could it? I had already spent most of my early twenties waking up every two hours through the night and heating up bottles and cleaning poop from my clothes and hair . . . or just leaving it because I was too tired. I'd probably raise a pair of wildlings just like how my mom raised me: carried in a sling on her hip or her back. I imagined my belly swollen, looking proudly at the faces of curly-haired, brunette children with funny little accents who pronounced the word "pen" like "pin" . . .

Whoa, boy. I was getting too much of the avocado tree magic.

That was a seed I couldn't plant in my brain. Was this the first sign of heat stroke? Logan was a vacation hookup, not the person I should imagine having babies with. I'd only known him for a few weeks. I was not making babies with him, no matter how good he looked taking care of baby monkeys.

"Okay," Mari said. "Let's keep going."

I didn't know if she'd checked her watch or had an internal "blessings" timer, but we stood up, dusted off our pants, and kept going. I looked back at the avocado tree and waved my hand up and down a couple times, waggling my fingers for good measure, all the while thinking to myself: *You better fucking grow and prosper. Don't make me look bad, tree.*

STAFF
PRICKLE
ISLAND
ZOO
ZOO

Lark

"There!" Mari grabbed me by the shoulders. My binoculars strap whipped my cheek as she twirled me in the direction of the troop. First, I only saw rustling trees. My focus went soft, searching for movement amongst the green, then finally, I spotted them.

"Yes!" I said with a gasp. "Look!" I passed the binoculars to Logan and squinted up into the canopy.

Now that I knew where I was looking, I could spot them easily, though backlit by the sun, it was difficult to tell their specific features. They were so high up in the trees that I didn't know how Mari could identify each of them.

"That one is a new male!" she exclaimed, pointing to one

of the larger monkeys in the middle of the treetop procession. "I wonder if . . . Ah!" She grabbed my shoulders again and jumped up and down. "There's a baby!"

"Baby!" I leapt up and down too, her excitement contagious. I squinted up into the trees but couldn't find the mother.

"She's toward the front of the troop," Mari said, excitedly jotting notes down in the margins of her logbook. "Use the binoculars."

I didn't wait for Logan to remove the binoculars strap from around his neck as I yanked them from his grip.

"Wh—" He let out a grunt as his head was unceremoniously pulled down toward me.

I peered through the binoculars, scanning for the troop, when my eyes finally landed on the little black bump on one monkey's back.

"Oh my god!" I whisper-cheered.

How amazing to see a relocated troop in the wild. How even more amazing that they'd successfully reproduced in the wild and incorporated a wild-born male into their troop. If I were Mari, I'd be crying right now. Okay, maybe I was getting a little misty-eyed. How many years of tireless work went into this troop's reintroduction? How many people had worked day and night to make this life for them?

This whole troop had started from five rescued baby monkeys, the victims of the wildlife trade. They were reared at a local wildlife rescue outside of Flores, rehabilitated and taught to forage, and relocated to the national park.

Mari pulled out her camera and affixed the telescopic lens to the end, snapping photo after photo of the troop. "Aw, look at this one!"

It was only then that I realized I was still holding the binoculars with Logan half crouched next to me so he didn't get guillotined by the strap. I peeked over to the side where his shoulder pressed to mine, his lips curved up as he looked at me. Our faces were so close that it would take nothing to lean over and kiss him, and I wondered if he was remembering what had happened that morning. His cheeks dimpled and his eyes filled with a mischief that told me he was thinking the same exact thing.

"No, this one's better! Look!" Mari's voice snapped our eye contact.

I swallowed, passing the binoculars back to Logan and dropping into a crouch next to Mari, where she pored over her photos. As I dropped, my hand reached out and trailed down Logan's calf. It was such a quick touch, there and gone, but I hoped it told him that I noticed that look in his eyes. God, I loved all these secret touches. The way his fingers kept accidentally bumping into mine, the way he sat close enough to brush against me, the way I'd press my knee into his.

I forced myself to stop thinking about how much I wanted to touch him again. The sounds he made in the hammock, the way he made me feel . . . it made my whole body turn to jelly just thinking about it. But as Mari shoved her camera in my face, I forced myself to quell my growing desire.

"That is an amazing photo," I said, admiring Mari's skill. "The details are so crisp. Look at that little hand and face. Ugh! So cute!"

She pointed her camera back up to the troop, who were nearly above us now, so high up in the canopy that we still needed to squint to see them properly.

"Scat!" Mari said with too much excitement as one of the monkeys dropped an aerial poo into the forest in front of us. Mari dug in her pack and produced two containers, wiggling them back and forth. "Who's turn is it to find the samples?"

"I'll do it," Logan said.

Mari passed him only one container and then handed me

the other. "You should both go," she said. "Whoever thought finding a needle in a haystack was hard has never tried to find monkey poop in ankle-deep leaf litter."

"It fell right over there," I said, pointing a few yards in front of us.

Mari snickered. "Then you should have no trouble finding it." She winked at me. "Let's make a bet. Whoever finds it first doesn't have to wash up the camp dishes for the week."

"Ooh!" I bolted into the forest, leaving Logan in my wake.

Mari let out a loud laugh as Logan exclaimed, "Hey!" and chased after me.

In a few long strides, I arrived at where the poo should be but found nothing but a thick layer of untouched leaves and dense foliage. Logan similarly pulled up short as he scanned around us.

"Shit."

"Literally."

We then proceeded to search high and low for the next *forty minutes*, while the troop wandered off from overhead and Mari sat there organizing her notes in her logbook and munching on a granola bar.

I paused from my scouring, wiping my brow. Our search had circled out farther and farther and still nothing. My chest rose and fell in heavy breaths. Who knew searching for poo could be so exhausting? But Mari had insisted we must find it and I understood. Poop could tell us all sorts of things about the health of the troop. It would be an invaluable part of this trip.

I took another breath, enjoying the feeling of not curling my neck to the ground for a beat. I glanced at Logan, who still had his chin tucked, searching the forest floor like a bloodhound that had lost a scent. My gaze lingered on him and he must have sensed it because he paused and looked up at me through the scrub brush and spindly trees that hadn't reached the light of the canopy. Our gazes hooked again for a second before our eyes widened simultaneously, our focuses shifting to the bromeliad blossoming on a branch between us. There, in a perfect swirl, just above our head height, was the monkey poo.

Logan and I looked at each other as I lurched forward. "Found it!" I exclaimed.

Mari cheered through a mouthful of granola bar.

I looked at Logan, surprised he didn't rush to claim the fecal prize.

He just folded his arms and smiled at me knowingly, saying, "Guess I'm doing the dishes this week. Good spotting, tails."

STAFF
PRICKLE
ISLAND
ZOO
ZOO

Chapter Thirty-Four

Lark

When I woke up in the middle of the night, my stomach was bubbling more than a scuba diver's regulator. And I was one hundred percent certain that I had just bridged into the territory of not being able to trust a fart.

Oh lord, I needed to get to the poop tree stat.

At first, I thought the rumbling was a sure sign I was going to vomit, but every time I fell back asleep and woke up again, that burbling had traveled farther south. Why had I let Logan do the chivalrous thing and take the now-fixed outside hammock, putting me square in the middle?

I rolled out of my hammock like a drunk gopher and

landed on top of my pack, feeling for my headlamp, which was tucked into one of my boots.

Please, dear God, don't let there be a spider or snake or something in my boot right now when I'm about to have a Niagara Falls incident in my pants.

I found my headlamp and turned it on in my hand, holding my fingers over it so only slivers of light peeked out from my glowing pink skin. The last thing I needed was for Logan or Mari to wake up and listen to what was about to happen.

I hastily shook out my boots. No spiders, thank God. I slipped them on, tied up the laces, pulled on my fleece because it was actually a little chilly tonight, and trekked off to the barbed-wire fence.

Reflective eyes beamed back at me as I walked through the scrub brush. Snakes, iguanas, even a couple of agoutis. It was awesome. If we saw a kinkajou, I'd officially freak out. If we saw an ocelot, I'd never shut up about it.

The horses' ears turned toward me as they continued to stand in their pastures, but they seemed otherwise unbothered. I carefully ducked between the barbed wires of the fence and jumped over the rivers of ants to the poop tree.

I'm a wildlife biologist. I'm not in the least bit grossed out by poop.

I spend a good chunk of my day triaging the state of excrement in order to decide if an animal is healthy or not. My family literally plays games about feces at the dinner table. It's not uncommon for pictures to even come out! So while I felt mildly grumpy about my current predicament, I was not concerned when my bowel movement was sloppy, but nothing dire.

I honestly felt relieved as I finished and farewelled the ant army, thanking them for carrying away the evidence of my secret midnight crap.

I climbed back through the fence, removed my boots, unzipped my fleece, yanked off my headlamp, flung myself back into my hammock, and drifted back to sleep . . . for ten blissful minutes before I awoke again—and this time, it was way more urgent.

I practically fell out of my hammock, didn't bother with the fleece or lacing my boots, while still trying to not wake Logan as I raced back to the fence. I muttered under my breath as I danced over the ants and avoided the remnants of my last visit.

This next round was like the aftermath of a spicy curry night from hell. All from that little shot glass of coffee, for fuck's sake! I should've known better than to drink it, but because it wasn't water, I'd forgotten.

The donkey in the nearest paddock had the audacity to turn and look at me while I was doing my shameful business, but at least it was over quickly, and I waddled sheepishly back to my hammock, falling asleep holding my headlamp in my hands this time, just in case . . .

"Just in case" came fifteen minutes later, and this one was a doozy of a sprint. I bolted, practically flinging myself over the barbed-wire fence and across the lava pit of ants to the tree, where I squatted for a good five solid minutes doing what could only be described in two freaking words: Jackson Pollock.

Kill me now.

About three minutes of shame-shitting later, I looked up to find that fucking donkey had wandered over to the fence and had its head hanging over the side, *staring* at me. The bastard didn't even blink, just watched me with what I swore was a look of disgust.

I flipped him the bird. This was one of the most embarrassing moments of my entire life and I had a judgy fucking donkey bearing witness to it all.

I lingered there for a long time, even after I was confident I was done because I didn't want to have to make the walk of shame over here again in another ten minutes. The literal jackass watched me the whole time, not blinking, just staring.

I don't know if you've ever had the pleasure of shitting your brains out while an animal gave you the most shaming look of your entire life, but it's a real treat. Ten out of ten would not recommend.

I didn't care how much Heron wanted donkeys for the petting zoo. They had officially become my least favorite animal.

"Fuck you, donkey," I muttered to him when I finally had the confidence to skulk back to my hammock for the third time.

It was only then I remembered the pills my mom had given me: some to make you go and some to make you stop going. I needed the stop ones ASAP. I tried to dig through my pack without making any sound, relief coursing through me when I grabbed the bag of travel meds without anyone waking. I popped the pills quickly and sighed with relief . . . but medicine didn't work that fast and it was time to run back to the tree . . . again.

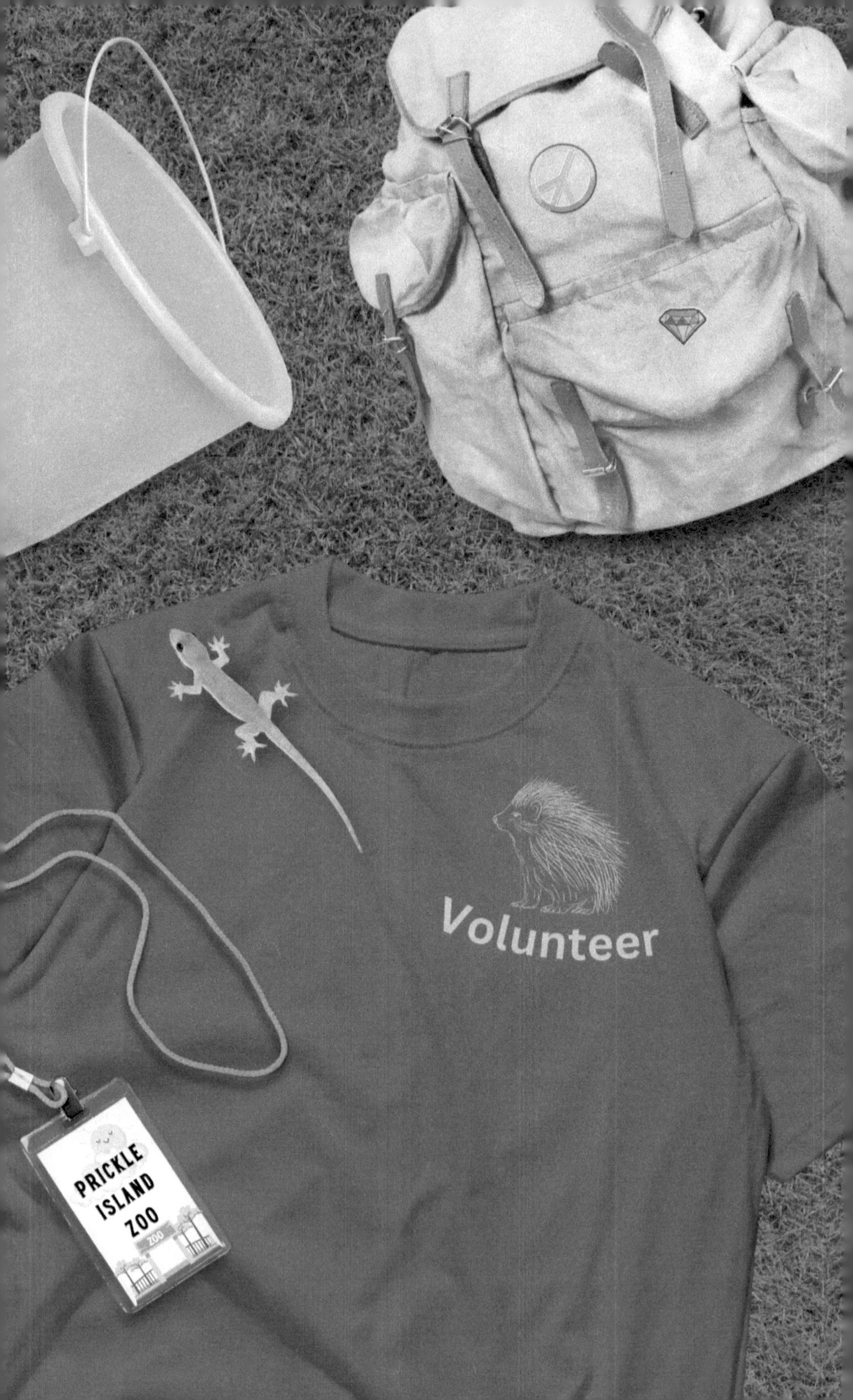

Volunteer
PRICKLE
ISLAND
ZOO
ZOO

Chapter Thirty-Five

Logan

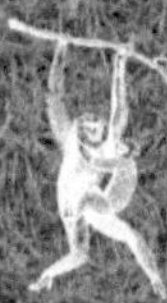

"You okay?" I asked, wandering up to Lark as she repacked her night clothes into her bag. A toothbrush hung from her mouth and she clutched her bottle of boiled water to her chest, staring vacantly like she'd just seen a ghost. "Is it your leg? You look a bit crook."

She completely ignored me until I waved my hand in front of her face, breaking off the staring contest she was having with the donkey in the pasture beyond.

"Wh-what?" She turned toward me and blinked. "Sorry." She held a hand to her stomach. "Rough night."

"Ah." I nodded, knowing she clearly didn't want to elaborate any further.

Mari walked up the hillside wearing her uniform, her hair wet from bathing in the pond, a towel slung over her shoulders. She looked fresh as a daisy, unlike Lark and me. I'd slept okay, but a mosquito had decided to hover around my ear for half the night, and the other half I kept getting woken up by these dreams of Lark muttering curses.

"You ready to do some tracking today?" Mari called over to us.

Lark rinsed her mouth and turned away from me to spit her toothpaste-y water into a bush. I couldn't help but chuckle. She was fine cleaning drains bare-handed but drew the line at letting me watch her spit out toothpaste? Probably because it was a more human than monkey thing to do.

"Ready!" Lark called back to Mari, swinging her arms back and forth like a boxer in a ring. As if she could will her upset stomach away through stubbornness alone. If anyone could, it was Lark Lachlan.

She squatted down and checked the laces of her boots again, her shirt riding up a little and giving me a straight sight down to the top of her underwear, which was gray with rhinos on it. My eyes stayed hooked on the sight for another breath before Mari cleared her throat and my gaze snapped up to meet hers.

"You ready, Logan?"

I patted my shorts pockets as if checking for my keys and wallet, my feet already hurting before I took a single step. "My toes are definitely going to fall off by the end of this trip."

"You'll be glad when you don't step on a scorpion," Mari taunted. She hoisted her day backpack, complete with something that looked like a TV antenna and a radio tracker that was eerily similar to an old-school gaming controller. "We've got a long way to go today. Make sure you're bringing two bottles of water. You won't be able to drink from the water catchments up at the lookout like I can, unless you want to be shitting your brains out all night long."

Lark's cheeks turned redder than a scarlet macaw at that, and her throat bobbed. Well, that explained why she only ate a corner of a rice cracker this morning. Lark shot me one of her infamous death glares, and I knew she was promising me she'd gut me and leave me to be picked apart by fire ants if I said a word to Mari. I knew Lark couldn't handle showing any weakness to her biologist friend. She wanted everyone to think she had her shit together . . . Didn't we all?

It made the way she'd confessed her dreams of a life outside the zoo even more intimate. She'd trusted me enough to not be perfect for once. The thought made heat bloom in the center of my chest, and I wanted to lift a hand and rub that pain away. I'd never felt this way about anyone before, like I just knew them without even trying. Years of attempting to figure Kelly out and it never clicked, and yet here was this woman I'd only known for a handful of weeks and I felt like I knew her better than my oldest friends.

Lark and Mari took off up the trail, pulling me out of my hazy daydream, and I sighed. I should be thinking about not getting heatstroke or being eaten by a jaguar, not about this innate inner knowing of a person, about how time wasn't linear when it came to the two of us . . .

Fuck it all to hell, there was no two of us.

I trudged up the path after them, taking the rear and trying to push the thoughts of Lark from my mind. But you know the worst activity for distracting yourself from the thoughts in your head? Walking.

The more I walked, the more I thought about her, the more I wanted her.

I didn't care if she was covered in monkey shit or being a stubborn perfectionist or trying so hard to live the life her family wanted her to live that she forgot to live her own. Whatever she was, I wanted to be a part of it.

I walked faster through the stretches of sunlight and slower through the patches of shade, creating a syncopated tempo to my gait as my thoughts of Lark consumed me. The buzz of insects and twitter of birds and rustling of trees in the wind created a constant din of noise that accompanied my steady boot steps. Sweat beaded across my brow, and I had to lift my shirt every few minutes to wipe my face again. I was about ready to take my shirt off entirely. The sun wasn't nearly as strong or burning here as it was in New Zealand, despite it being twice as hot and humid. But if I took my shirt off, Lark would probably give me that look she did when she thought I wasn't looking—the one where I was the most delicious dessert she'd ever seen and she was desperate to taste it—and then I'd have no choice but to grab her and fuck her against the nearest tree.

My dick enjoyed that thought a little too much, and I had to force myself to stare down at my boots instead of Lark's perfect bouncing ass in front of me before I was fully tenting my shorts. I needed to think of something else: Arctic, penguins, toasters, snorkels, fuck . . . But then one thought doused me in cold ice better than any other: all the fun of daydreaming about Lark ended in a short, sudden stop when I remembered there was no future between us.

I had to go back to New Zealand. My family would never ask me to, never even wanted to really clue me in as to what the fuck was going on with my dad . . . They were the opposite of Lark's family in that regard. The classic Kiwi stiff upper lip and the "she'll be right" attitude until the very end. But whether they told me or not, I knew something was wrong and I'd spent this entire trip waiting for the other shoe to drop. I knew the call would come at some point, the one I'd been dreading ever since I saw my dad's gray coloring and my mom assured me that everything was fine in that voice that told me everything was not fucking fine.

When the lookout appeared through the forest, the tension in my shoulders eased. No more walking. Time to get to work. At least now I could stop thinking about the gorgeous keeper who was slowly securing a place in my heart and all the reasons we could never make it work out.

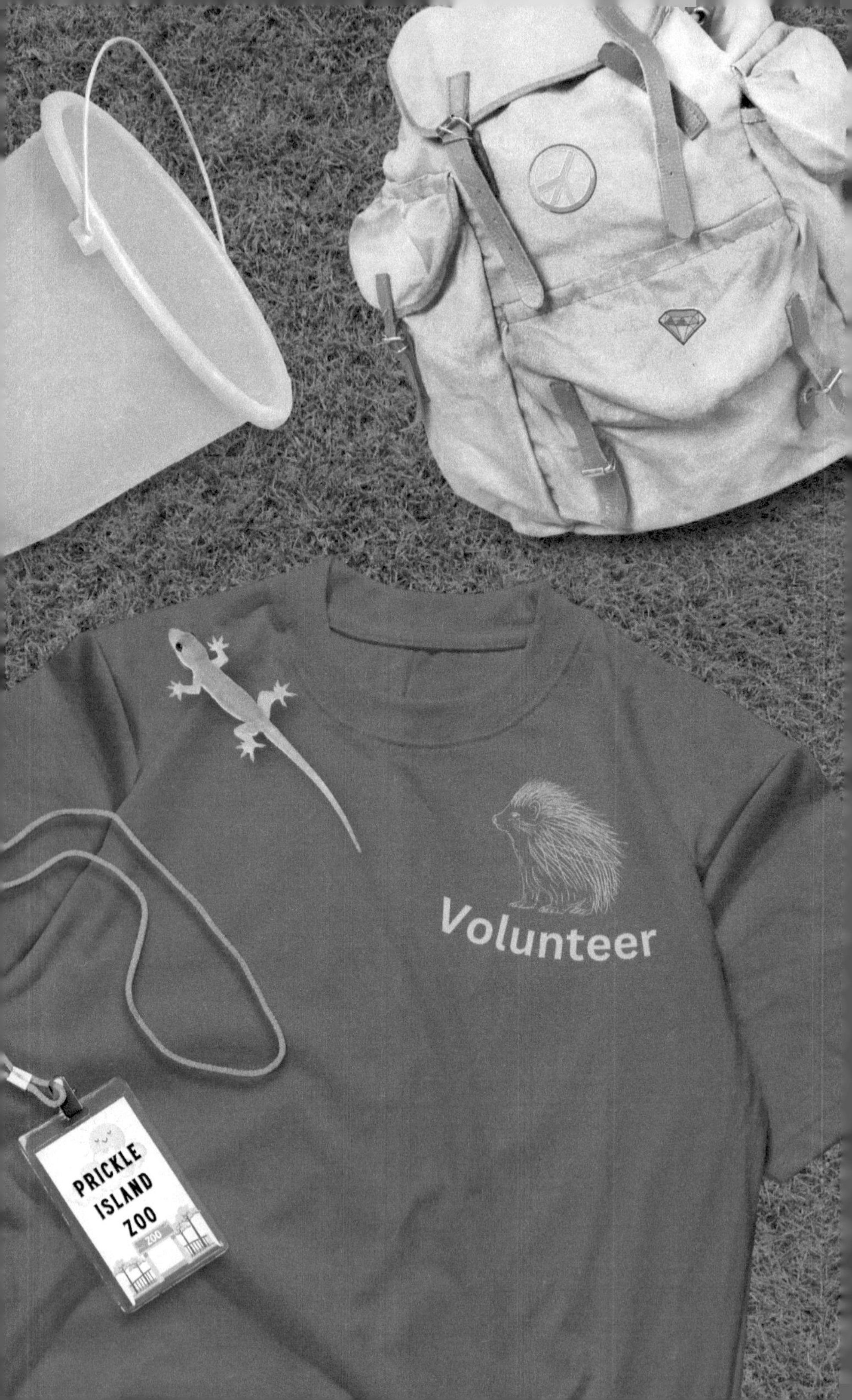
Volunteer
PRICKLE
ISLAND
ZOO
ZOO

Chapter Thirty-Six

Logan

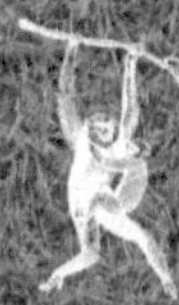

I spent the rest of the day trying *very* hard not to think about how much I wanted to pull Lark back to the nearest hammock and rove my hands all over her again. She spent the rest of the day doing that thing she does where she acts like she's tough and nothing's wrong, but if you look close enough, you can see she's limping, a little pale, and clearly tired from being up all night.

I kept refilling her water bottle and passing it to her in my not-so-subtle way of trying to rehydrate her. Getting severe dehydration out here would be a disaster. I'd probably have to throw her over my shoulder and run her all the way back down the mountain.

Still, I managed to sneak a few moments with her when no one else was looking: a brief kiss to her shoulder, a squeezed knee, a lingering hand . . . I just couldn't stop touching her. Each of the tiniest looks or brushes past me made me feel like a fourteen-year-old trying to constantly hide my hard-ons.

By the time three days had passed in the forest, Lark had consumed my every thought. By the time five days had passed, every single one of my senses was so tuned in to her, I felt like I had Lark-shaped blinders on.

When Mari had left to go check the trip cams and Lark had suggested a swim in the pond . . . I already knew I was done for.

We wandered down the sandy path that cut through the hills and switchbacked down to the pond at the bottom of the reserve. It was a beautiful turquoise swimming hole with reeds ringing the edges and dragonflies dancing over the white and red water flowers. I'd spent a lot of solo time submerged in this pond after the last few long days, the only way to seem to fully relax my muscles after hours of hiking. But when Lark stripped her top off and chucked it on the nearest rock, not a single muscle in my body was relaxed.

I swallowed the lump in my throat as she yanked her sports bra over her head and freed her breasts, only the slightest flash of them peeking from the side with her back turned to me. Before she could even start on her belt, I quickly stripped and dove into the pond to hide my erection.

I kept swimming over to the other side of the pond, waiting for the telltale sound of her splashing into the water before turning back around.

She dipped under the water and popped back up, smoothing her hair off her face. We watched each other for a moment, just treading water and taking each other in.

"What's her name?" Lark asked. Of all the things I'd expected her to say then, that wasn't it.

"Who?"

"The lock-screen girl."

"Ah. Kelly." I let out a long sigh through my nose, my hands slowly swishing back and forth through the water. "We were together since our senior year in uni. I found out she was cheating on me, and when we split up, I felt . . ."

"Heartbroken?"

"Relieved," I said, my shoulders drooping. "I felt relieved. She didn't want to be a small-town guy's wife. She wanted to live in the city and be an artist and go out to parties and shows every night."

"That sounds awful," Lark said with a snort.

I smiled, my heart cracking open a little more. "My parents hated her because she kind of turned up her nose at the family business, and I guess the only reason I stayed with her was because that's what everyone around me does—stays with the first long-term relationship."

She hummed. "That sounds sweet though."

"Does it?" I chuckled. "In a world full of people, I always wondered, what if?"

"What if what?"

"What if my person didn't live in my same university dorm, or my city, or my country, or even my hemisphere?"

"Is that why you're traveling around? To meet your person?" she asked hesitantly.

"No," I said with a laugh. "Just a thought. I went traveling because my dad's looking to retire in the next couple of years and I know he's going to need me back to help run everything. My younger brother, Matt, has already taken over most of the business but . . . you know, they'll need me, especially around the busy times of year."

"Of course," she said with a nod.

Of course. She said it so matter-of-factly. She probably really did understand. Lark had lived her whole life around animals, was more used to work boots than stilettos, was used to waking up at five a.m. even when she had a wicked hangover. She understood my life in a way that most never would. And I knew in that moment what this feeling was between us—far more than just a simple mutual understanding—even if I was too scared to say it even in my own mind.

I glanced up the hill one last time, hoping I wouldn't find anyone watching us from the hut, as I drifted closer to Lark. Mari was checking the cameras we set up on the lookout and would be gone for at least another half an hour, which meant . . . I drifted closer, my feet finally reaching the silty bottom of the pond.

Lark stayed where she was, her lips curling into a mischievous grin as my hands reached her sides underwater and pulled her to me. Her thighs wrapped around my hips, my cock growing harder as it pressed against her stomach. I ached to be inside her. She twisted in my hold, shifting herself against my erection, and my eyes hooded as my head dropped to her neck.

"I want you so badly," I murmured, rocking against her. "But I'm not sure if this pond is the best place for . . ."

She let out a little moan in response as she ground against me, and my mouth sucked and nibbled my way up to her earlobe.

"You're right." She groaned.

"This whole trip has been torture," I growled against her ear, my cock painfully hard as her peaked nipples rubbed against my chest.

"Torture," she hummed in agreement.

"When we get back to that hotel . . ." My teeth tested the

flesh of her earlobe. "I'm going to fuck you until you forget your name."

Her little moaning breaths were going to break me.

"Well, until then," she said, her hand sliding between us. She gripped my cock, and I let out a rumble of pleasure as she worked me up and down.

"Yes," I hissed through gritted teeth, all of that pent-up desire, those torturous days of wanting her . . . Finally—*finally*—we had this moment to ourselves.

She clung to my shoulder, my hands kneading her soft ass as she stroked me. The water around us sloshed as she moved over me faster.

"Lark," I groaned as she tightened her grip on me. I couldn't handle it. I'd wanted this so badly for so long—too long—and now she was finally touching me again and . . . "I'm—" The words died on a groan as she pumped me faster, urged on by the wanton sounds I was making against her lips.

She broke our kiss and lifted her mouth to my ear, murmuring, "Say my name when you come," and that made me shatter into a million pieces. I barked out her name as I fell apart, my mind homed in only to the look on her face and the feeling of her hand wrapped around my cock as I spilled my release.

My chest rose and fell in heavy, gasping breaths as I tried to regain control.

This was what she did to me. She was a fucking goddess. She was *everything*. And with that lust-filled look in her eyes, her teeth biting that full bottom lip, I knew I couldn't leave her wanting either.

My hands tightened their grip on her perfect ass. "Hang on," I said as I started walking to the shoreline.

She yelped as we emerged above the waterline, her naked

body slick against mine as I walked to the silty shore and dropped to my knees.

"What are you—?"

"I need to taste you." I laid her down on her towel, grabbing my own to wipe her down before dropping my mouth to her breast. She moaned again as I sucked her tight nipple, her breath gasping and desperate as I trailed kisses lower, across the plane of her stomach and down between her legs. "I need to hear you come."

"Logan," she panted as my mouth hovered between her legs.

God, the way she said my name, I was already getting hard again.

She writhed beneath me, clearly desperate for my mouth. Still, the first lick of her glistening, wet pussy made her gasp in the most satisfying sound I'd ever heard. I licked her again and her back bowed, her fingers threading into my slicked-back hair as she rode my mouth. I hummed my satisfaction against her clit and she moaned louder, seemingly uncaring if the entire jungle heard us now, so lost in her pleasure.

I worked her in long strokes, sucking and circling her clit until she was dripping for me. Then I added two fingers, pumping into her in the way I ached for my cock to fill her. *Soon,* I silently promised her and myself. Soon, I'd be inside her, claiming her, filling her in a way I'd been dying to since she first kissed me against that sea wall.

I curled my fingers inside her. Her shaking thighs clamped around my head in response as my tongue moved faster. I picked up my pace, knowing by the way her breaths were ratcheting up that she was so close, and I needed this, needed her to come on my tongue, needed to taste her release, needed to know that she was mine in every way.

I hummed again and her pussy clamped down around my

fingers, her breath catching and a hand flying to her mouth to stifle her scream. Her back arched and her fingernails dug into my scalp, holding me to her as she rode my tongue, coating my face with her release. The taste of her made me feral, wilder than any animal around us, the pulse of her muscles around my fingers the sweetest victory as her orgasm broke her apart.

My fingers and tongue stroked her until she collapsed back against her towel, her body still shaking in the echoes of her climax. I trailed kisses up her body, already ready to go again, wondering if I could do a naked dash up to my pack and grab the box of condoms burning a hole in the bottom of it. But that time would come soon. Soon was too fucking far.

I trailed my kisses up her glorious breasts and gave her one last, slow kiss to her lips. Holding her gaze, I gave her a look that promised this was only the beginning of her and me.

STAFF
PRICKLE
ISLAND
ZOO
ZOO

Chapter Thirty-Seven

Lark

When my jelly legs finally subsided along with the afterglow of that mind-blowing orgasm, I got up and noticed a trail of reddish brown something heading down my leg. I panicked for a split second that my stomach bug had somehow returned with a vengeance before my lower back muscles clenched as if to say, "It's me again, your monthly nemesis."

Of course, Logan stared directly at my legs before realizing what the fuck he was looking at and then quickly averted his gaze again. Shit, he'd just been down there. Did he know? I wanted to die right then and there. I started adding pecan waffles to the Cozy Moose Lodge menu in my mind. Where was a jaguar when I needed one?

"Sorry," I muttered. "I forgot it was this week."

Sorry? Sorry! What was I saying? Why was I apologizing? I didn't know how to freaking do this. This was just another perfect reason why I shouldn't be hooking up with men. Periods were a totally normal part of my relationships with women, but men . . . Some men got really weird about menstruation. They were like spooked freaking horses about it. It was bizarre.

My brain started jogging off down its own rabbit hole of the menses of different primates when Logan simply replied, "No worries. Do you need anything?"

Thank freaking God for this chill Kiwi guy. "Yeah," I said. "Can you just pop down to the shops and grab me a box of tampons and a bar of chocolate?"

It took him a second to realize I was kidding. "Did you bring tampons?"

"It's me. Of course I did," I said with an eye roll.

I'd planned for my period during this trip—planned like I was flying to the moon and not another country. I'd brought enough tampons to stock the bathrooms at a Reneé Rapp concert. Still, the middle of the jungles of northern Guatemala was not the ideal place to be hanging with Aunt Flo. Normally, this would be a great time to binge-watch Netflix and eat my body weight in chocolate-covered pretzels.

Logan stepped back into his boxer briefs and shimmied them up under the towel wrapped around his waist.

"Here." He unwrapped his towel and my mouth fell open as he stooped in his glorious, mostly naked form and *wiped* my leg. "Do you want me to go grab them from your bag?"

I bobbed my mouth open and shut again, flabbergasted. This was *not* the type of thing I was expecting when I started hooking up with a guy. Jumping jaguarundis, I thought I loved him from this alone.

That thought instantly panicked me.

This was not the moment to fall in love!

I needed to pick another one.

Shit shit shit.

It was probably just my hormones. My cramping ovaries were doing a happy dance right now, watching this muscled, gorgeous man standing in his underwear in front of me, offering to fetch me tampons. I might cry.

I absolutely could not freaking cry. Do. Not. Cry. Right now!

Stupid fucking hormones!

"It's okay. I got it," I finally said, still feeling weirdly sheepish around Logan, but for an entirely different reason now.

Logan just nodded and waited while I got dressed. He threaded his fingers through mine as we walked back up the hillside toward the hut, and my fingers squeezed his a little tighter—a silent acknowledgment of what we'd just done. He lifted my hand and kissed the back of it, and I had to shout at my period hormones *again* not to cry at the tenderness. Why did he have to be so freaking sweet right now? I trudged up the hill, equally swooning and angrier with every step, and I didn't care if it was hormones or not.

How dare he make me feel so many feelings right now!

STAFF
PRICKLE
ISLAND
ZOO
ZOO

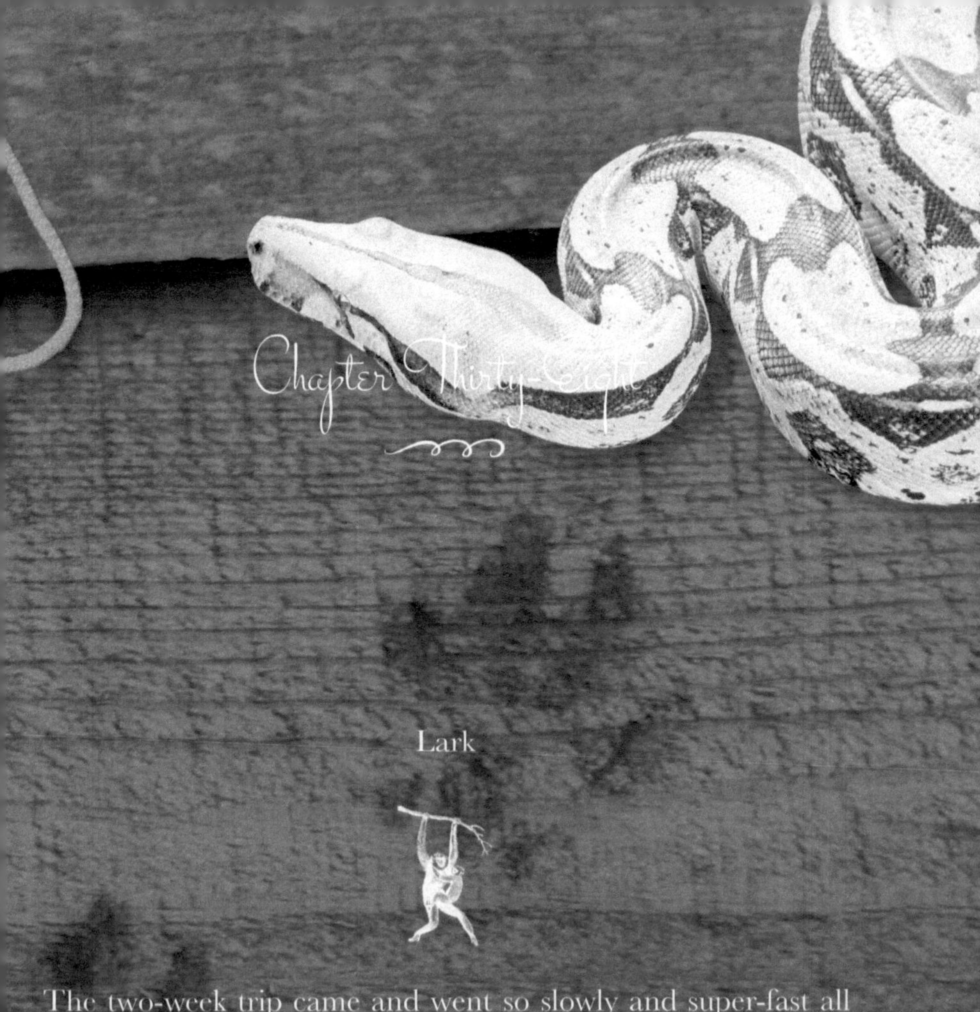

The two-week trip came and went so slowly and super-fast all at once. I was going to be sad to leave this beautiful, once-in-a-lifetime place, but I was also really, really ready for a shower, fresh clothes, and to throw away the trash bag of used period products at the bottom of my pack.

I wasn't easily grossed out, but having to keep all of my tampons in a Ziplock in my trash bag was a new kind of torture I wasn't prepared for. There were a lot of things the ants at the poop tree could tear apart and carry away, but period products weren't one of them. Why hadn't I looked more into a menstrual cup? Although, where exactly was I supposed to wash the thing? In the pond? That seemed like a yeast infection waiting to happen. Period underwear also didn't seem like my best bet considering there were a bunch of random carnivorous animals wandering around at night and swarms of flies . . . Luckily, I brought enough tampons for three heavy periods, even though we were only in the country for two weeks.

I had to wash my hands in the rainwater tap with soap after every not-so-subtle trip to the poop tree to change out tampons and tuck the old ones in my trash bag. I thought I was pretty outdoorsy, but after this trip, I had a new respect for people who menstruated and hiked for months at a time.

Logan had already gotten the shark week memo down by the pond and that had put a serious damper on my plans to sneak off and screw him at every available opportunity. Could you imagine attempting period sex out here? It would be like something out of *The Shining*. I'd briefly considered pond sex before thinking of all the fish and reptiles that frequented the pond and reconsidered. There was nowhere to shower. I had brainstormed a few creative logistical ways to do it involving buckets of soapy water, but finally, I just threw in the towel and decided this week was off-limits.

I was—as Logan would say—gutted. The first week's stomach upset had already slowed us to a screeching halt, and now the red tide . . . Fuck my life. We'd agreed we'd only hook up in Guatemala, and it felt like destiny was kicking us right in the balls for it.

I'd seen just about every kind of Guatemalan wildlife out here . . . well, besides jaguars, but I was kind of grateful for that. Logan had become just as excited as Mari and I with his animal identifications, and he'd nearly used up all the film on his disposable camera that he'd bought for the trip. At night around the campfire, he'd listen with rapt attention as Mari and I spouted off animal fun facts, which was honestly one of the sexiest things he could do—and did nothing to quell my constant horniness. I didn't know if he was actually interested or if he just enjoyed the way we both lit up when we talked about it . . . but delighting in my animal anecdotes was a better gift than flowers or chocolates any day.

At least the work kept me busy. My legs had gotten less Jell-O-y from all the hiking over the first week, and we all seemed a lot more confident in our little space. Logan and I would wander off up the trail alone without being terrified we'd forget the way back. I instinctively shook out my boots each morning without having to remember anymore. I had gotten used to brushing my teeth with a cup of water and had gotten a handle on how to quickly bathe with a bucket and a bar of soap.

I'd gotten to know Logan too—how he aggressively brushed his teeth like he was scrubbing a frying pan, the sounds he made while sleeping that oscillated from soft whistling to grunting, the way he stood Captain Morgan-style when his legs were tired and he really wanted to sit down . . . It felt like he and I had been living together for years. Nothing like camping in the forest to get to know the real underbelly of a person beneath all the pleasantries. No best feet forward out here. But instead of being put off by it, the more I got to know Logan's little quirks and idiosyncrasies, the more I liked him . . . In fact, that other period-induced L word kept jumping into my mind (and no, I wasn't talking about the word lesbian).

Mari passed me her water as we sat on the dry riverbed, waiting for the motorcycles to come take us the rest of the way. At least the hiking portion was done . . . although I knew now that the hours-long ride on the motorcycle would hurt my inner thighs more than an eighties Jazzercise workout. The burn on my leg was still gross, and I knew as soon as I got home, I'd have to see a doctor—or Finch—and pillage the medical supplies in the vet hospital.

Logan had wandered off down the riverbed to use up the last photos on his disposable camera roll. It felt like something had shifted between us as we descended the mountain. The pressure of our last days in this country was starting to grow. After the stomach bug the first week and the code red the second, we really hadn't had any time alone together—a few stolen kisses here, a few quick cuddles when no one was looking. All those tiny moments of affection were growing more and more lust within us, and I knew he was just waiting to get me back to the hotel. We had one more night together, only one, and then the vacation magic would be over and that would be it— the end of Lark and Logan, over before it even really began.

Mari seemed to wait until he was far out of earshot before she leaned over to me and said, "I bet you're dying to get back to the hotel to finally fuck him properly."

I snorted water out my nose, spraying everywhere like a geyser. "What?!"

"Oh, come on. I have eyes!" She leaned her elbows back on the smooth rock behind her.

"You knew?"

She gave me an incredulous look and then dramatically rolled her eyes. "Do you really think I needed to go checking cameras *that* often? I was trying to give you two some private time."

"Mari!" I swatted her with my hand. The sheen of sweat that had just started to ease came back anew.

"What's the problem? He's hot, you're hot. You're clearly into him, and he's *very* into you." She gestured between me and the curve of the riverbed. "What am I not seeing?"

"I . . ." I wiped my sweaty forehead on my shirtsleeve. "We have a 'no sleeping with volunteers' rule at the zoo."

"Does Finch know that?" She waggled her eyebrows at me. "I don't see why such a ridiculous rule should keep you from being with your person."

I stared at the forest like Logan might explode from the bushes and yell, "Gotcha!"

"He's not my anything," I countered, lowering my voice just in case Logan turned invisible or had planted a listening device on me. "We're messing around, but only in Guatemala. As soon as we get on the plane home, it's over."

"I thought you were intelligent." Mari slapped her forehead. "He's obviously crazy about you. Why don't you just see where this thing goes?"

"Besides the fact that it would break our very reasonable rules?"

"You and your rules." Mari frowned. "Seriously?"

I groaned and dropped my face into my hands. "So what do I do? Fall madly in love with him and then let him stomp all over my heart when he goes back to New Zealand at the end of the summer?"

"Why don't you just go with him?"

"To New Zealand?" I spluttered.

"Yeah." She said it like it was nothing at all to just pack my things and move halfway around the world at the drop of a hat. "You've always wanted to see more places than your one little island."

I kept my face buried in my hands as I shook my head. "I can't just leave. My family needs me."

Mari made a clicking sound with her tongue.

"What exactly does *shsct* mean?" I asked, trying to replicate the sound she made so easily.

"It means maybe your family can survive without you

better than you think they can." When I finally lifted my head, the look she gave me was so sharp, it could've cut diamonds. "Have you even asked them? Have you even *tried* to see what this could all be if you let it?"

My shoulders drooped. "I can't, Mari. I can't do that to them."

"You are hopeless!" She groaned, angrily snatching her water bottle from the ground and shoving it back into her pack. "You are being given the exact future you're asking for, friend."

The growl and whine of motorcycles cut through the distant forest, and Logan appeared from around the bend. He smiled at the two of us, making some sort of charades gesture of a bird. Maybe he spotted some macaws. He was beaming, his excitement unmistakable, and it made my stupid heart crack right open.

STAFF
PRICKLE
ISLAND
ZOO
ZOO

Chapter Thirty-Nine

Lark

When we arrived back at the *finca*, I dropped my pack and paced back and forth around the room like a trapped rabbit. Mari's words had wormed their way under my skin, and now I was on the verge of a nervous breakdown. None of this was supposed to happen.

Logan and I had one day and that was it, one day to have the hottest sex ever—sex we'd both been anticipating now for two whole weeks. And that was *way* too much pressure. *One day* and then all of our fun would be over and I'd have to stare at the way his shirt rode up and that cheeky lopsided smile all the while knowing exactly what he was packing under those khakis, and it would be complete, unending torture.

"What's going on?" Logan asked when he wandered inside after me. "Why are you pacing like a cartoon villain?"

I immediately stopped. "What? Shut up. I'm not."

"Okay," he said carefully, watching as I clenched my hands into fists. "Why are you angry?"

"I'm not angry!" I shouted, and he arched a brow at my hypocritical outburst.

"You're clearly mad."

"Fine." I threw my hands up. This was a fucking disaster. "I *am* mad. I'm mad at you and your stupid smile and your ridiculous body and . . . grrr!" I started pacing again, incensed even further by Logan's delight.

"I feel like I'm missing something here," he teased. "Why does that make you mad?"

"Because!"

"Because why?"

"Because I spent my whole life formulating this idea of who I would be with and it didn't look anything like you!" I shouted so loud that the doves perched on the balcony flew off. "I was supposed to be with Cate Blanchett or with the neckerchief French girl or . . . I don't know, someone with tits! And then I met you and *you*?" I waved to him up and down. "*You're* my person?"

Logan's bemused smile broadened as he took a step toward me. His cheeks dimpled as he asked, "I'm your person?"

My face burned worse than being bitten by a thousand fire ants as the fog of my panic spiral faded. Had I just said that out loud? I really needed to learn to keep my mouth shut after a full day of travel. "I-I didn't mean it like that. I just . . ."

Logan closed the distance between us and swept me up into his arms. I didn't care that he smelled like a skunk in a dumpster as I melted into his embrace. I probably smelled just as bad. It didn't matter. I loved the way I fit in his arms. I loved the way he held me. I loved the way he made me feel.

He kissed the top of my head and murmured into my hair, "I like being your person."

My arms tightened around him, squeezing his rock-solid torso. "But only in Guatemala." I said it half-heartedly, more to remind myself—a warning that this thing couldn't last between us.

Logan didn't immediately reply, just held me in his gentle, swaying embrace. Finally, when he spoke, the words came out as barely a murmur. "Only in Guatemala."

This was it. This was the moment. As the sun fell below the horizon, the pressure of this moment mounted in my mind. Time for the crazy, amazing sex that we'd been whispering about to each other for the last two weeks. My stress grew with each passing second as Logan held me tighter, seemingly contented just to hold me all night until I made a move. But what if sex with a guy was different? What if they changed all the rules from what I thought they were? Our chemistry was already amazing, and I knew he knew what he was doing, but . . . what if this fell flat? What if this moment we'd been torturing each other with, this carrot we'd been dangling for weeks, didn't live up to the hype?

I couldn't just stand there like that, slow dancing with a guy who was probably waiting for me to say it was "go time." I needed to move, needed to do *something*. I pulled out of Logan's hug, my anxiety spiral making me shoot to the other end of the room and pull out my headlamp.

"I'm going to go for a walk," I muttered, yanking my head-lamp on and practically fleeing out the door. *Great, Lark. Just great. Really smooth.*

"I'll come with," Logan offered and followed me out the door.

Awesome. He probably thought I was regretting everything. Maybe he thought I didn't want this at all . . . but those were the furthest things from my mind. *God, way to chicken out, Lark.* But I didn't know how to do anything else, so I just fled through the forest with the object of my desire tailing me.

"How are you so chill with all those moths flying at your face?" Logan asked from behind me as we walked up the trail. "Wouldn't this be more scenic during daylight hours?"

"More wildlife comes out at night," I said, scanning my headlamp across the thick forest.

"We've literally just been in the jungle for two weeks," Logan grumbled. "You'd think you had enough wildlife to last you a while."

"Calm down. Just appreciate some nature with me for a second, please." I scanned my flashlight back and forth. "This is our last chance to take it all in before we fly home." It was our last chance to do a lot of things . . .

Leaves rustled to my right. Probably an agouti, I guessed based on the sound.

"See. Check it out," I said, turning the beam of my flashlight. It sounded big, maybe a tamandua? A fox? I was excited. "Isn't nature beautif—oh fuck no!"

A dinner plate-sized tarantula started running at us through the underbrush.

This thing was straight out of *Arachnophobia*, so giant it kicked up leaves as it scuttled toward us. All of my calm, composed biologist professionalism flew right out the freaking window.

"Nope," I screeched, shoving Logan in the direction of the tarantula like a human shield and bolting up the trail with the only flashlight. Logan was now the sacrificial penguin that I'd shoved off the iceberg, and even though I knew that made me a giant asshole, I didn't stop running.

He'd be fine . . . ish.

"Lark!" Logan shouted as I ran at full speed up the steps of the lookout.

He muttered a bunch of what I presumed were Kiwi curses, even though none of the words made any sense.

"Thanks for leaving me without a torch, being chased by a creature straight out of Wētā fucking Workshop," he barked, racing to where I stood.

I shook my hands out, my skin rippling. "I don't do tarantulas."

Logan guffawed. "You don't *do* tarantulas?"

"Small spiders are fine, but when they're the size of a standard poodle, I'm out," I said, shivering against the feeling of a thousand tiny spider legs crawling up my back.

"I thought you were a wildlife biologist," Logan taunted.

"It is a stereotype that all wildlife biologists like all animals," I corrected, turning frantically in circles. Maybe that thing had a vendetta against me now and was running up the stairs to get us. "Have you ever met beetle biologists? They hate mammals. Don't get me started on the fish bros."

"Fish bros?"

"Ichthyologists," I whined, cringing at the sound of leaves rustling, but it was just a coati.

"Lark," Logan said. "Calm down. It's not chasing us."

He walked up to me and smoothed his hands down my arms, replacing the gross sensations of spider legs with the warm ripple of goosebumps.

"It's okay." I stepped out of his touch and cleared my throat. "I'm fine now."

"Okay, so can you please explain to me why we are up a lookout in the pitch dark when there's nowhere to, in fact, look?" He arched his sharply shadowed brow at me.

"I wanted to see some native bats," I lied, "and whatever else is awake in the jungle—"

"Except for tarantulas," he pointed out, leaning his forearms against the railing.

"Except for tarantulas," I said, my chest still heaving.

He waited a long beat before asking, "Could this have anything to do with the fact that it's our last night here and everything changes for us tomorrow?"

I hated the knowing look he gave me. My shoulders sagged. "It's too much pressure."

"It is too much pressure," he agreed.

"I feel like I have to be this amazing sex goddess because we've only got this one night and—" His hand reached out and he threaded his fingers through my own, silencing me.

"So let's just agree to go have not world-changing, earth-shattering sex and just go have fun, awkward, enjoyable sex instead, okay? I mean, if you still want to?"

My inner muscles clenched at that, the pressure and anxiety suddenly easing. "I could do that." The words barely left my mouth before Logan bridged the distance between us and kissed me again.

"Let's go have some fun," he murmured against my lips. "Unless you want to give Jorge another show?"

"Oh yeah," I said, grimacing as I remembered that he lived under the lookout. Poor Jorge probably got woken up all the time by hotel guests having quickies up here. "Good call." I turned, grabbing my flashlight when I remembered. "But . . . the tarantulas."

Logan squatted down and hoisted me over his shoulder. I let out a squeal as he playfully smacked my ass. "I would fight a fucking jaguar one-handed," he said, the fingers around my thighs squeezing. "That's how badly I want you."

"A jaguar would definitely win." I giggled as he jostled me down the steps. "They are one of the best apex predators. Have you seen—agh!" He smacked my ass again, silencing my animal anecdote as he took off running down the trail toward our room.

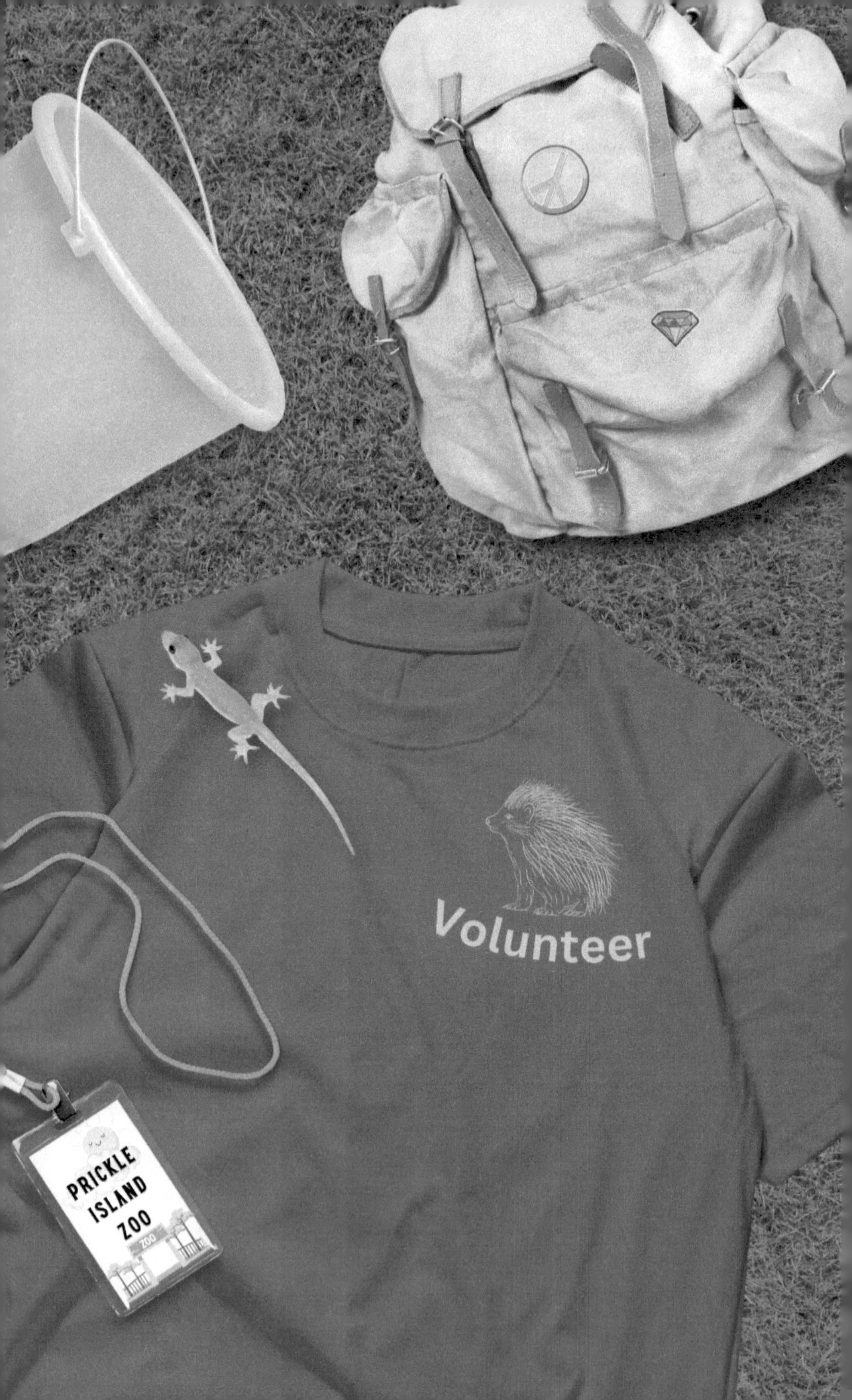

Volunteer
PRICKLE
ISLAND
ZOO
ZOO

Chapter Forty

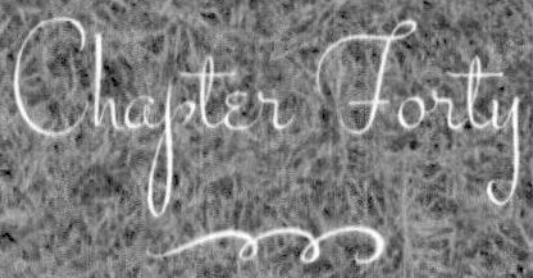

Logan

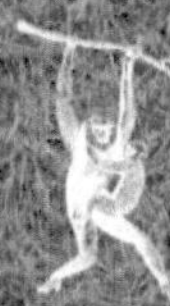

I kicked the door shut behind me and ate up the distance to my bed, tossing Lark onto the mattress. Her hair splayed out like a halo over the pillow, her eyes filled with playful lust.

I smiled, hovering over her for a second, taking in the sight of her. How badly I wanted this, to be on top of her, to be inside of her . . . The thought made my cock throb.

Once wouldn't be enough tonight. I would make every second of our last night together count. I would explore every inch of her body, know what each lick and touch did to her, what sounds I could pull from her mouth, how many orgasms I could give her before the sun came up.

"What are you thinking about?" she taunted, her lips curving in a devious smile.

"All the ways I could play with you," I murmured as my gaze trailed from her lips to the swell of her breasts peeking above her tank top. "All the *fun* we could have."

She let out a shuddering breath as my eyes promised all the things my mind was conjuring up. I dropped a knee between her legs, my hands bracketing on either side of her head as I slowly lowered and kissed her. Her lips were the sweetest sort of torture. The rightness I felt when we were touching was like nothing I'd ever known before.

She tugged on my shirt in silent command, and I reached back to haul it over my head. I lowered more onto her, my skin brushing against the fabric of her tank top, my tongue teasing hers, driving her mouth to move faster. Her nipples were hard and waiting as I lifted a hand and circled the one budded peak.

"Should I get a condom?" I whispered into her ear, and her head reared back. I loosened my grip. Did I misread this? Did I push this too far too fast?

"You brought condoms with you to the middle of the jungle?" she asked with a perplexed laugh.

"Is that a bad thing?"

"Did you think this might happen from the start?"

I shrugged. "Since the moment you said you wanted me to grab you and kiss you, I hoped this was where we'd end up." My confused eyes searched her face. "Does . . . that make you uncomfortable?"

"No," she said, and my anxious muscles eased. "I'm just impressed by your preparedness."

I barked out a rough laugh. "I'm just trying to keep up with you, tails," I said, dropping too quickly to give her another kiss.

Our teeth knocked together and we both laughed, our frenzied hands stilling for a second as we smiled against each other's lips. There was nothing more serious than my desire to have her, and yet, I loved the silly, sweet way we clumsily grabbed at each other too, learning each other's bodies, learning how the other moved. I wanted this, all of her, the funny and awkward and devastatingly sexy. I wanted this brand-new mixture of all the things that made Lark and I electric, her soul claiming mine as much as her lips were.

"Get a condom," she murmured, her hands sweeping down my chest to my belt buckle.

I closed my eyes and took a sharp breath through my nose, willing my cock to hang on as I got up and walked over to my pack. Just the command, the certainty in her voice, was nearly enough to make me come. I frantically tossed all of my things into a heap on the floor, making Lark laugh from behind me. I rifled through my belongings until my hands wrapped around the packet of condoms, then I yanked it free and whirled back toward her. But when I spun around, what I saw made me freeze.

Lark had undressed and was now lying naked on top of my bed. I scanned down her gorgeous, full breasts, her taut nipples waiting for my mouth, her round thighs pressed tightly together in a way that told me she was wet and desperate for me.

I prowled forward, shoving the condom wrapper into the pocket of my low-slung shorts. I dropped to my knees at the edge of the bed. Lark's breaths came out in rough pants as I slid my hands up her legs. I needed to taste her again, to make her as ready for me as I was for her. She seemed to know the exact train of my thoughts, her back arching as I grabbed her by the knees and pulled her down the bed.

I planted teasing kisses up the insides of her thighs, loving the exaggerated rise and fall of her chest as I got closer to her center. Her pussy was wet and glistening as I trailed a finger down her sex and parted her flesh.

"You're so ready for me, aren't you?"

She hummed, her hands fisting into the sheets on either side of her as I replaced my finger with my mouth. I stroked her clit with my tongue, and she released a sharp moan, her hips lifting off the mattress to meet my taunting licks.

"I'm too close," she whimpered, already dripping at just the softest strokes of my tongue. "Logan. I'm going to come."

I circled her entrance with my fingers, sliding one inside her, promising her just a whisper of the pleasure I was going to bring her.

"Then come," I said, "because I'm not stopping."

I lowered my mouth to work over her again, circling my tongue faster. She bucked, immediately shattering, her orgasm a bright, quick burst that I knew was only the beginning.

My cock stiffened as she came against my lips. I sucked on her swollen bud, pulling the last echoes of release out of her before dropping my hands to my waist.

Unbuckling my belt, I hooked my thumbs into my undershorts and yanked down my trousers and pants as one. I fumbled for the condom wrapper, ripping it open with my teeth, the taste of Lark's release still on my tongue as I slid the condom on. She watched in wanton fascination, her eyes hooded, her face not nearly as sated as it would be once I was done with her.

The thought made me thrum with desire as I prowled atop her, and I knew then that I'd never truly be done with her.

My lips trailed up her belly, her ribs, stopping to take her nipples into my mouth one by one and swirl my tongue around them. Lark's hips lifted again, rubbing her dewy pussy against me like she couldn't wait for me to be inside her. My lips trailed higher and closed over hers. I took my time kissing her, building her back up into the frenzy that I was feeling through every cell in my body.

I trailed the head of my cock down her folds, circling her wet entrance before slowly pushing inside her. Lark's breath hitched as I stretched her, her inner muscles flickering around me as I filled her tight core. Each inch was the sweetest ecstasy. I let out a shuddering groan as I sheathed myself fully inside her, the feeling of being buried in her even better than I could've imagined. I kissed her again, trying to go slow as I pulled out of her and pushed back in with rolling pumps. But she hitched her ankles around my hips and pulled me deeper. The way her perfect pussy gripped my cock made me choke out a groan as her hands clawed down my back, my arm muscles straining on either side of her head as I moved faster.

"Yes," she moaned, tilting her hips until I hit a spot that made her throw her head back. "Yes."

The sound broke me and I started moving my hips faster, fucking her tight channel with deep, long thrusts. I wanted this moment to stretch on forever, but my balls were drawing up and I couldn't hold on any longer. The sounds she made told me she was so close too, but I couldn't hang on, couldn't wait. The feeling of being inside her was too good.

With a barked groan, my head dropped forward and my orgasm whipped through me, my hips jerking as I rode her through my climax. Still inside her, I slid my fingers between us and rubbed Lark's clit, my mouth dropping to her nipple and sucking hard. That was all it took. She exploded around me, her inner muscles milking the last of my release from my sated cock. This orgasm was bigger and brighter than her first, stretching on and on as her muscles seized and a staccato cry pulled from her parted lips.

That sound. That sweet fucking sound. I would never get enough.

I sucked and rubbed her through the last waves of her orgasm and dropped down onto the bed beside her, pulling her against my chest. It had been everything I'd hoped it would be and more, and I knew we were only just getting started.

STAFF
PRICKLE ISLAND ZOO
ZOO

We stayed up until the sky was brightening before finally collapsing into the other still-made bed to sleep. We'd used half the box of condoms, and despite us both promising the not earth-shattering kind of sex, I had seven—*seven*—mind-blowing orgasms that I wouldn't be soon forgetting.

When I woke up, though, and heard the outdoor shower running, I checked the clock. We had an hour before we needed to be out of the hotel and on our way to the airport . . . One more hour and then this would all be a really hot, really vivid dream.

I didn't bother wrapping the sheet around me as I stood

and stretched. Three hours of sleep was not enough, but I'd sleep on the plane. I padded across the floor to the bathroom and opened the door a crack. It was unlocked.

When I peeked out and saw Logan showering, the sleepiness vanished from my mind, replaced with echoes from all the ways we explored each other the night before. He slicked the water off his face and peeked at me, a proud and wanton smile stretching his lips as his cock twitched to life again.

Well, good morning, sailor.

I stalked over to him, the cool of the water waking me even more. Logan wrapped his arms around me as he planted a wet kiss on my lips.

"Morning," he said, taking his time kissing me. "What time is it?"

"Eight," I said.

"So Lark Lachlan had a sleep-in," he mused, his hands idly roving down my back to knead my ass. He touched me with all the ease and claim of someone who'd done it a million times before, like we'd been together for years and not days.

"I had a busy night," I murmured, lifting on my tiptoes to kiss him before reaching for the body wash dispenser.

"Let me," Logan said, his voice dropping an octave as he got a handful of body wash and began lathering it in his hands. "Hmm." He made a sound like he was savoring every inch of me, his eyes roving where his hands followed. With sweeping circles, he washed me from the top of my shoulders all the way down to my calves, careful to avoid my burn wound.

I groaned when his hands barely skimmed over my pussy, wishing he'd give her a little of the attention that he'd doled upon her last night. Even though the suds had been long washed away, he worked his hands back up my body again, rising to stand. This time, his hand lingered between my legs as he dropped his lips to mine. I stretched up on tiptoes, trying to get him to touch me faster, quicker, but he only palmed me.

Fine. I'd take matters into my own hands.

I slid a hand down his muscled torso and wrapped it around his shaft, pumping him slowly in my fist. His eyes guttered, and he finally relented to my demands, parting my flesh and dragging a finger down my slit.

I hummed out a moan of pleasure as he touched me. He'd learned the exact tempo I liked. The exact rhythm probably coming to him now from muscle memory alone. God, I loved the way he touched me.

I held on to him tighter with my free hand, my legs already trembling as he worked me higher. His hand shot out and turned off the stream of cool water, and he twisted me toward the wall. He propped his thigh between my legs as his fingers slid inside me. My eyes rolled back as I leaned farther into the wall, rocking into his hand.

His free hand landed on my wrist and he murmured, "Wait." My hand stilled, and I wondered if he was too sore from our many rounds the night before, but then he said, "I want to finish inside of you, and if you keep going like that, I won't be able to."

I let out a smug laugh, delighting in the way I made him feel. His lips dropped down to my collarbone and then to my breast, sucking on my nipple. I moaned and threaded my hands in his hair, arching into his mouth. His fingers worked me faster. Fuck, everything he did to me set me on fire.

"Logan," I panted. "I'm going to come."

He kept his rhythm, his thumb working my clit while I rode his fingers. I let out a gasping moan as my orgasm pulled from my lungs. I'd never come so easily, usually needing everything to be just right in order for me to shut my mind off and focus on the pleasure. But with Logan . . . I swore he had a Lark remote control and kept pushing the climax button over and over and over. Easy as that.

He wrung out the last sounds of pleasure from me before grabbing a towel for me and then one for himself.

"Inside," he commanded, his lips swollen and eyes hooded.

He didn't wait for me to follow as he padded naked into the room. There were probably a few parrots getting an eyeful right now, and I prayed no one was about to do some gardening nearby. I dried myself off and left my towel on the hook. When I walked into the room, Logan was sitting on the edge of the bed, rolling a condom onto his hard cock.

I walked straight over to him, holding his gaze as I straddled him and hovered my entrance over his tip. My eyes began to close as I pressed him to my wet core.

His hand reached out and swept the hair off my face. "Look at me," he whispered.

I opened my eyes, holding his gaze as I lowered myself, watching everything that seemed to flash in the silence between one breath and the next. The words were right there. Right on the tip of my tongue. As I fully seated him inside me, I wanted to say everything that was screaming in the back of my mind, everything soaring and amazing and world-changing, everything I'd never felt in my heart before.

We stayed there for another moment, locked in each other's eyes, and I was certain that even though the words didn't escape my lips, he heard them. He knew everything I felt here, when our bodies were connected and our hearts were open. I lifted halfway up and slowly lowered again, rocking my hips as I worked his cock, watching the way his eyelids flickered with each of my movements. I tried to go slow, tried to string out this moment and make it last, but the feeling building within me was too good and, with each panting breath, I moved faster.

Logan's eyes dropped to where we were joined, watching as I rode him. He gripped my hips, meeting each of my movements with a thrust of his own. He groaned as he licked into my mouth, tasting me as he pulled me closer.

His arms banded around me and he stood, flipping us around to lay me flat on the bed again. My wet hair splayed across the sheets as he dropped over me, his mouth meeting mine. His hips pumped faster, making me moan. Grabbing one of my legs, Logan hoisted one knee over his shoulder, making him thrust into me even deeper. I cried out, the feeling so good as he bent me like a freaking pretzel and fucked my desperate pussy.

"Yes," I panted, tilting my hips with each of his crazed pumps.

"Lark," Logan growled, holding my ass even tighter. The headboard slammed into the wall with each of his wild thrusts, pounding me backward until I was screaming his name, so lost to the sensations that I didn't know where he ended and I began anymore.

I knew he was so freaking close, and I was chasing after him. When he licked his thumb, I knew he was determined to make me come for the *ninth* time in a single day. Oh fuck, I didn't know if I could handle it, but as his thumb dropped to my clit and he began circling me, I couldn't fight the building inside of me. Each circle of his thumb was met by a deep thrust of his cock, and I was making the most crazed fucking sounds, desperately hanging on.

When he dropped his mouth to my nipple and began sucking, I shattered. My soul left my freaking body, every single muscle in me vibrating, clenching, and releasing again and again. My vision spotted, my body filled with flickering heat as the most powerful orgasm I'd ever had in my life roared through me. Logan battled my clenching muscles, his own climax taking hold as we came together, over and over and over.

Nothing would ever be this good. Nothing would ever be the same. I loved him . . . and with that wonderful, terrifying knowledge, a question blasted into my mind: *how* was I going to platonically work beside him every day at the zoo?

STAFF
PRICKLE ISLAND ZOO
ZOO

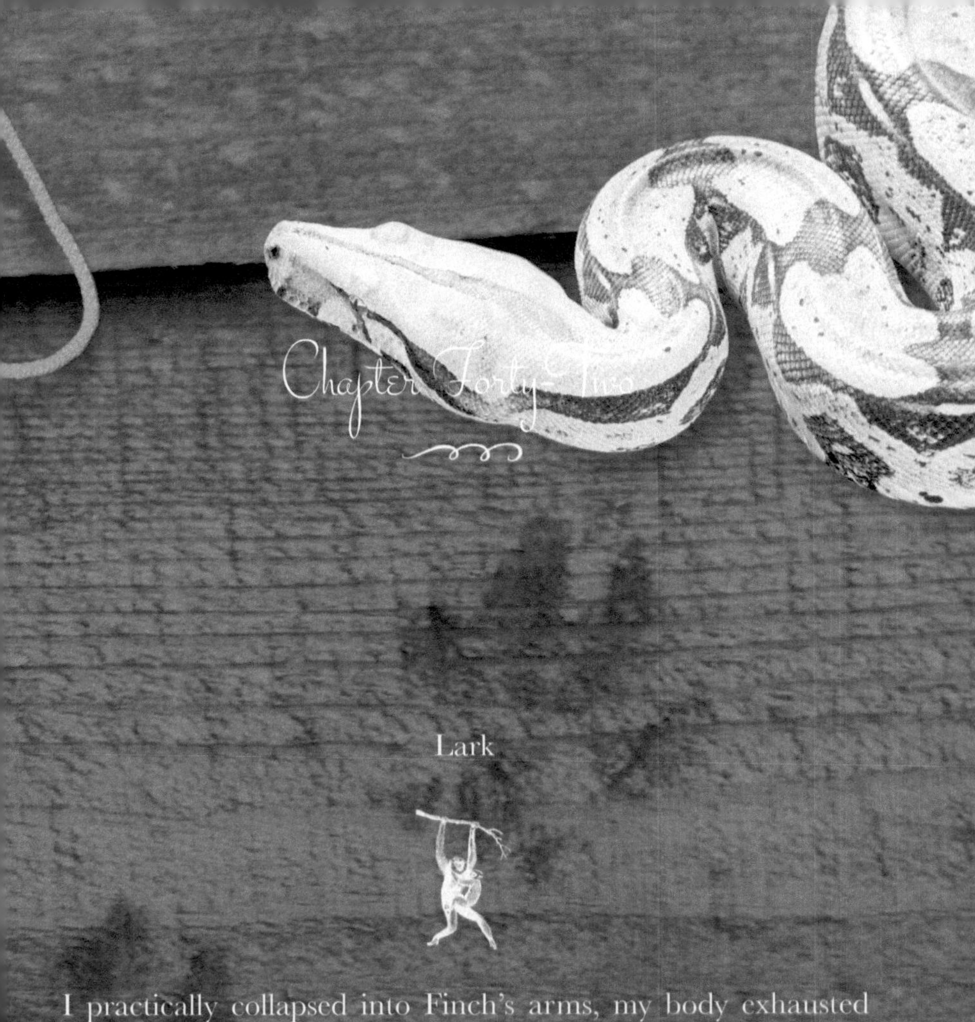

Chapter Forty-Two

Lark

I practically collapsed into Finch's arms, my body exhausted from the constant travel—and using my one rest day to have the nine best orgasms of my life.

"You smell like expired goat cheese and plane farts," Finch muttered into my shoulder.

"I love you too," I said, giving her one last squeeze before turning to Dove and giving her a slightly less aggressive hug. "How's Emma doing?"

"Let me show you!" Dove lit up, pulling out her phone and scrolling through photos. Finch recounted all of Emma's stats right down to the time of her bowel movements while Dove told me all about her personality and how cheeky she was getting—the difference between my sisters' priorities was clear. They were both in their work clothes, a few visitors still dotting the main paths through the zoo, the last stragglers making their way to the front. The café staff at the Peckish Peacock were pulling down the metal rolling doors and hefting the bags of garbage out to the giant dumpster behind a strategically placed billboard encouraging people to recycle. Heron and Crane drove past in their golf cart, waving and shouting their, "Welcome home!"s as they raced up to the top of the zoo to bring in the hoofstock animals for the night—late as always.

"How's the gala preparation going?" I asked, nodding to the streamers already strung up across the pavilion. "Has Mom—"

"I'm going to stop you right there," Finch said. "The gala will be great, and I've stolen the run sheet from last year so you don't even need to organize the animal encounters."

"Westworth is already up our ass. We need this to be perfect," I pushed. "Have you thought about—"

My sisters both launched into scolding me, recounting their different preparations simultaneously. As my sisters talked over each other, I kept stealing glances at Logan as he and Hawk chatted across the pavilion. They both leaned with their arms crossed against the porcupine playground, and I swore Logan was pushing up his biceps on purpose. No, I was just imagining it. His biceps were always that muscled. I just wanted him to still be trying to show off for me—which I shouldn't want at all since we were back in the US. My mind was still stuck on what Logan looked like without that T-shirt on.

My brother was laughing as Logan told him some story that I couldn't quite hear. Logan's eyes drifted to me and locked with mine for the briefest of seconds, his dimples deepening as he looked away and kept talking. Our last day in Guatemala flashed into my mind, and I forced myself to focus even harder on the photos Dove was showing me. Could everyone else tell we hooked up? I bet Finch had already guessed it, but at least no one had called us out.

"What the fuck is that?" Finch shouted, pointing down at my calf. "Is it infected?" She dropped into a crouch and pulled out a rubber glove from her pocket like she was inspecting a crime scene.

I cringed. "I burned my leg on a motorcycle muffler."

"And then rubbed dirt in it?" Finch asked accusatorially.

"We were on our way into the forest for two weeks," I hissed. "I kept it as clean as I could."

"You should come down to the clinic," Finch said. "Let me look at it properly."

"I am *not* coming down to the clinic." I shoved her back as she prodded the scabbing wound with her gloved finger. "Ouch!"

"Good. Doesn't seem to be any nerve damage," she murmured to herself.

"Finch, seriously." I took a giant step backward, and she stood with a frown. "It's healing just fine. I don't need a vet."

I looked again at Hawk and Logan, who were walking back down toward the volunteer house. Logan glanced one more time over his shoulder at me, and I felt the same familiar pull. It would be weird to say goodbye to each other, to hug or something, but we'd just been through this whole adventure together and it felt wrong for him to just be walking away back to the Bunny House.

This is what I wanted, I reminded myself, wishing I didn't feel like a tangled web of too many feelings.

Folding her arms, Finch leaned into my line of sight, breaking my wistful gaze at the back of Logan's head. "Please tell me you're using contraception?"

"Are you even on the pill?" Dove added.

A trickle of summer sweat ran down my spine as I gaped back and forth at my sisters and then frowned. It was that obvious, then. I couldn't even pretend convincingly for more than two seconds that I hadn't slept with Logan.

"We used condoms, yes," I said to Finch and then looked at Dove, thinking about how I'd slept with someone with the requisite parts to actually result in baby making. "And I've never needed birth control before because none of my previous partners had the required equipment for procreation."

"I am not ready to be an auntie," Finch said, shaking her head. "Even though I'd absolutely be the cool one." She shoved Dove, and Dove shoved her back. "Condoms aren't foolproof, Lars."

"They're fine," I grumbled.

"I can dart you with depo like one of the monkeys," Finch offered.

I let out a slow, frustrated sigh. This was exactly why I didn't want to talk to them about this. "I won't be needing long-term anything because there will be no *long-term* between us." I hated how bitter the words came out. "We agreed we'd only sleep together in Guatemala. Now we're here and it's over." Dove and Finch threw their heads back and cackled like hyenas. "Stop it," I snarled, shoving Finch so hard, she stumbled backward.

She wiped her fingers under her eyes, trying to catch her breath as Dove turned bright red with belly laughter. They laughed as if I'd told the world's funniest joke. Dove let out a little whimpering sound as she tried to catch her breath, smushing her cheeks together to release the strained muscles from laughing too hard.

"You two are ridiculous," I said. "It *is* over."

"Stop it." Dove's words barely came out through her laughter. "I'm going to pee myself."

Enough of this. I spun around and started stomping off when Finch caught up to me and finally tampered her laughter enough to say, "We're sorry. We're sorry. It's just . . ." She took a sip of air. "It's clear he absolutely wants to fuck you again and you absolutely want to fuck him again, and we've been working with animals for too freaking long for you to think you're going to override that desire."

"You're wrong," I snapped. "I am in complete control. Yes, in another world, I might want to sleep with him again," I relented. "But I'm more stubborn than I am horny, and I will deal with this like a professional."

"Then you'd better go charge your vibrator now," Finch said with a snicker. "Because you two are going to be besties for the rest of the summer."

"I'll go run a cold shower for you," Dove offered, and I punched her in the arm a little harder than necessary.

"Hey!" She shoved me back.

"Lars, stop taking your sexual frustration out on everyone," Finch chided. "Now, come on, I bet you want to go see Emma."

I perked up at that. The anger of my sisters' taunting abated as I thought about all the animals on my run. See, the job could keep me focused. I'd busy myself with work and forget all about the things Logan could do with his tongue . . . and his fingers . . . and his cock—

Fuck my life.

STAFF
PRICKLE
ISLAND
ZOO
ZOO

Lark

Why did everything turn me on right now? *Nothing* was safe. The way Logan swept the floor, the way he scrubbed buckets, the way he laughed . . . Dear God, I swore he was sweating more this week just to punish me.

I felt like I was perpetually wet, my pussy desperate for another rendition of that night we'd spent together. The echoes of that sexcapade were perfectly tattooed on the ridges of my brain. The sounds, the sensations . . . I swore when I turned the rusty handle of the enclosure door, I heard the groan of Logan coming inside me.

This was unbearable. I couldn't have him. But I couldn't send him away either.

We fell into what *seemed* like an easy routine, old friends who didn't need to speak to know exactly what the other was thinking, but I wondered if every noise, every movement I made tortured him just as badly.

I missed the simpler things too: the ease with which he used to reach out and hold my hand, the way he listened to me, how good it felt when he mindlessly bent and kissed my shoulder.

I went about my day, trying to focus on my routine, but instead, everything felt tinted with yearning. Aya had returned, which meant the diets were covered and we had a swing person for the keeper shifts again. Everything should've been faster, but I found myself dawdling, distracted by the man standing next to me.

"Tails." Logan snapped in front of my face.

"What?" I barked a little too harshly.

"I asked if you needed any help finishing early," he said. Damn, I needed help finishing alright. I blinked absentmindedly at him, and he carried on. "The gala tonight?"

"Oh, right," I said, my throat suddenly bone-dry. "No, I think we should be okay." I'd already sent Maddie off to go get ready. She claimed she'd need at least three hours to get "fully glammed," whatever that meant. I was both pleased and angry at myself that Logan and I were left hiding behind the bamboo hedgerow at the entrance to the monkey exhibit all on our own. I took him in, my eyes landing on his mud-splattered T-shirt. "Do you have anything to wear?"

"Hawk is renting me a suit when he goes to pick up his," Logan said, and my lady bits started clog dancing at the thought of Logan in a suit. He'd look like James freaking Bond, only scruffy and a million times better.

Tonight was the Westworths' annual zoo gala and fundraiser. The zoo shut early, and all the Westworths' rich friends were invited for drinks and canapés while they donated obscene amounts of money to different conservation funds. Most of the zoo revenue was made up from this one single night too. It was events like this that were the reason we could never seem to get out from under the Westworths' thumbs. We needed to dress up and show off all the animals to the wealthy guests and schmooze them until they footed the bill for the fancy apples and papayas that we had shipped over on the ferry. Maybe we'd even make enough to build a new lion enclosure.

If Finch was using last year's run sheet, I'd already scheduled my siblings down to the minute. I'd worked with the event planner to make sure there was always an animal for guests to touch and a keeper to ask questions to. Wherever the guests turned throughout the grounds, a Lachlan would be there, reminding them to open their wallets.

Logan stepped closer to me, and my neck craned back to meet his warm brown eyes and all thoughts of schedules seemed to evaporate from my mind.

"What will you be wearing?" he asked, his voice dropping an octave. Whatever suspicions I had that he was also being tortured were now confirmed.

"A boring dress," I said carefully, thinking of my dowdy plum dress that I wore to all of these events.

"Impossible," Logan said with a smile, and I had to take a shaky step away from him to not lift up on my tiptoes and kiss him.

It felt so natural, so right. It took no thought or effort. As easily as my body went through the motions of my job, it also knew how to mold into the curve of his own.

I closed the door to the monkeys behind me and swept my stray hairs behind my ear, my whole body on fire.

As Logan took a step down the path, his phone toppled out

of his pocket, and I bent to pick it up for him. He lurched for it like I might stumble across a dick pic just by touching it, snatching it from my grasp, but I already saw what he clearly hadn't wanted me to see: his lock screen photo was a picture of us, well, mostly him, but the head resting on his shoulder was most definitely mine. In the photo, he was looking at me with a half-smile. He looked happy. He looked . . . in love. Gone was the perky jumping photo of Kelly, and in its place was a photo of him and me.

Him and me.

I knew then this whole "only in Guatemala" thing was doomed from the start. I'd desperately tried to rationalize it, but we both knew that this photo meant something. I was about to say something about it when I stole a glance back at Logan, who was clenching his jaw so tightly, I thought he might crack a tooth. "What?"

He nodded to my shirt, and I looked down to see it had ridden up and my lacy black thong was peeking up from my shorts.

Yes, a thong. A very impractical and ridiculous undergarment to be wearing while I washed monkey poop off concrete floors. But I had worn it for this very moment, just for the thought of making Logan feel even the smallest bit of the torment I was currently experiencing.

"Please tell me you're going to be wearing that under your dress tonight." His hands were clenched into fists at his sides, and I knew it was taking everything in him not to close the distance between us and grab me.

I shrugged. "If I wear anything at all."

Logan choked out a growl. "Fuck me, tails."

God, I really, really wanted to. "Only in Guatemala."

The evidence of Logan's arousal was clear through his

shorts as he scrubbed his hand down his face and let out a frustrated sigh. "I'm going to have a shower," he said, whipping around and storming down toward the volunteer house.

"I'm going to find a sexier dress," I murmured to myself, marching uphill on a mission.

PRICKLE
ISLAND
ZOO
ZOO
Volunteer

Chapter Forty-Four

Logan

The pavilion outside the Peckish Peacock had been transformed with twinkling fairy lights, high-top tables, and silver and gold streamers. The TVs that normally played conservation videos were now playing montages of photos from the night itself, uploaded on a rolling basis by the roving photographers. The whole place reeked of expensive perfume and aftershave as the wealthiest people I'd ever seen waltzed around the space. It was all gaudy and overwhelming, and I considered, for a split second, taking my flute of Champagne and high-tailing it out of there . . . and then I saw her.

The sight of Lark was like a sledgehammer to the heart. The way that black lace dress hugged her curves, the deep V of the neckline, her hair worn down in soft waves framing her face, her smoky eyes and red lipstick . . . She looked like she'd walked out of the pages of a magazine, but it was the way she smiled at the cockatoo perched on her arm, busier chatting with the bird than any of the fancy patrons, that made me clench a hand to my chest. If ever there was a person so perfectly designed to be the other piece of my puzzle, it was Lark Lachlan, and I hoped right then I could be all the things she needed in a puzzle piece too.

As she walked down the stairs with ease, I noted she wore black Converse instead of heels and smiled. Smart. Don't want to go stumbling around with a cockatoo on your arm. Lark's gaze pulled from the bird and landed straight on me through the crowd, as if a spotlight were shining directly down on me.

Her soft smile widened into this brilliant, beaming thing, and I knew in that moment, I wanted to marry this woman.

It hit me all at once: the image of Lark walking down an aisle toward me in a white dress and matching white sneakers, a bird or monkey or some sort of animal perched on her shoulder. My whole body tensed with the yearning, and I wished I could manifest that image through sheer willpower alone.

Lark mingled with the patrons, letting them all feed Yellow sunflower seeds and give him pats on the head. She seemed at ease with the bird on her arm, as if small talk weren't as hard when it was about animals. I knew the exact tone she'd be using, the exact excited pitch of her voice as she told them about bird behavior, and I wanted to hear her talk like that for the rest of my life.

"Wow." The word snapped me out of my spell, and I glanced sideways at Finch, who'd managed to sneak up on me while I was ogling her sister. "You've got some serious heart eyes for Lark, huh?"

"I do," I said, unable to deny it anymore. There was no

point in arguing that Lark Lachlan had my heart in her hand . . . and a cockatoo in the other. "Is that a problem?"

"It depends on Lars." Finch shrugged, stroking her thumb over the head of the boa constrictor wrapped around her arm. "But I think she feels the same way about you."

"I doubt it," I replied a little too quickly. Lark liked being around me, liked sleeping with me for sure, but this kind of deep ache I felt in my chest . . . I didn't know if she felt the same.

"That's because you're too close to see it," Finch said, lifting the little boa, who flicked her tongue out at me.

"Do you think she'd say yes?" I mused, watching Lark mingle through the crowd, spouting her animal fun facts to the rich patrons. "If I asked her to come with me to New Zealand, do you think she'd say yes?"

Finch sighed, and I felt that sigh like a lead weight pulling me down into the ocean. "I don't know. Maybe."

Maybe. There was at least a flicker of hope with a maybe. I had the rest of the summer, two whole months, to convince her it was a good idea. I'd probably need to make a flow chart . . . She'd love that.

I nodded to the boa wrapped around Finch's forearm. "This must be the infamous Matilda I've heard so much about."

Finch moved her arm over to me so I could sweep a finger down Matilda's smooth skin. I let out a little "oh" of surprise at the sensation of her rippling scales as she coiled herself around Finch's arm.

"Right?" Finch said with a laugh. "Have you never touched a snake before?"

She asked that like everyone in the world was just running around touching snakes all the time. "One time as a kid at a zoo in Australia," I said. "But we don't have snakes in New Zealand, not even in zoos."

"I knew that," she said.

"Of course you did."

Finch chuckled. "You are so not the sort of person I would've picked for my sister," she said, and my gut clenched for a second before she added, "but I think you're perfect for her, Loganberry."

"Loganberry?"

"I'm workshopping nicknames," she said.

"What are you two talking about?" Lark asked, and I shot my eyes up to spy her sidling up beside me.

The way her hips moved in that dress . . . I had to ball my hands into fists to not reach out and touch her. I wanted to peel that fucking dress off. I wanted to grab those hips and . . . I cleared my throat. *Not the appropriate time, Logan.*

"Just telling Wolverine here about all of your embarrassing middle school stories," Finch said, elbowing her sister. Lark shot Finch back one of her "I'll kill you" glares, and it made me want her even more.

"Did you all even go to school?" I asked, looking around the pavilion. "How exactly did that work when you live on an island with no school?"

"Distance learning and homeschooling mostly," Finch said with a shrug. "I moved to New Haven to do my undergrad and had vet school near Worcester."

"I got my degree mainly online," Lark said. "After Dad, it seemed like the more sensible thing to do. Most of the work placements I could do through the zoo, so I didn't need to travel that much for coursework."

After Dad. That felt like a Spartan kick right to my sternum. Lark had given up everything, even her chance to have a university experience, to take care of her family. I thought about Dove and the twins and Wren . . . All of them had stayed back too—all the Lachlan siblings rallying to keep the zoo afloat in the aftermath of their father's death and their mother's grief. Lark's mom seemed like a happy, energetic person . . . but she had that look about her too. The kind that told you they'd gone through something terrible and were trying to fake it 'til they made it out the other side.

Lark seemed like she was about to say more before an older woman, flanked by two old men, approached us. I spotted how Lark's and Finch's shoulders immediately bunched up around their ears at the sight of the her.

"Mrs. Westworth," Lark said, her voice two octaves higher than it had been a minute ago. "How lovely to see you."

Westworth? Holy shit. *This* was the owner of the zoo that every plaque and signage was adorned with?

Mrs. Westworth was a short woman, five-two if I was counting the quail feathers sticking out from the top of her fascinator. She looked to be somewhere in her mid-eighties but had clearly had enough work done to look a decade younger, so who knew? She wore bright pink lipstick and heavy eye makeup that gave her a perpetually surprised expression. Her fashionable forest-green gown complimented the iridescent sheen of the feathers in her hat. She wore so much gold and emerald jewelry, from her brooch to her neck-laces to her earrings and a clattering of bangles, that I wondered if she had some serious guns from lifting her arms up and down. Everything about this woman screamed one word: expensive. I almost had half a mind to bow to her. How did one address someone like this? She seemed like royalty.

"When do you think the baby giraffe is coming?" she asked by way of greeting. She completely ignored me as she stared at the sisters.

Lark tried to smile at her, but it came out more like a grimace. "Zelda isn't pregnant," she said.

"Why not?" Mrs. Westworth looked like someone had just insulted her outfit.

"Because we don't have any male giraffes," Lark said with a considerable amount of restraint. I felt like she deserved sainthood for it.

"Well, can't you just acquire something artificially?" Mrs. Westworth blustered. Finch was about to open her mouth to probably explain that acquiring giraffe semen wasn't as easy as popping to the local supermarket when Mrs. Westworth continued her tirade. "And where is your brother? I was taking my friends"—she gestured to the two amused-looking men behind her—"for a tour around and the lions are all sleeping behind the rocks."

"Lions do love to sleep," Lark said, trying to smooth over the conversation. "Twenty hours a day. They—"

"Tell your brother to go over there and make them come down," Mrs. Westworth demanded.

My mouth fell open at that. What did she expect Hawk to do? Put them on a leash and walk them down to the glass? One of the many things I liked about Prickle Island Zoo was that all of the animals had a right not to be seen. There were always caves, bushes, and tunnels for them to be hidden from visitors. Most of them were either entirely unbothered or all too eager for the entertainment of people though. Still, no one was forcing these animals to do anything they didn't want to do.

"We'll throw some treats over," Finch said, nudging her sister in a silent reminder to plaster back on her fake smile. "We'll do our best."

"Well, do your best better," Mrs. Westworth sniped, ordering them around like they were her servants. I mean, technically, they were her employees. The Westworths owned the Prickle Island Zoo . . . and the rest of Prickle Island too. Everything on this rock was rented, loaned, or entrusted to its owners by the good grace of the Westworth matriarch.

"Yes, Mrs. Westworth," Lark replied tightly.

"Honestly," Mrs. Westworth said, turning and ushering her friends away. "I think it's time to take that Australian fellow's offer and sell this place."

Lark's eyes flared at that, and I stepped closer to her. The three of us waited in tense silence until Mrs. Westworth had moved to the other side of the party.

"I knew it," Finch muttered. "I fucking knew it."

"Knew what?" I asked, glancing between the sisters.

"Gaz Madigan has made an offer to buy the zoo," Lark said.

I reared my head back. "The Aussie reality star?" The advertisements for *Madigan Mountain* were splashed all over New Zealand media too. Gaz was one of the most famous people in all of Australia, although not in a good way. He wasn't known for his conservation efforts or winning charm; rather, he was known in the tabloids for his drunken brawls, illicit extramarital affairs, and generally being a public nuisance acting like he was God's gift to man. "Why would he want to buy your zoo?"

"Old rivalry with Dad. He wanted to turn this place into another Madigan Mountain Zoo," Finch muttered. "He wanted to stick cameras everywhere and make us into the American version of his reality TV show. Of course, he wanted his production company to run the whole thing and get a ninety percent cut of the profits."

"Smarmy business asshole," Lark said. "He and Dad had a falling out ages ago, before either of them was particularly successful. We never really knew over what. Since Dad died, Gaz has been pursuing ownership of the zoo every single year. Now he's gone straight to Westworth with his offer it seems."

"Do you think she'll sell?" I asked.

Lark's jaw clenched, and she gritted out, "I didn't use to think so, but the older and grumpier she gets, I'm starting to get worried. She told Dad that if he raised enough funds, he could buy the zoo from her and our family could own it outright."

"But that's *a lot* of money we don't have," Finch continued.

"Shit," I said.

"Yep," Finch replied. "So we have to keep kissing Westworth's ass like all of our ancestors. It's pretty much a family tradition."

Lark's body was wound so tightly, I thought she might snap and go off on a rampage. She'd given up everything to make this place run and this woman could take it all away from her in the blink of an eye. Yellow squawked and seemed to pull Lark out of her stewing thoughts.

"I should take him back," Lark said, sounding completely deflated. "The guests will be moving to the rainforest walk-through for canapés soon."

My hand drifted toward her a little as she stepped away from me, but I lowered it back down. There was nothing I could do or say to fix this for her . . . but maybe I could provide her with a little distraction.

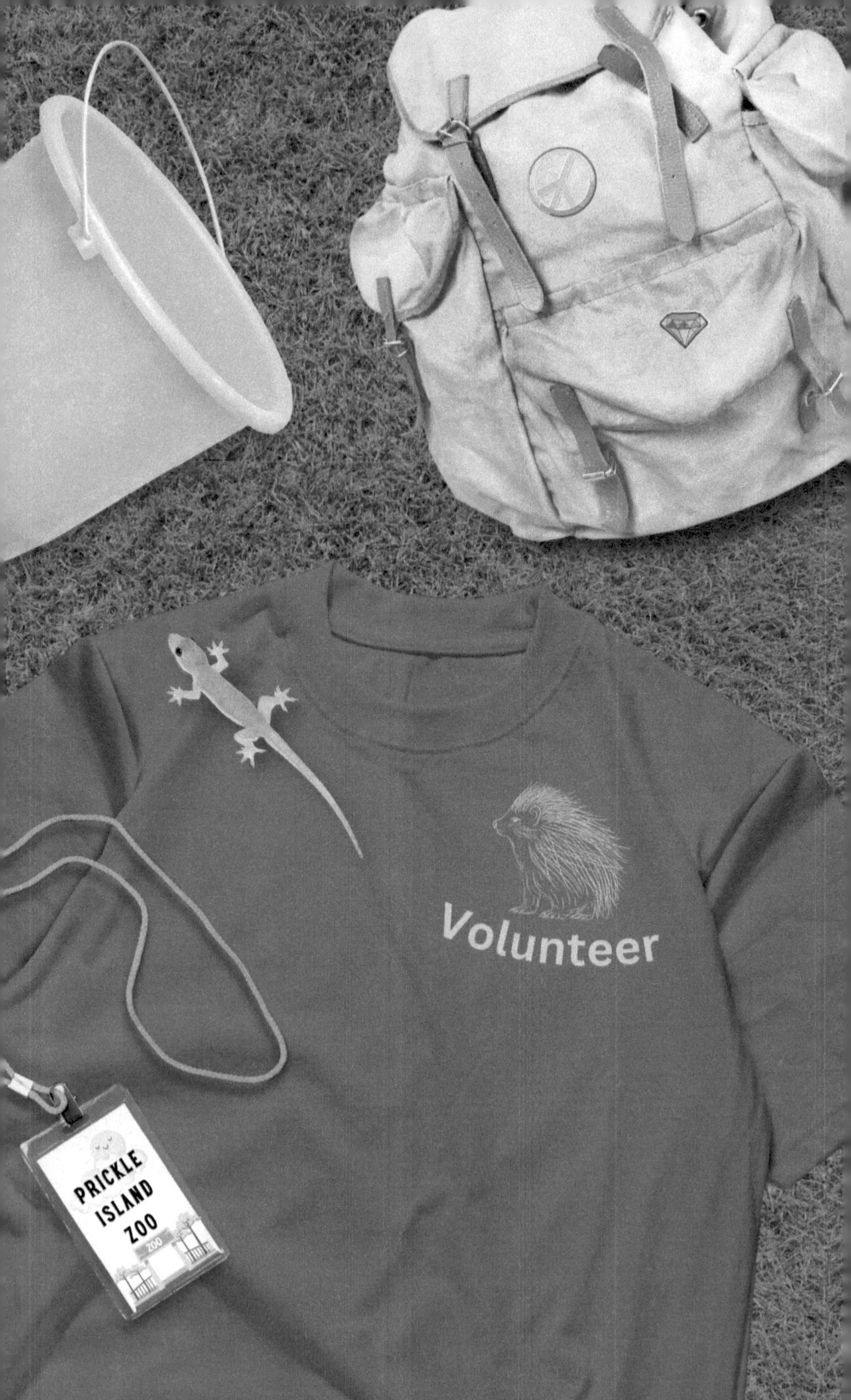

Volunteer
PRICKLE
ISLAND
ZOO
ZOO

Chapter Forty-Five

Logan

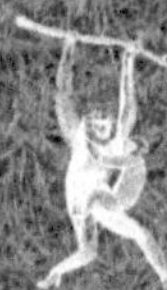

I waited for Lark to return Yellow to the aviary in the side alley behind the kitchens. The shadowed building to my back was skillfully hidden beneath the dense foliage that surrounded the reptile area. It was painted in camouflage for good measure. You'd never notice the giant building was even there if you weren't looking for it. I was beginning to realize the zoo was an elaborate maze of well-hidden pathways that led behind the scenes. Now that I was getting accustomed to being here, I started spotting them everywhere, hiding behind rubbish bins and ducking around corners.

All thoughts of the artistry of hiding things in plain sight fell out of my mind when Lark sauntered back down the path to the pavilion. Her hips swished more when she thought no one was watching. Even the contemplative look on her face that I'd first read as grumpy was entirely endearing now.

She was nearly past me when my hand shot out and circled around her waist.

And that was a mistake.

Her elbow flew backward, and I had just enough time to twist my head so I copped it in the ear instead of her breaking my nose.

"It's me." I groaned, clutching my ear as I released her.

"What the fuck are you doing?" she whisper-hissed at me, her eyes darting from side to side as if she were worried that a guest might see that she'd just clocked me good. "You can't just go grabbing people out of the darkness."

"I was having a lark."

"You can't just *have* me," she snapped.

"It's an expression," I grumbled. "It means making a joke."

"Bullshit. There's literally a Kiwi expression called 'having a lark?'"

"Yes."

"And you thought jumping out at me would be funny?"

"I was trying to be romantic," I said, rubbing my ear a few more times before straightening.

"I don't know what romance is like in New Zealand," Lark teased, and I snickered. "But in the US, we save that shit for haunted houses."

"Okay, okay," I replied. "Roses and chocolates next time. Not grabby hands in the dark."

"Right." Lark's smile fell and she rubbed the back of her neck. "Except there won't *be* a next time, Logan, because we agreed that once we left Guatemala, this"—she gestured between us—"was over."

My fingers stretched out on either side of me. Even they

couldn't help but want to touch her. That fucking black dress was going to be the death of me.

"Right," I agreed. Lark nodded but lingered, twisting her body from side to side as she stared at the cement floor. "But you know——"

"Yes?" She perked up instantly, and heat flooded through me again.

She wanted this. She wanted *more*. Just as badly as I did.

"We didn't really get to use all of our time in Guatemala," I hedged, seeing how that suggestion might land. "So maybe we have, um, two weeks to make up for?"

She tipped her head back and forth as if weighing the logic of that statement. "Not the most sound argument ever . . . but right now, with you in that suit, I'm very easily persuaded," she said and flung herself at me.

We stumbled backward into the dark kitchens, feeling our way along the hall as our lips stayed connected, our tongues battling each other's, as we finally found the metal edge of the table. I hoisted her up, yanking the hem of that fucking lace dress up around her waist. A flash of her black lace thong made me groan.

I palmed her pussy, and her eyes hooded. "You did this for me, didn't you?" I asked. "You were trying to kill me today, weren't you?"

"Yes," she moaned, tilting her hips into my touch.

"And what did you fantasize about me doing to you with these on?" I pressed one finger tighter into her folds. My cock strained in my pants at the feel of the soaking wet fabric.

"I imagined you pulling them off with your teeth." She moaned as my fingers stilled.

"And then what?"

She could barely get her words out as she panted. "And then you ate me out like a fucking feast. And then you flipped me onto my belly and fucked me until I was screaming your name."

I instantly dropped to my knees, desperate to make her fantasy into a reality. Her legs trembled as I trailed my lips up the insides of her thighs and buried my face against the wet lace. Lark gripped the edge of the table tighter, her breathing frantic as I bit into the fabric of her thong. She lifted her hips off the table as I dragged the fabric down, letting it fall the rest of the way to the floor.

There was no taunting or teasing this time, only carnal need as I gripped her by the thighs and spread her wider, lowering my tongue to claim her with my mouth. Her moan echoed off the cold steel as I tasted her tangy wetness, lashing her with my tongue until her breathing was ragged. She was so wet for me, so ready for my cock, I could barely take it. I licked her until I was about to come in my pants, and I thanked every fucking star in the sky when she gasped out my name.

I held her gaze as my hands dropped to my belt buckle. I freed myself and pulled a condom from my pocket, hastily rolling it on. That condom had been burning a hole in my pocket all night long, a desperate long shot of a hope that it might be used. A flash of a smile crossed both of our faces, peeking out from the lust storming between us. God, I loved her. She was sweet and passionate and fun, and then this sexy vixen came out and I knew she loved playing this little game with me too.

"When you imagined this, did you imagine it gentle or rough?" I rasped, loving the way her mouth fell open at my question.

"Rough," she panted without missing a beat.

I grabbed her by the hips, my fingers digging into her soft flesh in a way that elicited the most delicious gasp and smile from her, Lark clearly enjoying every second of this manhandling. I flipped her around, pushing her chest down against the steel workbench and kicking her legs apart until she was spread open for me. Wanting to give her every single one of her desires, I smacked a hand across her ass, eliciting another moan as the skin pinked up.

Dragging the head of my cock over her slick entrance, once, twice, I thrust into her until I was fully sheathed in her tight, wet core. A broken groan pulled from my lungs and Lark cried out in unison as I curled forward, the feeling of being inside her the best in the fucking world.

I didn't care how I had to contort logic. I didn't care what rules I needed to bend. I never wanted this feeling to be the last.

I grabbed her hips, my fingers digging into her soft skin as I pulled out of her and slammed back in again, making her cry out. The sound unleashed me and I moved faster, clenching her hips tighter, pulling her back onto my cock, driving into her again and again as she slid across the metal workbench.

"Fuck," she moaned, the sound stretching out as I filled her. "Logan. Yes."

I picked up the pace, the sound of her moaning my name spurring me on as I fucked her hard and deep. It was utter torment the last few days, wanting to be back inside her tight pussy. I poured every ounce of that frustration into moving inside her now. She was dripping wet for me, the carnal sounds of our bodies slapping together echoing across the vastness of the room. I couldn't hang on much longer.

I grabbed Lark by the back of the neck and pulled her upright, burying myself deeper inside her as she teetered on her tiptoes. My other hand slipped around to her swollen clit, circling her as she cried out, the sharp sound so loud that I paused, and she let out a groan. Any louder and they'd probably hear us all the way at the rainforest walkthrough, and while I didn't give one flying fuck if everyone heard the way I made Lark come, I knew she would.

I pulled out of her.

"Wh—"

Before her question could even be asked, I spun her around and dropped to my knees, pulling her down with me. She straddled me as I pulled her onto my cock. Her eyes rolled back at the sensation, this angle even deeper than before.

"I want to consume your every sound," I said before dropping my mouth to hers and kissing her roughly as I thrust back up.

Her legs circled around my hips, her arms wrapping around my neck and her fingers twisting in my hair. She bounced up and down, meeting each of my thrusts with a rock of her hips. I greedily pulled one of her breasts from her black lace bra and then the other, needing to see them bouncing as she rode me. She chased her release faster, her breath hitching. My balls tightened and I was desperate to hold on, wanting to come with her. I gripped her face with both hands, letting her ride my cock with wanton abandon as I kissed her deeply, drinking in every one of her ratcheting breaths. Her sounds grew louder, higher, and then with a cry, she shattered, her pussy clamping around me, gripping me so tightly, pulling my release from me as I came.

I growled into her mouth, pumping into her as my orgasm roared through me, riding each wave of pleasure as spurt after spurt spilled from me. It was endless. Time seemed to slow, to bend and warp, the release going on and on until finally, we came down from those shattering heights together.

I swept Lark's hair from her face, my kisses becoming softer, my touches more soothing, coaxing us back into our bodies as that burning lust within us was finally sated. I wanted to stay there, buried inside her all night. I never wanted to return to my body, to the world, to the responsibilities I knew would be waiting for us.

Lark's hazel eyes roved my face, her fingers, still trembling from her release, traced my features, and I wondered if this was the moment. She was so open and raw, her eyes carrying with them such depths. I silently willed her to say it: say the words I was so desperate to say back.

Instead, a faint siren wailed in the distance, growing louder and louder. We both paused, confusion crossing Lark's face as she said, "Is that?"

She stood quickly, and I felt bereft without her warmth. I wanted to pull her back down, to bury my face in her hair and hold her all night, but when she gasped, I stood too. We looked out the window of the kitchens as a boat with flashing red and blue lights sped up to the jetty in the distance.

"Oh my god," Lark said and ran.

STAFF
PRICKLE
ISLAND
ZOO
ZOO

Chapter Forty-Six

Lark

"What happened?" I shouted, bolting down the hill while Logan chased right behind me, pocketing my thong as he ran. I really wished I were in work clothes right now or at least underwear . . . a sports bra even. One of my boobs was about to give me a black eye.

We careened down the hill, spotting the flashing lights of the ambulance boat pulled up to the wharf just below Kangaroo Point.

Two paramedics were rolling someone on a stretcher down to the boat. All of the air was knocked out of my lungs at the sight. Someone was hurt. Someone was hurt so badly that they needed to get *off the island* for emergency medical treatment.

The memory of the day my father died flooded back into me as unfettered panic shot through me like shock waves. I couldn't do it. I couldn't handle losing another person I loved. Was it Mom? Was it Finch? Who was that little dot of a face in the distance being rushed off to the paramedic's boat? How had no one contacted me sooner?

Fuck. Shame burned up my throat. I'd been too busy screwing Logan to do anything else. I'd left my radio in the house and was going back for it when Logan had pulled me into the kitchens. They were all probably trying to contact me. They needed me and I hadn't been there for them.

Thundering toward the spider monkey enclosure, I saw Mom first, then Hawk and Finch, all gathered around the entrance to the primates exhibit. My shoulders eased a little at the sight of them.

"Who's hurt?"

Mom spotted me first and ran over with her hands held out. "It's not one of us. It's not one of us," she repeated, relief washing through me so keenly, I thought I might cry. "Everything's going to be fine, honey." We all knew "everything's fine" was mom code for everything was not at all fine.

I darted around her and then skidded to a halt when I spotted Finch holding a limp spider monkey wrapped in a towel.

"What happened?" I screamed, bridging the distance and seeing it was Jacob in her arms.

"He's okay, Lars," Finch said tightly, her mouth clenched around a syringe cap and anger threading through her normally composed voice. "I've sedated him so I can check him for injuries, but so far, he looks okay. I bet the bastard who grabbed him doesn't though."

My heartbeat drummed so loudly in my ears, I was sure my entire face was pulsing with the rush of blood. "Grabbed him?

What's going on? Why wasn't Jacob inside his enclosure? Did he escape?"

Hawk held up a flashlight, inspecting the outer door to the monkey enclosure. A piece of black fabric hung off the top of the chain-link fence, waving like a flag. "Someone broke into the exhibit."

"What?!" I yelled, so loudly that the troop inside started hooting and whooping again.

"Some drunken party guest broke in," Hawk said. "When I heard the commotion on my way back to the house, I came to check what was going on and a man was screaming bloody murder inside. I managed to get him out and call the ambulance. Where were you? I tried to radio . . ."

My whole face ignited with shame as Logan took a step in front of me and said, "It was my fault."

But my siblings all knew what that meant. I shoved Logan to the side. He might've been trying to take the fall for me but, in doing so, just announced to everyone, including my *mom*, that we'd been fucking.

"How badly was the guy injured?" Logan asked, trying to fill the awkward silence.

I'd put good money on really freaking badly. Monkeys seemed like cute little toys until you were up close with one and they started biting you and ripping your hair out with their little shit-covered hands. Now imagine fifteen of them doing that at once and that was probably what this guy was dealing with.

"I think he broke his leg and dislocated his shoulder trying to get back out," Hawk said. "There was so much blood, it was hard to tell."

"So he jumped the fence," I said, staring at the swath of fabric again. "But then, how did he get the main door open? Did he have wire cutters? Did he break the lock?"

Hawk's face warred between pained and furious as he pinned me with a look. "The door wasn't locked."

All the racing blood drained from my face at that, and I thought I might throw up. I felt like someone had just kicked me out of a helicopter without a parachute, my stomach still free-falling. It was every keeper's worst nightmare, the thing that kept us awake in the middle of the night: trying to remember if we'd locked a door or if we were just recalling locking it the day before. I'd never forgotten a lock. Never. But on the first and only day in my entire life that I did, a bastard decided to check if they could find a way into the monkey enclosure?

"I . . . I'm sorry," I murmured, my voice shaking with adrenaline and restrained tears. I knew an apology wasn't enough. I might lose my job over this. Worse, I'd failed my family.

"Save it for later," Hawk said, angrily pushing past me. "I need to go speak with the police about this. If we thought Westworth was going to sell the zoo before, she's going to be thinking twice as hard about it now."

"I'll go try to smooth things over with the guests," Mom said.

Panicked tears fell from my eyes, my lips wobbling. "I'll go recount and do another perimeter check."

"I'm taking Jacob to the vet hospital to do a proper exam," Finch said. "Meet you there?" I nodded as more tears streaked down my cheeks. "It'll be okay, Lars," she murmured in a way that told me she knew as well as I did that I'd be tormented by this mistake for the rest of my life. "It wasn't as bad as the tiger incident."

Logan waited until she started walking away to ask, "Tiger incident?"

I shook my head, more tears falling, forcing me to cover my face. Now wasn't the time for that story.

Logan stepped into me immediately, his arms sweeping around me in a tight hug. He buried his head in my hair and kissed the top of my head. "Breathe. Breathe," he coached me. "The animals are safe. Your family's safe. You're safe."

A sob shook my whole body, my tears staining his shirt. "But they almost weren't safe. Jacob almost got taken. That piece of shit could've been killed by them, and then we could've had a bunch of police at our doorstep and lose our accreditation. What if he left the door open and they all ran away and got hurt and—"

Logan gripped me by the chin with his hand and tilted my face up to meet his as his lips pressed onto mine. It was a warm, arresting kiss, the kind that quieted the other parts of my mind long enough for me to take a single deep breath.

"I need to go count them again," I said, my lips wobbling against his. "I need to fix this. My family depends on me and I let them down. I need to make this right with them."

"You will," he murmured against my mouth and pulled me into one more quick, burning kiss, his arms around me feeling like the safest place in the world. Even when he released me, he kept a reassuring hand on my back and walked with me toward the exhibit. That feeling of his hand was the one quiet spot, the one tiny shred of peace through the hurricane raging inside me.

STAFF
PRICKLE ISLAND ZOO
ZOO

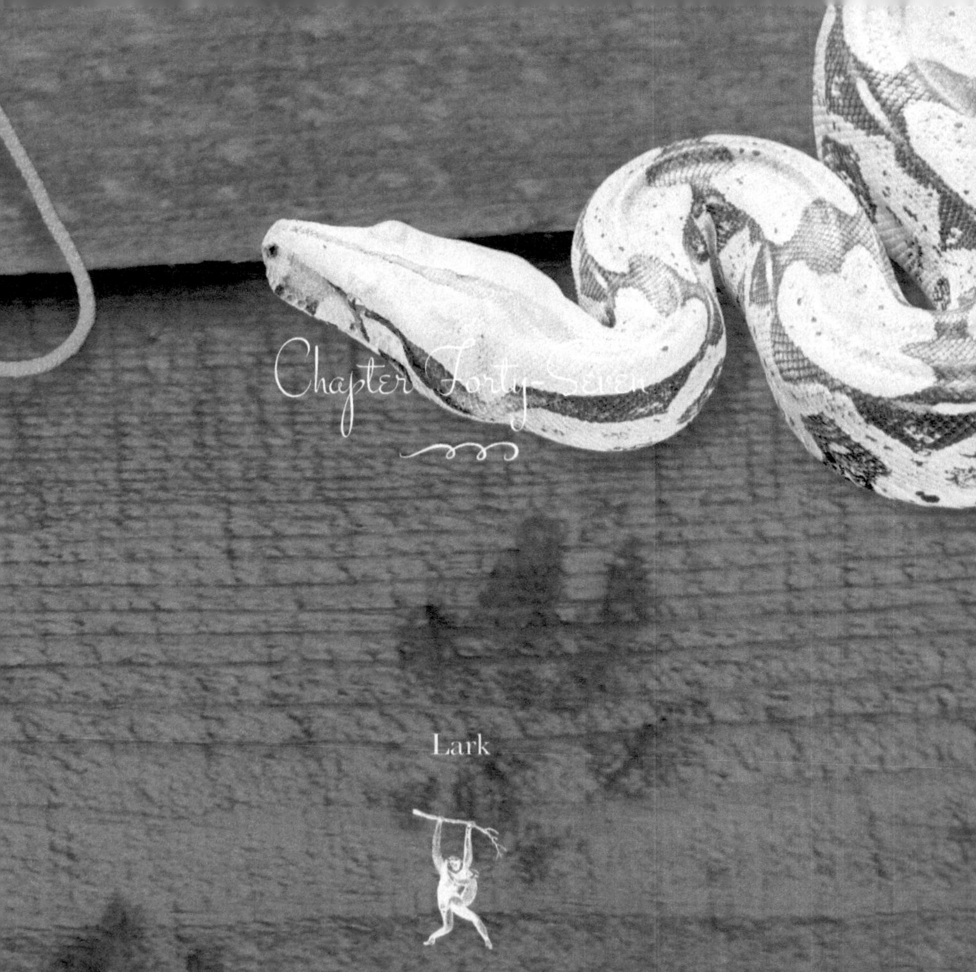

Logan and Finch worked together to coax me out of the monkey exhibit to Mom's house for a very late post-gala dinner. Jacob was still in rough condition, and Finch was worried he somehow sustained a concussion when that piece of shit grabbed him. Luckily, the Westworths were going to be filing charges against him and they had the best lawyers in the entire country, so I felt confident that he would be punished for hurting Jacob and scaring the life out of the rest of the troop . . . but it also meant I would need to give testimony and be scrutinized by dozens of people. I would be reliving this awful night for a long time.

"People are really clueless," Crane muttered, passing the

pasta bowl down the table. "Probably thought he would make a cute pet."

The break-in had become the main topic of conversation over the family dinner, understandably, but I muttered, "Can we *please* talk about something else?"

There'd been many times over the years that I thought one of the mistakes of my siblings would be the reason the zoo got taken from us . . . but I never thought I'd be amongst them. As Logan's hand gave my knee another squeeze, I shifted in my chair and pulled out of his touch. This would've never happened if I hadn't been so distracted with him. I was acting foolish and irrational and so not myself.

Logan hid the look of discontentment as I edged away from him, but I could tell from the way he studied his Caesar salad like the *Mona Lisa* was painted on it that he was hurt by the action. There was a reason I'd said "only in Guatemala," and this, *this* was the reason and had come to bite me in the ass.

"So, Logan," Mom said, breezily changing the subject with the air of someone who'd been a front-facing zoo manager for over four decades. "Tell us about you."

I clenched my hand tighter around my fork, spearing my croutons and praying that my family didn't interrogate him.

He shrugged. "There's not much to say."

"I doubt that," Dove said with a smile, propping her elbow on the table and resting her chin in her hand like she was a swooning princess. "You seem plenty interesting to me."

"Garlic bread?" Mom quickly interjected, passing the tray to Logan while Finch yanked Dove's elbow off the table.

Hawk leaned over toward Logan from the other side and started asking him about the All Blacks. I was grateful to my brother in that moment for rescuing me.

"Seriously?" Finch scowled at our little sister while Logan

was distracted while talking to Hawk. "He's obviously with Lark. Will you cut it out?"

Crane shrugged. "Yeah, but Lark's going to mess it up like she always does, and then Dove will sweep in."

I placed both hands on the table and leaned across it. "Will you stop being such a child?" I snarled at Crane so quietly, the words barely made a sound. "If you say one more word, I'll stab you with my fork." The irony wasn't lost on me that that was a rather childish thing to say . . .

"Careful, Lars, or I'll put maggots in your bed."

"You've already done that," I hissed.

Crane shrugged. "Again."

Being in charge of the reptiles and invertebrates at the zoo meant Crane was also in charge of keeping a steady supply of mealworms and maggots coming for all of his animals. If he ever became a serial killer—which some days, I still wondered about—his calling card would definitely be a pile of maggots. He'd ruined a lot of perfectly nice dates for me and all of my siblings by slipping a handful of them in our pockets.

"If you do that, then I'm keeping Matilda and never returning her to reptiles." His mouth fell open at that, and I nodded. "Yeah, that's right. You heard me."

"Bitch," Crane muttered and went back to eating.

I wasn't sure how many siblings threatened to keep a boa constrictor as punishment, but I knew where to cut to the core of my little brother, and Matilda was it. He'd already been perfecting her exhibit, getting the substrate and humidity just right, growing the plants . . . but if I decided she wasn't "ready" for her big day on display, then he and I both knew that everyone would side with me—the ridiculously responsible one . . . well, on every day of my life apart from today.

Heron tossed me the bag of parmesan cheese. It had been

their job to set the table and they decided that it would make less work for everyone if the cheese wasn't put into a serving bowl. "I still can't believe you, of all people, forgot to lock a door," they said. Mom swatted them with the dish towel. "What? It's true."

The panic of what could have happened gripped me all over again and Logan's hand found my knee under the table and squeezed. I pulled away again.

"That's enough, Heron Lachlan," Mom said, her eyebrows lifting into her hairline in a facial expression that, if she were a baboon, would've been called "flashing." "Need I remind you of the time I woke up to find a zebra's head sticking through my kitchen window, licking the dirty dishes in the sink?"

Crane burst into laughter. "Oh, yeah."

"Or the time we nearly had to call the conservation department because you thought you left the praying mantis terrarium open, Crane?"

Crane instantly sobered. "We found all three of them still inside the house, Mom. It wasn't the same."

"It could've been just as bad for us," Mom chided.

Dove, to my surprise, added, "Remember when Monty got out during that storm and it took us two weeks to catch him?"

The whole table—except a bewildered Logan—groaned in unison. That had been a really rough two weeks. It had been springtime when all the trees were freshly green, and trying to find a military macaw hiding in them was like trying to find a needle in a haystack. We'd set up bait traps all over the zoo, trying to get him down, and had someone tailing him constantly for two whole weeks all around the island before one day, we woke up to find him back in his enclosure like nothing had happened. Needless to say, we were a lot more careful about macaw-proof locks after that.

"And don't get me started on Finch," Mom continued. "I still have nightmares about the ferry incident."

All of my siblings started laughing, and even I was forced to crack a smile.

"What happened on the ferry?" Logan asked.

"Finch was probably eleven or twelve at the time and thought she would take one of the meerkats with us on our trip to New Haven," Mom said, eyeing Finch and shaking her head.

"No!" Logan gawked around the table at all of us stifling giggles.

"The meerkat was burrowed up the sleeve of her puffy jacket, and she thought no one would notice until—"

"Until he wanted to get out and started burrowing in my armpit," Finch continued, her whole body shaking as she tried to contain her laughter.

"People were staring at you jumping around all strangely," Hawk added with a chuckle.

"So we played it off as an impromptu family dance party." Mom had tears of laughter streaming down her face, and my abs hurt from laughing so hard.

"That Lady Gaga song was playing on the ferry radio," I said, rubbing my cheeks. "We all looked ridiculous trying to copy Finch's 'dance moves.'"

Mom shrugged as she wiped under her eyes with a napkin. "Nobody ever knew, just thought we were that strange zoo family."

"We *are* that strange zoo family." Finch cackled.

The whole table was laughing so hard that we could barely breathe, trying to take sips of water and fan ourselves and wipe tears out of our eyes. That was the power of our family. When we joined forces, we were ridiculous but strong, and we made it out of that incident without anyone finding out about the stowaway meerkat. We teased and we taunted. Sometimes, we were downright mean, but we always had each other's backs.

"We survived all of those things. Just as your grandparents and the ones before them did," Mom said, finally able to catch her breath from her laughing fit. "We'll survive this too." She met my eyes. "Together."

STAFF
PRICKLE
ISLAND
ZOO
ZOO

Chapter Forty-Eight

Lark

"Your family is lovely," Logan said, putting his hands in his pockets as he walked beside me. "Wilder than any animal in the zoo, but lovely."

"Uh-huh," was my only reply as I rushed down the path, forcing Logan to trail me like he had his first weeks at the zoo.

"What's wrong?" he asked as he hustled after me.

Everything. Everything was wrong.

"I mean," he added hastily, "besides the incident. Are you okay?" He reached for my elbow. "Talk to me."

I moved out of his touch and kept speed-walking downhill where to, I didn't know. I just needed to keep moving forward, to keep moving *away*, to put some distance between me and the pain I already felt from the words I needed to say.

Guilt. Lust. Shame. Desire. They all coalesced into one now.

"Lark," he said. "Tails. Come on, talk to me."

Tears pinpricked my eyes. A burning invisible hand squeezed my windpipe, and I coughed roughly. "You know why the door was left unlocked?"

"Because you're human," Logan said, jogging now to keep up with me. "Because everyone makes mistakes."

"I don't!" I barked. "I don't make mistakes. Not like this."

Logan bolted in front of me, placing his hand on my belly to stop me from racing forward. Even then, as he crowded into my space, I wanted him and knew I'd never allow myself to have him again.

"Please. Tell me what's going on."

"All I could think about this whole week was *you*," I rasped. Logan bent down to kiss me, and I yanked away. "Don't," I commanded, and his eyes brimmed with pain, as if he already knew what I was going to say. "I was more focused on fucking you than doing my job. You distracted me, and there is no room for error around here or bad things happen—lives could be lost."

Logan's brows pinched together. "You blame me for what happened to Jacob?"

"I don't blame you," I snapped, an angry blush prickling across my face. "I blame *me*. I should've known better." I balled my hands into fists. "We said only in Guatemala. It was a rule for a reason. This is what happens when we break the rules."

"It was just a mistake, tails."

"Don't call me that." I hated myself more with every angry word. "Whatever this was, Logan, should've ended the second we got on that plane. I had to learn the hard way, even though I knew better. It's over now."

"No—" Logan's voice cracked, and I swore I'd never forget the sound.

"Tomorrow, you'll be on Heron's run. I can't have you around me anymore." I swallowed, willing the tears not to well in my eyes. I knew if I started crying, I'd never be able to go through with this. He'd wrap me up in his arms and I wouldn't ever be able to step away. I forced resolve into my voice as I said, "I can't keep thinking about you more than I think about anything else."

He stepped back into me, moving me backward until I was pressed against the brick wall behind me. I forced myself to crane my neck up at him as he loomed over me, making him believe I meant every hateful word.

"Please don't do this," Logan pleaded, searching my gaze for a spark of hope. "Come on. It doesn't have to be like this. I'll double-check locks with you. I—"

"My family needs me," I said resolutely. "The animals I care for depend on me. I can't be distracted with some random summer fling."

As his eyes welled and he shook his head, I wondered if he, too, was thinking about that moment in Guatemala when our gazes locked as our bodies joined and we both knew then for certain what this was. We both knew . . . and I'd called him a random summer fling just to hurt him.

"It could be more than that, Lark," Logan whispered, his hand splaying across my belly as his head dipped.

"No." I stepped around his body and out of his hold. His hand drifted toward me but didn't reach out for me again. "This job. This family. This zoo. I can't fuck this up. *This* is all I have."

"It doesn't have to be all you have!" he shouted. His face

fell more with every step I took backward, away from him, until he was left in the floodlight of the kitchens and I disappeared into the shadows. "Please."

His breathless final plea made me want to fall to my knees, to beg him to take all of my doubts away, to kiss me until I forgot why we were fighting, but instead, I said, "Goodbye, Logan," and walked away, choking back tears.

STAFF
PRICKLE ISLAND ZOO
ZOO

I sat perched on a stack of boxes filled with zoo flyers from two years ago that now doubled as litter substrate under the nesting boxes. Nothing went to waste here. I bounced my knee, listening as Hawk relayed the same story to the fifth police officer.

"Okay, okay, uh-huh, right." He set the phone down and jazzy saxophone music rang out from the receiver.

"Hold again?" I groaned, rubbing my eyes. Every time Hawk had to recount what happened the night of the gala, my soul died a little bit . . . especially the part about *me* leaving the door unlocked. I knew my brother couldn't lie to the police, but every time he said it, I wanted to leap off the boxes and run to the phone and word vomit all over the officers about how it was an accident and it would never happen again and I'd ended things with the reason for that distraction. I was better than that . . . normally.

I tried to ignore the white-hot pain in my heart—the giant Logan-shaped hole that had been there since our conversation. How was I going to face him without bursting into tears? Everything felt so sensitive, like the tiniest thing could tip me over the edge and I'd be crying again.

I tried to hide my devastation from my siblings, but they all clearly knew. Hawk had moved Logan to Heron's run, which already felt really awkward, but at least I hadn't seen him around yet. Surprisingly, Heron decided to pause being a chaos demon and very strategically switched their shift so that Logan was always at the opposite end of the zoo to me. Heron, of course, would never admit it was for me, but I knew.

Still, I couldn't just ignore Logan forever. At some point, we'd bump into each other. Something had happened to us during our trip. We drifted from casual hookup to something more without even knowing. At least this horrible break-in could distract me from having the crushed look on Logan's face occupying every one of my thoughts.

"Bureaucracy at its finest," Hawk said, stretching his arms over his head. "You don't have to be here for this, Lark."

"I know," I said, my knee still jiggling. Technically, it was my lunch break, but I couldn't handle waiting to hear what was happening with the break-in. Would the man even be charged? Would the Prickle Island Zoo be splashed all over the local newspapers? Would everyone think worse of my family's legacy because of my mistake?

"How's Jacob?" Hawk asked, and I knew it was his way of trying to nudge me out the door.

"I just came from the clinic," I said, shooting him a "nice

try, asshole" look. Hawk's shoulders drooped. He wouldn't be getting rid of me that easily. "We had to pull him from the troop again last night. He's still acting strange and the others were picking on him. Finch said she'd run some more tests but . . . short of an MRI, we won't know for sure."

"Do you want me to call my friends at Yale?"

I rolled my eyes. Hawk loved saying he had friends at Yale. We'd had to do an MRI for one of the ocelots and it was all over the news. It got a lot of publicity for the zoo, but it also cost us a bajillion dollars.

"Could we even afford it?" I asked, and Hawk frowned. "I doubt Mrs. Westworth will fork up the funds when it was *my* mistake that got him injured in the first place."

"I don't think that's how she's going to punish us."

Were we going to be punished? Mrs. Westworth had been furious when she heard the news. She'd threatened—*once again* —to sell the zoo that my great-great-grandfather built to Gaz fucking Madigan, and anyone who was permitted to stay on as a Madigan employee would have to follow his rules, which would probably include his kind of drama-filled reality TV show.

You know, when over the course of a few seasons, you go from mostly normal zookeepers with minor drama to Kardashian wannabes in full makeup and having fake chaos plastered across the screen every single episode. No zoo had as much drama as the Madigan Mountain Zoo. If even half of it were true, the government would've shut them down ages ago.

We watched that evolution happen with the Madigan family, much to the delight of most of the world but in horror to us. Now, the eldest Madigan daughter had an animal-themed yoga pants line—which, yes, fine, I did own three pairs because they were really freaking comfortable—and the eldest son's face was on everything from barbecues to toilet cleaning products. They *did* manage to single-handedly buy a huge chunk of protected rainforest larger than the size of Connecticut from a palm oil plantation developer with that money though, so . . . maybe there was some method to their madness after all. Still, I could barely take the scrutiny of one person, let alone millions of weekly viewers.

"You okay?" Hawk asked. I looked up to see him studying my face. "About Logan?"

"I don't want to talk about it," I said roughly, afraid if I even said his name, I might cry. This pain was still too new. I couldn't let anyone see or touch the rawness that I felt right then. Everything felt like it was crashing down around me, worsened even more by the fact that I'd failed to do the one thing in my life I was confident in: being good at my job. "I won't let a guy, of all people, distract me from my job again."

Hawk's brows pinched together, and he opened his mouth to say more when a grizzled, bored voice came back on the phone. The jazz music abruptly halted as Hawk picked up the phone again. "Yes, hello," he said, drumming his fingers on the desk in annoyance. "Yep, sure." He put the phone back down and the jazz music rang back to life.

"Seriously?"

"Why don't you go do something else?" Hawk offered. "You helicoptering over me is not making this any easier."

"Do you think they'll charge him? Will they punish me for it?" I rubbed a hand down my face. "Do I need to be on observation to make sure I'm doing my job correctly?"

"Lars." Hawk gave me that "stop being totally unhinged" older brother look.

A red light on the old beige phone blinked—a call from another line. Hawk switched it over and put on his forced customer service voice. "Thank you for calling Prickle Island Zoo. This is Hawk speaking. How can I help you?" I mimed dry heaving at his fake voice, and Hawk flipped me the bird. "Oh," he said, his smile faltering. He kept listening, his face growing more concerned. My pulse picked up speed as I watched his happy mask slip. I knew that face, and I knew whatever was being said to him was something really bad. "Okay. Okay. I'm so sorry. Alright. Okay. I'll tell him. Right. Okay. Bye."

Hawk switched back to the other line, the jazz music still playing, as he shot up from his chair.

"What was that—"

Hawk cut me off, pointing to his office chair. "You talk to the cops," he said.

"What!" I exclaimed as he ran to the door. "What's going on?"

"I need to go do something," he growled, pointing at the phone emphatically one more time before racing out the door.

I stared, blinking at the weighted door as it slowly pulled shut behind him. What was that about? And why couldn't he tell me? My anxiety doubled in size as I stared at the door and then back to the phone.

When a brand-new officer picked up, my whole body slumped forward like a puppet whose strings had been cut. I guessed it was my turn to recount the story of the worst mistake of my life.

PRICKLE
ISLAND
ZOO
Volunteer

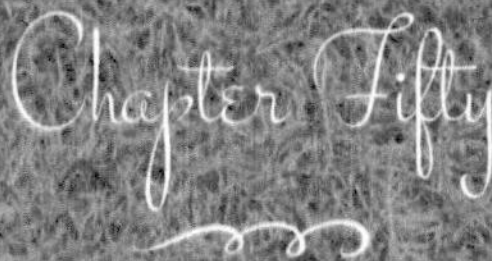

Chapter Fifty

Logan

I sat on the splintering wharf, looking out at the roiling Atlantic Ocean. The sky was filled with a gray haze as a summer storm rolled in. The spray from the choppy waves misted against my legs from where they dangled off the wharf. I stared down at my phone in my hands, turning it over a few times as Hawk's words replayed in my mind. The moment I saw him running toward me, that look in his eyes, I knew.

This was it. The end of my adventure. Time to go home.

Finally, I summoned the courage to unlock my phone and ring my mum. Hawk had offered me use of the office phone, but I wanted to be far away from the other volunteers and especially far away from one person in particular in case I couldn't contain my emotions. The roaming bill would be astronomical, but I needed this call to be private.

My heart drummed away in my chest as the line finally connected and Mum picked up on the first ring.

"Logan," she said by way of greeting, and the way her voice went down at the end, I knew it was bad. "We need you to come home, son."

"What happened?"

Mum paused, her heavy breath crackling down the line, as if even now she couldn't bring herself to say it. "Your father had another heart attack."

"Another?" I shouted, gripping the phone so tightly, I thought I might crush it beneath my hand. "When did he have his *first* heart attack, Mum?" I knew it. I knew this was what they were hiding from me.

"Two years ago," Mum said.

"Seriously? Seriously, Mum?" I offloaded all the last two years of fear and anger, wondering why Dad had looked so unwell, why they kept excusing his absences and making up stories about it just being a stomach bug. "This was what you were keeping from me?"

"We didn't want you to worry—"

"Well, I did worry!" I barked. "I worried constantly! I just didn't know about what!"

"He had some complications with his surgery, Logan," she said, and my whole body went numb with fear.

"Is he . . . Is he okay?"

"He's hanging in there right now, darling . . . You know how stubborn he is." Mum's voice cracked, and my eyes filled with angry tears at the sound. "They don't—" She sucked in a sharp breath. "They don't know when he'll be back on his feet though." I heard the unspoken "if" in her words. "It's going to be a long road to recovery."

I pinched my eyes, pushing so hard I saw spots, as if I could shove the tears back into the sockets. "Why didn't you tell me about this sooner? Why did you let me come here?"

"He didn't want to hold you back," Mum said. "After your breakup with Kelly, we both thought a little travel would do you some good."

"I wanted to move home straight away and help with the café, but you let me come here," I gritted out. "If I had been there, maybe Dad would've rested instead of worked himself into another heart attack!"

I could hear the heartbreak in Mum's voice as she said, "This isn't your fault, Logan."

"You let me go," I cried. Tears slipped down my cheeks and dripped off the end of my nose, and I knew some of them weren't just for my father and the fear of something happening to him. No, as I pulled the phone away from my ear, I saw my lock screen—the selfie I took of Lark sleeping on my shoulder—and let out a broken sob. "I should be there with you right now, and I'm all the way around the world—"

"We thought we had it under control—"

"Bullshit!"

"Logan," Mum scolded, as if I were a child again. Even now, she couldn't help herself. "We wanted to make sure it was something worth worrying about before we made a big fuss about it."

"You would've waited until he was dead," I muttered. "I might not even have had a chance to say goodbye. You let him go into that surgery without me even knowing." I stood up, my shirt whipping out behind me as it caught a gust of wind. "I'm getting on the first flight out of here," I said. "I'll text you the details. I gotta go pack." I wanted to hang up right then and there, but I forced myself to add, "I love you, Mum. Tell Dad I love him too and to hang in there for me."

"Love you," Mum said. "We'll see you in a few days."

The *we* brought me a little comfort, as if my mother's confidence would be enough to make it true. I prayed Dad would be out of the hospital and back home by the time I arrived. Wiping my tears with my sleeve, I tried to huff in a few breaths to steady myself as I roughly shoved my phone back into my pocket. I needed to change the lock screen again.

When I turned, I found Hawk's red pickup truck parked at the end of the wharf.

I quickly made my way down to him, knowing he wouldn't judge me for my blotchy face and red-ringed eyes. "Wh-what are you doing?" I called to him.

He leaned out the window. "I took the liberty of grabbing all your things," he said, hooking a thumb toward the back seat. "You need a ride to the ferry?"

"You're a bloody saint, Hawk," I said, clearing my throat again, trying to keep it from wobbling. But Mum had told Hawk enough that Hawk knew the seriousness of what was happening too.

I was grateful to him right then for that first week when he let me prep diets in the kitchens with him. He and I had become good friends in such a short space of time. I realized that by leaving, I wouldn't just lose the woman who held my heart. I'd be losing this friendship with him too. Everything these last several weeks had meant to me was all falling like sand through my fingertips now.

"She's going to meet us at the ferry terminal," Hawk said, his voice quieting as I closed the distance to the truck. I already knew which "she" he was referring to and it made an invisible rubber band tighten around my chest.

"I don't know if I can talk to her right now." My shoulders tensed, and I wondered if he'd told her everything.

"I asked her to bring down some of the boxes that we need

to mail to the mainland," Hawk said. "You can't just disappear without saying goodbye to her. However things are with you two is between you and Lark but . . . you'll regret not saying goodbye."

I hung my head as I reached the truck. He was right.

I opened the passenger door and slid in. My backpack was all lumpy and misshapen, as if it had been hastily packed. I guessed I'd be traveling in work boots and khaki shorts back to New Zealand . . .

"Hey, do me a favor?" I asked as I slammed the door closed and looked at Hawk.

"Anything," he said with a shrug.

"I'll say goodbye, but don't tell Lark about why I'm leaving," I said.

"I haven't, but . . ." He frowned as he shifted the truck into gear and started driving around the coastal road. "But you're not going to tell her?"

"I wanted her to come with me," I hedged, watching as Hawk's hands gripped the steering wheel tighter. "But now . . . it's clear she's made her choice. If I tell her my father's not doing well, she might just say yes out of guilt or obligation. I don't want to manipulate her into a yes."

"I think there's a difference between honesty and manipulation," Hawk said carefully.

"I can't be the guy that says 'move halfway around the world with me because my dad is sick,'" I pushed. "I can't do that to her. It's clear she doesn't want to come with me, even if she feels half as much for me as I do for her."

Hawk sighed. "You're a good guy, Logan."

"Do you hate me for wanting her to come with me?"

"No," Hawk said. "If anything, I'm sad that she made the choice she did. I mean, I'd miss her. We'd all miss her. We'd have to hire someone to take over her shifts. Hell, we'd probably have to hire *three* people to take over her shifts." I chuckled and nodded in agreement. "But the way she looked at you . . ." I hated the way he said "looked," like it was already long in the past. It still didn't feel over to me, which made it all hurt even more. "She was happy with you. I don't want to be the one telling her to throw away the first thing that's lit her up like that in years."

The truck pulled around the bend, the little strip of Prickle Island shops coming into view in the distance. We passed the Salty Dog and the spot along the path where Lark had ambush-kissed me those many weeks ago. God, it felt like a year ago. More maybe. Something about us had felt inevitable from the moment I first laid eyes on her . . . even if her arm was up a drainage pipe.

"Ask her again," Hawk said.

"What?"

"Ask her to come with you again."

"I . . ." I shook my head.

"She was upset the night of the gala," Hawk continued. "Being the best keeper is her way of making sense of the world. What happened to Jacob devastated her, but she didn't realize you'd be leaving when she said all of those things. If she knew you'd be gone today, maybe it would've been different."

"Do you think she'd come with me?" I asked, the tiniest spark of hope flashing back to life within me.

Hawk's fingers tapped out a rhythm along the steering wheel. "There's only one way to find out," he said, nodding to the little spot on the horizon.

Lark sat on the seawall in her work uniform, two boxes beside her, as she watched the ferry taxi in. My heart flipped at the sight of her, and as we drew nearer, more details of her came into view. Tendrils of her hair had escaped her ponytail and were whipping across her face as she idly kicked her legs.

She looked beautiful, contemplative, vulnerable . . . I mean, she always looked beautiful, but this was different: catching her so in her element when she thought no one was looking. It wasn't the sharp, sudden impact of her half-naked in a hotel room or the jaw-dropping looks of her gala dress. This was just Lark, exactly as she was, and God help me, I loved her.

Nerves banded around my chest again, tightening their grip on me as we drew closer.

"Our dad isn't around anymore to ask any sort of permission or anything, not that Lark would ever allow that," Hawk said as he rolled into a parking spot and cut the engine. "And I don't think you're planning on getting down on one knee or anything. But I'd give you my blessing one day, Logan, for what it's worth."

I leaned over and gave Hawk a giant bear hug. He clapped me on the back with a laugh.

"Good luck, brother," he said. "I hope your dad recovers quickly."

"Thanks, mate," I said, giving him one last shake by the shoulder and opening the truck door. I grabbed the pack out of my seat and turned to go ask the girl I loved one last time to run away with me.

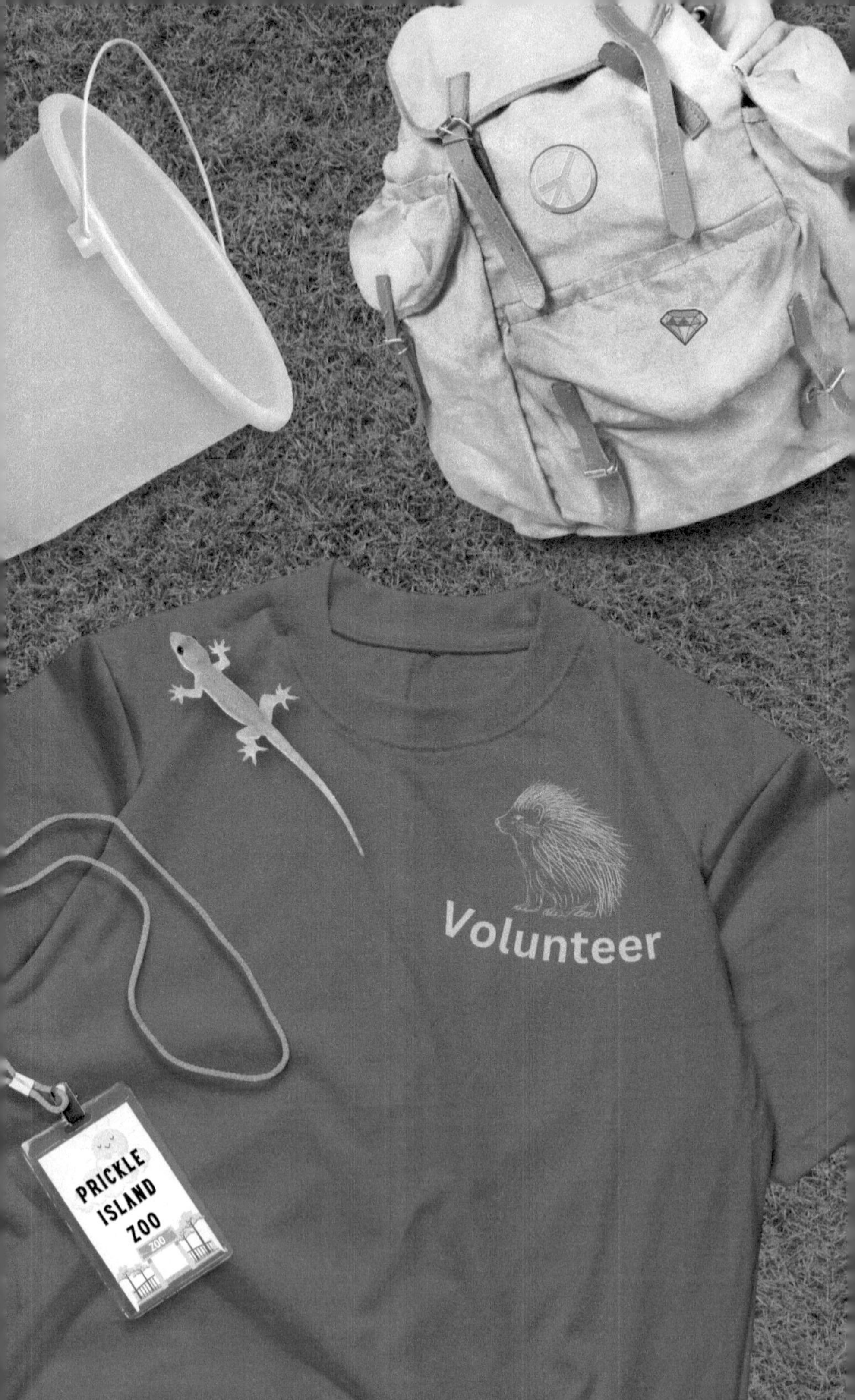
Volunteer
PRICKLE
ISLAND
ZOO
ZOO

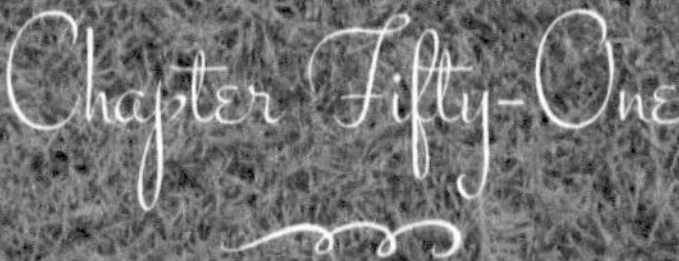

Chapter Fifty-One

Logan

I hated the way Lark did her best not to look in my direction, even though she'd clearly seen Hawk's pickup. I hated even more the way her face fell when she spotted my pack slung over my shoulder. The same pack we'd hiked through jungles together with. The one we'd shared as a makeshift seat on many hot days in Guatemala. Now, it was free from the red dust and clusters of insects and smell of humid jungle air, but still, those memories were so inextricably intertwined with the woman standing in front of me, I knew I'd never be able to think of the country without thinking of her.

"What's going on?" Lark's eyes darted between my face,

the pack on my shoulder, and Hawk's truck pulling out of the parking lot. "What happened? What's wrong?"

She spoke as if she'd forgotten everything she'd said the night of the gala. The concern in her voice seemed to supersede the knowledge that she'd wanted us to go our separate ways. I clung onto that flicker of hope as I held out placating hands to her, holding her by both shoulders to steady her. The zing of her warmth under my fingertips eased my nerves.

"I need to go home," I said to her slowly, crouching down a little to meet her worried hazel eyes. "There's an issue with my family, and I need to go back."

Issue was putting it lightly, but I really didn't want to get into all of it. I knew she'd just panic more on my behalf. The chaos of the last few days caught up with me, and my words got lodged in my throat for a second. *Come on, Logan. Just ask her.*

"I want you to come with me to New Zealand," I said, wanting to cry and drop to my knees and pull her against me but, instead, just letting the statement hang between us.

I love you. I need you. Please.

I couldn't bring myself to say the words—to guilt her into coming with me. I couldn't let her know how scared I was, how desperate I was to have her by my side as I went through all this shit with my dad. I needed her hand in mine. I needed the way she rested her cheek on my shoulder. I needed her comforting words and lavender scent and the unwavering presence of her love. And I wanted to spend my life making her feel as safe and warm and loved as she made me feel.

"What?" Tears welled in her eyes as her hands found my forearms.

"Come with me," I said, trying to not sound pleading. "Come visit New Zealand. See my home. Let's go have another adventure together."

"I . . . I can't just go," she said, shaking her head.

"You might need to organize visas and things, but a visitor's one won't take long and—"

"I can't just leave!" Lark yanked out of my grip and stared at me wide-eyed. "Even if I wanted to."

A hard lump formed in my throat. "Do you want to?"

Please say yes. Please say yes.

"The call Hawk got in the office." Lark's gaze drifted to my shoulder strap. "Is this what that call was about?"

"Yes."

"Tell me what's going on," she demanded. "You can't ask me to fly to another country with you and not be honest with me."

The way she said it was like a kick to the gut. It all came crashing down on me at once. I was doing the exact same thing to Lark that my parents had just done to me: keeping her in the dark, trying to protect her from the truth, trying not to tell her I needed her in the fear it would guilt her into making a choice she didn't want to make. But I wished I'd known about Dad. I wished they'd let me feel that pain and make my own choices with all the information.

I cleared my throat, trying not to cry as I said, "My dad had a heart attack. Another one." All the blood drained from Lark's face, and I knew she was reliving her own father's passing. I hated that I was the one to put those memories back to the front of her mind. "There were complications with his surgery and . . . they don't know when, or if, he'll be back to normal . . ." My bottom lip wobbled, and I clenched my jaw so hard, I thought the muscle might rip in two.

Lark shot forward, wrapping me in the hug I so desperately needed. I buried my face in her hair and let the tears I'd been holding in fall. My hands fisted into the fabric of her shirt as I fell apart, feeling like I didn't need to explain any further for her to understand.

She swept that soothing hand down my back. "I'm so sorry," she murmured into my chest, and I felt the wetness of her tears stain through my shirt. I banded my arms around her tighter and breathed in the smell of her hair.

"I have to go," I choked out.

She nodded into my chest. "Of course you do. I understand."

"I want you to come with me," I whispered, my voice cracking.

Lark pulled away again, and my fingers pressed into her soft flesh for an extra second, as if relishing the feel of her one last time. I knew what she was going to say by the look on her face before she even said it. I knew through the tears and the pinch in her brows and the look of utter devastation.

"I can't go with you," she said, her tears now clearly not just for me but for her own broken heart too. "My family needs me here. We just had a break-in and the Westworths are two seconds from selling the place, and it's impossible to find staff, and there's no money to——"

"It's okay," I said, stepping into her and wrapping her back in a hug even though nothing—*nothing*—about any of this felt okay. "I understand."

"I'm sorry," she cried, holding me tightly again. "I'm sorry, Logan."

"No worries, tails," I said, dropping a kiss to the top of her head. "We always knew it would end like this."

God, I had been such a fool thinking she would actually say yes and drop her entire life and all of her responsibilities to come with me. I knew this would happen. I shouldn't feel like I was shattering into a million scattered pieces. It was my own damn fault.

I wanted to tell her I loved her, wanted to tell her that she was *my* person, but I knew that would only make this a thousand times harder for both of us.

The ferry horn blasted. The sky was still gray, and the old skipper waddled down the docks to collect the boxes Lark had brought down to the terminal in his yellow rain suit despite there not being a drizzle—he seemed to know better than us.

She gave me one last tight squeeze and said, "You should go. I'm sending your dad all of my well wishes right now. Message me when you get there and let me know how he is."

I nodded and wiped the tears from my eyes. I adjusted the pack on my shoulders and took two steps from her before turning back around, grabbing her by the forearm, and yanking her into one last, burning kiss.

She let out a cry as our lips fused, her hands cupping my face. We melted together into a kiss that I hoped would tell her everything: I want you. I love you. I'll miss you. Goodbye.

STAFF
PRICKLE ISLAND ZOO
ZOO

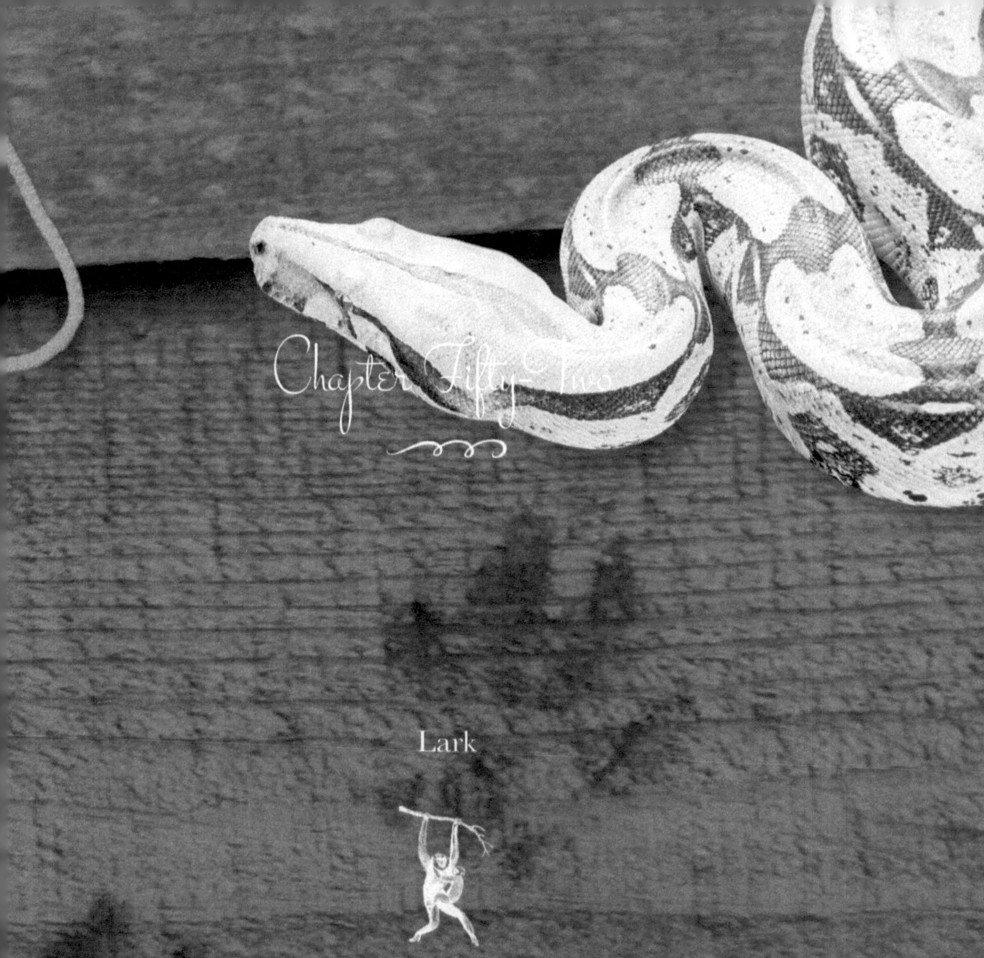

Chapter Fifty-Two

Lark

I kept myself so immersed in work, I couldn't think of anything else. I'd replanted enclosures, reorganized the food storage, and squeegeed every freaking window in the entire zoo. If I was too exhausted to think about *him*, then he never existed. I refused to pick apart that logic.

My siblings clearly knew what I was doing but let me keep going, processing through hard work just as I always had. I exempted myself from the next Sunday Funday Fondue Day and tried to speak to my siblings as little as possible. I knew at some point, something had to give, but right then, I could at least pretend that I was coping. I would pretend I was okay until I was. I'd done it the last time my world fell apart, and I could do it again.

As I walked double-pace through the pavilion, the sight of my reflection in the enclosure glass made me pause. I looked at the person staring back at me: purple half-moons under her eyes, greasy hair in a messy bun, stains on a shirt she hadn't bothered to change in three days. I could walk as fast as I wanted, work as hard as I wanted, but she . . . she wasn't looking great.

Still, the eyes, the nose, the mouth, even the uniform. I looked so much like my dad when he was my age. I hadn't really thought about that before. Strange to think about it now when I looked like an absolute dumpster fire. But it was there —a little piece of my father in me.

"What now?" A voice groaned.

I glanced over to see Crane hiking up the steps to the pavilion, scrubbing a hand down his face. It was only then I realized I'd stopped in front of the enclosure he'd designed for Matilda. I knew my brother was already on the defensive about it . . . and I knew it was my fault. I'd made him feel that way. Not because he was doing a bad job, but because I felt like I needed to be doing a good one.

The memories of the break-in, Logan leaving, and the aftermath hit me like a wave. I balled my cracking hands into fists, the skin red from scrubbing too many buckets. I couldn't keep acting like this, like a one-woman show. Too much of who I was had gotten wrapped up in this job, and it was breaking me.

I thought about what Logan told me the day we hiked that mountain in Guatemala: *I think you're working yourself raw trying to make someone proud and that someone isn't you.*

I glanced back at my reflection as a hot brick formed in my

throat. This wasn't what my dad would've wanted for me. He would've hated me breaking myself for his legacy.

"I've got the temperature perfect," Crane continued, closing the distance between us. "The plants are just right. I built this awning for the winter sun angles and—"

"It's ready," I said.

Crane stumbled a step backward. "What?"

"It's ready." I shrugged. "It's been ready. *I* haven't been ready." I cleared my throat to shake the wobble out of it as I looked at my little brother. "I'm sorry I made you feel like it wasn't good enough. You're a great keeper, Crane."

Crane's gray eyes widened, his brows bunching together. "Who are you and what have you done with my sister?"

"I know I've been too controlling. I thought I'd found a healthy way of coping with everything." I sniffed and looked back at the sad woman in the glass. "But I don't really think that's true anymore. I just wanted you to know I'm trying not to be like that."

Crane shifted his weight back and forth, clearly uncomfortable with this sudden burst of emotions. He finally settled on cracking a grin. "So does that mean I can start the gecko breeding program—"

"I'm still a little controlling," I corrected, wiping my eyes and smiling at him. "Baby steps."

He chuckled. "Baby steps." He stopped fidgeting and took three steps toward me and wrapped his lanky arms around me. It took all of the willpower I had left to not sob in his arms. "Thank you."

I hugged him back just as tightly, a silent conversation seeming to pass between us. His chin rested on top of my head, and I couldn't believe he was tall enough to do that now. It felt like just yesterday, he and Heron were in diapers, and now he was a full-grown man.

"It's going to be okay, you know?" he added, and I nodded into his shoulder.

"Who died?" Finch's voice called.

Crane and I ended our hug and turned to look at her. "No one died," he said, rolling his eyes and turning into a teenager again.

"So . . ." Finch gestured between us. "You two are just hugging of your own volition?"

Hawk walked through the pavilion, and I noticed that both he and Finch were wearing their zoo jackets—the ones that they only wore to special events when they were trying to look presentable.

"Where are you two going?" I asked, pointing at their clothes.

Hawk and Finch exchanged glances, clearly debating whether to tell me.

"Mrs. Westworth has requested a meeting," Hawk said.

My mouth fell open. "And you weren't going to tell me?"

Finch looked me up and down. "You seemed a little preoccupied, Lars."

I was about to open my mouth to demand I join them, but then I remembered the conversation Crane and I just had. I still felt responsible for this situation with Westworth and wanted to see it through. It was my mistake. I needed to be accountable for it, even if my siblings were trying to shield me.

Instead of demanding to come, though, I settled on, "Can I tag along? Please?"

Finch stared at me like I'd just told her I was a unicorn. "*Please?*" she asked incredulously. She let out a huff as she shook her head, took off her jacket, and passed it to me. "Well, I'll be damned. Here," she said. "To hide . . ." She waved at me up and down. "All of this."

My frown deepened as I tried to subtly sniff my armpit, but I took the jacket anyway.

"I'm going to get Matilda!" Crane called and scampered off toward the house in what could only be described as a frolic.

"Wow," Finch said as we headed toward the parking lot. "You're finally letting him take Matilda?"

I let out a long sigh as I stared down at my boots. "It was time to let go."

STAFF
PRICKLE
ISLAND
ZOO
ZOO

Hawk sat next to Finch and Mom, bouncing his leg so aggressively that water trembled in the glasses on the desk. Finch elbowed him in a silent command to quit it while Mom gave Finch a "knock it off" glare. I remained tucked off to the side by the bookshelves filled with old leather-bound first editions. Maybe my stink would be hidden by the smell of old books? I'd finger-combed my hair into a low ponytail, but I knew I still didn't look like the best representative of the zoo.

"It will be fine," Finch murmured more to herself than to us. She anxiously picked a mint off the silver tray in front of her.

Mom, Finch, and Hawk sat on one side of the mahogany

desk in upholstered chairs with intricately carved legs that looked entirely uncomfortable. Mom had a pinched expression, shifting her weight as we waited for Mrs. Westworth. The room looked like a set piece from a Regency film. Everything from the oil paintings to the lace doilies over the backs of the chairs screamed old money.

"I hate this place," Hawk whispered, looking around the room suspiciously. "Every time Dad brought us here as kids, it felt like walking straight into a horror movie."

Finch chuckled, leaning into Hawk and whispering, "If a creepy little girl in a white nightgown walks by, run."

Hawk shuddered. "Don't."

Mom opened her mouth to reprimand my sister when the door creaked open and Mrs. Westworth doddered in. My family rose and, one by one, shook her weathered hand. Today, her red fingernails were filed into what could only be described as talons. She looked more tired than the night of the gala, but her clothes and hair were fastidiously maintained, styled in the latest fashions of the 1960s, as if time stopped after that moment.

"Lachlans," she said by way of greeting, her voice scratchy and wet.

Mrs. Westworth had always seemed like something straight out of an old Hollywood film, probably from her poise and mid-Atlantic accent.

"Please, do sit." She gestured back to the chairs as she rounded her giant desk. I tucked tighter into the bookshelf as she gave me a cursory glance, and I swore her lip curled. "How are things at the zoo?"

Finch nodded. "Very well, thank you."

I had to give my sister credit—Finch could camouflage herself in high society shockingly well for someone with a bunch of face piercings and sleeve tattoos. It was probably her

Ivy League education and propensity for mirroring the people around her. That combined with the air of importance she so readily exuded, and she could have just about anyone believing she was an aristocrat. It didn't hurt that she wore a sky-blue button-down and tie today either.

Hawk was too gruff, with dark hair and a stubbly, short beard. He wore his khakis emblazoned with the park logo under his jacket . . . a working man. Unlike our sister, the veterinarian, who could rub shoulders with the rich elite.

"I'm glad to hear it," Mrs. Westworth said, her hands shaking slightly as she took a sip of water.

"And you, Mrs. Westworth?" Mom asked, narrowing her eyes to that shaking hand so subtly, you'd blink and miss it. "How have you been?"

"Now that the headache of this break-in is finally being dealt with," she said, squaring me with a look that had a chill running down my spine. "I'm much improved. I just bought a beach house in Watch Hill." She set her clasped hands on her desk, her bracelets clanging together. "I'm planning on residing there by my ninetieth."

"Not on the island?" Hawk asked, bemused.

"It's too far from my grandchildren," Mrs. Westworth said, straightening her collar. "I'd like to be closer to them, though I'm sure I will still visit Prickle Island on occasion."

Finch nodded. "Sensible."

"Yes, well." Mrs. Westworth spoke so slowly that Hawk started bouncing his leg again. I cleared my throat, and he stopped. "This is the last year I'll be officially summering on the island. I want to wrap up my affairs here."

"Understandable," Finch said measuredly while Hawk clenched his jaw.

"Let's cut to the chase." Mrs. Westworth leaned forward. "How are your finances?"

"Very good," Hawk said immediately.

Her pencil-thin eyebrows lifted. "Did you bring any statements like I asked on the phone?"

"We didn't." Hawk cleared his throat, and Mom shot my brother an anxious look. Did she even know about this? My heart started pounding faster. Why hadn't Hawk told me about this meeting? I could've printed them out— "We felt they don't accurately reflect the earning potential of the zoo at this time."

"He's just like your late husband." Mrs. Westworth huffed, looking at Mom and pointing flippantly to Hawk. "He had a way of dancing around the truth too."

"We just need a little more time," Finch pushed. "We can prove to you over the next few years that we *can* keep ourselves afloat without the Westworth Trust patronage."

"So I am to assume then that you aren't *currently* able to fully support yourselves without my aid?" My siblings paused, looking between each other as my gut clenched. "I'll take that as a yes."

I took a step forward. "We can do it—"

"A notable patron would do the zoo good," she said, holding a hand up to me that had me stopping so fast, you'd think we were playing freeze tag. "It would protect you and your family."

"You told Simon you'd leave him the zoo," Mom said, and the way she said Dad's name made me have to battle the swelling of tears behind my eyes. She said his name like it still hurt a decade later to even think of him . . . and I cursed myself to a thousand hells for thinking of another name that broke my heart anew: Logan.

"Regrettably, Mrs. Lachlan," Mrs. Westworth said. "Your husband is not here to claim that promise." She hacked a wet cough into her hand. "And I have yet to see enough aptitude from those he left behind." What were the etiquette rules around slapping an old lady? "The Westworth Trust was not set up to run a zoo, and I am certain the people who will control it after my death will not know what to do with you," she said. "Therefore, I have taken it upon myself to find another patron to take my place in funding the zoo."

"We can fund it ourselves," Hawk pleaded. "Please. Just give us some time."

"I've had a very generous offer from Mr. Madigan."

"No," I croaked. "You can't be serious."

Mrs. Westworth smirked. "He may be a bit over the top, but he knows how to run a *profitable* zoo. He's made his family quite famous for it."

"We're zookeepers, not reality stars," Hawk grumbled.

The matron's watery eyes pierced into Hawk. "Would you prefer I sell it to some developer who would level the place and turn it into another golf course?"

"Mrs. Westworth, please," Finch said, flashing that easy, charming smile of hers. "If we can prove that the zoo can turn a profit without your aid by your ninetieth, will you promise us you won't sell it? Surely that's many years away."

"My ninetieth is next year."

Finch flashed her megawatt smile. "That can't be possible."

"Your flattery is noted, Miss Lachlan."

Finch frowned and leaned back in her chair at that. Apparently, there was an upper age limit to her charms, and that number was eighty-nine.

"I'm doing this for you." Mrs. Westworth sighed. "So you scramble this year, but what about the year after that, hm?"

"We'll make even more," Finch said with a confident nod. "We have plans. We can show you."

"I am trying to protect the legacy that our families built together." She shook her head, and that pressure behind my eyes built again. We were going to lose everything. "I know it seems better to own it yourself, but if the zoo goes under for it, I'd never forgive myself."

"Please, just give us this time," Finch pleaded. "We'll show you that you have nothing to worry about."

Mrs. Westworth paused for what felt like an eternity before looking up at me. She studied my tear-stained cheeks, her Grinch heart finally seeming to crack. "Fine. You have one year to prove me wrong." She stood slowly, pushing up from his chair. "But if by next year's gala, you aren't self-sufficient, I'm selling the zoo to Gaz Madigan."

Volunteer
PRICKLE
ISLAND
ZOO
ZOO

Chapter Fifty-Four

Logan

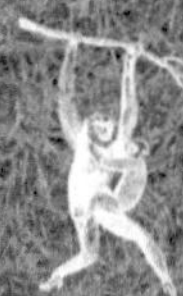

The swinging door of the café bathroom shut behind me with a loud thud. My phone buzzed in my pocket, and I picked it up to see another update from Mum: *Doctors say vitals looking good. Might be discharged by Friday. Fingers crossed.*

I gave my phone a sad smile, my eyes looking past the message to the photo behind it, which felt like a gut punch every time I saw it. Still, I didn't change it. Couldn't. I just kept spiraling, punishing myself with the pain of her memory, her laugh, her scent like a fucking sadist.

A knot formed in my windpipe and tears pricked my eyes, welling until her face was blurred. I wanted to scream. I

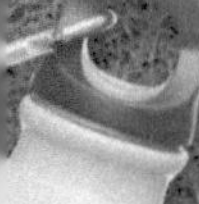

wanted to throw my phone across the bathroom and stomp on it until it shattered. But then what if Mum called with an update about Dad and I missed it? What if a café patron walked in and called the cops on me or, worse, left us a bad review? What if I let the world see how broken I felt without her?

The door to the bathroom swung open, and a patron lingered there for a second, watching me stare at my phone like it was fucking kryptonite. He gave me an awkward smile and quickly turned and fled. Great, I was scaring the customers away.

Clearing my throat, I roughly wiped my sleeve under my eyes, shoved my phone in my pocket, and hustled to the back stockroom.

I swore I heard Lark's voice in the general din of loud café conversations. Her voice always hung in the air around me. Maybe I was going crazy. My brain just couldn't make sense of her not being there.

I yanked the cord that switched on the one flickering light above me. Stretching up to reach the crate on the highest shelf, I gingerly lowered the heavy container down. But what I found were jars of hot sauce, not the bottles of tomato sauce I'd been searching for. I reached for the next crate, but I knew from the lightness it was serviettes. The next crate was empty.

My first thought was that Lark would've had this place organized in a single day. I'd bet she'd have a perfect system for the whole thing: regular stock takes, clear labeling . . . That knot formed in my throat again. I couldn't fucking cry over a lack of organizational systems.

Everything reminded me of her.

I tore off my forest-green apron, wadded it into a ball, and threw it into the nearest crate, kicking it again for good measure. My toe throbbed, the nail still bruised from our trip to Guatemala. Guatemala . . . fuck. *Here we go again.*

"Hey, Matty," I shouted to my brother.

He poked his head into the storeroom with an arched brow. "You summoned me?"

I reached for the last crate. "Nope. Too heavy."

"You playing three little bears with the crates again, Logie?"

I couldn't help but crack a smile, and Matt's grin doubled in size.

My little brother knew the second he saw me my heart was broken. It must've been written across my forehead in permanent marker. He handled it like he handled most things: with humor and alcohol.

"Are we out of tomato sauce?"

"Fuck." He drew out the word, looking around the storeroom as if he could summon a bottle from midair. "I forgot to put the order in."

"I'll shoot down to Johno's and grab one for now."

"Thanks, bro."

I gave him a half-wave. "No worries."

It was a good excuse for some fresh air. Something about the cold winter wind seemed to help stymy the overflow of emotions. I found myself pacing up and down our little strip of shops for one reason or another every single day. I worked double shifts in the café every day too, which Matty tried to stop, but I kicked up so much of a protest he let me. He'd been handling everything solo for so long and never once asked me for help. The least I could do was show up for him now . . . and it also helped me not think about her.

No. Fuck. I wasn't going to think about her. The dream girl with a funny name and a ridiculous, lovable family. The one who made me tie up into knots every time I smelled lavender. The one that was prickly on the outside but really sweet and soft on the inside.

The one that got away.

STAFF
PRICKLE
ISLAND
ZOO
ZOO

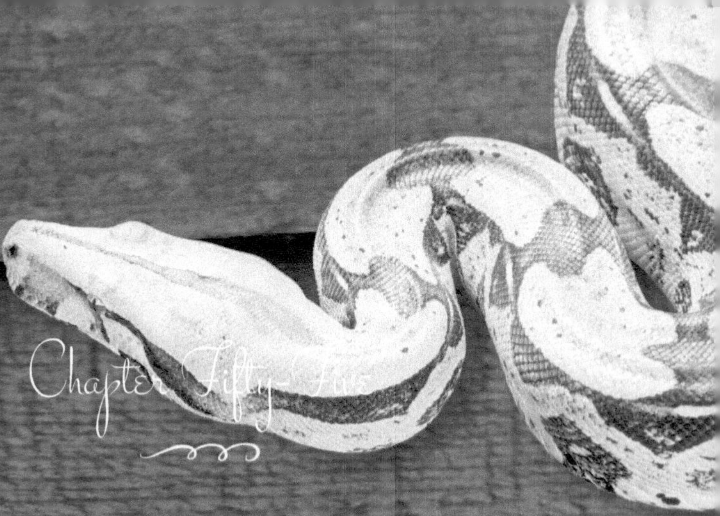

Chapter Fifty-Five

Lark

Four weeks passed. *Four weeks* where I did my absolute best to look like my world hadn't tilted on its axis and never returned. We were all stuck in this weird post-Logan existence—a world where everything felt broken and wrong. I doubled down on my routines. Went even harder on myself to do more and be faster and poured myself into my work enough that I collapsed from exhaustion at the end of the day just so I could sleep.

I was determined to act like everything was alright until it actually felt that way . . . and then Mom staged an intervention and forced me to take a day off. The first day in two weeks. The first breath without Logan, and I picked up that grief right where it left off, all of it blooming within me anew.

"Larzy Larson," Finch sang as she danced through the door. "I have a surprise for you!"

When she saw me sobbing at the reflection of my tattoo in the mirror, she threw her hands up in the air. "Is this a hormonal thing? Or is this about a guy who makes the word *deck* sound dirty?"

More tears fell down my cheeks, and I let out a shuddering sob.

"Yep. The guy," Finch said, walking into the room and gingerly shutting the door. "Definitely the guy."

She spotted the movie paused on the screen and ran over and shut the TV off like it was on fire. "Are you seriously watching the extended cut *Two Towers* AGAIN? *Why* are you trying to torture yourself?"

"Because I wanted to." I sniffed, feeling caught in the most pathetic wallowing of my life. "Because I deserve it."

I mentally apologized to every single person I ever judged for doing the exact same thing after a breakup. We couldn't help ourselves. The sweatpants and messy buns and bowls of ice cream and ugly crying just miraculously appeared when our hearts got stomped all over . . . except Logan didn't stomp all over my heart. He wanted me to go on an adventure with him and be there for him when he was going through a terrible time, and I said no. It was me. I was the asshole who did all the heart-stomping. I didn't have the right to be so upset. We weren't ever really even a couple . . . I wished someone could tell that to my whiplash of emotions.

I finished my shift and immediately changed without even bothering to shower. I relegated myself to my den of self-pity with an industrial-sized box of ice cream bars I stole from The Peckish Peacock and a baggy, zoo-branded hoodie with a giraffe embroidered on the front.

"Stop it," Finch said, yanking the blanket off me where I was puddled on the living room floor by the mirror.

Yes, I was watching myself cry and crying harder. I was upset. Sue me.

"Stop what?"

"Stop this." Finch waved her hand up and down over me like she was afraid she'd get an infection if she touched me in my current state. "You were the one who didn't want to go with him."

"Of course I wanted to go with him!" I shouted. "But I couldn't just go. I have responsibilities!"

Finch rubbed her hand across her temple like I was giving her a migraine. "Lars, listen. I don't know how to tell you this because I love you and it seems like you need to believe we all can't survive without you, but we *can*." Finch held up her hand and plowed forward before I could protest. "We can't replace you as our sister or as the best zookeeper on the East Coast, but we *can* find someone who will take good care of your animals even if they're not as fast or skilled or routined at it as you."

"You'll never be able to find someone who will work here year-round," I protested. I'd finally dismounted off my high horse after that conversation with Crane, but this was a realistic concern. "And with what money are you going to pay them?"

"I have a few ideas." Finch waggled her eyebrows. "You know people apply for jobs here all the time. There are a million twenty-somethings who would love to spend a few years living here and working at the zoo. Are you kidding?"

"And the money?"

"We have connections. We have people who want to support us. I'm not saying it's not going to be hard, but we *can* get there by the end of the year."

"But Mrs. Westworth—"

"Look, I'm stopping you right there." Finch pinched my lips together, and I batted her hand away. "You can argue yourself out of this a million different ways, but this is all semantics if you really want to go. The Lachlans always find a way. So tell me: if Logan asked you again and there were no financial constraints or family or zoo to worry about, what would you say?"

"Yes," I said, another tear sliding down my cheek. "I would say yes. Instantly."

I wanted to live in a new country, have new experiences, make a life for myself that wasn't predestined for me . . . but most of all, I wanted to feel Logan's arms around me again. I wanted to hear him murmuring into my hair as I fell asleep. I wanted to see those dimples when he caught me in my stubborn antics. I wanted to watch him aggressively brush his teeth and hear his little whining sounds in his sleep and listen to his jokes filled with words I was only starting to understand. And most of all . . . I wanted to see what we could become with a little more time just the two of us.

"Good," Finch said.

"Good?" I asked. "How is that good? It's awful! What I wanted to say and what I *did* say were two different things, and it's going to torture me for the rest of my fucking life!" I wailed and buried my face dramatically into my pillow. Finch merely chuckled. "Stop laughing at me!" I hurled the pillow at her, but it just bounced off her body as she arched her brow in amusement.

"I love seeing you fall apart like a middle schooler. It's nice knowing that even with all of your cleaning routines and organization, you're as messy in love as the rest of us." Finch reached into the pocket of her scrubs. "But that's not why I said good." She pulled out a folded white piece of paper. "I said good because I already applied for your working holiday visa and have taken the liberty of booking your flights."

I exploded up into a sitting position, pillows and blankets and a very discontented Matilda being flung to the side. I quickly chucked a blanket over Matilda and leaned to the side to hide the snake. She was meant to be in her new exhibit, but I'd stolen her out for emotional support. If Finch noticed, she didn't say anything as I whirled toward her and shouted, "You did WHAT?"

Finch shrugged. "Mom gave me your passport. It was actually not that hard to fill out." She passed me my booking confirmation, and I gaped down at the paper. "It gives you twelve months to explore the country and spend some time with Logan and—" She held up a mocking finger to my lips again so I couldn't cut her off. "And if it all falls apart, you can come home and be ready for next summer. And if it doesn't, then it doesn't."

My mouth was still hanging open as I looked up at Finch and back to the paper, and then to Finch and then to the paper at least three more times, before I said, "Oh my god, what if it doesn't?"

She grinned. "What if it doesn't?"

I couldn't even wrap my brain around the thought. What if this was it? What if I left for New Zealand and never came back? I mean, I'd come back for Christmas and things but— *Whoa, whoa, whoa.* A better question was: what if I got there and Logan was already over me and told me I'd made a huge mistake coming and—

Thwack!

A pillow smacked me across the face, and I glared up to see Dove and Hawk standing there too. Dove's arms were crossed, the corner of a second pillow pinched in her fingers, waiting to be unleashed upon me.

"Whatever you're spiraling about, stop," Hawk said. "I'm taking you to the ferry tonight. Go start packing."

I glared at Finch and raised my booking confirmation papers. "Does everyone know about this?"

Finch shrugged. "I don't know that Crane was paying much attention at the emergency family meeting, but I'm sure he'll figure it out when you're not at the next Sunday Funday Fondue Day."

"I always thought I'd be the first one to fly the nest," Dove said pointedly.

I stood up, swept the stray hair from the messy bun behind my ears, and straightened my twisted hoodie. As I stomped over to Dove, her eyebrows raised more with each step as if calculating if I might smack her, but instead, I pulled her into a tight hug.

She squeaked at the embrace. When was the last time I'd hugged her like this? A real, honest hug? She and I had always been at each other's throats our whole lives, but I was going to miss this. Miss her.

"Uh . . ." Dove twisted her head to look from Hawk to Finch as I clung to her like a baby monkey. "Is this a normal breakup thing or . . . ?"

"She's a hugger now," Finch said. "It's official. Caught her hugging *Crane* a few weeks ago."

"I'm sorry," I murmured into Dove's polar fleece vest. "I'm sorry I always made you feel like you were abandoning us if you ever wanted a life outside of this place. I was just jealous that you always thought it was a possibility for you and I didn't. Never stop being brave, Dove."

Dove's arms finally circled around me, and she squeezed me just as tightly. "You were always superhuman to me," she said. "I felt like I could never compare to you and your perfection, or Finch and her academics, or Hawk taking over after Dad and . . ."

Her voice wobbled, and Finch and Hawk unanimously let out an "aww" sound and circled in on either side of us to form a giant group hug.

"I'll watch out for Emma for you," Dove said, making more tears well in my eyes again. "And Jacob and everyone else. I've been wanting to take over the rainforest walkthrough for years, but I thought you would never give it up."

I hugged her tighter until I was certain all of our bones were creaking from the fierceness of our embrace.

Finch was the first to pull away. "You've got to go pack, Lars," she said. "Your flight leaves in eight hours and we've got to catch the ferry."

"Oh my god!" My hand flew to my rat's nest hair. "You couldn't have given me more than a day's warning that I was moving countries for the next year?"

"Or possibly longer," Finch taunted.

"Finch!"

She just shrugged. "The airline had a sale on."

"Oh my god," I said again, rushing to the stairs.

"I'll help you pack!" Dove called, running after me.

"I'll go grab the truck!" Hawk declared.

"I'll go return Matilda to her terrarium, you snake thief!" Finch shouted.

STAFF
PRICKLE
ISLAND
ZOO
ZOO

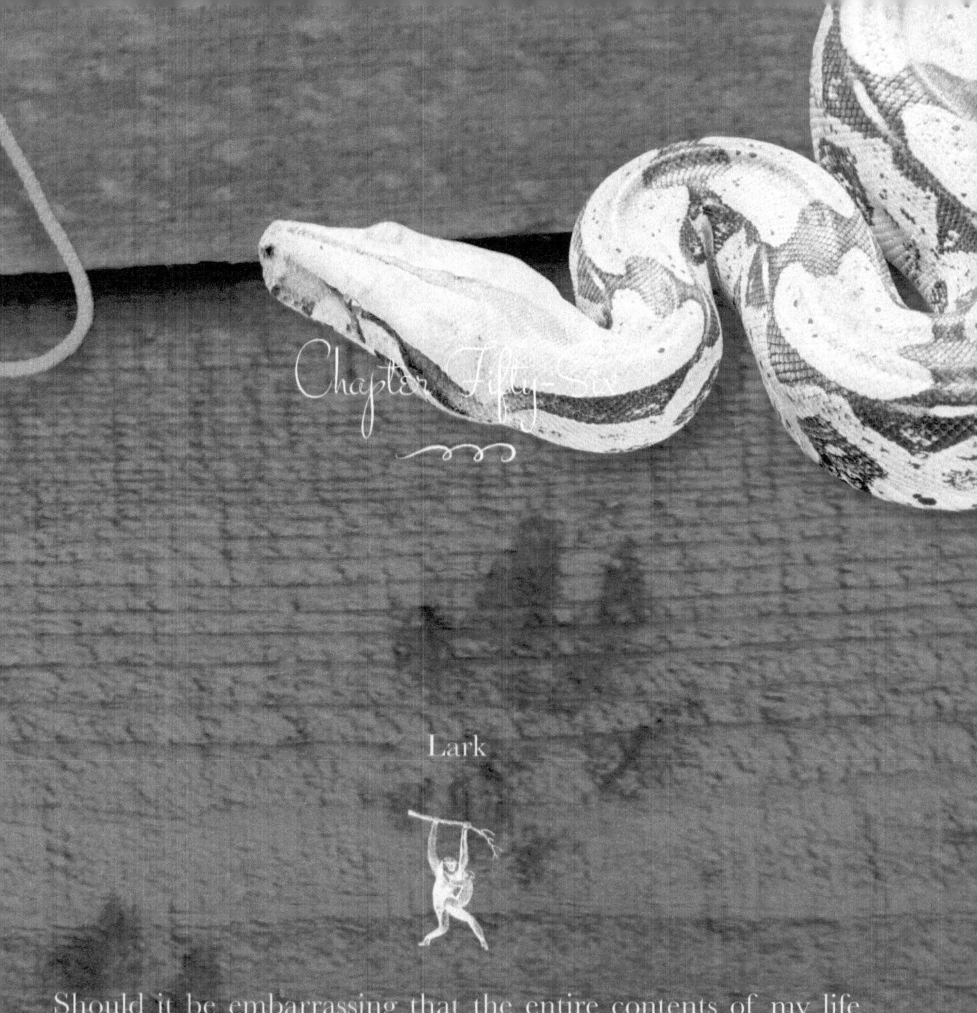

Lark

Should it be embarrassing that the entire contents of my life easily fit within two suitcases? The minimalists would be so proud. I managed to snag a single middle seat to LAX, where I seemed to be the only person on the plane sympathetic to the mother with a crying baby. I may have pulled out a few of my baboon-rearing techniques on the little dude, and the mother seemed eternally grateful. I enjoyed bouncing him around and pulling silly faces at him for a few hours since it was the only thing to keep my mind off the fact I had just decided to drop everything and follow a guy I barely knew halfway around the world.

I literally didn't have time to wash the clothes I was

wearing and had to triple-bag my monkey poo-stained hoodie to bring with me. I had dumped all of my dresser into two old suitcases that were held together by duct tape and a prayer. Dove had helped me, which I thought had been because of our newfound friendship but was actually so she could scope out the new room that she'd immediately staked her claim to before I was even out the door.

When I got to LAX, I hopped on an Air New Zealand flight to Auckland. The flight was *long*—like three director's cut *Lord of the Rings* films long—but after having hiked for two days straight up a mountain with a giant burn hole in my leg, it was no big deal by comparison.

By the time I pulled up to the front of the "something to declare" line at New Zealand border security, I was an odd mixture of exhausted and anxious, which I was sure made me seem even more like a drug smuggler to the surprisingly friendly Nathan. He was a middle-aged man with sandy brown hair, glasses, and a mischievous look in his eye.

He flipped over my declaration form. "What is it that you are declaring?"

"Farm animals," I said, suddenly feeling like I was on trial. All the big warning signs around me plastered with pieces of fruit made me feel like if I produced an orange right then, an entire SWAT team would come rushing over. Border security seemed like they'd be more upset if I produced a banana than a kilo of cocaine. "And wildlife. I-I work at a zoo . . . I think I have some dirt on my boots and—"

"Well, why don't we just take those boots, give them a wash, and then you don't have to worry?" he said with a smile, nodding down at the metal table where my two bags sat.

"Oh," I said, surprised that the answer wasn't: we're going to charge you a million-dollar fine and burn all of your luggage. "Okay." I fished through my bag and Nathan passed my boots off to a man in a white button-down with blue rubber gloves. I really wasn't in the States anymore. Why were people being nice to me? At the *airport* of all places?

"He'll just be a minute," Nathan said. "Do you have any other things that could be potentially contaminated by wildlife? Clothes you haven't washed, et cetera?"

"Oh." I looked at the ceiling and pulled a face. "I do have a dirty sweatshirt in here."

I reached through the bag until I was elbow-deep and my hands landed on the plastic. When I pulled it out, the stench of it was enough to make even *me* gag. It smelled like it had fermented over the last day of travel. Great, I'd arrive at Logan's doorstep reeking of monkey shit . . . At least I was consistent.

"You know what, maybe just burn this," I said, pinching the bag by the corner and dropping it in the trash can with a giant red X on the cover.

"Good idea," Nathan said with a chuckle. He leaned casually on the podium, flipping my card over a few times while he waited for my boots to be cleaned. "Working holiday, eh?" he asked with a nod. "Got any plans for your trip?"

"Besides following a guy I fell in love with over the summer?" I meant it as a joke and cringed.

Nathan just chuckled. "Ah yep. My missus is from London. We met on my OE," he said. "Classic."

"Yeah, well, he might already be over me. Who knows? I kind of broke up with him before he came back," I blabbered. "So maybe I'll just do the Wētā Workshop tour."

"Ah yep, the ones that do the CGI for *Avatar*?"

"That's WētāFX. They're different." I realized that it was probably not a good idea to correct a border security officer, even one as friendly as Nathan. "Anyway, maybe I'll just do that, visit Mount Doom and then fly home."

"Yeah nah," he said, leaning his elbows on his podium as if there weren't a whole line of sleepy people waiting to pass through. "What about Milford Sound? Queenstown? *Lord of the Rings* fan, are ya? You've got to see Hobbiton."

"Are you secretly working for the tourism bureau, Nathan?"

"Nah," he said with a smile. "I just think you're going to fall in love with Aotearoa and find a way to stay, even if this bloke ends up being an egg."

I laughed as the person with my freshly washed boots came back. Man, they must've power-washed them or something because I hadn't seen them so clean since the first day I put them on.

"Thank you," I said.

"Good luck, Ms. Lachlan." Nathan stamped my declaration and gave me a wink. "I hope you have an adventure."

Having my Frodo leaving the shire moment, I hefted my backpack onto my shoulders and headed through the plexiglass doors. Bolstered by the border security man's blessing and my fresh boots, I grabbed my bags and strode out of the line and into the bustling international airport in search of a taxi . . . and that was when I remembered: I didn't have Logan's address.

"What the fuck was I thinking?" I cried to Finch from my cheap airport hotel room. I clutched the landline to my ear.

"You were thinking you were going to run off into the sunset with your Kiwi boy toy," Finch said. "Just chill for a sec. Hawk is finding his address from the volunteer files."

"Isn't that illegal or something?"

"I think it stopped being illegal when he started putting his dick in you—ouch!" Finch snarled, and I knew one of my five other siblings had either punched her or thrown something hard at her.

"I don't have enough money to just roam around New Zealand for a year searching for him," I said, flopping onto the too-hard mattress and covering my eyes with the crook of my arm. "Which would also be the most pathetic thing ever. And it would be super creepy to text him and randomly ask for his address. You would never do this."

"That's because I'm someone who likes to play the field and will never be tied down," Finch said proudly.

"One day, you're going to find the right girl who makes you regret saying that and I'm going to *love* rubbing it in your face," I replied.

"Never going to happen."

"I give it less than a year."

The conversation paused as Finch muttered something to Hawk about having a better organizational system and what decade was it.

"How's Jacob?" I asked.

"The reintroductions are going great," Finch said. "I messaged you a video of him." I made a mental note to go find a SIM card. "This will be his third overnight with the troop. I think he'll be set."

"Oh wow," I said, the bittersweetness twanging through me like a minor chord being strummed. I hated that I was going to miss it. "Will you—"

"Dove is already planning on sleeping in the anteroom just to keep an eye on everyone," Finch said reassuringly. I wished I could bear hug Dove all over again. "We'll keep you updated. Don't worry."

"How's she doing with the primate run?" I asked, fiddling with the bedsheets.

"A natural, just like her sister," Finch said with a laugh. "She's given some of the birds to the twins, and we're thinking about implementing the zone system we've been talking about for ages."

"That's awesome," I said, feeling another strum of sadness. I'd been suggesting that we divide some of our animals based on exhibits and locations for years. It didn't make sense for an enclosure with birds, primates, and reptiles to have three different keepers coming in and out. "I miss you."

"We miss you too," Finch said. "But you know who else I bet is missing you? Logan."

"This is a completely serial killer-level of crazy girlfriend move, isn't it?" I whined, wiping a hand down my face. "Do you really think this is a good idea?"

"It's a bold move, Lars," Finch said. "But you've played it safe your whole life. Now is the time for bold moves. What's the worst that could happen?"

"He looks at me like I'm Bigfoot and says I shouldn't have come and he wasn't ever really that into me and—"

"And you say 'okay whatever' and fly home," Finch said. "And you know you'll never randomly bump into him again on our little island and you can find the next neckerchief French girl to fall in love with instead, alright? Either way, it's going to be okay."

I slumped into my bed. "I love you."

"I love you too," Finch said in that matter-of-fact way of hers. "Now go talk to him. I've got his address. Are you ready?"

I held the phone between my ear and shoulder and grabbed the notepad from the bedside table. "Roger. Go ahead," I said like I was taking a radio call.

Finch snorted. "You can take the girl out of the zoo . . ."

STAFF
PRICKLE
ISLAND
ZOO
ZOO

Chapter Fifty-Seven

Lark

Flying into Wellington was like riding the worst roller coaster ever. All the people around me didn't even bat an eye while I was nearly hurling into my hands on the landing. It seriously was like something out of an action movie. I was pretty sure we landed sideways in what I called "a giant fucking hurricane" and the captain called "a light wind."

I got a taxi to the train station and a train out to the end of the coastal line. My stomach tied itself into a bigger and bigger knot with every hour that passed. At least I had time to shower the night before and no longer smelled like monkey poo . . . although the hotel shower only had a quarter-sized bar of soap and an all-purpose wash that I'd had to make work as a shampoo. I didn't bring makeup—I didn't even own makeup. The only time I did wear it, I stole it from Finch or Dove. I'd considered running out in the middle of the night to find a drugstore, but they were all closed and I thought it would look even more crazy if I was showing up at Logan's rural family home wearing a full face of makeup. He'd probably think I was there to axe murder him.

I didn't bring any cute clothes—those were also stolen from my sisters—so I opted for a pair of ripped jeans and my least-stained Arctic Monkeys T-shirt, which, yes, I mostly bought because it said monkeys on it. I hefted my backpack and two rolling suitcases off the train and realized what an absolute mess I looked like rocking up at Logan's address unannounced with my life's worth of stuff. Was this what romantic gestures were supposed to look like? Maybe I should've bought him flowers? Ew, no. That would be even more cringey.

The train station was no more than a slab of concrete with a sign and a little covered area—not a single taxi in sight. I kept searching down the little row of shops for a potential taxi stand or . . . Did they have Uber in the middle of nowhere New Zealand? I was about to roll across the street to ask at the little café when I spotted something that made my heart leap into my throat.

Logan.

He was standing outside the café. Oh my god, that *was* probably his family's! Why did I bother finding his home address when he had a freaking café I could've just Googled? But I would shout at myself about that another time because all of my energy was focused on the gorgeous woman he was talking to. I'd seen her before. She was the happy jumping screensaver on his phone! Kathy? Katy? Kelly! Ugh, that was her.

She had gorgeous blonde hair fashioned in beachy waves

that looked like she'd just walked straight out of a salon. She wore a cream-colored sweater, blue jeans, and riding boots. Of course she was an equestrian, of fucking course. She laughed and playfully touched Logan's arm at something he'd said, and I wanted to be abducted by aliens in a beam of shining light right then and there. I ducked behind a lamppost, which did little to actually conceal me, and watched as Kelly stretched up on her tiptoes and placed a kiss on Logan's cheek. Logan smiled back at her, and I wanted to simultaneously cry and strangle Finch for making me come here just to endure this embarrassment firsthand.

He'd gotten back with his ex. I was just a fun little American fling, and now he was back with the real girl who was meant to be his puzzle piece.

I tried as stealthily as possible to roll my suitcases toward the little covered bench seat and wait for the next train to roll in. Rain misted the gray skies, and I shivered, remembering that August was winter in New Zealand. Should I fish my jacket out of my suitcase and risk never being able to duct tape it closed again? After taping it up again this morning, this thing was on its *last* last legs. I decided to just sit as still as possible with my back to the café, praying Logan wouldn't see me.

I stared out at the wide-open paddocks on the other side of the tracks, thinking about what a fool I was, when I saw my own personal harbinger of evil.

There, standing at the edge of the paddock staring at me, was a motherfucking donkey.

"You've got to be kidding me." The donkey just stood there in the pelting rain, staring at me, and I began to wonder if instead of crows or black cats, donkeys were my bad omen. "Stop. Staring. At. Me. Donkey," I gritted out to the donkey, as if it were the same one from Guatemala and it had been magically airlifted off the mountain and teleported to New Zealand.

Was this the universe's sick practical joke? I really didn't feel like being judged by yet another hooved mammal right now.

The rain began pelting down cold, icy droplets, and the shelter did nothing to protect me. Did rain fall sideways in the southern hemisphere? It was bone-chillingly cold, and I was about to be soaked completely through. I peeked back over my shoulder and saw Logan had gone back inside the café, disappearing somewhere behind the counter.

Fuck it.

There was a place that looked like a corner shop but for some reason was called a "dairy" two stores down from the café. Then I remembered Logan using the word before, and it made me want to start crying.

I really shouldn't be here.

If I crossed at the end of the road and cut back over, I'd keep out of sight of the giant glass café windows. With the *Mission Impossible* theme music playing in my head, I rolled my suitcases down the train platform and across the street, getting soaked more with every step. I was just about to step back onto the curb when my Converse sneaker squelched into something and I winced. I'd felt that exact same sensation too many times to count over the years. Every zookeeper had.

Please be mud, please be mud, I chanted as I looked down and saw that I was standing ankle-deep in rain-sodden manure. Why did the universe hate me? It was probably from one of perfect Kelly's perfect horses or that judgy fucking donkey.

At least it's not carnivore poo, I told myself, which was pretty much a Lachlan family mantra. In the hierarchy of shit you didn't want to step in, horse shit was pretty low down the list. I wiped my sneaker on the gravely road, but it was already seeping into the fabric and up into my jeans. I debated taking the shoe off and just limping into the dairy, but every second I deliberated, I was getting more and more soaked. Finally, I decided that I would just apologize for my stink—like I'd had to do for most of my life—as I sheltered inside.

A bell rang as I opened the dairy door and hustled into the room.

"It's absolutely pissing out there, eh?" an elderly man said by way of greeting without looking over his shoulder. He was busy restocking a shelf with red wine, the fluorescent light above him blinking on and off.

"Uh-huh," I said, trying not to cry. "Um, do you know when the next train back to Wellington is?"

"Not until six," he said, and I gaped at the bald spot on the back of his head for a second before I realized he'd said the number six and was not, in fact, soliciting me for sex.

"Okay, thanks," I croaked.

"The café round the corner makes a mean fry-up if you need a place to wait," he offered.

I just stood there, dripping brown water all over his tiled floors, trying to decide between dying of exposure and facing the man I'd traveled here for, who was already back with his ex-girlfriend. I swallowed and nodded. Exposure it was. I manhandled my wet suitcases around and turned toward the door just as the bell rang and a man said, "Hey, Johno, have you got any more oat mil—"

I whirled and came face-to-face with Logan.

Volunteer
PRICKLE
ISLAND
ZOO
ZOO

Chapter Fifty-Eight

Logan

"I'm sorry," were the first words out of her mouth, and I had no idea why this hallucination was apologizing to me.

I was frozen to the spot, unsure if maybe I'd been struck on the head by a giant hailstone on the walk over here and this was all a figment of my imagination.

Lark Lachlan stood there looking like she'd just swam across the Pacific with two suitcases that at the youngest were from the nineties. Water dripped off her hair. An Arctic Monkeys shirt clung to her curvy figure, and I was sure she bought that T-shirt just because it had the word "monkeys" on it. Goosebumps covered her arms, and her whole body trembled. My mouth dropped open as I looked her up and down.

again and again. This couldn't be real. She couldn't really be here, could she?

"This was a mistake. I shouldn't have come," Lark croaked again, her cheeks redder than a scarlet ibis. "I'm sorry."

She moved to push past me and slipped on the wet tiles. Her arms wheeled as she tipped backward. I shot forward, landing hard on my knees to catch her in the same exact way I'd caught her in the howler monkey enclosure weeks ago. Her head rocked back against my forearm, and she looked up at me breathlessly, her eyes too wide in her head.

"You okay?" I asked as my fingers gripped her tighter. She was really here, right now, beneath my fingertips.

This was real.

"Yeah," she said. "Hi."

I let out a sound that was half laugh, half cry, my voice strangled with emotion as I said, "Hi," back, pulling her tighter against me until my shirt was soaked through too. "Why shouldn't you have come?"

"Kelly," she said, her eyes darting everywhere but my face, which was hard considering our faces were only a few centimeters apart.

My gut clenched. Fuck. She'd seen me with Kelly and must've assumed . . .

"It's not what you think," I said so quickly, it sounded like one run-on word. I scrambled to rectify whatever scenario she was creating in her head. "She was driving down from Palmy back to Wellington and just stopped by to drop off some things I'd left behind at her place."

"She was flirting with you," Lark said, crunching up into a seated position. She shifted away from me, but my hand lingered on her arm, as I was unwilling to not be touching her.

She was here. She was really fucking here.

"Yeah, I know," I said with a grimace. "She floated the idea of us getting back together. She said we could make it work somehow. Her in the city. Me out here."

Lark's voice grew all quiet as she said, "Oh."

"I told her no. Obviously," I said, and her eyes finally lifted to meet mine again. God, that hopeful little look in her eyes made my heart do a backflip. "I told her . . ." I took a breath. Just say it. She was here. There would be no other time. No more regrets. "I told her I was in love with someone else."

Tears welled in Lark's eyes, and the sight of them made me break. I grabbed her by the knees and pulled her forward across the wet floor until she was back against me. I cupped her cold face in mine and kissed her wet lips. Fireworks exploded through my whole body at the feeling of those full lips against mine again. The little breathy sound she let out made me thread my hands through her dripping wet hair and pull her even closer, melding the two of us together. How I dreamed of doing this again.

"Hey, Martha!" Johno called out. "Come here! Logan is down here pashing some chick!"

Lark and I broke our kiss, laughing as we leaned our foreheads together.

"You're here," I said, tucking a wet strand of hair behind her ear.

"I'm here," she said, her smile beaming like a ray of sunshine breaking through the clouds. "And I love you too."

I pulled her back in for another kiss, not caring that Johno was pulling out his phone to snap a photo that would probably be sent to the entire town. I needed to kiss her, needed her mouth on my own, needed to know she was finally mine and I was finally hers.

The bell rang again, the door nearly smacking me in the back as my brother said, "What do you mean Logan is necking a . . . Holy shit!" I cringed. "Is this the American chick? *The one?*"

"Lark, meet my little brother, Matt," I said through clenched teeth as she bashfully waved up at him.

She gave me one last chaste kiss and whispered, "I think we should get off the floor now."

I laughed. "Good idea."

I helped her to a stand and slung my arm over her shoulder, not letting her out of my reach, as if she might just vanish into thin air if I didn't hold on to her. She shook Matt's hand, and he gave an impressed look from Lark to me like she was way out of my league. I nodded in agreement.

"Nice to meet you," she said, adding with a cringe, "I'm sorry for the smell."

We both looked down at her suspiciously brown sneaker, and I guffawed, pulling her into my side. Even soaking wet and covered in horse dung, she was still the most gorgeous woman in the entire world . . . and she was here for me.

I kissed the top of her head. "We just wanted to make you feel at home."

STAFF
PRICKLE
ISLAND
ZOO
ZOO

"And look who this is," Dove sang out, twisting her phone to the howler monkey enclosure. A round, little black puffball sat right by the fence, munching on her morning leaves.

"Emma!" I exclaimed, and Logan gave my hip a squeeze and dropped a kiss on my shoulder. I swore he couldn't keep his lips off of me for more than five minutes. He knew how hard it was for me to say goodbye to Emma, but it clearly looked like she was thriving with Dove. It seemed like she'd doubled in size over the last month.

"And here." Dove swirled around and flourished a hand, dancing down the path and across the pavilion. "Matilda is loving her new home."

"Look at her!" I shouted, shoving my face closer to the screen. Her enclosure was like a reptile Disney World. Her little tongue flicked out, and I'd like to think it was because she recognized me. "Crane has seriously outdone himself."

"She's obviously loving her new space," Dove said, zooming in on a curled-up Matilda basking on a warming stone.

"Is that Lars?" Finch's voice called from somewhere nearby.

"Yeah," Dove said, and we caught a brief glimpse of her rolling her eyes before the phone was unceremoniously yanked from her grip.

"Lars!" Finch was panting like she'd run the last stretch uphill to snag the phone. "How's Murray doing?"

Murray was our pet Kunekune pig. Finch had sent over a detailed treatment sheet for his minor skin rash on the crease of his floppy ear. It was my sister's way of showing love, so I didn't mention that we could just ask our local vet, but the treatment did work straight away so . . .

"He's good!" I said brightly. "All better now. Thanks for that treatment plan."

I already imagined three decades into the future when Finch was still messaging me remedies to all of our animal ailments. As much as I missed the zoo animals, I still managed to get my fill of animal love. Behind the café was Logan's family's farmland, which included three houses and a mishmash of farm animals that had either been rescued or re-homed from the surrounding farms. We had all sorts of sad-looking animals needing some love: goats, ducks, chickens, sheep, alpacas, pigs . . . and, yes, one actually very sweet donkey named Eleanor. You can take the keeper out of the zoo, but she'll find a way to care for animals anyway.

My days were still filled with waking up at the butt crack of dawn, hauling heavy bales of hay, and scooping poop . . . just under completely different skies and stunning constellations.

"How's Matty and Kaia?" Finch asked. "Tell her I don't appreciate her slick moves on Words With Friends."

Logan's brother, Matt, was really lovely, but Matt's wife, Kaia, had instantly become like another sister to me and my sisters. I was immediately welcomed into Logan's big extended family, who all lived in the area. It felt just as joyful—and just as chaotic—as my own family back home. Logan's dad had spent three weeks in the hospital but was finally back in his house, and it felt like the whole town let out a collective sigh of relief.

I snorted. "You've got to up your game, Finchy."

"Finchy?" She cackled. "You've been in the land of nicknames for too long. Give the whole fam love from me."

I beamed at her. "I will."

"Ooh, I found another brewery you need to add to your South Island trip . . ."

She carried on with her info dump, telling me all the coolest places for me to go so she could live vicariously through me. The café was in a perfect jumping-off point to explore different parts of the North Island. We had a South Island trip planned in the spring and then a trip to Australia with Matt and Kaia planned for next winter during the slow season. I *might* have funneled all of my need to organize and schedule into the itineraries for these trips, which were already color-coded and stuck to the fridge with a magnet.

Finch walked me around the zoo, showing me more things: the new playground, the new ice cream truck, the plans to renovate the old lion exhibit. Dove chased after Finch, demanding her phone back as Finch swatted her away.

"Okay, fine," Finch finally relented. "We'll see you at dinner on Sunday, your Monday?"

"Yep, see you then."

"Okay, love you, bye," Finch said.

"Love you!" Dove shouted from behind her.

"Love you too," I said, raising my voice an octave.

I still attended the Sunday Funday Fondue Day via Zoom. They happened at my ten a.m. on a Monday since I was a whole day ahead. Scheduling time to call family had become a Herculean task with "your times" and "my times" and different days and something that you had to either be a mathematician or wizard to fully comprehend. But I made it to dinner every week, still nursing my second morning coffee while everyone else ate fondue. Thank God for video chatting. I didn't feel so far away.

Logan swept his hand down my back and dropped a lingering kiss to my cheek. "Is tonight a eat leftover café macarons and watch *Taskmaster* kind of night or . . ." He dipped his finger in the neckline of my slouchy T-shirt and pulled it down to kiss the skin above my collarbone.

"Or?" I asked with a catlike grin. I turned into him on our little couch, sliding a hand up his arm. Matt had renovated the little cabin at the corner of the property for when Logan returned. It was cozy—and in need of a little extra love—but it wasn't an old wildlife enclosure, so it was already a step up from the last place I'd lived.

I swept my hand up to the back of Logan's neck and pulled him into a kiss as he lowered me onto the couch. His hand slid under my shirt and cupped my breast, rolling my nipple between his fingertips as he settled his hips between my thighs. I moaned as he licked into my mouth and my hands dropped to his belt.

A loud braying sound made us both jolt.

"Shit," I said. "Did you feed Eleanor?"

"No." He dropped his forehead onto my shoulder in resignation. He started kissing up my neck again. "Maybe we could just—"

Eleanor started braying again, so loudly that the windows shook. It would only be a matter of time before his mom or brother was at our door, asking what was going on.

"Fine. Fine!" Logan threw his hands up, and I giggled. "She's really getting on my tits." He pointed to me and said, "Keep thinking all those dirty things you're thinking."

"Something about my tits?" I asked, trying to hold in my laughter.

He dropped one knee back onto the sofa and grabbed my cheeks and kissed me hard. "Only you would put up with all of this."

I snatched a handful of his shirt before he could pull away and yanked his lips back to mine. "Um, excuse me, I *love* all of this."

"And that's why you're a keeper," he said, kissing me one last time before darting off before someone called the donkey police on Eleanor.

I followed him to the door and pulled on my gumboots.

"Okay, okay, miss," I called to Eleanor, who was waiting very impatiently at the fence. Logan laughed and threaded his fingers through my own as we marched off to feed the animals.

STAFF
PRICKLE
ISLAND
ZOO
ZOO

Chapter Sixty

A few years later . . .

Lark

As winter drew nearer, the heavy rains turned the ground into thick mud. I stared out at the fern-covered mountains on the horizon. Even after years, the beauty of the New Zealand land-scape, the sound of its birdsong, the way the mist lifted off the land and the storms rolled out to sea still awed me. Some deep, churning part of my soul had settled here. I hadn't known how I'd find it here in this corner of the world, but I now knew it with an unerring certainty: this place was home.

The sound of Logan's litany of muttered curses from the stables pulled my gaze from the misty horizon. I slogged through the wet earth toward where he crouched, two chickens and a cheeky baby goat following in my boot steps. The rest of the farm animals had the good sense to hide out in the barn or under the thick branches of the old pōhutukawa.

Soon, it would be summer in the US and The Prickle Island Zoo would be opening its doors for visitors again, along with another new batch of volunteers. We were planning a trip back over at the end of the year, and I was so excited to see all the animals . . . and my family too, of course.

As I got closer to the stables, I saw Logan kneeling in the mud and hustled over faster, worrying for a second that he might be hurt. But then I realized the grate of the stable drain had been removed and he was fishing for something inside. He'd taken his jacket off and was in a T-shirt in the pouring rain, the awning of the stable doing little to protect him. His shirt sleeve was rolled up, and he had his arm shoulder-deep in the putrid water.

"Did you drop your keys down there again?" I called, squelching over. I was looking forward to the trip to Rarotonga to get some sunshine after the last four weeks of wet winter weather.

"I've got it under control," Logan said. "You go inside and get dry."

I folded my arms and leaned against one of the beams, enjoying the sight of Logan's muscled back and arms from this angle. "I think I'm good right here."

"Seriously, tails," Logan grumbled, and I laughed.

"What exactly did you drop down there?" I asked, arching my brow as Logan dug through the brown muck. "Whatever it is, we're going to have to burn it because it's going to be soaked in pig poop." Logan ignored me and kept fishing around. "We can get you a new wallet," I pushed. "Nobody's going to take that money anyway—"

"Aha!" Logan let out a victorious shout as he yanked his arm back and quickly tucked the poop-stained item back into his pocket . . . which we'd definitely need to wash before he stepped foot in the house. But stealthy as he was, I saw it.

A ring box.

"Is that?"

Logan whirled toward me, holding his arm out under the guttering to wash off his arm. "Nope," he said too quickly.

"It is, isn't it?"

"I have no idea what you're talking about."

"Are you going to—"

"Not like this, tails."

I bounced up and down on my toes, pouting my bottom lip. "Oh, come on! I want to see it."

Logan shook his head and flashed me a sheepish grin. "This isn't exactly the romantic way I had planned."

"We can lie to everyone and tell them a different story," I pushed.

Logan chuckled, pulling the box back out and rinsing it off in the deluge from the guttering. "Okay, okay, let me rinse it at least."

"You know I'm not squeamish."

"Oh, I know." Logan laughed, weighing the box in his hands as if debating with himself. "Screw it." He turned to me in a whirl and dropped down onto one knee, splashing mud and who-knows-what-all over the place. The farm animals all drew closer, intrigued by his antics as my hands flew to my mouth. "Lark Lachlan, will you marry me?"

He opened the soaked velvet box and produced a beautiful diamond ring with a sapphire band. I sucked in a breath, surprised by the overwhelm of emotions that flooded through me, especially considering where that box had just been. I guessed all the big moments of our life together had to be covered in some form of animal poo.

My eyes misted as I said, "Yes."

Logan shot up from where he knelt, reaching for me with both hands, but then thinking better of the poo-covered one, he tucked it behind his back.

His lips landed on mine, his kiss deep and burning as he let out a long sigh.

"I love you," he murmured against my mouth. "I love our life together. I can't wait for the next chapter."

"I love you too." I sniffed, threading my fingers through his wet hair and holding his face to mine.

A goat bleated, and that got the chickens going, and soon the whole farm was alive with a racket of noise as if they, too, approved of this proposal. We both broke our kiss with a laugh. Logan pulled out the mostly unscathed ring and slid it onto my finger. A tear slid down my cheek as I looked at the diamond perched there, but my tears were hidden amongst the rain.

"So, how are we going to tell people this happened?" Logan asked as he studied the look on my face while I admired the ring.

"Beach at sunset?"

"Beach at sunset," he confirmed with a laugh.

I stepped forward, careful not to accidentally step on a chicken, my boots squelching in the mud as I rose up on my toes. "I love you," I said again. "My person."

"You know . . ." Logan smirked down at me. "I just heard from one Wren Lachlan that the Prickle Island Zoo is now doing weddings."

I gaped at him for a second. A wedding back home! A wedding all of my family—both furry and human—could attend. I tried to contain my excitement as I put on my best serious face and said, "Only if I get to wear Matilda around my neck as I walk down the aisle."

With his warmest, beaming smile, Logan bent and kissed me again. "Deal."

THE END

Want to read a bonus epilogue set at Lark and Logan's wedding *and* get all the latest Zoo news? Scan the QR code on the next page to join my newsletter!

- Ali xx

SIGN UP
FOR ZOO NEWS

ALSO BY

Ali K. Mulford Books:

The Prickle Island Zoo Series:

She's a Keeper

Easy Tiger

Party Animal

Maple Hollow Series:

Pumpkin Spice & Poltergeist

A.K. Mulford Series:

The Five Crowns of Okrith

The Okrith Novellas

The Golden Court Trilogy

Acknowledgments

To all of the real life people and animals who made it into this story! Since I was a kid, I always wanted to either work with animals or write books. I've loved having this opportunity to bridge the world between my two great passions!

Thank you to all of my amazing readers for coming on this new adventure with me. I am so humbled by your support and all the ways you champion my books out in the world!

Thank you so much to all of my Patrons! I love writing new stories, commissioning spicy art, and getting to connect with you on Patreon! A very special thank you to Audrey, Lauren, Amy, Ciara, Jaime, Kristie, Linda, Marissa, Alyssa, Bri, Divya, Hannah, JeNaya,

Jessica, Kat, Kelly, Lindsay, Mandy, Latham, Samantha, Sarah, Stacy, Tatiana, and Virginia!

Thank you to Sara Kingsley from Adore Editing and Norma from Norma's Nook Editing

Thank you to Enni from Yummy Book Covers for designing the gorgeous covers for this series.

Thank you to Holly Dunn for designing the Zoo Map.

Thank you to all of my zoo friends for Beta reading this story!

To my PAs, Treece and Hannah, thank you for helping me launch this new pen name and keeping Team Mulford going! I love working with you!

To my book wifey and publishing bestie, Kate, thank you

for formatting this book, designing the gorgeous interiors to this book, and running the Zoo Gift Shop!

Thank you to my agent, Jessica Watterson and the whole team at SDLA for supporting me when I said I wanted to self-publish this series. Looking forward to many more wild adventures together!

And to the real life Emma (who won't be reading this because she's a howler monkey . . .).

I'm so grateful I got to be a small part of your life and I forgive you for suction-cupping yourself onto my face while covered in poo when I was really, really hungover.

About the Author

Ali K. Mulford (also known by their bestselling fantasy pen name A.K. Mulford) is a rom-com author and former wildlife biologist who swapped rehabilitating monkeys for writing novels. A US and NZ citizen, Mulford now lives in Australia rearing two human primates, writing lovable characters, and making ridiculous TikToks (@akmulfordauthor).

www.akmulford.com